Don't let them get me!

A shadow fell over him, travelling slowly across his back and bringing a paralyzing chill with it. Taverik sensed a presence, seeking him, calling him. He crawled faster. It was hard to see; twilight was deepening awfully fast.

Taverik collided with a thornbush. He jerked back and swore softly, cradling his cheek. Suddenly Taverik understood and his blood went cold. He'd felt that same presence in the alley behind the pawnshop; the *mahiga* of the Black Eagle.

As if in answer to his recognition, he felt a voice inside his head. "Come."

"No," he said aloud. Shielding his face with one hand, he pushed blindly through the thorns. The darkness thickened to more than night blackness. It pressed in on him, hindered him, clouded his mind. The Black Eagle stalked him, voices whispered on either side of him.

He heard the horsemen moving along to his left. He fell flat and listened.

Other voices echoed inside Taverik's head. "Go to them," they whispered, louder and louder until he couldn't be sure they weren't audible. They pulled at him as if they'd planted hooks in his thoughts. The darkness pushed. Taverik buried his face in the snow. "No," he whispered, and added with the simplicity born of desperation, "Zojikam, don't let them get me!"

CAROL CHASE

HAWK'S FLIGHT

A Baen Books Original

Baen Publishing Enterprises
P.O. Box 1403
Riverdale, N.Y. 10471

ISBN: 0-671-72064-3

Cover art by Studio H
Maps rendered by Eleanor Kostyk

First printing, June 1991

Distributed by
SIMON & SCHUSTER
1230 Avenue of the Americas
New York, N.Y. 10020

Printed in the United States of America

Acknowledgments and Dedication

Many thanks go to three friends who helped me and rooted for me: Marian Bray, Maureen Taylor, and Larry Clark. I also want to thank Perry Culwell and Peter Chase, who gave me hours of their time when I needed consultants. And finally, I want to thank my mother, Myrna Kern Chase, who knew I should write before I did, and who provided the means and the encouragement. To her this book is most lovingly dedicated.

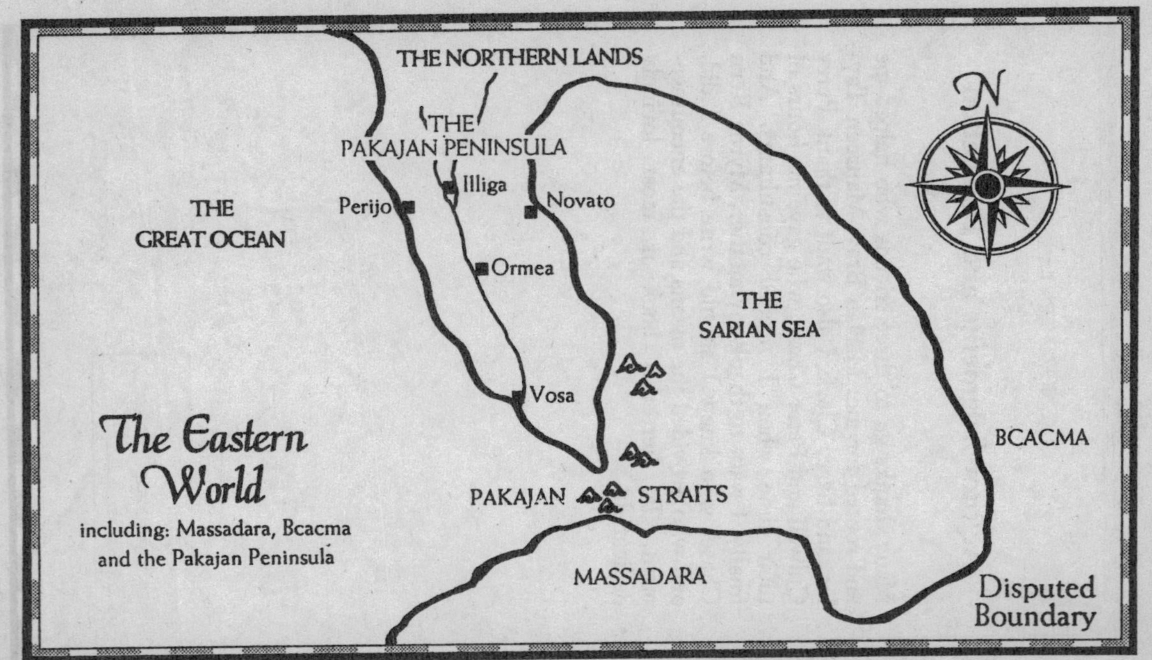
The Eastern World
including: Massadara, Bcacma and the Pakajan Peninsula
N
THE NORTHERN LANDS
THE PAKAJAN PENINSULA
Illiga
Perijo
Novato
Ormea
Vosa
THE GREAT OCEAN
THE SARIAN SEA
PAKAJAN STRAITS
BCACMA
MASSADARA
Disputed Boundary

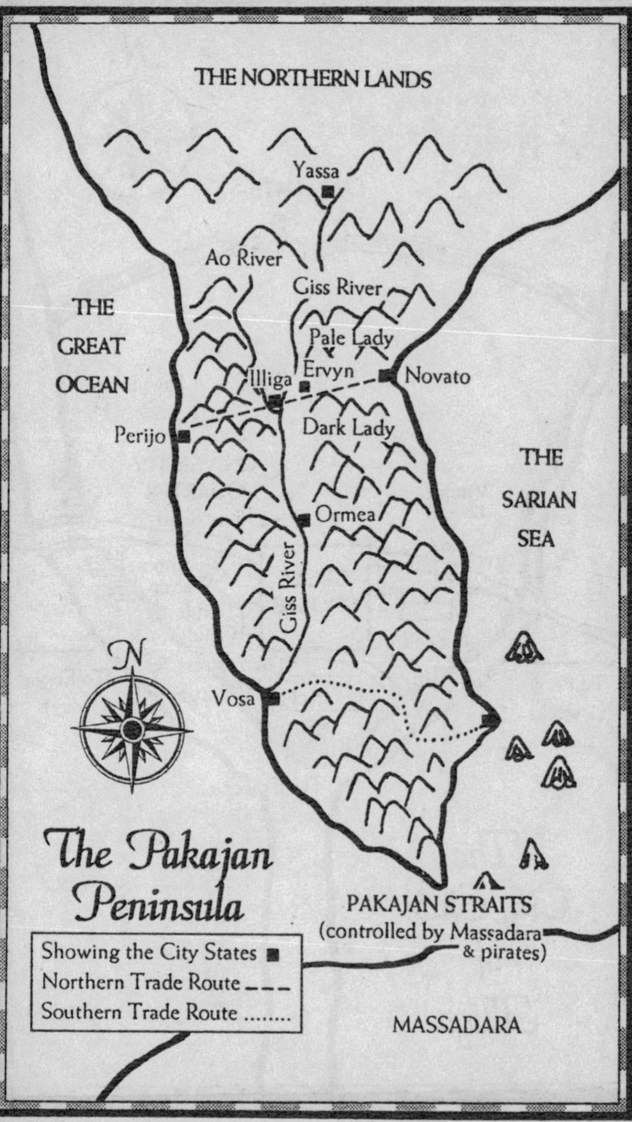

THE NORTHERN LANDS
Yassa
Ao River
Giss River
THE GREAT OCEAN
Pale Lady
Illiga
Ervyn
Novato
Perijo
Dark Lady
THE SARIAN SEA
Ormea
Giss River
Vosa
N
The Pakajan Peninsula
PAKAJAN STRAITS
(controlled by Massadara & pirates)
Showing the City States
Northern Trade Route
Southern Trade Route
MASSADARA

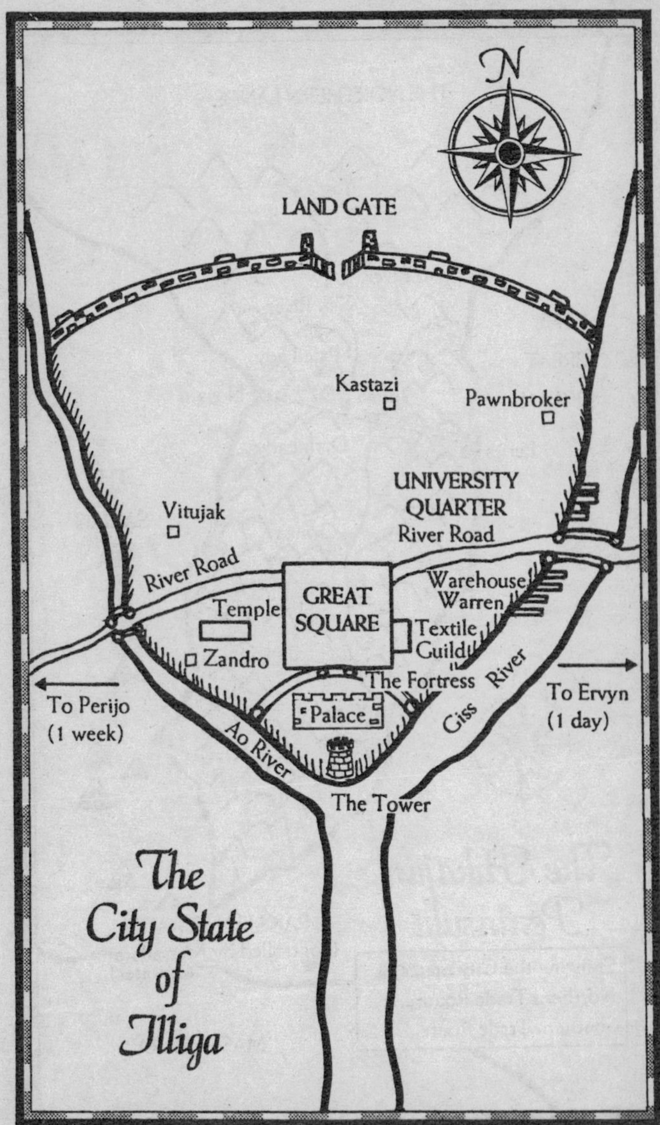
N
LAND GATE
Kastazi
Pawnbroker
UNIVERSITY
QUARTER
River Road
Vitujak
River Road
GREAT
SQUARE
Temple
Warehouse
Warren
Textile
Guild
Zandro
The Fortress
River
Giss
To Ervyn
(1 day)
To Perijo
(1 week)
Palace
Ao River
The Tower
The
City State
of
Illiga

Part I

Chapter 1

Taverik

"Bandits," mumbled the old man. He plunked his elbows on the splintery table and buried his nose in the bowl of ale Taverik had bought him. Taverik met Marko's eyes across the bent white head. With the incredible din in the tiny mountain tavern, he couldn't be sure he'd understood the old man's toothless Pakajan. But Marko's gray eyes had gone wary.

"Bandits! Where?" Taverik pressed, voice hoarse from the smoky room.

The old man surfaced and wiped his mouth on his filthy sleeve. "I told you, but you can't understand your own language anymore. You want I talk Massadaran, you boot-licking merchants? In the pass. Just above us."

"How many?" Marko asked.

"Dunno. More and more all summer. Attacked the last caravan ahead of you. In the gorge. You know it?"

Taverik nodded. He'd travelled the gorge dozens of times, a narrow, high-walled defile about two hours climb up the mountain from the village. "Any survivors?"

"Not many."

"Not *any*," Marko said grimly. "Or we'd have heard about it in Illiga."

Taverik saw the old man's quick scowl and looked a warning at Marko. Several of the villagers had quieted suddenly and edged closer. He didn't like their expressions. They might have finished off the survivors themselves, and looted whatever the bandits didn't take. Either that, or they'd attacked the caravan themselves and made damn sure no one survived to warn later travelers. Times were hard under Massadaran rule and who knew what these last few pockets of ungoverned Pakajans would turn to for survival. Best get out of there.

A young man swaggered over, hand on the sword he wore at his belt. Just making sure, Taverik thought with faint amusement, that we two "tame" Pakajans notice it. If caught, a Pakajan could spend a year in prison for wearing a sword. If caught.

With a sneer that heated Taverik's blood, the young man planted his knuckles on the table. "It's said that they are Bcacmat."

"The bandits?" said Taverik. "Oh, come on. You're trying to scare us."

"It's true," said the old man, puffing beery breath into Taverik's face. "We call the leader Red, and not for his hair, 'cause *that's* black. So's his beard. And he don't hardly speak no Pakajan. Nor Massadaran."

"And he comes here each night to relax," Marko said tartly.

"Yup," agreed the old man.

"No," chorused the others hurriedly. The old man thrust out his lip sulkily and buried his face in the bowl.

Taverik caught Marko's eyes and gave a slight jerk of the head toward the door. Marko nodded and flipped a coin to the table with a casual yawn. "Well, guess it's time to turn in," he said.

Taverik backed away. "Nice meeting you all." To his relief the crowd parted and let them cross the round room to the door. And why not? Taverik thought as he followed Marko under the reeking hide in the doorway. What's a few pelli from two merchants tonight, when tomorrow a whole merchant caravan might be for the taking?

A few snowflakes swirled through cold blue dusk. He

took a deep breath and his lungs gave a twinge from breathing smoke. "Phew!"

"No wonder the others refused to come with us," Marko said, leading the way past silent stone houses. "Lucky thing we went, though."

"Yes," Taverik agreed. "Now we have *some* warning, at least." They rounded the last house and Taverik could see the twinkle of the caravan's five campfires on the mountain almost directly above them. A cold gale roared down the slope, flattening his boot-length surcoat against his shivering body, and whipping his long yellow hair into tangles. "Going to be tough sleeping."

"First day of winter," Marko said into the teeth of the wind. "We'll be the last caravan through the pass this year."

"*If* we get through," said Taverik, then wished he hadn't, for Marko's shudder was not from cold.

"Who goes?" sang out a sentry in Massadaran.

"Taverik Zandro," Taverik called. "And Marko Kastazi."

The soldier abandoned formality. "You crazy, Zandro? You went down there?"

"Where's the captain?"

"Over there." The soldier pointed up at the second of the fires.

"Taverik," said Marko, "you go ahead. I'm going to take a walk."

"Take a walk?" repeated the soldier. "You want to get picked off?"

But Marko merely waved and continued on past the mules toward the pine grove on the other side of the trail. The soldier looked at Taverik with his jaw dropped, but Taverik only shrugged. Marko *liked* solitude. He was forever slipping off by himself. Taverik had given up two caravans ago warning him to stay in sight of camp. Marko would smile and agree it was dangerous, and the next moment off he'd go again. He was a strange one, Marko, and oddly close-mouthed about his past.

The captain stood up as Taverik strode toward the fire. "What's wrong?"

"Bandits," Taverik said, pulling off his cap as *Sadra* Law required. In the sudden silence the wind roared through the spruces around them. Even the loud-mouthed merchant from Perijo found nothing to say.

"They attacked the last caravan," Taverik added. "In the gorge. The villagers say it's a band which has been growing throughout the summer and fall."

"Don't believe it," said the Copper Guild man. "It's probably them, themselves, the flea-ridden thieves."

"They do seem on pretty friendly terms with the bandits," Taverik admitted.

"We must not go on!" declared the loudmouth from Perijo.

The captain made a rude noise. "You can stay in this forsaken village if you like. I intend to spend the winter in the comforts of Illiga."

"Well, you just see we get there!" said the loud-mouth. "We paid the zoji through the nose for your protection. So if I'm murdered by bandits, I'll report you!"

Taverik joined the roar of laughter and laughed even harder at the furious scowl on the loudmouth's face. The captain wiped his eyes and said, "Well, I'll warn the others. I've no doubt we can beat them off. We're a good size and have more soldiers." He strode toward the next fire.

Taverik sat down next to his mule boy. Twelve-year-old Uali shuddered and pressed closer to Taverik's leg. Tough for him, Taverik thought, his first caravan. He was the son of the family stableman and had never even been out of Illiga before. His face, white in the gathering darkness, turned up toward Taverik. "Maybe we shouldn't go, Kali Taverik."

"Don't worry," Taverik said bracingly, ignoring the tensing in his own stomach. "I've run off bandits before. It doesn't take much to scare them."

One of the Massadaran students condescended to speak Illigan Pakajan. "No, don't worry, boy," he said and glanced pointedly at the man to his right. "They're probably just a bunch of northern Pakajans who don't know what end of a sword is which."

The brunt of the barb was an immense Pakajan with the long red beard and braids all Pakajans had worn before the Massadaran colonists had arrived. He defiantly wore the colorful embroidery and sword belt, but his scabbard was empty. "Notice," he said in pure Pakajan, which the student probably couldn't follow, "first they impose *Sadra* Laws forbidding Pakajans to use a sword then they ridicule us for not using a sword. In the north, life is hard, but we are free from *Sadra* Laws. We haven't submitted to the Massadaran yoke."

"Barbarians!" retorted the other Massadaran student, poking his long nose from his furs—also forbidden to Pakajans under *Sadra* Laws. His sneering glance included Taverik, whose yellow hair and wide cheekbones proclaimed him Pakajan, and the Copper Guild man, with his light red hair and freckled face. "All of you."

"And you," Taverik returned, "are *ikiji*."

The student flushed and shoved the amulet he'd been fingering into his surcoat. Taverik had never seen anything like it before, a circlet with an odd claw-like design in it. Ugly. *Ikiji*—second best—indeed.

The Copper Guild man saw it too. "What are you doing?" he cried. "You'll bring the bandits upon us as punishment. You know the Creator forbids worship of anything made by man."

"Zojikam doesn't care a hoot about anything," said the student. Karaz, his name was. The Viti Karaz. "If you need help, turn to someone who *will* help."

The loudmouthed merchant from Perijo wrung his hands. "You mustn't say things like that!"

"Things like what?" Marko squatted down next to Taverik and spread slim, chapped hands to the fire.

The Copper Guild man reached across both Uali and Taverik to thump his knee. "You'll have to stop creeping off into the dark like that now, lad. Not safe no more!"

The loudmouth nodded solemnly. "The bandits will get you."

"So no more maidenly modesty!" cackled the Copper

Guild man. "Take your leaks against a tree like the rest of us."

Everyone guffawed at his words, then laughed again as Marko calmly told him what he could do with his leaks. Only Taverik saw the faint flush creeping up Marko's beardless cheek and wondered, not for the first time, how old he actually was. Young enough to have trouble growing a beard, but with the self-containment of an older man. He had the dark hair, high cheek bones and hawk nose typical of the Massadarans, yet he had the gray eyes of the Pakajans, and supported himself, his sister, and housekeeper as a merchant. Odd.

Sanisman, the only other Textile Guild member in the caravan, strolled over from the next fire. "Figures *you'd* go down to the flea-hole, Zandro," he said. "So tell us more about these bandits."

"They say the bandit chief speaks neither Massadaran nor Pakajan. Claim he's a Bcacmat."

"Bcacmat!" gasped the loudmouth from Perijo.

Taverik snorted. "The boogy man. More likely he's a merchant from Perijo."

"Will you be serious?" demanded the Perijan.

Sanisman laughed and squatted closer to the flames. "You're asking the wrong one to be serious. Our Taverik here's as crazy as they come. He's the one who dressed up a goat in the Textile Guild president's robes."

Not that story again. "That was three years ago," Taverik protested above the laughter. "And it was a pig, not a goat. Ittato campaigned for election saying a pig might as well hold the office as his opponent!"

"So," Sanisman said, "he tethers it in old Ittato's chair just before a meeting. And here's dignified old Ittato, opening his mouth to commence the meeting, and this pig starts squealing!"

Everyone hooted. Sanisman gasped out, "Then Ittato tries to drag it from the chair and it gets away and runs across the dais. And Donato Zandro—that's Tav's father—stands up and shouts, 'Hey, that's our pig!' "

A fresh wail of laughter arose.

"And when he realizes what he said, he shouts, 'Where's Taverik?' "

"Nowhere near," said Taverik.

"Next day, here comes Tav with both eyes black and a nose the size of a turnip!"

The men laughed again, but the smile faded from Marko's face. "That's nothing," Taverik said quickly. "The worst was Ittato's lecture. My ears ached for a month."

The Copper Guild man shook his head, still grinning. "Is that Zandro the one in three guilds and with all the warehouses? You're his son? Aye, I'd rather face an angry bull than cross Donato Zandro."

"So would Taverik!" said Sanisman, and they all laughed again.

"Glad you find bandits so funny!" called a merchant heading for the mule string.

Taverik's stomach flopped like a fish at the reminder. He caught Uali's worried eyes and stretched casually. "You set for the first watch?" he asked.

The boy nodded. "As long as there's plenty of firewood."

"Good lad. Wake me next, and I'll wake Marko." He looked the question at Marko and received a nod in return. They'd worked together for the last three journeys and barely needed words to communicate. Tossing a blanket to Uali, Taverik strolled into the cold to check the mule string one last time.

His five mules huddled on the far end of the picket line, their breath misting. Taverik ran his hand down the leg of the little one who had developed a limp that afternoon. The leg felt puffy and warm.

"You did this on purpose to plague me, you little idiot," he muttered. He'd have to repack everything the next morning to give her a rest up the switchbacks. He patted her and moved on to his riding mule, a huge, big-hearted beast. *Sadra* Laws forbade him horses, but he'd found himself the best mule he could afford. Better than any horse he'd ever seen, he thought, gently pulling the long silken ears. But still, low status.

A little apart stood the horses ridden by the caravan guards and the two Massadarans. Taverik paused to stroke the warm neck of the dappled grey nearest him, admiring the broad chest and powerful shoulders. The grey bent his head and nuzzled Taverik's fingers.

Suddenly a hand seized his collar. "Get away from my horse!" shouted Viti Karaz. Before Taverik could react, the student spun him around, kicked him in the rear and sent him sprawling to the rocks. Furious, Taverik surged to his feet, pulling his knife.

Arms circled him from behind. "Easy, easy," said the caravan captain, and to the student, "Put that sword away. I'll have no brawling."

Recalled to his senses—he could spend a year in prison for threatening a viti—Taverik relaxed and allowed the captain to push him away from the student. He turned into the darkness hearing the captain's low voice saying in Massadaran, ". . . not doing any harm, no need to humiliate him like that," and the angry mutter of the student's reply.

Marko watched from near his wagon, hands buried in the thick mane of his giant white mule. "They are pigs," he said.

Though seething with resentment Taverik merely shrugged. "I should have known better," he said lightly. He draped his arms over Whitey's bony back and tried to forget the incident. After all, during this entire trip the two students had reviled the Pakajans—including Taverik—in Massadaran, completely unaware that Taverik, and Marko too, spoke it fairly fluently. Not that they'd have cared if they'd known.

He stole a look at Marko, who was staring off up the pass, hands still under the warmth of Whitey's mane. Scared, but holding it in, Taverik thought.

He'd met Marko at the Textile Guild last year when the youth had attended his first meeting. Marko had only just earned enough money for the guild fee, and from his gaunt look, must have starved himself to do it. He'd plainly been on the edge of going under, and the other merchants, who had their own snobberies, had avoided him. Taverik had felt sorry for him and invited him along on the next merchant caravan as his mule boy. He'd offered to lend him money for purchases, too.

Older merchants had immediately closed in around Marko, obviously warning him about the Zandros. But to Taverik's surprise, Marko had gone with him and brought back excellent rugs. He'd immediately repaid Taverik with interest, and on the next caravan brought his own wagon, a huge-wheeled farm cart, though he and Taverik had still worked together.

Taverik couldn't exactly explain why he'd first put himself out for him. Maybe the determination and guts of the lad. But there was more to it, something about the way Marko seemed able to see Taverik for himself, instead of as one of those damn Zandros. Well, that wasn't it exactly, but he gave up trying to untangle it and tried instead to think of something to say to encourage the lad.

Cold darkness settled around them as the camp quieted for sleep. The twin peaks of the Guardian Ladies loomed high against the starry sky, and the wind poured down their talus slopes like fingers seeking entry in every crack of clothing. "Tav," said Marko softly.

"What?"

"If, hmm, if—"

Marko stopped there so Taverik finished it for him. "If anything happens to you?"

"Yes, damn you," Marko said, laughing softly. "Would you take care of my sister?"

"Of course," Taverik said. Though what, he privately wondered, would he ever do with a quiet, intellectual, self-contained young woman like Oma?

He said good night and went for his blankets, feeling hollow inside. Marko had people he loved waiting for him. What could he himself say? *If anything happens to me, would you tell my uncle I love him?* He hadn't seen his uncle since his seventeenth birthday, four years ago. Ah, how about, *Commend me to my brother Chado?* Taverik laughed sardonically and forced his mind to get sleepy.

* * *

The next morning dawned gray and grew no lighter. Clouds hung low, hiding the pass. As the caravan began its way up the trail, Taverik pulled up his hood against the cold damp wind. He rode tensely, moodily, at the end of his string.

Below him, the round stone houses of the village seemed to disappear into the rocky slopes from which they were made, their window holes staring blankly. Above, the first of the caravan rounded a switchback, the two students in the lead of course, flanked by watchful soldiers. The trail grew steeper. All too soon they were approaching the gorge. The captain rode back along the caravan. "Close up!" he said softly. "Stick together."

Uali hunched miserably on the lead mule, reins slack, and the string began to lag. The lame mule just ahead of Taverik balked suddenly. Taverik's big mule threw up its head with a snort as they almost collided.

"Will you get moving?" said the loudmouthed merchant just behind Taverik.

The captain trotted past. "Quiet! Don't get separated."

"We'll get left behind for the bandits," whined the loudmouth, "and it will be all your fault."

Taverik ignored him. "Uali! Keep them moving! Go on."

Uali looked back, then urged his mule on. They gained on Marko, whose cart had slowed at the steep turn of the switchback. Marko jumped down to lead the straining Whitey and Uali followed them around. Taverik gave the lame mule a touch of the whip and then his own big mule carried him up the rocky curve.

Ahead, six vultures struggled into the air. They'd entered the gorge.

To each side of Taverik lay the remains of carts, a dead mule, and scraps of cloth—the debris of a ruined caravan. Two more vultures hopped awkwardly away from an unidentified carcass. Taverik looked away.

High walls lifted overhead, echoing back hoof beats, the chink of rock and the creak of the wagons. If only they didn't make so much noise. Not that any bandits wouldn't have known exactly where they were at any point all morning. Taverik sat tense in the saddle, scanning the cliffs, his face tight, his buttocks tight, even his toes curled tight in his boots.

Gradually the trail rose. The cliffs receded and the switchbacks began again. They'd made it through the gorge. Nothing had happened. Taverik took a deep shuddering breath of relief.

They reached the top several hours later. The forest thickened here—the west side of the pass caught the rain from the sea and hoarded it, while the east went dry. Fog and spruce needles muffled the creak and clop of the caravan. To each side the White Lady and the Dark Lady rose into the clouds and disappeared, their presence almost human. The twin mountains had Massadaran names, but it was the old Pakajan names that stuck, the White Lady for her almost continual snow cap, and the Dark Lady for her south-facing rock field. Together they were the beloved guardians of Illiga.

Now that he could relax, Taverik became aware of his hunger. He reached back and dug in his saddle bag for the hunk of cheese stowed there.

With a dry woosh, an arrow struck the bag.

Taverik stared at it for one uncomprehending moment. Then the spruces on each side of the trail came alive with men. A high wavering yell exploded about the caravan. *Damn* Sadra *Laws,* Taverik thought, *leaving a man defenseless.* Then a man with a long knife leaped at him.

Taverik kicked a booted foot at him, and the man disappeared under the mule's hammering hooves. Some of the hired guards fled into the brush.

"Cowards!" shouted the captain, then fell from his horse, an arrow in his side.

"Taverik!" screamed Uali. Three men had surrounded him, dragging him from his mule.

"Hang on!" Taverik shouted and drummed his own mule forward.

A man on a white-eyed roan plunged between them. Behind the black beard the man's teeth gleamed as he roared something in a language Taverik couldn't make sense of. He swung a club. Taverik ducked under it. The man swung again, just as the mule reared bringing Taverik well in range. The club caught him a glancing blow, exploding the world into slivers of light and pain. Taverik grabbed for the mule's mane but it wasn't there.

Chapter 2

Taverik

He became aware he was lying on his face in the freezing mud. His head ached until he thought it would shatter, and he wanted to vomit. He swallowed and swallowed again.

Men shouted back and forth, but the battle was apparently over. Taverik lifted his cheek from the ooze and tried to see, but his eyes seemed glued shut. He rubbed at them—they felt sticky and his hand numb and stiff with cold.

"What about this one?" someone asked in Vosa Pakajan. The ground shook and footsteps crunched by his ear. Taverik forced himself limp. If any of the bandits realized he was still alive they might simply knife him. A booted foot kicked him ungently onto his back. He lay where he fell, trying not to screw up his face in defense. Hands patted his surcoat, felt the lump of his money bag, pulled it from his undercoat. His warm mantle was stripped away. Rough fingers found his chain and yanked.

"Hurry it up!" a man shouted in a strange and heavy accent, directly over Taverik. He recognized the voice of the black-bearded man who had struck him down.

"Get his ring," said another.

His ring! Oh Zojikam, his ring! It always was too tight. They'd cut off his finger for it. Taverik stiffened then again forced himself limp. Better than losing his life, better than losing his life, he thought over and over in rhythm with his throbbing head. Someone lifted his hand and he grit his teeth. But his fingers were cold and the ring loose. A tug, then his hand was dropped into the mud. Hooves thudded past. "Hurry!" shouted the bearded man again.

Footsteps crunched, then faded. The trail was silent.

"Zojikam!" groaned someone nearby. "Help me!"

Taverik struggled to his knees and wiped his hands over his eyes. His lashes parted painfully and he stared blurrily at his fingers. All there.

He looked up. His favorite mule lay dead beside him. The rest of the string was gone. And Uali?

He pushed himself to his feet. Around him lay broken wagons, dead mules, and twisted bodies. The loud mouth from Perijo sat on the ground shaking his head back and forth like a bewildered bear. Uali sprawled on his face. Taverik rolled him over, then turned abruptly away. His stomach twisted, then heaved.

He straightened slowly, wiping his mouth on his sleeve. Suddenly he stiffened. What about Marko?

The farm wagon still stood just ahead. Taverik stumbled past it and saw why. Whitey lay in the traces, red stains bright against his creamy coat. "Poor thing," he murmured. At his voice, Whitey lifted his head and looked at Taverik then laid it tiredly down again.

Climbing over the tangle, Taverik found Marko curled up against the front wheel. He dropped to one knee beside him, allowing himself no hope.

"Marko?" he said softly. He lifted him away from the wheel. Marko groaned. Blood darkened the front of his black surcoat, red on Taverik's fingers as they found the gash in the fabric. Marko opened his eyes, focused on Taverik and gasped. He struggled away.

"Stop it," Taverik said. "It's me. Tav."

Marko stared at him a moment then relaxed. "Your face."

"Bloody, I know. Let me look at you." Taverik eased him down and began to unbutton the quilted undercoat.

Marko's cold fingers closed around his hand. "I'll be all right," he said. "Just take me home and Sahra will take care of it."

"Who's Sahra?"

The fingers tightened. "I mean, Oma."

"Let me bandage it, Marko."

"No, I'll be fine. Just help me up."

"Hold still, will you?" Taverik said, exasperated. He pulled his knife and slit the linen undershirt. Marko caught his hand with surprising strength. "Are we friends, Tav? Truly?"

"Of course," Taverik said. "You know that."

Marko met his eyes for a long moment. Delirious, Taverik thought. Finally Marko nodded and turned his face aside. Wondering at his tension, Taverik tore open the linen shirt. "But . . ." he said in surprise. "You're already bandaged?"

"Taverik," Marko began resignedly.

Taverik slit the bandage. He stared in astonishment, then understanding flooded him. "You—you're a, a . . ."

Marko met his eyes again. "A woman."

Taverik stared back, anger quickly replacing his amazement. A woman! All this time, all these trips, she'd made a fool of him. Here she was, walking brazenly around, her hair uncovered, the Guild, Taverik himself taking her for a man, talking to her like she was a man—

"Take me to my sister," Marko said. "And don't let anyone know . . . and *don't* take me to a doctor! Promise!"

Promise? How could he promise that? Yet, he thought, he, no, she, was the same person he would have given his life for in a street fight, and he could have sworn Marko would have done the same. Why was she pretending to be a man?

Marko shook his arm. "Promise!"

What should he do? His father would hand her over

to the authorities, denounce her at the Textile Guild and put in a claim for her property. The end. His brother, Chado, would do no differently. That thought awoke the stubborn core within him. "Father always did despair of me," he said slowly. "All right, Marko, or whatever your name is. I promise."

Marko gave a little sigh and relaxed, eyes closed. Grimly Taverik set to work, stanching the blood and tying a dressing tight. No air bubbles, he thought as he pulled the gory linen and undercoat back into place. He'd heard that meant the wound had missed the lungs.

He stood and took Whitey's reins, clicking encouragingly. The mule obediently heaved himself to his feet and stood trembling. Taverik untangled his near back hoof from the traces and led him forward, pulling the wagon a few paces. He might do, Taverik thought.

He went back for Uali, wrapping the boy's body in his cloak. Poor thing. Taverik dreaded the moment he gave him to his father. Lifting him, he staggered through the wreckage to the cart.

The short day was passing fast, the cold intensifying. The Copper Guild man limped toward him. "The captain's dead," he said. "So's our poor free Pakajan. He should have stayed in the north where he was allowed to defend himself. I'm counting survivors. Will that wagon go?"

"Yes." Taverik laid the body in the cart. "Help me with Marko Kastazi, will you?" They settled Marko beside Uali and Taverik wrapped her with the rugs the bandits had found too heavy to carry off. She was not conscious.

The student with the amulet strode up to the cart, his heavy-browed face unburdened by any pain or shock. "You going down the hill? You'll take me."

"Yes, my Viti," Taverik said neutrally.

"That's five for this wagon, then," said the Copper Guild man. "Only one other wagon is mobile. That other clothie, Sanisman, and that fellow who talks all the time can go in—"

"There's a body in here!" exclaimed Viti Karaz. "I'm not riding with any body! I will be defiled for ten days!"

Where had he gotten that odd idea? "You can go in the other wagon, Viti," Taverik said.

"No. You get it out of the cart, Pakajan."

"I will not," Taverik said, reckless with a splitting head and worry about Marko. They had no time to stand arguing, and he wasn't about to tell his stableman he'd left his son in the road. He saw Sanisman and nodded. "Want a ride?"

"The sooner the better," Sanisman said. Taverik helped him in and touched Whitey with the whip. They rolled forward, Taverik guiding the mule around the wreckage. Sanisman looked back. "If looks could kill, you'd be in the road, Zandro."

"I may be yet if he reaches Illiga still with his grudge."

"Well, I'll say one thing for you Zandros, you don't lack for courage whatever else they say about you. I'm glad you gave it to him. Do you know, when the attack began he held up that disgusting *ikiji* of his and none of the bandits touched him! They only took his horse. He didn't have a scratch on him."

A village had grown up on the west slope of the pass, an easy day's journey from Illiga. Taverik's heart always lifted as Ervyn's steep slate roofs appeared around those last switchbacks—once more he'd come home to the beautiful Giss Valley.

The clouds cleared as they descended, and just as Whitey's trembling legs brought the cart into the temple yard, the sun's last rays blazed across the iron work and stone towers of the temple. Taverik caught his breath at the beauty of it.

"Zojikam be praised," murmured Sanisman beside him.

"Thought we'd never get here," complained the loudmouth from the freight wagon behind. The Copper Guild man pulled it in beside Taverik and limped to ring the temple bell. A crowd gathered, talking excitedly and listening to Loudmouth who for once had an enthusiastic audience. The priest, a Pakajan with white-gold hair, helped Sanisman clamber stiffly over the rolls of rugs.

Taverik leaned his elbows into his knees and cradled his aching head. He felt terrible. Nothing would be nicer than to allow the priest and his readers to care for his needs. To eat—well, maybe not to eat, his stomach churned as it was. But to sleep . . .

He'd promised Marko. No doctor. Take him—her—home. Maybe the promise didn't count. But no, it would be impossible to conceal her identity here. He'd rest and then go.

"Kali, won't you come in?"

Taverik woke with a start. The street was deserted. Darkness had cloaked the village, and the priest beside him stood in a pool of yellow from the lantern in his left hand.

"No, but thank you," Taverik said. He roused himself and climbed stiffly over the seat to kneel beside Marko. "I promised my friend I'd take him home."

The priest lifted his lantern and peered over the high wheel. "Your friend needs medical attention. You do too," he said in pure Pakajan.

Taverik chewed his lip. It was true. Marko breathed shallowly with a catch each time she inhaled. Her skin felt clammy. Maybe he could swear the priest to secrecy. Let him tend them both.

"There's a visiting doctor even," the priest went on.

A doctor! "No, I promised," Taverik said firmly. He broke off and stared as the priest squeezed shut his eyes and held his breath. "Are you all right?"

The older man looked hard at Taverik. "There's more to this than you're willing to say. But, young man, I trust you. Water your mule. I'll bring you food and a jar of blessed water infused with healall."

The man put down the lantern and was gone before Taverik's slowed mind took in all he'd said. The priest knew something was odd. What if he'd gone to fetch the village headman? Maybe Taverik should sneak away before he came back. Yet Whitey stood with his head down. They wouldn't get far.

He fetched water in the bucket from the courtyard well, and held it while Whitey drank gratefully. Frigid water sloshed and numbed his hands. Whitey finished and snorted a wet cold spray into his face. "Beast!" he sputtered. But the shock woke him up.

"Here," said the priest, hurrying down the flagstone path from a side door. He thrust a jar and a bundle into Taverik's arms and waved aside his thanks. "Listen," he said, coming close. The lantern's light cast shadows upward across his face. "Last night I dreamed. A black eagle chased a hawk. The hawk fled, but wherever it hid, the eagle was always there before it. Somehow I knew that if the black eagle caught that hawk, all comfort, justice and truth would depart from our land."

Cold dread tightened Taverik's stomach. The priest's words pierced like arrows, aimed at him alone of all the people in the universe. The safe material world seemed to ripple until he felt exposed, unsafe—as if all the unseen spiritual beings in the cosmos had suddenly become aware of one Taverik Zandro.

"All day," the priest was saying, "I have asked Zojikam what he meant by that dream, and what he wanted to do about it. But all was silent until you said, 'No, I promised.' Then a thrill went across my soul, and I knew, somehow you were part of that dream."

"No," Taverik said hoarsely. He cleared his throat. "I mean, I'm just a merchant. There is nothing."

"There is something. Something afoot. Whatever it is, my son, remember that Zojikam is a tower of defense. Now let me bless you."

Taverik pulled off his soft cap, wondering if he should kneel Massadaran style or stand Pakajan style. But the priest merely reached up and covered Taverik's hair with his warm hands and poured out the familiar, comforting words. The unseen world retreated.

"Thank you," Taverik said. He climbed into the driver's seat and picked up the rein. The priest went to Whitey's head and Taverik watched, puzzled, as he whispered into the mule's long, silky ears. Whatever he'd said, Whitey responded by arching his neck and pawing with one huge hoof.

The priest stepped back. "Go with Zojikam," he said, then as Taverik snapped the reins, "Wait!"

Taverik pulled up and looked back. The priest dragged off his own warm mantle and thrust it into Taverik's hands. "I can't—" Taverik began, but the priest had already gone.

The road dipped and rose over gentle hills, past farms and orchards lit silver in the light of the moon rising behind them. Dogs barked sleepily as he passed each silent vidyen with its round stone rooms and numerous conical roofs. Taverik wrapped the reins over the brake and let Whitey pick his pace. Once more he climbed over the seat—damn but he was tired! Kneeling awkwardly on the rolls of rugs, he untied the bundle the priest had given him.

"Marko," he said. He felt her neck for her pulse. Her skin felt cold. Taverik's face tightened. He should have stayed. She needed a doctor.

She stirred and groaned something. Taverik leaned closer. "What?"

"Black eagle," she said. "Sahra!"

"Marko, wake up," Taverik said, feeling helpless and hating it. "Here, drink this."

"Water?" she said more normally.

He helped her drink. "Blessed water with healall in it."

"Where are we?"

"The road for home. Hours away though. Listen, there's a doctor back at Ervyn. I think you need it. And the priest is a good man, why don't we go back and—"

"No, please, I must hide. The fewer who know about me . . ." She trailed off and squinted up at him. "Unless you won't make it?"

"I'll make it. Can you eat?"

"No."

He drank some blessed water, and his head cleared. Biting off a piece of the bread, he chewed with distaste, staring at the road rolling out behind them. She'd mentioned the black eagle, he thought. Was there really such a thing, or had she overheard the priest's dream?

"Marko?" he asked, but she didn't answer. He pulled the rug higher and crawled back over the seat, resigned to grinding hours of travel.

The nearly full moon rose from behind the mountains, flooding the Valley with silver light. A fey mood fell upon Taverik, and he turned the priest's words over and over in his mind in time to Whitey's hooves: Something afoot, something afoot. Behind and before, the bare peaks of tall mountains gleamed blue-white in the moon glow. Pinned so in the silent white and black landscape, Taverik again felt exposed—a sole human in a world of unseen powerful beings suddenly aware of him. Something afoot . . .

He woke suddenly and found the cart stopped by the side of the road and Whitey dozing, one hip cocked. He climbed down and got the mule going again. He walked beside the cart to keep awake and warm.

He could see Illiga now as he topped each gentle rise. The moon, nearly overhead, gleamed faintly on its beautiful towers which climbed the stark cliffs between the Giss River and the Ao. At the very peak stood the tallest tower, where Zoji Balanji ruled. Built by Pakajan river barons, the tower now served generations of Massadaran zojis, part of the growing trade empire built by powerful Massadara to the south. The Pakajan Peninsula blocked the mouth of the inner sea like gritted teeth, and whoever controlled its narrow, mountainous length controlled trade with the rest of the world. Massadara held it tight against its rival nation, Bcacma. And the Pakajans suffered.

Illiga herself lay midway on the only northern pass across the mountain ranges, and at the confluence of the two major rivers running nearly the length of the central valley. Raw ore and wool came down river from the mountains, and merchants crossed the passes or travelled the river by barges, all carefully controlled and taxed by the Zoji Balanji. The city prospered.

The farms Taverik now passed were of the square-built Massadaran type, the Pakajan farmers trapped in the semi-feudal system imposed from outside. As the road began its descent to the Giss River, Whitey stepped up his pace eagerly. Taverik climbed into the cart again, unable to keep up with his head spinning and aching so. They covered the last miles to the bridge in less than an hour.

"Who goes?" sang out the sentry.

Taverik squinted against sudden yellow light of a lantern. "Taverik Zandro, citizen of Illiga and—"

"Papers."

Taverik pulled them from his belt and was waved on. "Get up, Whitey," he said and the mule started across the bridge. Above them rose shadowed cliffs, blending imperceptibly into ancient city walls. Below, barges rocked silently at the city docks. The spill of light from the inner guard house crossed Whitey's flanks, Taverik's face, then at last they were in the city. Whitey leaned into the harness and struggled up the steep River Road. Taverik's eyelids felt heavy and gritty, but he forced himself to keep vigilant. He'd be a tempting target for thieves.

They passed the silent university and entered the square with its homeless sleeping under the stars—Marko had told him that she and her sister had lived like that their first year here. In this very cart. On his own, Whitey turned down silent narrowing streets and finally stopped before a shuttered store front, and gate.

Taverik pounded on the gate. No answer. He took his knife and pounded with its hilt. The racket echoed down the silent street and he couldn't resist a quick look over his shoulder. Next door a dog began to bark.

At last he heard timid footsteps. A woman said, "Who's there?"

"Taverik Zandro," he said softly. "Open up, Bibi. I've brought Marko home."

The bolt slid back and the gate opened. Whitey crowded past the servant woman into the tiny courtyard. Bibi shut and locked the gate behind them. "Where's Kali Marko?" she asked, raising the lantern until the courtyard glowed.

"Here," he said, unrolling rugs. "She's been hurt pretty bad."

"She . . ." Bibi whispered, her eyes wide.

"She," Taverik repeated firmly. He slid his hand under Marko's shoulders. Only then did he see what he had missed—for how many miles? Marko had bled and bled, the thick wool pile of the rug thirstily soaking up the blood.

Chapter 3

Taverik

Taverik stripped back the rugs. "Hurry," he snapped at the round-mouthed Bibi. "Help me lift her."

Bibi started, then helped him lift Marko's dead weight to the edge of the cart. "I'll get the kala," she whispered.

"Wait!" Taverik hissed. But she had already snatched up the lantern and flurried around the back of the house.

Left alone in black and silver light, Taverik looked up at the shuttered windows of the next house and realized his indiscretion. *She's been hurt*, he'd said aloud. Had curious ears heard? He'd have to guard his tongue from now on.

Carrying Marko, he staggered across the tiny courtyard to the back door Bibi had left open. He stepped into the dark tiny kitchen and looked around uncertainly. He'd always entered through the shop in front, or through the side door, where the front stairs led to the second floor. This was Bibi's domain. Red light from the embers played across blackened cooking pots and a basket of dirt-clodded potatoes. Strings of onions and garlic hung from the low rafters. Beyond, a door with an ancient, hand-hewn lintel led to the hall and the shop. Bibi's bed, linen trailing, was tucked snugly under the steep stairs to his left. Maybe he should set Marko down there; his arms ached from her weight.

A stair creaked above his head and he looked up into the glow of the lantern. Marko's sister, Oma, peered at him around the narrow landing. She wore a green wrapper over her nightdress. Her black hair, uncovered like a prostitute's, rippled across her shoulders. "Is he dead?" she whispered, her eyes frightened pools.

"No, she's not," Taverik said, harsher than he meant because his shoulders burned under the strain. "Where do you want her?"

Her startled eyes focused on his face. Her hand flew to her hair, then she turned. "Up here," she said.

Taverik followed her around the narrow landing, Marko's boots scuffing the whitewashed wall. He passed the tiny room where he'd eaten many a relaxed meal completely unaware of the trick they were pulling on society. On him. Winter chill struck his face as he followed Oma into the front room. Bibi knelt by the hearth, coaxing flames from the embers. "Put her here," Oma said, pushing forward a padded couch.

He lowered Marko gently down and collapsed into the wooden armchair opposite, breathing hard. His head throbbed. He wanted nothing more than sleep.

"She won't stop bleeding!" The panic in Oma's voice brought Taverik's head up with a jerk. He *had* slept. Bibi was fumbling with a new bandage already stained shockingly crimson. Marko's face looked waxy white, almost transparent, the circles dark under her eyes. Oma knelt beside the couch and chaffed a limp hand. "Oh, what'll we do?"

Taverik forced his aching head to think. They couldn't lose her now. Not after all that. "Bibi," he said, "down in the wagon is a bottle of water. Blessed water with healall in it. Will you bring it?"

"Yes, Kali," she said and thudded across the bare floorboards.

"We've got to keep her warm. Do you have another blanket?"

"Blanket? Yes." Oma whirled away and he heard her feet on the steep stairs, then overhead. Bibi brought the water and Taverik gently spooned some into Marko's mouth. It merely ran out. "Zojikam!" breathed Bibi behind him.

Taverik sat back on his heels, frustrated. Afraid. "We've got to bring a doctor," he said.

"No!" cried Oma, returning with blankets.

He met her eyes. "Look," he said, "I don't know who you two really are, or why you're playing this crazy game. But Marko will probably die if she doesn't get help."

"We have no money."

"You have a cartload of rugs."

"We don't know any doctors."

"I'll find one."

"But what if he sees she's a woman?"

"Let him," Taverik said. "Put her in a nightdress. Get her hair covered respectably. He'll suspect nothing."

Chewing her lip, Oma stared from him to Marko's white face, to Bibi's frightened one. At last she thrust out her hands as if explaining herself to someone not there. "All right then."

Taverik pushed himself wearily to his feet, remembering a tattered doctor's sign near the market square. He'd have to double the usual fee, though, to get a doctor out at this time of night.

In the end he had to triple it. But, he thought as he stabled the doctor's mule, at least one of the rugs had been acceptable payment. None of them had anything else.

The cart still sat in the courtyard. Sour disquiet settled over Taverik as he remembered Uali, lying silent in the cold. He trudged upstairs.

Oma's stricken eyes met his when he entered. Something was wrong. She'd dressed, and now stood by the fire, hands clenched so tight her knuckles shone.

"Well?" said the doctor. He sat on the wooden armchair, the ends of Bibi's bandage in his hands. Bibi hovered across from him, clutching a steaming bowl of water.

"Well what?" Taverik said.

The doctor swiveled around. His eyes glittered indignantly. "This is clearly a wound made by a sword."

Taverik's vision narrowed. "Yes," he said calmly enough, though his mouth went dry.

"How is a young woman receiving sword wounds?"

"We were attacked by robbers."

Marko murmured something and the doctor bent to listen. Taverik crossed to the foot of the couch. He found himself looking at a stranger. She now wore a nightdress, her hair pulled back and decently hidden under a cap. Even in lace she did not make a pretty woman; her high cheekbones, arching nose and firm chin were too strong for current definitions of beauty. Without the humorous gray eyes she looked pure Massadaran, remote and aristocratic. The quiet friend who had made the last year bearable was gone. Taverik felt disjointed, as if he were looking down from the ceiling at himself and an unknown vita.

Again she said something. The doctor cocked his head. "What's this about black eagles?" he demanded.

Water splatted on the floorboards. Bibi righted the bowl with horrified apologies.

"That reminds me," Taverik said, speaking quickly, saying anything to ease the sudden tension. "We've got some blessed water you can use. Yes, where? Ah, here it is." He snatched up the bottle and thrust it towards the doctor. "Try some of this."

The doctor smiled. "Blessed water," he said, at last beginning to work on the wound. "You poor innocents. You really think Zojikam has blessed that particular jug? I doubt the old fool was even aware of your prayer."

"Some people say so," Taverik said stiffly. The mockery of the Holy Creator pressed in on his aching head. Yet he had to admit the doctor's hands were skilled and he managed to at last stop the bleeding.

The old man pulled out a needle and black thread.

"I'll just take a quick stitch here and there," he said. Oma paled and turned away.

"Now, just as I must take a stitch—so," continued the doctor, bending over Marko but talking to Taverik, "to make sure the shoulder mends right, so must we all take our own steps to make sure our lives go right. There are many lesser spirit beings in this universe who, correctly addressed and appeased, are much more willing to help us than the so-called almighty Zojikam in—"

"That's *ikiji*," Taverik said.

"Second best? Being cheated?" The doctor snipped the thread and thrust the needle through his sleeve. "The concept is merely an abrogation of materialistic merchants. More sophisticated, learned men know many sides to the matter. Hand me that dressing. Hold her up."

Taverik knelt by the couch and half-lifted Marko as the doctor deftly rebandaged her shoulder. Her face looked gray. "Will she be all right?"

The doctor pulled the shears from his bag and snipped. "Depends. On infection. Strength. We should know by morning. Set her down. Now, just to be on the safe side, I have this little charm."

From around his neck he pulled the circlet containing a three-clawed talon symbol. Oma gasped.

"So odd she should mention the Black Eagle," the doctor said. "I have just returned from Vosa, where I purchased a powerful charm of the Black Eagle." He looked down at Taverik, still kneeling by the couch, the circlet winking in the firelight. "You desire a spiritual dimension to my healing craft. Since Zojikam is powerless, I shall invoke the name of the Black Eagle."

"No!" cried Oma and Taverik together.

"It won't take long," the doctor reassured them.

Oma pushed between Marko and the doctor, suddenly fierce. "It's evil. Put it away!" she said.

"My dear . . ."

"She told you to put it away." Taverik stood up beside Oma, more than a head taller than the doctor.

The old man shrugged. "So be it," he said, slipping

the charm back into his surcoat. "And now, let's have a look at your head, young man. I want you in bed, yourself."

"I'll stay here."

"Surely—"

"I'll stay here," Taverik insisted, aware the doctor thought them all crazy, but filled with the odd notion he ought to guard Marko. Maybe he *was* crazy. Guard her from what?

The hours crept past. Marko tossed and muttered in her fever. Often she cried out for her father and mother. She seemed to be searching for a strong box. She called again for Sahra. Oma knelt beside her. "Hush, Mar," she said, sponging her face and soothing her.

"We will know soon how it shall go," the doctor said. He sat beside the couch; his hooded eyes seemed to Taverik to be watching them all.

Taverik sat opposite him in a straight chair, struggling to stay awake. Absurd that he not let himself take a nap. Yet he felt an odd sensation of being locked in a silent battle with the doctor over Marko; as if she'd be lost if he slept. He wasn't sure what the battle was about—it felt like grappling shadows. But even stronger than before he felt the disquieting sensation of exposure, as if every being in the spiritual world watched him. Zojikam!

To keep himself awake, he began to recite the opening prayers of the temple service. He'd forgotten large parts—he hadn't attended the temple in years—but he struggled on, the words like a thread leading him through the night's confusing maze. He'd made it past the Confession to the Promise before the doctor stirred and laid a hand on Marko's brow. "The fever has gone down," he said.

Oma lifted her head, hope filling her dark-circled eyes. Bibi thudded across the room and opened the shutters. In the soft pre-dawn light Marko's face had regained some color.

"Yes, she'll do," said the doctor. "And you, young man, get some rest."

He stood up, and Taverik stood with him, searching his seamed face. The man seemed unaware of any contest between himself and Taverik. It must have been morbid imagination, coupled with the concussion.

"I will bring your rug tomorrow," Taverik said.

"I'll send a servant for it today," the doctor amended, and started down the stairs. Taverik followed, saw the doctor off, then stood in the courtyard as the first sun crept across the roof. Hard to think what to do.

"I caught you in time," Oma said breathlessly. Her cap had gone awry and fluffy strands of black hair floated in the morning breeze. Taverik pretended not to see them. She pressed his hand. "Thank you. I can't thank you enough."

"That's all right," Taverik said.

"Please, you won't tell anyone?"

"I won't tell," Taverik assured her. With effort he dragged his thoughts together. "May I borrow Whitey and your cart to take Uali home in?"

"Yes, yes, certainly."

His muscles grated against each other as he dragged rugs from the cart and threw them into the storefront, then labored the reluctant Whitey into harness once more. Ahead lay the unpleasant task of bringing Uali's body to his family. After that, confessing to his father that he'd returned with less than he'd started with. He'd be blamed of course. And after that?

Chapter 4

Marita

A line of light shone under the door ahead. Marita crept down the dark hall toward it. Her heart beat so hard she could hear it. Against her will, her fingers closed around the knob, turned it. She peered in.

The terror engulfed her. Her hoarse cry echoing forever, she fled a presence she couldn't see—had never seen. Black corridors opened on each side of her as she ran. Another door ahead. She scrabbled toward it, willing suddenly sluggish muscles to move, panting for air. There! She was safe, she was free.

Sahra! Sahra was still trapped in the house and would never be able to escape that evil presence alone. Marita had to go back. For an eternity she clung to the door that led to safety. The war inside her grew to agony. At last she mastered herself and turned. Three steps into pitch blackness.

She immediately felt the presence like a black, buzzing cloud about her. "Sahra!" she shouted.

Sahra answered close by. "Mari! Here."

The black cloud engulfed Marita. She choked.

Sahra's voice sounded right in her ear: "Mari, stop it! You're scaring me!"

Marita was being shaken and it hurt. She opened her eyes and found Sahra bending over her with frightened eyes. Her throat felt raw and her linen shirt clung damply to her neck and arms. Sahra released her. "You scared me," she repeated.

"Scared myself," Marita said. She was lying on the couch before the fire, the morning rain pecking steadily at the thick glass in the window. "I had the nightmare again."

Sahra sat back on her heels. "I thought it had stopped."

"The bandits must have stirred it up."

"Maybe some brandy would help," Sahra said.

Marita wiped stinging sweat from her eyes as Sahra crossed the room, the dark tendrils of the nightmare still clinging to her mind. She'd dreamed it first in an alley in Vosa, huddled with Sahra and Bibi behind a broken cart while flames from her parents' home roared to the sky.

She'd dreamed the dream every night for almost a year afterwards. Not until they'd fled to Illiga did it begin to fade; she only dreamed it when things went wrong or when she'd gone too long without food. Lately she'd almost forgotten about it.

Sahra came back with Bibi. Marita snorted when she saw the tray loaded with food and watered wine instead of brandy. It was the closest Bibi would ever come to disobeying.

"Let me help you sit up," Sahra said. Gritting her teeth, Marita struggled higher. Though it was but the third day after she'd received the wound, she'd insisted on dressing. She'd learned early to guard against the tempting trap of self-pity.

"You have recovered fast," Sahra said, pouring a glass of wine.

"It was the blessed water," Bibi said, curtseying at the door. "Zojikam is so good." Marita closed her mouth on her retort: if Zojikam was so good, why had he let this happen in the first place? Why were they struggling and starving because of their parents' death and a murderer still seeking them?

Sahra sat once more at her table, her head bent over her books, her special love. Sometimes it seemed Sahra could exist in a world of books and never need human companionship—or realize Marita might need her companionship. Their new life had been hardest on Sahra, Marita thought, so very bright, yet unable to adjust to constant uncertainty and danger.

She watched her younger sister's pen scratch across the paper under the steady glow of the oil lamp. Open books circled her like planets around the sun. Several were Sahra's own, volumes of poetic philosophy, currently the rage. Since a book by a woman would never have been published, let alone read seriously, Marita had told the publisher she was an agent for an author who wanted to be known as "The Humble Kali." The books had caught on, selling well even among the viti. The publisher had happily agreed to keep their address secret, providing the manuscripts kept coming.

Sahra's other two books were written by a rival author, who also seemed to prefer anonymity. The Gentle Philosopher's humorous, peppery answers to each of Sahra's works stirred her to write more than ever. The public loved the debate, demanding more and more books from the gleeful publisher. Sahra had almost finished her next manuscript, a reply quite adroitly done, Marita thought.

Still, Marita felt wistful as she watched Sahra's face, serene in the warm lamplight. Only when Sahra became engrossed in her private world did fear and tension seem to ebb from her. Marita had tried her best to provide security yet nothing but books seemed to stave off the memory of terror. So Marita bought books, even if she had to skip a few meals to afford them.

But Marita's near death had this time frightened Sahra so badly she'd retreated deeper than ever. For that matter, Marita thought, balancing her watered wine on her stomach, it frightened her too. Two new players had joined in the game.

To save her life a doctor had been called. Who knows what secrets he might have ferreted out? What if she were to meet him again? Would he recognize her even in men's clothes? And now Taverik knew her secret. What would come of that? Men in more than one guild claimed no Zandro could be trusted. But Taverik was different from his father and brother. Wasn't he?

He'd kept her secret after all, and taken her home, that jolting, disorienting journey through the dark, the stars wheeling overhead, the eagle's claw wheeling in her mind.

She'd been oddly aware of his presence in her delirium, when the dark cloud engulfed her, just as in her nightmares. She'd been hardly able to stave the dark off, her strength failing fast. "Help me!" she'd cried into the night. At that, something had seemed to brush her hand. A thread. Her fingers closed around it and it tugged her gently forward. She followed it but found it harder and harder to feel. She'd clenched her hand tight but the thread was gone. The darkness closed in.

Light. A thin ray of golden light gleamed across her palm. She'd followed that desperately, until it faded, leaving the dark darker. But immediately she heard a faint melody, as from a pipe. The sweet, reedy sound seemed to go before her until it, too, began to fade. "Don't go!" she'd cried, and plunged stubbornly after it. Gone. But once again the thread brushed her hand. Thread, light, melody—or all three at once. Whatever it was, she hung onto it tightly, and it led her safely through the burning anger in that dark presence.

When she woke she found herself in lace, her hair pulled tightly back under a cap. It had been more than three years since she'd worn such clothes. To one side of her sat an old man in a black surcoat, to the other, Taverik Zandro, a pair of lions with eyes fixed on her face to search out all secrets. Taverik's shoulder-length yellow hair was dark and spiky around a scalp wound. She puzzled over it then fuzzily remembered all that had happened. He'd gotten her back just as he'd promised, though he'd apparently broken his promise not to call a doctor. Was she that ill? She'd felt too weak to worry about it and had merely gone to sleep.

But now, three days later, she felt good and worried. Taverik knew. Nothing could turn back time. Things would be different from now on.

"Sahra," she said, and waited while her sister surfaced reluctantly from her private world. "You haven't heard from Taverik since that night?"

"No. Why?"

"That's not like him. It worries me a little." A lot,

but she wouldn't scare Sahra by saying so. "I'm wondering if we should slip away to another city. Novato, maybe."

Sahra swallowed hard. "The books. And oh, I couldn't face another year sleeping in the wagon in a slum, doing mending forever."

"We won't have to do that," Marita said soothingly. "We'll plan ahead and not get taken by surprise again. I love this house too."

She loved it fiercely. Tiny it was. Sparsely furnished. But *hers*. She bought it with money she'd earned by her own work. She was proud of that, of the rug on the floor, the books and the few knickknacks that told her they were not so poor anymore. Even the wood keeping them warm was something *she* had achieved.

Sahra rose and went to the window, staring through the thick, distorted glass. Rain pattered and guggled in the eaves. "Do you think Taverik will ever come back?"

Marita turned her head sharply at the wistfulness in Sahra's voice but her sister stood against the light and Marita couldn't see her expression. "It would be a good thing if he didn't," she said all the more firmly because she herself depended on his friendship more than was safe.

Bibi's voice rose from the gate outside, and the next moment a hollow clopping resounded in the courtyard. Sahra squinted through the rippled glass. "That's him now." She smiled roguishly, like in the old days. "Shall I tell him it would be a good thing if he went away?"

"Brat!" The side door opened below and Marita struggled to sit up. "Hurry, hide your manuscript!"

Sahra gasped and stacked her books and papers. "What are you going to tell him?"

"I don't know, I haven't had time to think. My boots, Sahra, I can't reach my boots."

Sahra crawled half under the couch. "Got them," she panted as she surfaced, her cap knocked half off.

Marita thrust her feet into their stubborn depths. "Your hair's gotten loose," she said. "Hold still." But the wayward strands would not properly tuck.

A knock sounded at the door and Bibi entered. "Kali Taverik," said Bibi.

"No, wait!" Sahra cried, hands to her cap.

"Good morning, Oma, Marko," said Taverik. He'd quietly followed Bibi up, and stood in the doorway behind, head and shoulders taller than the servant. Bibi gave a startled bleat and hastened away. Taverik met Marita's eyes, amusement giving way to a fleeting expression she hadn't seen before. Uncertainty? Distaste? Then he laughed and flung his wet felt cap to the chair in the corner. The faint aroma of damp wool drifted over to Marita as his cloak followed it. "You're looking better than the last time I saw you," he said.

"You look better too," Marita said.

"Two days and two nights of sleep helped," Taverik said. He fingered his head ruefully. "Best of all, I haven't seen either my father or Chado in all this time."

"Sit," Sahra said, pushing forward the armchair and retreating to the straight chair at her table. Taverik pulled the armchair closer to Marita and peered quizzically at her. "Did you drink the rest of that blessed water?"

"Yes," she said shortly. She'd heard enough about blessed water.

"Thought so. You were at death's door two days ago. Now you're yelling for your boots and looking sassy." He looked into her face. "Hmm, yelling for your boots, at least."

"Oh, go jump in the Giss," she said, laughing in spite of herself. Then as he kept staring at her, she growled, "Well? Do I look like a man or a woman?"

Not a whit abashed he said, "Like both. Now I know, I can't see how you fooled everyone. But when I'm not actively thinking about it, you look like a young man. Almost too young to be on your own. How old *are* you?"

"Twenty-one," she said.

"My age? It's preposterous. How do you get away with it?"

"People see what they expect to see. As long as nothing happens to make them *really* look."

"And you do have an uncanny ability to make yourself invisible. Three journeys with you and I never knew."

Bibi brought brandy for Taverik. He sipped it slowly, his blue eyes bright with curiosity. "Why are you doing this? Who are you really?"

Sahra's alarmed look flashed from behind Taverik's back. Now the inevitable questions. Marita had to tell Taverik enough to satisfy him, but not too much. She rubbed her forehead with her thumb, thinking. "I won't tell you who we are," she said slowly, "not merely for our safety, but yours."

"What do you mean?"

"People who have tried to help us have ended up in trouble," she said. "I don't want to bring that on you."

"My choice," he suggested.

She smiled but shook her head. "My father," she said carefully, aware of Sahra's tensing, "had the misfortune to make a ruthless enemy. One night this enemy attacked the house, but his plans went awry. My sister had stayed up far into the night, reading in the library. I came down to persuade her to bed. That's how we survived, we weren't where they expected us.

"We heard the loud voices of strange men and hid—I was in my nightdress, after all. They came in, dragging Father, yelling at him to reveal something. He wouldn't and they murdered him. Mother was already dead."

"I'm sorry," Taverik said. "I had no idea. I know it's inadequate, but I mean it."

"I'm sure you do," Marita said. "It's not so bad anymore, it's just this is the first time I've had to tell anyone about it."

"Grief unmourned is grief unhealed," Taverik quoted. "Who was this man?"

"We're not sure. We have only guesses."

"How'd you get away?"

"They sacked the house," Marita continued. "But as soon as they left the library I got Father's strong box from behind the books and we slipped out the window and hid in the garden. Bibi and Ot, my father's stableman, helped us get away. We hid in an alley while Ot found some clothes for me, his own it turned out because the house was burning. I've worn a man's ever since.

"The next night the zoji of Vosa and all his family were assassinated by the zoji's marshal, Soza. The rest you know. We got away because all Vosa was in turmoil, and our enemy was looking for two women, not a brother and sister."

"He kept looking for you? What does he want?"

Marita shrugged her good shoulder. "Don't know. Bibi took us to her family's farm outside Vosa. But the man found us. We'd gone on an outing into the hills, came back and found the farm in charred ruins. The family with it.

"So we moved back to town, this time with the farm cart and Whitey. We slept in the cart and began trade. I discovered I enjoyed it. Also," Marita added shyly, "I found I was good at it."

"Very."

"Things went well until one day Bibi came searching for me. She forgot and asked every vendor for me by my real name. I'm sure that's how we were discovered. The next day Ot and I were attacked just as we reached the cart. We drove them off, but Ot was badly hurt. I got him into the cart and we left right then. Travelled all night. But Ot died. We came here to Illiga. I think maybe now we've lost our enemy, but you see how careful we must be. We must hide from him the rest of our lives." Marita found herself shaking from suppressed emotion. She clenched her teeth, exhausted.

"No wonder," Taverik said gently, "you're so closed-mouthed and standoffish."

"Befriending us carries a jinx," Marita said. "No one else shall suffer because of us."

"And your secret is safer if fewer people know you. Safe but lonely." Taverik rediscovered his brandy glass and tossed down the last mouthful. The gleam returned to his eyes. "You should try a false beard."

Marita's fist clenched involuntarily. He had no idea

of pain or terror, she thought, but all she said was, "A false beard invariably falls off at the wrong time."

The crinkles deepened in the corners of his eyes and she suddenly realized he'd been pulling her leg. She blushed and added more lightly, "Just as I'm talking to the guild president, Frez Ittato, for instance."

Taverik gave a great laugh, and she found herself chuckling too. It felt good. Oh, she'd miss Taverik terribly if they had to flee.

He took her hand. "What's your true name?"

"Marko Kastazi," she said firmly. "And this is my sister, Oma Kastazi."

He looked disappointed, but accepted it. "Marko Kastazi, your secret is safe. Don't be anxious because of me."

"Thank you," she said. "Thank you for—helping me, that night." So much for prepared speeches, she thought, suddenly tired.

He stood up. "I'll come again when you are stronger," he said. She nodded, feeling pale. Taverik's parting conversation with Sahra slid past her ears without sticking. Finally the room fell quiet and again she could hear the peck of rain on the window and the crackle of the fire. Sahra's skirts rustled. Marita opened her eyes and found her sister sitting, hands folded, in the wooden armchair.

"Do we stay?" Sahra asked.

Chapter 5

Taverik

Taverik turned the old mule up city, squinting against the drizzle. Marko's story clung to his mind like the thick mist now rising from the river. He had no doubt it was true—he'd heard of strange happenings in Vosa ever since it had fallen to its former marshal. But who, he wondered, was this enemy of Marko and Oma? Was he actually still looking for them, or was it just their frightened imaginations? And if he sought them, why? And why would they still fear him, more than a week's journey north of Vosa? Odd, odd, odd. The whole affair was odd.

When he'd finally surfaced this morning, his driving thought had been to find out if Marko lived, and to satisfy his raging curiosity about her. He'd also felt faintly depressed about the whole affair, his comfortable friend being supplanted by a remote, Massadaran-looking woman. But when he'd visited, he'd found merely Marko there on the couch, quietly humorous and reserved as usual. Only when he probed too closely did he see flashes of the hidden person underneath with tragedy, secrets and fears. And now, he admitted, "Marko" wasn't enough for him. He wanted to know the real person.

In the square, market vendors huddled under dripping canopies, bright colors beside the gray stone buildings. The walls of the fortress soared above, insubstantial in the mist, the ancient tower disappearing into a cloud. The cranky old freight mule balked, ears flat out in protest to the wet. Taverik raised his quirt, then hesitated. Where would he go? Home lay just a few twisting blocks west, but tired and headachy though he felt, Taverik didn't want to go there. Time enough to listen to his father roar about the loss of the mules and goods. He wanted quiet to think. He'd escape to his own warehouse and see how things had gone while he was away. Turning east, he entered the steep warrens of warehouses above the Giss River.

The sleeper boy let him into the barren front room. "Kali Taverik! I'm so glad you're alive."

"I'm glad of that myself," said Taverik, stepping past him and throwing off his cloak. He wrinkled his nose at the mustiness of the place. "Keep the fires lit from now on, boy," he said. "Not good for the fabrics."

"Yes, Kali, sorry, Kali. I'll make up the fire in your office," the boy said, diving into a closet for wood.

"Any trouble while I was gone?"

"One night someone rattled the door," the boy panted, emerging with a load of kindling. "But he ran when I yelled. I checked next day and found rasp marks on the window bars. But I haven't heard anything since."

"Good work." Taverik picked up the lamp and led the way down the flagstone corridor to the office. He unlocked it and let the boy pass with the wood. The room held only a trestle table that served as a desk, and two chairs. The whitewashed walls were bare, the floorboards scrubbed for so many years the grain stood high.

The boy dumped the kindling before the fireplace. "We heard you got back alive, though it was too bad for Uali," he said.

"You were the same age?" Taverik said.

"Yeah, we was pals." The boy wiped his nose on his sleeve and plunged on. "Then we heard you was dying after all, what with you taking to your bed and never moving for two days and nights, and nobody being able to rouse you. And the Kali—your father—in a terrible temper and near beating the doctor."

"Well, I'm fine," said Taverik, lighting the lamp on his desk.

"There. Done." The boy stood, slapping his hands together. "The big logs were here already what with Kali Chado using the room so often."

Taverik looked up sharply. "Chado used this office?"

"Yes, Kali. He was doing your work for you while you were gone." The boy lingered and Taverik slipped him a coin as he gave him back the lamp. The moment the door closed behind the boy Taverik strode to the desk and unlocked its drawer.

The ledgers were still there. Taverik pulled out the latest one and thumbed through it suspiciously. Yes, Chado's sloppy figures filled the last few pages. "Damn and blast," he muttered.

He sank into the wooden chair and pulled the lamp closer, scowling as he ran his eyes down the columns. Chado had pulled some deals with the silks and with a moth-eaten wool Taverik had intended for charity. But what? The figures didn't even make sense. But whatever he'd done it was bound to be dishonest.

Taverik clenched his teeth in anger. Bad enough Chado pulling shady deals with his own accounts. But when he started in on Taverik's domain that was the limit.

The Zandro firm had well earned its bad reputation. Back when Taverik's mother was still alive, it hadn't been so bad. Or was it that he hadn't begun to buck his father yet? After all, as soon as he'd grown enough to hold an oar against the current, his father had taught him the secret of guiding a small boat down the Giss by night, slipping through the blind spots of the customs watch. He'd gotten good at it, better than his older brother Chado, who couldn't sustain the attention needed for safety. He'd even enjoyed the danger to an extent, but found himself caught tighter and tighter in his father's illegal webs.

His mother had suspected what Donato was teaching the boys and tried to hold him in check. Meddling, Donato called it, and took out the resulting tension on the boys. Their constant black eyes became the joke of the guilds.

When things got too bad Taverik took refuge with his

mother's brother. Much younger than she was, Nikilo Vitujak still lived in the house where the two had grown up, children of a respected Pakajan merchant. Nikilo, however, had small taste for business and made his living tutoring the sons of Pakajans and other non-viti not allowed to attend the university. Taverik's mother insisted Nikilo tutor Chado and Taverik. "I want you boys to know manners," she'd said privately. "Manners, integrity and the love of Zojikam." Chado sneered, but Taverik had seen the difference between the way men reacted to his father and the way they reacted to Uncle Nik. He preferred to imitate his uncle.

It wasn't easy. Taverik entered his teens shamed by the tainted business his father was teaching him, but desperately keeping it secret from his uncle. The double life increasingly tore him apart; only his mother's death gave him courage to do something about it.

The day after the funeral, the fourteen-year-old boy told his father he wouldn't run the river anymore. And he'd stuck to it, though it cost him the first of many beatings before Donato finally gave up trying to force him. It meant that Donato increasingly favored Chado and gave Taverik dirty work. But worst, Taverik also suspected it caused the first rift with his uncle.

Uncle Nikilo visited one evening, and had smiled at the boys and squeezed Taverik's shoulder, then immediately closeted himself with Donato. Soon their voices rose into a ferocious argument. Taverik and Chado had hovered close to the door but could make out no words, and when the door had opened abruptly, Nikilo strode out and left the house without so much as a glance at either of them.

"And if I catch you here again," Donato roared down the stairs after him, "I'll beat you to a pudding." And to the boys, he'd said, "I forbid you two to ever go to Vitujak's house again. He's a meddling fool and I don't want you two influenced by him." And from then on, Donato had never mentioned Nikilo's name without appending a curse to it.

Taverik, of course, went immediately to Uncle Nik's

house. But when he'd asked Nik what had happened in the roundabout way he approached everything vitally important to him, Nik had merely looked sadly at him and said, "My house is yours. You may come whenever you please and stay as long as you want. We can even continue your education, if you desire." Still, Nikilo would never discuss the cause of the argument.

The boy thought he knew, however. Donato must have accused Uncle Nik of forcing Taverik to quit running the river; and Nikilo, hearing about it for the first time, had been shocked and disappointed in him. That must be why Nikilo hadn't looked at him when he left.

But though Nikilo never again came to the Zandro house, he never made any comment about smuggling. His love continued steadily, now the only source of love in Taverik's life. Taverik secretly continued his studies as much to be near that source as from a desire to learn. When his father found out and exploded with rage, Taverik merely became more careful.

In those days Donato ranted more and more against the viti and the *Sadra* Laws, coming sometimes, uncomfortably close to sedition. He always seemed to have some new scheme that would make the Zandros' fortune or secure them a higher place in Illiga's rigid social structure. But ironically, his business became shadier and shadier until the firm had well earned its unpleasant reputation.

Taverik hated it. He hated the expression in the eyes of guild officials whenever Taverik had to do business with them. He hated the whispered sayings such as, "When you shake hands with a Zandro, count your fingers." His pride, however, wouldn't allow him to show he cared. He threw off the embarrassment with clowning and pranks and volunteered more and more for the caravans.

The affair four years ago with the buyer from Ormea brought on the second big crisis. The man was from out of town and hadn't known any better than to prepay on a shipment of brocade from the Zandros. Taverik's father had unloaded on him the brocade with the green weft threads rotting out.

Instead of slinking back to Ormea, the shamed victim of *ikiji*, the merchant had protested to the Textile Guild. The Zandro firm had been publicly reprimanded and fined. They lost a lot of business, and many in the Textile Guild began to snub them.

That's when Taverik made his second move for independence. "Give me one area of the Zandro firm to manage totally," he'd demanded. "I'll be responsible for its success or failure. But I'll run it my own way."

Donato exploded. Taverik walked out on him, and slammed the door, two actions which he knew he'd have to pay for later. Maybe. He'd had an idea, and had gone straight to Uncle Nikilo's house intending to ask if he could move in for good.

But Nikilo met him with his eyes alight. "I've been given a wonderful opportunity, Taverik," he said. "I'm to go to Vosa as secretary of Zoji Balanji's ambassador. I leave in three days."

"That's wonderful, Nik," Taverik said, forcing a smile. "About time they saw how valuable you are." He'd listened with a show of enthusiasm to Nikilo's plans and never mentioned his own dilemma; it would be just like Nik to decide he ought to cancel the job and stay and help Taverik. After supper Taverik said the toughest good-bye of his life, then grit his teeth and went home to Donato's anger.

Somehow his stubborn pride would not let him abandon his demand and to his surprise, Donato began to come around after a week. "Less work for me," Donato said. "Good for you boys. Maybe that will keep you out of my way."

"I'm oldest," Chado said. "I pick first. I want the Gem Guild."

"You'll fit right in," said Taverik. "It's famous for its double-crosses and intrigue."

"You want a fat lip?" Chado said.

"Give it to him later," said their father. "Taverik, since you're so smart, you get the Textile Guild, which put this damn idea in your head in the first place."

A not so subtle revenge, but Taverik took it, filled with an awakening sense of controlling his own destiny.

He dug in, relieved to work hard at something that didn't make his conscience wince. And though his double reputation as a clown and a Zandro worked against him, lately he'd had the satisfaction of overhearing a guild member say, "Well if you *must* deal with them, stick with young Taverik. He's the best of that bunch." Which wasn't exactly lauding him to the skies, but it was better than before.

But now even that tenuous repute might be shattered forever. Taverik glared down at Chado's sloppy columns. They didn't add up. Nothing added up. And his lingering concussion gave everything the effect of swimming upward. He rubbed his forehead with the heel of his fist. He'd kick Chado from here to Vosa.

A faint tap at the door. "Come in," Taverik said, sitting back with a sigh.

The sleeper boy peeked in. "There's someone here to see you, Kali."

"Who is it?"

"He wouldn't say, Kali, he just asked if you were alone."

"Send him in," Taverik said. Probably someone about Chado's dirty business. He'd kick him all the way to Vosa, too. He stood up as the tall man entered, and had started forward before he took in who it was.

"Nik!" He grabbed his uncle in a great bear hug, pounding his back and laughing at the same time.

His uncle pounded back. "Easy, easy," he said. "Remember my advanced years."

"Hogwash," Taverik said. Nikilo's red hair had but a few white strands, and his long, freckled face looked the same as ever. Taverik pulled his desk chair around to the fire. "Sit down, sit down. How many hours will you be in town this time?"

"Quite a few," said his uncle, folding his lean form into the chair. "I've been called home."

"Good!" said Taverik calmly, though his heart leaped happily. "What will you do now?"

Nikilo lowered his voice. "I will work as secretary to Zoji Balanji himself. He wants someone experienced with Soza."

Taverik stared in amazement. "Don't tell father! He'll suddenly become your loving brother-in-law and demand introductions at court."

"That's just what I'm afraid of," said Nikilo ruefully. "I want to ask you, Taverik, not to say anything to anyone about this."

"Promise," Taverik said. "Ah, Nik, I missed you these four years."

"Four years. You're twenty-one now, aren't you? And still getting knocked about, I see."

"This was bandits, Unk. Didn't you hear they're attacking caravans in the pass from Novato?"

Uncle Nikilo's mobile eyebrows shot upwards. "Tell me about it."

Taverik swung the other chair around and straddled it. "Their leader is called Red but has black hair and doesn't speak either—" He broke off listening.

"What is it?"

"Someone's here." He turned his head to hear better, disappointed at the interruption. The voices grew louder and unmistakably, his father's was among them. Taverik got up quickly and went to the door. "I'll head them off and get right back to you."

"Taverik!" The familiar bellow resounded in the hall.

"Coming!" Taverik squeezed out and tried to shut the door behind him but Donato pushed him back into the room. He was a huge, bull-like man made larger by the padded shoulders of his red surcoat. His blue eyes were set in a ruddy face which flushed purple whenever he became angry.

It was purple now. "Where have you been this morning?"

"Keeping the books. Which would be a lot easier if you'd keep Chado out of them."

Donato wasn't listening. He glared over Taverik's shoulder and shoved past him to the middle of the room. "Vitujak. What are you doing here?"

Nikilo rose slowly. They were of a height, but Nikilo stood slender and poised, Donato beefy, truculent. "I am visiting my nephew."

"Get out."

Taverik thrust himself between them. "You can't barge in here and—"

"You keep out of this!"

"I will not!"

"Taverik," said his uncle, shaking his head and raising his hand slightly.

Taverik turned to him hotly, but held his tongue. Without another glance at Donato, Uncle Nikilo went to the door, reaching it just as Chado slid through. "Good afternoon, Chado," Nikilo said as he left, just as if he'd seen him only yesterday.

Chado had the same intensely blue eyes and yellow hair of all the Zandro men, but his shoulders stooped and his hands, manner, even his hair seemed limp. He stuck his head into the hall and called, "Why Uncle! Have you come back to teach us some more? Perhaps we could teach you, now."

"Chado," Taverik said, "you keep your long drippy nose out of my account books."

Chado leaned against the door frame. "My, my, little brother. I was only trying to help."

"You were only trying to pull a dirty deal," Taverik said.

His brother straightened at that, an ugly look in his eyes. "Prove it."

"I don't have to," Taverik mocked. "Nothing balances in the books. You don't even have the smarts to make a decent embezzler."

Chado swung. Taverik ducked easily and thumped him on the chest. "So stay out of my books."

With a growl of rage Chado closed in. Taverik swung back, releasing pent-up frustrations.

"Stop it!" roared Donato. "Chado! Tav!"

Taverik had been able to beat Chado ever since he'd grown enough to match him in size. He'd have bested him now except that Chado managed a lucky blow to his concussed head. His headache thundered and he lost his balance. He grabbed at Chado and they both fell against the desk which went over with a lingering crash. Books, ink, pens, the lamp and Chado, all on top of him, Taverik curled up and covered his face against the rain of blows.

Suddenly Chado was no longer there. Taverik opened his eyes. Donato had pulled him off by his collar and was shaking him. "You stop when I say stop!" he yelled. Donato concealed his origins as a dock laborer, but he still had arms the size of clubs. He could take on either of his sons, who had inherited the lighter Vitujak frame. He cuffed Chado behind the left ear and sent him reeling to the door.

"Taverik started it!" Chado yelled.

"Get out of here. Go home!"

Taverik scrambled up. "And stay out of my books!"

His father's hammy fists closed on the front of his surcoat. "And you stay away from Vitujak!"

Taverik stayed stubbornly silent and received another shake. "Hear?" His father pushed him away. Sullenly, Taverik straightened his ink-stained coat and righted the desk. His head throbbed and he hurt all over. It grated that Chado had bested him, and it grated that Nikilo had been treated like a beggar.

And it grated that he'd lost his temper. He'd learned long ago he couldn't win a head-on collision with Chado and his father. He had to outthink them, outtalk them, keep them off balance. He breathed deeply, fighting to get back self-control.

Donato watched him pick up the ledgers. "I'm deducting the price of the mules and goods from your accounts."

Taverik paused, fallen lamp in hand. This would wipe out the money he'd been saving to make his break with the Zandro firm. Not that he hadn't expected it.

His father seemed disappointed in his lack of response. "Did you hear me?"

"Yes, Father," Taverik said. "You are as generous as usual."

Donato grunted at the irony. "That's not why I wanted to talk to you. Shut the door."

Taverik shut it and found his father staring moodily at him. "Dula Familo has rejected Chado," he said.

"I don't blame her. I reject him myself," Taverik said.

"Don't get smart. She wants you."

Taverik gaped at him then burst into laughter. "Me? I've only met her once."

"Apparently that was enough. She remembered you." Donato looked him over through half-closed eyes. "You are invited to her house for dinner Thursday night. You will entertain her and charm her and do all you can to win her."

"I don't want her."

"You will marry her. Damn it, you fool! Her father is just one step below the viti. Do you know what this means for us?"

"Yes. Being the despised Pakajan merchant in-laws of an impoverished and powerless Massadaran family. No thank you."

His father locked eyes with him. "You will woo her and marry her."

Taverik stared back stubbornly. The marriage could quite possibly be a death sentence, once the Familias gained control of his wealth.

"Do you hear?" His father's voice rose.

Never butt heads with an angry bull. Surely he could figure out something by Thursday. "Father," Taverik said, suddenly cheerful, "I will go to her house and woo her. If she still wants me after that, we'll talk about weddings."

Donato glared at him suspiciously. "If only you were Chado," he uttered, and stalked out.

Taverik remained, staring blankly into the fire. Donato had already spent a fantastic sum entertaining Dula's father, trying to win her for Chado. Taverik had no doubt that fantastic sums would continue to be spent, once the two families were linked, in order to refurbish the fading Familo glory. But the provider of the wealth would live in a wretched state, despised and unaccepted. He'd figure some way out of this mess.

"Kali Tav?"

He looked around. The sleeper boy stood beside him

holding up a note. "Kali Vitujak told me to give this to you privately."

"Thank you," Taverik said, fingers reaching for a coin. He dismissed the boy and tore open the note.

"My dear nephew," Nikilo had written, "would you honor me by attending the temple service with me on Friday, and dining afterwards at my home?—Nikilo. P.S. I assume the horrendous crash I just heard is the desk going over. I trust you will be recovered by Friday."

Chapter 6

Marita

Whitey's enormous ears flicked forward when Marita led him out into Friday's crisp morning. Snorting, he pulled her into the tiny yard and split the heavens with his magnificent bray. Marita laughed and patted his silky shoulder. "I feel the same, old friend," she told him, gazing up into the cloudless, cobalt sky. The first rains of winter had ended, giving them a day so clear she could see shadows on the distant mountains to the west and east. Brisk wind whipped her cheeks until they glowed, and the air tasted good with each breath. The day had exhilarated her until nothing would do but to get out in it.

Sahra stood under the apple tree, hugging her arms about herself. Over her head the tree's long branches whipped and rattled in the wind. "It's too soon," she repeated.

"I feel fine," Marita said, ignoring the twinge in her shoulder as she heaved the saddle over Whitey's tall back. "Wonderful."

"You lost so much blood. Wait a few weeks before you go careering all over the countryside."

"I don't think Whitey would career all over the countryside even if I asked him to," Marita said, reaching under his belly for the cinch. "And I'll go crazy if I'm cooped up here one more day."

"I don't like it!"

Marita looked over the saddle and met Sahra's eyes. The worry in them rankled—was she to be confined from now on? Sahra had even begged Marita not to go on any more caravans ever again. Well, she'd have to, to get the rugs that were keeping them afloat. Besides, the thought of never travelling again made life stretch out flat and dull into a cramped future. Ironic, considering how she lay awake before each trip worrying. "Sahra," she said, trying to frame feelings into words, "this is what makes life worthwhile, and—"

"What if something happens?"

Marita mounted carefully, favoring her shoulder. "Look, I'll deliver your manuscript, I'll ride a bit, then come home. What can happen?"

Plenty, Sahra's cross expression said, and Marita was glad when Taverik's voice hailed them through the half-open gate. "Hello! Good morning! Where are you off to?"

He rode a dark, hammer-headed mule into the yard. Sweeping off his soft cap he gave Sahra a grand bow. "Good morning, Kala Oma."

Sahra smiled back. "Good morning, Kali Taverik."

He looked at Marita, the dark blue of his surcoat setting his eyes alight. "Where are you off to this fine day?"

"Errands and a ride."

"You need some help?" he said.

"No, I don't," she replied. She didn't want him coming to the print shop. Before Sahra could protest, she prodded Whitey into his ambling walk.

Taverik followed, leaning down as he passed Oma. "Don't worry, Kala. I'll bring him back as soon as he gets tired."

Marita gave him a good scowl, but he only laughed

and wheeled his mule alongside. "I've renamed this beast Frez," he told her as Sahra closed the gates behind them.

"After the guild president? Does he have gout too?"

"No, he's merely the worst curmudgeon I've ever had the misfortune to ride. Beware his back legs. His teeth too. I'll never find another like my old mule. Where are we going?"

"A bookseller near the Giss. Then across the bridge for fresh air."

"Glad you invited me," he said and before she could retort, added, "Do I smell like garbage?"

"Like what?" she gasped.

"Garbage. I ate dinner at the Familo's last night for the purpose of wooing and winning Dula, better named Dulla, if you ask me."

"Taverik, I know by now when you are pulling my leg."

"I'm not!" he protested. "They're poor as rats, you know, and my father has been spending enormous amounts of money trying to marry Chado into the family and improve the Zandro status. Only once she checked Chado's teeth she decided I was a better bargain."

"Don't marry her, Taverik!" Marita said in dismay. "That family will eat you up and spit out the pits."

"My thoughts exactly," Taverik said. "But I couldn't get out of the banquet. So I went and twitched."

"Twitched?"

"Like this." Taverik shrugged his shoulders quickly, then let his jaw drop. He twitched again, and lolled a leering look sidewise at her.

"Oh stop it," Marita said laughing. "That's awful."

"Dula thought so too. Oh, and I chewed black olives and talked with my mouth full, picked my teeth and wiped it on the table cloth and—"

"Stop, stop!"

Taverik laughed. "Dula left the table in tears, her mother went to comfort her, her father went to drag her back because they need the Zandro money, and being left alone with me, her three brothers took the opportunity to throw me out the kitchen door onto the garbage heap. Heard this morning the Familos withdrew their offer. My father couldn't figure out what went wrong."

"You're lucky nothing worse happened to you."

"Nothing could be worse than Dula. Even if they are related to Viti Malenga."

"Odd," Marita said. "Malenga is at court, and powerful. Why would the Familos need even consider a Pakajan merchant?"

"Money," said Taverik. "For all their grandness, the viti don't have much money under their high pretense. That's why they always slap on new *Sadra* Laws. Keep us under control. What a lot of students loose today."

Marita looked up at that. They'd entered the University Quarter where Sahra's publisher kept shop. The university was the only one in the Peninsula, and more and more viti sent their sons there, settling for just a finishing tour of Massadara. Though open only to Massadarans, Pakajan influences had crept in until the education received there had quite a different flavor than that received in Massadara itself. Many of the old guard cried out loudly about it, but the trend proved impossible to reverse.

The students themselves, however, felt arrogantly superior to Pakajans and often made trouble for them. Marita viewed warily the unusual number of black-robed youths filling the street near the book shop. "Must be a holiday."

"Bet there's an uproar before the day's over," Taverik said. "I'd best stay out here with the mules."

She'd been worrying how to keep him outside. Relieved, Marita climbed gingerly off Whitey and handed Taverik the reins. "I'll only be a minute," she promised taking the package from the saddle. She turned and nearly ran into a bent old woman in pitiful rags. Avoiding her eyes, Marita dodged the outstretched hand. She shut the shop door behind her as if it could shut the beggar out of her mind.

The printer came forward wiping his hands. "Ah,"

he said. "Another volume from the Humble Kali. His books sell well, they do."

"And you will therefore increase the payment."

"Not that well," amended the printer hastily.

Marita pressed, falling easily into the pattern of bargaining. The first payments had been small, as befitted an unknown whose books might prove liabilities rather than profits. But surely the publisher made quite a profit on them now. Marita easily talked him into a more generous royalty by reminding him he wasn't the only printer in town. Satisfied, she tightened her fist around his advance. Money was the only bulwark that stood between her and the fate of that wretched woman outside.

The years camped in the wagon in the slums of two cities had instilled in her a horror of poverty. Bent, shaking old women, on their knees scrubbing rich men's floors, old men sitting oblivious to the squalor around them, children with frostbite in winter, rat bites in summer. Thieves, prostitutes, muttering wanderers—they all filled her with anxiety and despair. So little kept her and Sahra from a like fate. So little. Theft, sickness, bandits, any one of myriad disasters would land them right back among them.

But she had herself well in hand as she stepped back into the wind once more. The beggar woman had sunk down into the shelter of the shop steps and was exchanging banter with Taverik. Marita gave her a large coin.

"Ah, so generous," cried the woman. "Thanks be to Zojikam!"

"And does Zojikam help you?" Marita asked ironically.

The woman drew herself up, dignified despite her rags. "Zojikam provides, though you are the means," she said. "He upholds me."

Her eyes burned as fierce and independent as Marita's own. Embarrassed, Marita turned away and took the reins from Taverik.

"You look gray," he said as she got up.

"I'm fine," she said. "Just remembering." She

pushed her disquietude aside and threw back her head to the sun. This day was too good to waste. They reached the steep slope running down to the east bridge where the Giss glinted silver. The mules braced themselves, planting their feet carefully between the worn cobbles. The jolting ride bothered her healing wound, and she stiffened her shoulders against it, only to straighten when she noticed Taverik covertly watching her. Three years in disguise taught her an instinctive dislike of any attention paid to her.

At the river front they dodged laborers loading and unloading barges, piling huge sacks, crates and bundles of raw cotton. From the barges men whistled and shouted directions to those above. Students jostled among them, horsing around, getting in the way. A few jeered at a merchant standing on the dock overseeing a half-loaded barge. He turned to exchange words with them and Marita recognized Sanisman, who had also been in the caravan. He waved. "Glad to see you up!" he shouted over the din.

"Thank you," she called.

"You're welcome," mocked a student, giving a grand court bow. The others gave awkward country bumpkin bows back.

"They're like overgrown kids," Marita growled.

"There'll be trouble if this keeps up," Taverik said.

"Hope not," she said, but she could almost taste the tension among the dock laborers. She felt relieved once they crossed the bridge to the quiet farms on the opposite side. She rode contentedly, the silent companionship between her and Taverik like old times. With unspoken accord they turned onto a trail leading up a low, pine-forested hill.

Below them spread the Giss Valley, stretching gently back to the abrupt line of the mountains. The Pale Lady and the Dark Lady looked down on them, neither yet wearing her snow cap. The air was so clear Marita could make out the details of the rockslides on their slopes. "Remember the time," she said, "we galloped out that trail and rounded a bend only to find a farm cart smack across the middle?"

Taverik laughed. "I jumped it, but Whitey planted his feet and skidded. You landed in the potatoes."

"And got the biggest tongue-lashing of my life from that Pakajan farmer." She chuckled, remembering.

The wind soughed through the pine branches, and the scent of sun-warmed needles filled the air, clean and good. "It looks so normal and peaceful," Taverik said. "Different from the night we came home. With the moon out turning everything silver, I kept feeling like all around us were spirit beings—some good, some bad, but all of them aware of me and you, as if we were somehow involved in their business. Gave me the shivers. Must have been that priest that put me in mind of it."

"What priest?"

"The Pakajan priest in the village under the pass. The one who gave us the blessed water. He said, let's see, 'I dreamed a black eagle chased a hawk.' "

Marita's breath went out of her and didn't want to return. So that's where she'd heard of the Black Eagle that night. The words sent a sickening feeling through her.

Taverik continued, squinting at her as he spoke. "The priest said, 'The hawk fled, but wherever it hid, the eagle was always there before it.' And he said something about if the black eagle caught that hawk all comfort, justice and truth would depart from the land."

She found her vision darkening. Whitey jerked his head as her fingers tightened on the reins. With an effort she loosened her hold and clutched the saddle instead.

"What's the matter?" Taverik said. "What's this eagle to you?"

The wind whipping their hair into tangles now felt cold instead of exhilarating. She didn't want to talk about the Black Eagle. Talking about it always brought the darkness near. She turned Whitey back down the hill, saying lightly, "It's nothing to me."

Taverik caught up, brushing under a pine bow and bringing down a spray of chilly drops. "You kept muttering about black eagles when you were delirious. And when the doctor brought out his Black Eagle amulet Oma and your servant looked like Pakajan warriors until he put it away. And now when I mentioned it you nearly fell off your mule."

"I did not nearly fall off my mule," she said. "Leave it alone, Tav. Or are you always going to be hounding me with questions from now on?"

Her outburst quivered in the silence. "I'm sorry," Taverik said finally. "I let my curiosity get out of hand."

His handsome apology shamed her but at the same instance she remembered how much she owed him, and felt trapped. If only they could return to their old uncomplicated friendship. "I'm sorry, too. I'm snappy because of my wound, I guess."

"You don't need to apologize."

She eased her tense shoulders then said, "The men who murdered my parents wore the Black Eagle's claw, and apparently adhered to that *ikiji* cult. That's why my sister and I tend to react to it. That's all."

Taverik didn't speak again until they neared the bridge. "Funny," he said, "the priest said he had the feeling the dream was connected with us somehow. At first I thought he meant I was the hawk he was talking about, because for a long time I've dreamed of changing my name and going somewhere where I could throw off the old Zandro curse."

Marita looked at him in surprise. Taverik had never opened himself like this before.

"I'd get rid of the Zandro and call myself Taverik Tazur," he went on. "That's old Pakajan for hawk. So I thought the hawk in the dream meant me. But now I think it means you."

The mules' hooves resounded on the bridge. "Me? I'm no hawk." The wind off the river cut right through Marita's cloak and she gave up trying to pretend. "Taverik, my sister was right, though I'll beat you up if you mention it to her. I've got to stop for a while."

"How about we go to the River Front Inn and get a bite to eat?" he said. "It's past noon anyway."

She followed him through the jostling crowd to the inn, and gave Whitey to the ostler. Inside the warm darkness, a deep murmur of conversation rose about her. As her eyes grew accustomed to the dim light, she made out three students, heads together, lounging against the bar, their black robes almost indistinguishable against the smoke-darkened wood. Near the fire a cluster of flushed and laughing students looked over their shoulders at Marita and Taverik. One made a low comment and they all laughed raucously.

Five dockworkers, exiled by this influx of arrogant viti, sat along a bench in the far corner. Muttering together, brawny arms on knees, they cast sullen glances at the revelers. Taverik chose a table in the dim back, near the kitchen door, and sat with his back to the wall. Marita slid gratefully onto the scarred chair opposite.

The kitchen door flew wide before the innkeeper, letting out a blast of warmth and cooking smells that brought water to her mouth. With a scuff of cloth shoes, the innkeeper veered their way, his white shirt gaping across his paunch as he bowed. "Kali Taverik, haven't seen you in months. On caravan again? What can I bring you?"

"Stew," Taverik said. "Bread, ale."

"Excellent, excellent." The man smiled jovially at them, but his eyes looked tense. Behind Marita, the students at the bar pounded the counter and clamored for more wine. The innkeeper growled something under his breath and shuffled to the bar.

Taverik raised an eyebrow. "Drunk at this hour!" he said in mock disapproval.

"I just hope they keep to themselves," Marita said. She noticed Taverik's suddenly-narrowed eyes. "Anything wrong?"

"Don't turn. Not wrong, maybe. Just that one of those students at the bar is our friend Viti Karaz from the caravan."

"Delightful," she growled. "Don't attract his attention." The kitchen door swung open again and the innkeeper set steaming crockery bowls of soup before them. A moment later he brought cheese and crusty bread.

Marita ate hungrily. The warm soup revived her and the hollow feeling in her core began to ease. She sank her teeth contentedly into the thick bread.

"I've been thinking," Taverik said.

"Thought I smelled smoke."

He smiled but pressed on. "About what you told me of your enemy."

"Oh?" she said warily. More questions.

"It seems like he's going to enormous trouble to find you."

"And?"

"And I imagine he thinks you have something he wants, or which could injure him. Maybe because you can identify him?"

Laughter burst from the students behind her. Taverik's eyes shifted to them, then back to her face. "If you could figure out why the matter is so important to this person, you might be able to take steps to free yourself. Was your father anybody important?"

She shook her head impatiently. "My father was a bastard," she said succinctly. "A bastard son whose family cast him off. Any other questions?"

Taverik winced. "I don't mean to—"

"Pry?"

"Bring up a painful subject," he amended. "But wouldn't you like to be free of this shadow?"

"Yes," she said. "Yes, it would be nice to be free. The trouble is, I don't want to get near enough to him to find out the truth of the matter."

Taverik leaned forward. "Who is he?" he began, then broke off, staring past her.

She turned. Before her glinted a golden circlet with that obscene claw symbol. Her eyes travelled up to the hook-nosed face of Viti Karaz who wore it. Beyond him two other students leered unpleasantly. The finely carved lips of Viti Karaz curled into a sneer. "What have we here?" he said.

The room hushed as people became aware of the confrontation. "I'd wondered at that smell," the student continued. "Two stinking little Pakajan merchants defiling our presence."

Chapter 7

Marita

Taverik nudged her under the table. She pulled her eyes from the glinting amulet and realized he'd risen in deference to the viti. Belatedly she got up too, pulling off her cap and edging farther away from them. The glint was back in Taverik's eyes again, but his face wore the bland non-expression Marita had seen on him when he bargained. "Greetings, noble viti," he said, bowing respectfully. "It is our honor to converse with such fine and obviously intelligent young men."

The irony seemed beyond them. Viti Karaz bared his teeth. "Fah!" he said to the others. "This is the Pakajan I was telling you about. Laid his filthy hands on my horse. I'd have skewered him then and there if it weren't for that damn captain." His expression implied he'd finish the job today given half a chance. The amulet gleamed.

The other two scowled drunkenly and moved in closer. Marita spoke quickly and soothingly. "Allow us the pleasure of buying you all a drink," she said. Her conciliatory gesture brushed the knife hidden in her sleeve. Zojikam forbid she should need it; it was unlawful to even threaten a viti. She would spend her entire purse to get them drunk enough so they could just walk away. "It would be a great honor, my viti."

"Join money grub merchants?" said the one nearest her, who had watery eyes. He crowded Marita and she backed away quickly with a warning glance at Taverik, who had moved out protectively. The watery-eyed one mimicked Marita's light tenor. "Why their lust for money has emasculated them."

Karaz and the other, a plump little fellow, guffawed and dug each other in the ribs. Taverik's jaw tightened. At the fire the students leaned over each other to watch, grins over their faces. The laborers had sat up, and one had risen to see better. The landlord sidled from the bar. "Viti! More wine for the viti. Won't you step this way?"

He held up a bottle but Karaz waved it away. "I don't drink with inferiors," he said. His hand went out and took gentle hold of Taverik's collar. Marita tensed. "Especially insubordinate Pakajans who prefer dead bodies to their betters. The smell nauseates me."

"Tav," Marita warned. Too late.

Taverik's fist flashed up, breaking the student's hold. Viti Karaz narrowed his eyes and struck with his open hand. Taverik knocked him into the arms of the plump student behind him. With eager grins the two surged forward.

The watery-eyed student dodged around the table at Marita. She upended it, dishes and all, in his path and turned to help Taverik. Karaz had pinned him against the wall. Taverik kicked off the plump one rushing in. The student staggered back and Marita thrust her chair in his way, hammering him in the nose as he stumbled. He dropped to his knees clutching his face.

Marita caught a glint in the corner of her eye and ducked. A chair swung by the watery-eyed student just missed her head. It struck her instead in the chest, throwing her against the wall.

The breath went out of her at the pain. The watery-eyed student scrambled over the table and came at her. *Move!* she commanded herself. Braced against the wall she aimed the low, swift kick to the groin that Ot had taught her. He doubled. Got him good, she realized with satisfaction. She hit him in the jaw with both fists and he fell, writhing, to the floor.

Even as he was falling, Marita saw in a quick flash the other students and the sullen dockworkers locked together in battle. Spilling out into the street, both factions clamored for reinforcements. The tension building throughout the day had broken like a dam, flooding the entire waterfront with violence.

"Viti, I beg you!" cried the landlord. "Kali, Kali, please, my inn!"

"Marko!" shouted Taverik, beset two against one. The plump student had grabbed him from behind. Taverik, his hair wildly disheveled and a long rip in his blue surcoat, backed hard against the wall. The student grunted like a pig but hung on. Karaz bared his teeth once more in a wolfish grin and leisurely drew back his fist.

Marita sprang. She seized the fist and hung on like a bulldog, pulling back and down, and at the same time winding her leg around the student's. He fell, the Black Eagle charm knocking Marita in the cheek. She gasped at the unpleasant thrill that coursed through her. What was in that thing?

"This way, Kalis! Hurry!" The innkeeper. Marita risked a look over her shoulder. He held open the kitchen door.

"Tav!" she shouted. Taverik backed the overweight student against the wall again and at last loosened his grip. She pointed. "Door!"

Karaz climbed to his feet, eyes on Marita. "Stinking dog," he snarled and pulled his knife.

Marita went cold with dread. With shaking hands she drew her own knife and held it ready to throw. The student's lips curled as he saw it. He advanced, blade held loosely before him.

She retreated. She was dimly aware of Taverik and the plump student pummeling each other, then her world closed down to that gleaming knife and the face behind it. Viti Karaz lunged. She sidestepped, and he laughed. But she saw his sluggish reactions and her hopes rose. He'd drunk too much. He was backing her though. Farther and farther away from Taverik, farther from the door.

With his free hand he suddenly seized the amulet. Holding it high, he actually began to call for help from the Black Eagle. He was hard to understand, or had he shifted to another language?

Marita panted for air. The glittering of the charm confused her, and she barely avoided another clumsy thrust of the knife. The room seemed to darken, and she couldn't remember, was this real life or her nightmare? The terrifying presence that haunted her dreams merged with the student, and once more she knew she had to get past him, though she couldn't remember why. She'd never done it before, she'd always fled.

"Marko!" Taverik bawled. "This way!"

Just in time. The student lunged. She flung herself aside, heard the ripping of cloth, then found herself on the sticky flagstones, tangled with a chair. Above her loomed the hook-nosed face.

She'd seen it before. Behind the curtain, in her nightmares, was she her father? Or had it happened to her in the first place and the last three years a flash dream? The claw swung before her. "Zojikam!" she screamed.

With a roar, her hearing returned. Karaz hesitated and Taverik jumped between them, throwing up the arm holding the knife. Marita rolled out of the way and scrambled to her feet.

The student flung Taverik off. She grabbed up the chair and brought it down on Karaz's head with all her strength. He crumpled, knife ringing on the flags.

Marita doubled over, panting for air, her arms wrapped around the agony reawakened in her chest. Taverik's fingers closed hard around her shoulders. "Let's get out of here," he said, propelling her through the door.

The kitchen. Taverik propped her against the greasy wall and forced the door shut with his shoulder. A bottle splintered against it from the other side.

"Mercy on us!" cried the cook. The little wizened man cowered in the chimney corner leaving a half-plucked chicken on the table.

"The troops will be here any minute," Taverik said. One eye was purple and swollen shut. "We've got to be well out of this."

"Give me that chair," Marita said, straightening. She felt oddly dizzy, but managed to shove the sturdy kitchen chair under the door knob before following Taverik to the back door of the inn.

Strange to see the afternoon sun still pouring down. Chickens pecked in the straw and dung, oblivious to the shouts and breaking glass in the street outside the wall. Taverik whistled through split lips. "The entire waterfront must be in on this."

"When we start something," panted Marita, "we do it good. Let's hide in the stables."

Inside, Whitey stuck his pale nose over a stall and flicked his ears in surprise. Frez kicked the partition. Leaning against the stone wall, Marita rubbed her eyes. Everything looked smaller and darker than usual.

Holding his left side, Taverik paced down the line of stalls. "This last one is the hay mow," he said. His voice sounded distant. "We can hide there."

Marita tried to join him but her muscles wouldn't obey. The room blackened and broke into crazily dancing spots. She'd better sit down, she thought, and felt her knees buckle.

Taverik

Taverik only just managed to keep her head from striking the stone floor. Despite stabbing pains in his ribs he half-carried her to the last stall and settled her gently in the hay. Slumping down beside her, he rested his forehead on his knees.

A good thing the students were drunk, he thought, listening to the swelling riot outside. They'd have never escaped otherwise. Zojikam grant the students remembered no names to give the law.

He began a mental list of his aches and became aware his hand was sticky. He lifted his head and looked at it. Blood. In sudden fear he crawled over to Marita. No, the bandage around her chest was still white. He took her right hand and found a cut on her forearm. He sighed in relief; it had already stopped bleeding.

Still holding her hand, he leaned over and looked at her face. Sun from the window traced the faint lines etched around her mouth and in the corners of her eyes. What a burden she carried. He liked her grit. But then, he had liked her from the first he saw her, at the guild. Chado had cheated at cards the night before, and the outraged players had surrounded Taverik in the Textile Guild Hall the next day, on the theory, he supposed, that any Zandro would do for revenge. The situation had been tight, but he'd managed. Then, just as he'd gotten them all to stroll out for a round of beer with him he'd looked up and seen that the newest guild member, a starved-looking youth, had watched everything. Just looking, but the look had accepted him.

Curious, he'd gone out of his way to meet Kastazi, and found he must be older than he looked, though getting him to say anything about himself was like trying to drag a mule where it didn't want to go. Marko had often invited him home, shared meager meals and uncritical quiet. But throughout their growing friendship, Marko had never made any reference to his dubious reputation.

He liked her wry humor. And her quicksilver moods, changing like sunlight and shadow flashing across the Giss Valley. And her intriguing background.

As a woman she was the opposite of foggy Dula Familo. He'd done his best to rattle Dula last night, and he hoped it was enough; she'd had strict orders to capture him. The thought of marriage to her revolted him. If only he could find someone like Marko.

Why not Marko, herself? The thought took his breath away. Why not? She never would, that's why. Perhaps he could persuade her. What would Uncle Nikilo think of her?

He stared down into her face. She looked more vulnerable asleep. Maybe she would welcome marriage. He thought about her fierce independence and doubted it. In fact, he'd have to be very careful or she'd get nervous and quietly disappear before he could win her around.

She stirred. He drew back feeling faintly guilty, as if he'd been reading a private diary. Then, on quick impulse, he bent and kissed her lips.

Marita

Marita opened her eyes and stared in bewilderment at sunbeams, weathered boards and broken bits of straw caught in cobwebs.

"How do you feel?"

She turned her head. Taverik sat against the stall, his face bruised and swollen, dust powdering his torn blue surcoat. "Sick to my stomach," she said. "Did I pass out? How embarrassing."

"Lie still a while," Taverik suggested. He stretched out his legs and crossed his ankles. "We can't leave for a while anyway."

She became suddenly aware of the ring of shod hooves on stone, the screams echoing above the roar of the riot. "So, they've called out the troops," she said then stiffened with a sudden sour memory. "Taverik, did I scream?"

He nodded. "Just once, though."

"That's enough. Damn!" If anything would betray her as a woman . . . She might have just jeopardized the freedom of three people she loved. More care, more prudence. She shouldn't even let Taverik so close, she thought. But dammit, she had to have a friend, especially with Sahra acting so withdrawn.

"It was just a soft scream," Taverik assured her. "Probably no one heard it over the noise of the fight."

"I have this recurring nightmare, you see," she explained sheepishly. "And when Karaz began that Black Eagle chant, I couldn't tell nightmare from reality. There was something odd going on."

"What is this Black Eagle?" Taverik demanded.

She shrugged. "Some *ikiji*. I saw it a lot in Vosa right after Soza took over. Our attacker adhered to it."

"Well, don't worry," Taverik said. "Those students

won't remember a thing. They were too drunk. Besides, they think we're emasculated."

"How could they have thought that?" she said wryly. "They *must* have been drunk."

Taverik snorted with laughter. "You're pretty handy in a fight," he said. "Your father teach you that?"

"Hardly! My father's stableman, Ot, taught me a lot before he was killed."

"I'll teach you more if you like. You hold your knife funny."

"That's the way we do it in Vosa," she said, a little nettled. "We throw them."

"You do? I'd like to see you do it." Taverik picked hay from his sleeve and flicked it away, speaking without looking up from this seemingly absorbing task. "My uncle is back in Illiga. Would you like to attend the temple service with me tonight, then dine with him?"

"Thank you," she said warmly, knowing that his uncle was the only bright spot in Taverik's family. "But all I want to do is go home, close the door and curl up. Maybe when I'm feeling better."

He looked stricken. "Of course. I forgot."

"It sounds quieter out there now," she said, struggling to sit up in the prickly hay.

"Shall we go?" He clambered groaning to his feet and offered his hand with its torn knuckles.

Marita grasped it and was pulled easily to her feet. "I dread telling my sister about this," she said. "She will suffer agonies."

Taverik threw out his chest and thumped it. "Courage! Face your guilt like a man!" His eyes slid twinkling to her exasperated frown. "At least try."

"Go jump in the Giss," she said, annoyed at his careless reference to her sex.

The riot had been quelled, and mounted army patrolled the waterfront. A burly pikeman gave Marita and Taverik a hard look as they picked their way through the mess, but no one stopped them. "Perhaps," Marita said as they turned into the steep River Road at the bridge, "perhaps we should avoid the University."

Taverik's answer was drowned in the rumble of many hooves crossing the bridge. Marita turned in the saddle. Six horsemen galloped headlong across the bridge, the guards diving left and right to get out of their path. The riders never slowed. They crossed the wharf area and headed straight up the hill at Marita and Taverik. In the lead plunged a foaming dark horse ridden by a woman. "Make way! Make way!" she screamed. Her voice was shrill with terror.

Chapter 8

Marita

Make way? There was no place to go. Wooden crates and huge bales of cotton closed in the narrow street. Marita squeezed Whitey against the wall. Taverik tried to follow her but Frez half reared and pivoted him into the road. Taverik swore and brought him back just as the riders thundered upon them.

The first horse plunged past, the woman beating him rhythmically. Lather whipped from his foamy shoulder and splatted against Marita's cheek. She wiped it without thinking, her eyes meeting the vita's for a seeming eternity, sharing the raw fear she saw there. Memories awoke and clamored inside her until she wanted to spur Whitey and flee with them. Run anywhere. Escape.

Then, veil askew and hair flying like a man's, the woman was past. Five viti clattered after, their gorgeous raiment stained and crumpled, one man pale and swaying in the saddle. The pavement trembled. The last man carried a boy before him, the little hands clutching the scarlet surcoat in a whitened grip, the eyes dark holes in a pale face. The powerful haunches of the great black horse pulsed and surged, propelling them up the steep hill. They were gone.

Frez burst from among the cotton bales, bucking and plunging with stiff legs. Taverik controlled him then shook his fist up the hill. "Damn them!" he roared. "Just because they are Massadaran! Just because they are viti! They think they are ordained by Zojikam to do whatever they want!"

"What's the use of fussing over viti?" Marita said from the imperturbed Whitey. "They do what they want, that's just the way the world is."

Taverik brought the dancing Frez alongside. "You should have incarnated yourself as a viti," he said. "Then you'd have fewer problems."

She faced him quickly. "Have you no discretion?" she demanded.

His startled expression changed to swift comprehension. "I'm sorry. I didn't think."

Leaning forward, she gripped his wrist. "Listen, Taverik. You've several times made a careless reference to—to me. People might overhear and understand. The danger is real, not just to me, but to you, too. Bibi used my real name in the market place and Ot died because of it. It could have been all of us."

She gave another glance up the road, strangely troubled by those others' misfortune, whatever it might have been. "It could be you. Please, believe me, you run danger the more you associate with me."

He put his battered hand over hers. "They say nothing good comes easy," he said warmly.

She pulled away. "What do you mean?" But Taverik had already urged his mule up the hill. After a moment she followed.

The late afternoon sun shone in her eyes as they reached the plaza. The glow touched the stones of the tower with orange, and blazed blood red from the windows of the palace until the building seemed to be on fire. People swarmed around the gate like ants around a stirred-up anthill.

"I think," said Marita, "that I'll just head home from here."

"You'll be all right?" Taverik asked. His hair was tangled, and he'd pulled down his soft felt cap against the chilling wind. His face looked puffy and tired.

"I'll be fine," she said. "You?"

"Oh, I'll be fine. Until the next mess then," he said cheerfully and struck out diagonally across the plaza.

Marita turned down city, steeling herself to meet her sister's horrified reaction to her disastrous escapade. Bibi opened the gate so quickly that Marita knew she'd been waiting. Weary, she slid from the saddle and came face to face with Sahra, pale and anxious. Marita stiffened, ready for deserved recriminations.

"Thank Zojikam you're back!" Sahra cried. "Oh, Mari, have you heard? Soza has taken Ormea! He assassinated the entire zoji family, and many of the leading viti in one night!"

Marita's breath caught. "Just like Vosa. So now Soza is one step closer to us."

"Only the zoja and her child survived," Sahra said. "She's escaped here, to Illiga."

Taverik

The sun slipped behind the mountains as Taverik reached the temple. The clock tower pointed a lean finger against the luminous green sky, and the bells rang out above him, joined by fainter peals from the temple across the city.

One of Illiga's oldest buildings, the temple had thick Pakajan walls and heavy gates which now stood open. Taverik hesitated outside, weighing what to do. His muscles had stiffened, and his face must be a sight. Not to mention his torn surcoat. He hadn't been to a temple service in a long time either—three years. Maybe he'd better just go home.

Frez champed and sidled at the delay. "Damn you, mule," Taverik growled, clamping his free arm against his sore ribs. "Aren't you tired yet?" Shivering in the evening's chill, damp air, he nudged Frez toward the gate. If he didn't go, he'd miss Uncle Nik.

More mules filled the yard than Taverik had ever seen there. Quite a number of horses, too, which meant viti present. Taverik felt faint surprise; viti usually attended the temple at court or the one across the Ao where most of them had property. From the temple door soft light spilled, warming the purple dusk. Three young boys squabbled in the entry over who got to pull the bell rope, just as he and Chado had years and years ago. He squeezed past them into the vestibule, aware both of warmth and the presence of many people in the hall beyond. Where would he find Nik in that crowd?

Someone came in behind him. He heard an exclamation, then a hand clamped onto his shoulder. "I've got you, Zandro!"

Taverik turned, removing himself from the man's grip in the same motion. A heavy-jowled stranger glared at him then looked puzzled. *Iron ore,* Taverik thought, taking in the leather clothes. "You have the advantage of me, Kali," he said smoothly.

"No, you have the advantage of me," said the man. "But I intend to make it right. 'Go to Taverik Zandro,' they said. Bah! I say, you're all a pack of scum and I'll have the law on you. You'll never set foot in a guild hall again!"

Swift comprehension set Taverik's blood pumping. "Kali, may I take it you had some dealings with my brother Chado in the matter of—"

"Stout wool!" the man bellowed. Taverik wished he'd keep his voice down. "Stout wool filled with moth holes and paid for twice."

More fool you, Taverik thought, but he smiled gently. "Kali, I regret the error. Next time you will have to deal with me personally, if you wish full satisfaction. My brother is not, er, experienced with the textile trade."

"Not experienced! *Too* experienced, I say."

"As it may be," Taverik soothed. "If you'll bring your woolen goods to my office tomorrow early, I will make good your money."

"You'd better," said the man, starting away. "I won't back down! I'll have the law on you if you don't. You're all alike, you Zandros. Damned if I deal with you again."

He pushed past Taverik to the hall. Feeling sour, Taverik turned to follow him and found his uncle waiting in the doorway. "What was that all about, Tav?"

The blood rushed to Taverik's face. Of all the conversations for Nik to overhear! Yet despite the heat radiating from his cheeks, he felt oddly defensive about Chado. "Just a misunderstanding the man had with my brother. I'll straighten it out tomorrow."

He'd come forward into the softly lit temple. Nikilo's eyebrows flew up as he caught sight of him, and his hand gripped Taverik's shoulder with a concern that warmed deep. "What happened? You weren't caught in that riot?"

"Caught in it?" Taverik gave him an affectionate grin and leaned closer. "I started it."

"What!"

The murmur of voices had died down, and singing had begun. "Tell you later," Taverik whispered.

"You'd better," Nikilo said, rolling his eyes. "And tell no one else. Let's sit."

"Where?" Taverik could see no empty bench in the packed room. The benches, each with a low kneeling rest before it, groaned with the weight of elbow to elbow people. Men and women crowded the aisles, and stood in the back.

"We'll have to worship standing," Nikilo whispered. "Pakajan style."

Taverik followed him to the back of the men's seating where several people made room for them against the wall. One of them was a viti, in furs and jewels. Taverik took off his cap and bowed. The viti nodded gravely at him, then gave him a long second look. Acutely self-conscious, Taverik stared at the front where the priest in a white robe had begun to sing the Invocation.

There'd been changes in the last three years. The priest sang in Illigan Pakajan instead of archaic Massadaran. The Pakajan gave the words a curious stalwart feel, almost too down to earth to be holy. Yet their meaning struck him as the half-understood archaic Massadaran never had.

Or was it, he wondered, the odd experiences he'd had lately that made him more sensitive. No matter, he felt the presence of Zojikam like a cloud over the assembly, and that made worship awkward.

The people worshiped differently than he'd remembered, too. Many sang with eyes closed, with smiles on their faces. He wondered what they were getting out of it that he wasn't. He stole a glance at his uncle. Nikilo stood with his eyes closed, just listening.

At last they reached the Repentance. It wouldn't be long now before he could get out of there. With the others he sank awkwardly to his knees on the unyielding flagstones and bowed his head. He felt exhausted. The flagstones bit his knees, and his ribs ached.

Arms lifted, the priest sang through the promise. ". . . and Zojikam will come to you and walk among you, and you shall see him face to face—" Suddenly the man stiffened. "My children," he said slowly.

A prophesy! Silence fell on the temple, until even the constant undercurrent of rustling stilled. "My children, you will be tested. Hold firm, or night will come upon you. An eagle chases a hawk—"

Taverik's head snapped up. His hands and feet went cold.

"—The hawk flees, but wherever it hides, the eagle is there before it. Pray the eagle will not catch the hawk or darkness will fall for a time, another time and a long time."

The priest remained a moment in silence. Then he dropped his arms and walked back to the altar. Taverik stared after him, oblivious to the chant of the Creed now filling the room. What did it mean? And why was it following him around?

Nikilo's fingers closed gently on his shoulder. He looked up and realized everyone had stood. He'd missed the entire Creed. He climbed slowly to his feet. Nikilo leaned closer. "Are your ribs broken, Taverik?"

"Don't think so," he whispered back. His uncle gave him a long look from his brown eyes, but said nothing more. Taverik leaned against the wall willing the Repentance to hurry. But even with several assistants, it was a long time before Taverik's turn came to kneel in the aisle before the priest and receive blessing.

The priest paused, the silver bowl on level with Taverik's eyes. Under the singing of the worshippers, he said, "It has been long since I've seen you here, Taverik Zandro."

"Yes," Taverik said. Just *do* it, he thought impatiently.

"Your family has earned a hard reputation," the priest said, his eyes searching Taverik's swollen face. Taverik remained silent, but inwardly he seethed. He was always blamed for the things his family did, no matter how he tried. He'd go away, change his name to Tazur. He caught his breath. There it was again: *Tazur*. Hawk.

The priest at last began the ritual. "Do you truly repent of your sins?"

"I truly repent," Taverik said. Of his *own* sins, he added stubbornly under his breath.

"Then I administer to you, because of the Promise, this token of repentance." The priest dipped his finger in the bowl containing the ashes mingled with blood from the morning sacrifice. He placed his finger on Taverik's forehead. Instantly, he gasped. His fingers curled around Taverik's face. "Flood and darkness," he said, his eyes looking right through Taverik. "Flood and darkness and—fire."

Chapter 9

Taverik

Taverik jerked away. "What do you mean?" he demanded.

"I don't know," said the priest. "The moment I touched you, that's all I could see." Rubbing his fingers together wonderingly, the priest considered Taverik with his grizzled eyebrows knit. "Young Zandro," he said at last, "lay your life down before Zojikam, for there is much at work in you that is of the spiritual world, and I know not if for good or for ill."

No easy joke rose to Taverik's lips to ease the awkward situation. He stared back at the priest, stiff-jawed and stubborn. It wasn't fair. There were hundreds of men who were worse than he, and the priests didn't go around embarrassing them with prophesies. He stood up abruptly and stalked back to his place, refusing to meet his uncle's questioning eyes. As the Benediction began, he leaned against the wall and inwardly sought the presence of Zojikam. "What does it mean?" he asked silently. Then, from the depths of his soul, he added, "I don't want it!"

A damp, chill wind coursed smoothly through the streets, carrying with it the river smell. Taverik lifted his collar, wishing for fur. Wishing Nikilo would speak. But his uncle remained silent and the sound of the hooves echoed even louder because of it. A man carrying a yoke of tinware rattled past, then the street was again empty and silent. Faint lights glowed behind shutters.

If Nikilo would only say, "What was all that about?" Taverik could tell him he didn't know. That it was as surprising to him as it probably was to Nikilo, and that it wasn't the only weird thing that had happened lately. But Nikilo's face remained thoughtfully fixed on his mule's ears. And after four years of keeping his own counsel, Taverik couldn't break the restraint between them.

Not until they drew up beside Nikilo's narrow four-story house did his uncle speak, and then on a complete non sequitur. "Taverik, you haven't seen Viti Malenga hanging around the guilds, have you? Talking with merchants?"

"Hanging around the guilds?" repeated Taverik incredulously. "A *viti*? Are you crazy?"

"No, just curious," Nikilo said casually. "Let me know if you see him, will you?" He kicked the locked gate with his stirrup. "Mano! Hurry up!"

"Coming, coming." The gate swung open and Manokichit's battered old face peered out, lit from the bottom by an oil lamp. He'd been a beggar by the temple gate for years until Nikilo had declared he was tired of tossing coins at him and dragged him home—much to the distress of Nikilo's prim housekeeper. Mano had responded in devotion if not in industry, and had been responsible for much of Taverik's nonformal education.

The fringe of hair around his bald pate, Taverik saw with shock, had turned completely white. An unpleasant awareness of mortality washed over him. Had it been that long?

Mano lifted the lamp higher and recognized him suddenly. "Taverik!" he yelled. He sprang forward, causing Frez to throw up his head with a snort. "Hee hoo!" he shouted, pounding Taverik's thigh. "You tricky devil, it's been years!"

"It must be years, you old street rat," Taverik said, locking his elbow against his aching ribs and forcing the curvetting mule into the alley. "You look as white as the Widow Pardi now!"

"And every hair her fault," Mano shouted, rattling

the bolt and padlock behind him. "And yours too, I'll have you know."

Taverik grinned in the darkness and dismounted gingerly beside Nikilo in the backyard. His uncle clasped his shoulder briefly, warmly. "Manokichit," he said, "when you're through here, bring up poultices and check the tricky devil's ribs for me."

"He do look a sight," Mano said.

The back door opened. A stooped woman darkened the light flooding from it, calling in a quavering mouse's shout, "Kali Vitujak! Is that you? Shall I begin your supper?"

"Supper for two, Kala Pardi," Nikilo said, striding to the house. "I've a surprise guest for you."

The woman shaded her eyes and peered past him as Taverik drew near. "It never is!"

"Never," Taverik agreed.

"Taverik! Gracious, and so tall! Such wide shoulders! So handsome!"

"Handsome!" snorted Nikilo. "You can't have gotten a good look at him yet."

"Oh mercy!" she cried, pulling Taverik into the kitchen with knobby fingers. "Your poor face. And that lovely surcoat, all ruined. I don't think I can mend it to good as new. Whatever has happened?"

"Don't worry about it, Kala Pardi," Taverik interrupted gently. She looked frail enough for him to blow over, and so stooped now his own back ached for her. He slipped a coin into the pocket of her starched white apron. "Your good dinner will fix me fine."

"And a little peace and quiet," shouted Mano from the yard.

She clung to Taverik's sleeve to get past him to the door. "Get on with you, Manokichit!" she cried.

Laughing softly, Taverik followed Nikilo past Kala Pardi's room in the front of the house and up the wooden stairs. The house, though only one room wide and two deep, had four stories. From the road it looked crooked and ready to tumble into the street, but it had stood firm for generations. When Taverik was a boy, the house had seemed to wander upwards forever, each set of stairs growing steeper and ricketier until he'd be climbing the ladder into Mano's attic to look over the slate roofs of the houses crowding each side.

Nikilo topped the stairs and strode through the salon without stopping. Taverik stumbled over a tiny footstool and came slower. It was a dark, formal chamber with oak furniture and mementos of Taverik's white-bearded grandfather whom he could just barely remember. His mother had liked that room, and Nikilo let it remain just as it was, kept depressingly tidy by Kala Pardi.

Soft light filled the front room. Taverik felt his way towards it, and into the familiar smell of leather, ink, and books. His uncle knelt by the fireplace trying to light the fire.

"Cold in here," Taverik said, edging past the table piled with rolled up maps and an astrolabe. He shivered. "Draft like a gale. How can you work?"

"Fire will do it. Let me clear that chair for you." Nikilo got a promising flame going and stood up. Picking up the pile of books on the sag-bottomed chair, he looked vaguely around for an empty surface.

Taverik snorted. "Try the floor," he suggested. The stuffed owl still glared furiously at him from the mantle. Taverik pushed it aside and set down the lamp, grimacing as he caught sight of his face, hideously distorted, in the ox-eye mirror on the wall above it. The rest of the mantle was taken up with jars of dark liquids, the bust of a Massadaran poet, seashells, a bear skull and a clock whose pendulum wound first one direction then the next. As a boy, Taverik had stood on the horsehide chair and stared at that pendulum until half entranced.

"Let me show you my new book, Taverik."

Taverik turned. Nikilo had piled the books on the floor and was thumbing through the top one, a slim red volume. "It's my answer to the "Humble Kali," whoever he is. Just came out a couple of weeks ago. You'll remember his discussion of the philosophy of true beauty."

"Uh," said Taverik.

The door opened and Mano stumped through the

salon. "I can't see a thing in here!" he complained. Lamp light gleamed on his bald pate as he came in with a steaming bowl. "Take off your pretty blue mantle, boy."

Taverik obediently unbuckled his belt. Nikilo peered over the book at him. "Listen here, Taverik. I had said earlier, 'beauty is perfection,' and he says . . ."

"Manokichit!" called out Kala Pardi, "You come take this tray. I can't see a thing!"

"You're the one who leaves them stools everywhere to trip on," Mano said. "Here boy, hold this."

Taverik found the warm bowl thrust into his battered hands as Mano tramped back into the salon. Nikilo looked up again. "Taverik, you'll have to clear off the table."

Balancing the bowl on the slippery horsehide, Taverik gathered the maps together and tossed them on the window seat at the casement windows. Mano thudded the heavy tray onto the table. "There. Now get on with it, boy."

"How do you ever carry these things up the stairs, Kala Pardi?" Taverik asked, pulling off his surcoat and tossing it over the chair. He shivered and moved closer to the fire.

"I make do," she said. She crept over to the surcoat, holding on to the furniture for balance. "Such a lovely color, that blue, just like the young gentleman's eyes."

"Yes, yes, thank you, Kala," said Nikilo. "Now, listen, Taverik—"

"Take off your shirt, let me see them ribs."

"Put another log on," Taverik demanded, stripping and shivering.

"Seems like yesterday he was a little youngster, and now a fine tall lad, with broad shoulders . . ."

"—I had said beauty is perfection, and he answered, 'Imperfections can make an object more poignant, and therefore more beautiful.' "

"Ha!" crowed Mano. "Then I guess our Taverik is the prettiest of them all!" He gave Taverik a prod with a stubby forefinger.

"Ouch!" Taverik pulled indignantly away.

"Hold still!"

"Don't poke around like that!"

"However, I've got him now! For if you say imperfections make beauty, then . . ."

"You ought to be grateful, you ought. It's not everyone I'd waste my talents on. I've got a remedy here I wouldn't waste on the likes of Kali Chado. So sit still, damn you!"

Taverik sat as still as his shivering would allow, what with the fire searing his left side and the draft chilling his right. Nikilo closed the book triumphantly. "So we'll see what he says to that! Wish I could meet the fellow."

"Nothing broken," said Mano.

"You sound disappointed!"

Mano scowled. "It would be more than you deserved. Didn't I teach you better than that?"

"Two against one. I did use your finger trick. Worked pretty well."

Kala Pardi folded her hands under her apron. "He always was a bright one. Though he did manage to wiggle out of whatever he didn't want to do. Many's the time . . ."

"Many's the time you talk too much, woman!" Mano scowled terribly as he slapped a poultice into Taverik's hand. "Stick that on your beautiful imperfect eye."

The widow straightened herself as much as her back would allow. "Look who's talking about talking! As I was saying, many's the time I'd . . ."

"Go back to your kitchen," said Mano gathering up bowl and towel. "The kalis wish to talk philosophy and you keep interrupting them."

Kala Pardi shook with determination. "*Many's* the time I'd . . ."

Taverik broke in. "You're a dear, Kala Pardi," he said, planting a kiss on her soft wrinkled cheek. "Many's the time you hid me in your pantry to escape my father's caning."

"Go on with you. You probably deserved every one of those licks. Though I do think the Kali beat terrible hard and long."

"Your pastries made up for it."

Her eyes brightened. "You ate a few!" She straightened her apron with arthritic fingers and started for the door. "How I do run on. You kalis shouldn't encourage me like that." From the darkness of the salon Mano gave an expressive snort.

Overwhelmed by their noisy love, Taverik lowered himself gingerly into the horsehide chair. He found himself grinning foolishly, stopped, then grinned again. He looked up and found his uncle watching him with a strange expression on his face. "What's the matter, Nik?"

Nikilo shook his head and put down the book. "I should never have left," he said. "I should have taken you with me."

"I've been all right," Taverik said lightly. Feeling faintly defensive he pulled on his shirt. "Where's my surcoat? Did the widow take it? Help, give me one of yours before I freeze."

They ate, and Taverik hadn't realized how hungry he'd been. He dug in enthusiastically, telling an edited tale of the waterfront riot, reminded by Nikilo's elegant good manners not to talk with his mouth full, or wipe his lips on his sleeve. He'd forgotten a lot in those four years.

When he couldn't eat another bite, Nikilo called Mano to clear the dishes. Taverik settled back with a sigh. "Mind if I sleep here tonight, Nik? I think Mano will have to take me home in a wheelbarrow otherwise."

"I'd be glad to have you," said Nikilo, pouring a thick amber liquid into two tiny crystal cups. "Will they worry?"

"They won't notice."

Nikilo's eyebrow went up, but he merely handed Taverik one of the cups. Taverik sniffed it suspiciously.

"An acquired taste, nephew."

"Certainly not natural," Taverik said grimacing. He took an experimental sip and at last brought up what he'd been turning over and over in his mind.

"What do you know about black eagles, Unc?"

Nikilo took his time, pulling forward the sag-bottomed chair and seating himself. He placed his fingertips together in a way that warned Taverik that he was about to hear everything his former tutor knew about black eagles.

"The black eagle," Nikilo said softly, quoting, "is a bird of ferocity and not to be tamed. For when he misses his prey, he turns in his anger to attack his master and his horse."

"Fierce," Taverik agreed.

"Yes," said his uncle in a brisker voice. "And because of its reputation the black eagle has always fascinated the war-like Bcacmats. In fact, I suspect Bcacma is where people first turned from worshipping Zojikam to worshipping his creatures. The tlath himself, of course, is believed to be a personification of the black eagle."

"A personification?"

"Members of the black eagle cult undergo a ceremony in which they invite the 'eagle' to reside within them. What they receive, of course, is an evil spiritual being, a *mahiga*."

Taverik shuddered. "*Ikiji.*"

"Decidedly second best," Nikilo agreed dryly. "Furthermore, devotees of the cult entice the lesser *mahigas* associated with the black eagle god into jars and seal them. The jar is kept near and is supposed to confer powers on the owner."

"Does it?"

Nikilo shook his head. "Quite the opposite. The owner gives *it* power and in the end it consumes them."

"That's awful!" Taverik said, revolted. "How can they bear to do that?"

"To Bcacmats, the Black Eagle represents their military might, of which they are so proud. It certainly sums up the character of that particular nation. To them, they are not living unless they are fighting. Massadara has had to defend its mutual border since before history, and we ourselves felt their cruelty a generation or so ago when they swept from the north."

"And that's why Massadara so determinedly hangs on

to the Peninsula," Taverik said. "Prevent them from getting an easy route to the sea."

"That and other reasons."

"How do you know all this, Nikilo?"

"I looked into it when I began seeing the cult's symbol in Vosa."

"That claw amulet? I've seen it here in Illiga."

Nikilo stilled. "Here?"

"Yes. A student wore it, the one who jumped me. And a doctor tried to use it to heal a friend of mine."

"So it has come here," Nikilo said softly. In the firelight the freckles stood out on his lean face and his lips compressed to a grim line. "I had hoped it wouldn't. But that must have been what the priest was prophesying. It was all over Vosa, of course."

Taverik squinted at him. "Of course?"

"Soza has a black eagle on his coat of arms. Of course the cult spread when he took Vosa."

"On Soza's coat of arms," Taverik repeated slowly. A whole lot of things suddenly fit together—the way Marko and Oma jumped every time the Black Eagle was mentioned. They were from Vosa, a man wearing the Black Eagle amulet murdered their parents, the next day, Soza assassinated the zojis and took the city. Could Soza be the enemy they fled? If so, no wonder Marko was so cautious! No wonder . . . "Who is Soza?" he demanded.

Nikilo spread his hands. "That, my nephew, is the very heart of the matter. During my four years in Vosa I did my discreet best to find out."

"I thought he was marshal of Vosa."

"That's right. He worked himself up through the ranks by mostly foul means. Anyone who opposed him met an unexpected death. I found it hard to merely get anyone to talk about him. But it is supposed he is a Pakajan nobody. He looks more Massadaran to me, but I also have other suspicions."

"What are they?"

"I can prove nothing." Nikilo slapped his hands together. "Nothing! But it's interesting that suddenly a nasty *ikiji*—there's rumors they use human sacrifice, by the way—a nasty *ikiji* begins to spread in the Peninsula as soon as Soza arrives. An *ikiji* peculiarly Bcacmat. I suspect Soza has some connection with Bcacma."

"Bcacma!" The blood drained from Taverik's face. "How could he cooperate with them?"

"I don't know. But if proved, it might be enough to once more unite the Peninsula against a common enemy. And so I wrote the Zoji Balanji."

Taverik gave him an affectionate smile. "And here I thought you sat meekly writing down whatever the ambassador told you."

Nikilo's eyes crinkled in response. "I did that, too."

"And of course that's why Zoji Balanji recalled you and made you his personal secretary."

"When it became obvious Soza wouldn't stop at Vosa."

"He hasn't," Taverik said, "managed to quell Vosa entirely. A lot of riots."

"A lot of riots," Nikilo agreed. "He didn't manage to get the entire Vos family and the city knows it. The people cling to the hope that the Voses will again rule, and Soza has moved heaven and earth trying to find them."

"That sounds like him," Taverik growled. No wonder Marko was afraid. How had she taken it when she heard that Soza was now in Ormea, just two days' ride south? A wave of disquiet washed over him; what if she reacted by fleeing on? Would she tell him? Would she even be there the next time he visited?

"The same situation has happened in Ormea," Nikilo said. "Except Soza knows exactly where Akusa and her son are. A second attempt was already made. One of her men was a traitor—Soza likes to work from the inside—and he tried to finish the job on the Giss Bridge before Akusa could make it to the fortress."

"So that's what we saw this afternoon. Maybe," Taverik said hopefully, "maybe Akusa can keep Ormea from falling entirely into Soza's hands. She could spearhead a revolt from here."

Nikilo shook his head. "Taverik," he said heavily, "right now I wouldn't bet a chicken feather on Akusa's life."

Chapter 10

Malenga

"Damn river fog," Malenga muttered, nearly frantic. He'd blessed it at first—it hid this little trip from prying eyes. But that was before he'd thought he'd heard someone following him, and had plunged his mule into the warehouse warren. He'd promptly gotten lost in the predawn dark and milky fog. All the streets looked alike, he couldn't find the right door, time was passing, and with his luck he'd be caught out here on this humiliating mule. Damn if he'd do this again! There had to be a better way. The worst part would be dealing with the vulgar fool he was supposed to meet.

He turned up a street so steep it had steps. This looked familiar. He pushed on and soon found the warehouse with the sign of the spice bush and the Zandro name over the door. At last! His fading fright left him irritable and headachy. Breath misting around his face, he dismounted the shameful beast and knocked.

The door opened immediately, Donato Zandro, huge and bull-like, bowing and bowing and blocking the way. Malenga pushed past him without a word, dragging the mule right into the flagstone hall. Zandro bolted the door behind him. "Did you have problems finding your way, Viti?"

"No," snapped Malenga. He winced as he took in the effect of the over-rich purple velvet surcoat with Zandro's yellow hair and ruddy face, gaudy even in the lantern light.

"Excellent," said Zandro. "Now, if you'll be so kind as to follow me, Viti, we can be private in my office."

The oaf lifted the lantern and led the way into the darkness.

Rich scents delighted Malenga's nostrils as he followed. Cinnamon, cloves, myrrh, cedar, and another scent—what was it? Ah, the pungent leaf from the newly discovered western isles. "Your warehouse is large," he said in spite of himself.

Zandro looked back, the lantern grotesquely lighting his jowls. "This is but one of them," he said, his chest expanding visibly. "I have several others and two shops in the city."

He lifted the lantern to let its light play across sacks of aromatic beans, scented boxes of spice, and rare herbs. "I started in spice and have since expanded—textiles, jewels, you name it. I am now a member of more guilds than any other merchant in the city."

"You do deal in many commodities."

Zandro smirked. "More than most people would guess," he said and winked conspiratorially. A bitter-iron taste tinged Malenga's mouth; the man was crude. Sometimes he wondered if this would all be worth it in the end.

Zandro's office was square and dark despite the fire struggling in the grate. Iron-reinforced oak boards shuttered the high windows against cold and thieves. "Please be seated, Viti," Zandro said, setting the lantern on a table covered with an exquisite knotted rug.

Malenga stepped over a bundle of furs and wool on the floor, hating Donato for the careless way he'd dumped the lantern down on that beautiful rug. Bloodsucking merchants. They had the money, sure, but with it all the aesthetic sense of pigs. Damn barbaric Pakajans. And damn Zoji Balanji for allowing Pakajan influence to creep in more and more. Zandro pushed forward a chair for him but he kicked it away irritably. "Have you got the money ready?" he demanded.

Zandro chuckled and settled insolently into the rejected chair. "Right at your feet."

Startled, Malenga looked again at the bundle. "It's in there?"

"That's right. Anyone who sees you leave will think

you were merely picking up some clandestine presents for your sweetie." Zandro laughed at his own cleverness.

"Cunning," Malenga admitted reluctantly. Belatedly he remembered his prepared speech. "Soza will be pleased," he said. "He rewards generously; a man of your skills surely will find a prominent place in his new kingdom. There are no limits. Only play your part well."

He stopped, frowning anxiously at Donato Zandro's reddening face. Had he laid it on too thick? Or was the man having a heart attack?"

"Wonderful!" Zandro exclaimed, actually rubbing his hands together like a theater merchant. "But there's something I want *now* in exchange."

Malenga's mouth pulled down with distaste. "What?"

Zandro leaned forward, the chair squawling with his weight. "I want a good marriage for my oldest son. A vita."

"You forget yourself!" Malenga snapped. "Unthinkable! Disgusting! That a vulgar dockworker—"

He cut himself off. Zandro had gone purple with rage, and Malenga suddenly remembered his cousin Familo had been angling for one of the Zandro sons. After all, Familo had reasoned, the son didn't have to last long once they'd gotten hold of the money. Besides, Soza needed Zandro's money badly, as well as the contact within the city. With an effort Malenga controlled his revulsion. "I will consider what may be done," he said smoothly. "Now I must go to meet Soza's emissary with your gift. Soza thinks highly of you, and I'm certain his reward to you in the end will be beyond what you expect."

Zandro seemed content with that, missing the dry irony that Malenga couldn't keep out of his words. Malenga returned his over-effusive bows with the stiffest of nods. Poor fool, he thought.

Balanji

The morning sun had burned off the fog by the time the zoji's hunting party entered Illiga's North Gate.

They clattered splendidly up through the twisting streets, passing citizens squeezed desperately against the walls but still bowing low and humbly pulling off their hats.

Zoji Balanji himself rode in the lead, carrying his own hawk. He'd long ago noticed that the people showed little affection or enthusiasm for him despite their great respect. It bothered him today too, but mostly his thoughts circled around Akusa of Ormea, and Soza.

Despite the cold, he wore no cloak, and he'd even loosened his collar. His viti followed, their haughty splendor comically diminished by their cold-pinched faces and reddened noses. Balanji had laughed secretly as he watched those who'd adopted the latest style, the *hama* craze which had filtered north from Massadara. Their legs, warmed only by silk hose, dangled under ridiculously short coats. Even their buttocks must be frozen, he thought with delight. None of them seemed to realize that only the southern heat of Massadara gave the style any sense.

The party swept into the fortress, scattering chickens, children, grooms and servants. Balanji gave his hawk to the hawk master and firmly waved away the hovering viti. He wanted to talk to the stablemaster about the lameness of his favorite horse and knew that the Pakajan would become about as communicative as a rock in the presence of arrogant Massadarans.

The two of them were alone then, when the hooves sounded in the doorway. The stableman looked up and Balanji swung around, annoyed at the interruption.

Malenga. He'd stopped short, almost in a crouch, red-rimmed eyes startled. His face registered a quick succession of fear, then hate, then the familiar obsequious expression that never failed to irritate Balanji. "Good morning, My Zoji," he said, straightening and bowing low. "I trust the hunt was successful?"

Malenga's smug tone grated Balanji's nerves. He bowed a fraction in return, smiling urbanely. "Quite."

He looked pointedly at Malenga's heavy furred cloak and mud-splattered horse, and raised an eyebrow.

"And you, my noble viti, had business which kept you from the hunt. I trust you had a successful morning?"

Malenga returned the smile with a shuttered one of his own. "Ah yes, quite," he said. "Quite satisfactory. Thank you, Zoji."

Balanji narrowed his eyes slightly at the ironic tone but he hid his counter thrust in a lazy drawl, aware of the stablemaster watching stolidly behind him. "Success attends you so rarely, Viti Malenga. Its presence at last gives me great joy."

Malenga bowed. "I'm flattered."

"Of course you are."

Malenga's face darkened at the snubs and Balanji decided to have done. "Good day, Viti," he said, noting the faint look of relief on Malenga's face. Taut with anger, he stalked from the stable. He hesitated in the yard, then avoided the palace. Instead he entered the ancient tower and crossed the ground floor to the room on the far side. From there a tiny door led to the edge of the cliff.

Balanji opened it and stepped out into the wind and sunlight. He was standing on a narrow rim of rock running between the tower and the precipice. This was the back way out—a series of foot holds, rings, ledges and caves that safely led those who knew the way down to the bottom of the cliff. Not that it had ever been put to the test. The city hadn't seen an enemy since his grandfather's time, when Bcacmat armies had swept from the north. Those times had been the only period in history when the factious city states of the Peninsula had worked together.

There was another way down. Only Balanji knew it, and when the time came his two young sons would know. Hollowed into the cliff was a tortuous passage twisting down through the dark. One branch exited in the city, under the paving stones of the temple. The other branch worked down to the very base of the cliff, almost at the confluence of the rivers.

The wind blew back Balanji's dark hair, cooling his face and calming his anger. Above him the tower soared to the blue sky, the rushing clouds giving it the feeling of forever toppling forward. Hundreds of feet below, the churning Ao met the smooth waters of the Giss. Both rivers ran muddy, swollen with winter rain. But no snow yet, Balanji thought, his eyes lifting to the Guardian Mountains across the valley to the east. The Pale Lady's glacier shone white as usual, but the Dark Lady carried no snow. Winter, but the pass still open. Strange.

Strange times. Soza had just bloodily overrun the nearest city downstream, and here his court was, dithering about the latest foolish fashion in men's clothing. For the first time in his reign Balanji had sent an army to the field, and here his court was, demanding he strengthen the *Sadra* Laws because certain merchants could afford finer clothes then they could. Forbid velvet indeed! Balanji ground his teeth and felt alone.

Grandfather, he thought, *you had the Bcacmat hordes. Father, you managed to keep Illiga free from Perijo's domination. Now I've got Soza. How did you know what to do next?*

A cough sounded behind him. Marshal Yuot Kintupaquat's weathered face peered through the low door. "Ah, my Ironbiter," Balanji said with a smile. "Come enjoy the fresh air."

"Confound these small doors," Kintupaquat grumbled, stooping to pass through. The huge Pakajan was one of Balanji's most trusted advisors, combining a stout loyalty with a shrewd knowledge of Pakajans that enabled Balanji to keep relative peace between the two factions. His name meant "iron biter" in Pakajan, and Balanji thought it humorously appropriate.

The wind flattened Kintupaquat's red wool cloak against his mail as he came near. "I have the report for you," he said in a low voice, throwing a glance up at the tower windows directly above them.

Balanji matched his tone. "Where did he go?"

"Across the river. He met a stranger, exchanged his horse for a mule and went back into the city. One of my men stayed to watch the stranger, the other followed, but lost him in the maze of warehouses just above the docks."

"Remind me to raze that area someday. You think he met a merchant?"

"Must have. He returned with a huge pack on his mule. Went straight back to the stranger and they traded mule for horse. Then he just rode straight back here."

"And the stranger?"

Ironbiter gave a grim, satisfied smile. "We got him. He'd headed straight for Ormea. Now he's gone without a trace and we have 5,000 vidlas. And this."

Balanji unfolded the square of paper Kintupaquat handed him. Its contents hit him like a kick in the stomach: a carefully drawn map of the fortress, palace and the town's defenses. He met his marshal's dark eyes. "So Malenga is our traitor."

"Without doubt. Shall I arrest him, My Zoji?"

"Does he know of your surveillance?"

"No."

"Let him remain then, until we discover who this merchant is. Then we'll clean out the whole rat nest."

Kintupaquat bowed. "We may also learn something from the stranger. Meanwhile, My Zoji, I beg you will take proper precautions."

"Such as?"

"Let no new servants be hired, no new men stand guard. Watch any newcomer. Remember, Soza took Ormea from inside. And please, wear the mail shirt I gave you."

"I will rely on your excellent judgment, Kintupaquat," Balanji said, calmly enough, for all he felt exposed and defenseless. *Zojikam, help us,* he thought.

He remembered his seventh birthday suddenly. His grandfather had just broken the Bcacmat siege on Illiga and driven them from the valley. In gushing rain, unself-conscious before the entire city, his grandfather had knelt and cried thanks aloud to Zojikam. And because he knelt, the entire city knelt. In the square before the fortress, and crowding down the twisting roads, the people had knelt and given thanks. Balanji had knelt too, the cold water soaking through his surcoat at the knees, listening, watching, wondering if his grandfather was admirable or embarrassing.

He still wondered. He gave one last look up at the bottomless sky and thought, *High Lord, Zoji of Zojis, what am I to you?*

"Or you to me?" he added aloud.

"I beg your pardon?" asked Kintupaquat.

Balanji blinked, then recovered. "You have done excellently," he said smoothly. "I'm very pleased. Let us go." He led the way back to the palace and went in search of the exiled Zoji Akusa of Ormea.

He found her in the south salon, but he paused long in the doorway, unwilling to enter. The room was grossly overheated and the scent of mingled perfumes stung his nose. Akusa stood opposite him, staring out the window. In her grief she made a beautiful picture, black and stark against the light. Very poetic, his more cynical self thought, watching her lift her hand languidly to brush her forehead. He disliked patently overacted emotion.

At the far end of the room, across an expanse of black and white tile, several vita clustered near the fire with embroidery stands, their voices low murmurs, and their frequent glances at Akusa nervous, uneasy. Balanji was about to withdraw when Vita Nalama raised her head and saw him. "Zoji!" she gasped.

The other vita looked up like startled deer then quickly rose to bow, gracefully clutching to their bosoms the ridiculous length of material that proved to the world they were not required to do anything useful.

Akusa made no sign that she noticed. Balanji waved back the women and crossed to her, aware of many eyes on his back. He touched her elbow. "Cousin."

She cringed away with a muffled cry.

"It is merely myself," Balanji said soothingly. "You need have no fear."

She seemed to return from some far inward country. Her hand dropped. "I beg your pardon," she said in her deep, throaty voice. "I was thinking of . . . something else."

"I understand completely," he said, though he knew he lied. "My deepest sympathy."

He caught the attentive eye of the servant by the door and signaled for a chair, studying Akusa's face as he seated her. The winter sun mercilessly picked out her dark-circled, red-rimmed eyes. Deep lines ran from nose to mouth, lines that had not been there last summer. Balanji realized he had done her injustice; she by no means consciously acted the romantic figure. She was filtering the horror of that night of assassinations through her emotions, instead of intellectually as he would. What would it be like to experience life so viscerally? He himself analyzed everything until he almost forgot the whole in chasing parts. He was often plagued by the feeling of watching himself from the outside, even when he made love to Ela, though Zojikam knew how much he loved her.

"I trust you have been made comfortable?" he asked.

"Yes," Akusa said. "You are so kind."

"Do you feel well enough to discuss the future?"

She turned her head listlessly and stared into the sunlight. "Whenever is convenient."

"Very well, then. I'm concerned for your safety and the safety of your son while you are here," he said. "You must know that Soza will probably make another attempt. The continued restlessness of Vosa will have taught him the loyalty of our cities to their zojis."

"Yes."

Unpromising, but Balanji pressed gently. "I would like to make arrangements to hide you. I will send a trusted advisor to find a secret villa in the country where—"

Her head whipped around. "No!" she exclaimed. She leaned forward and caught his hand. "It's safer here. There are guards, people. The country, no, anything could happen!"

"Keep your voice down!" He held her panicked eyes with his until he saw caution return. "It *will* be safer. You'll take another name. We can control who enters."

And she wouldn't lead Soza to his palace, he thought, though he'd never say it aloud.

"It's safer here."

Balanji observed her whitened knuckles with concealed exasperation. If only she had Ela's ability to set aside her emotions and *think*. What would reach her? Her eyes, black and anxious in her whitened face, fixed on his. He smiled with reassurance he did not feel and disengaged his hand. "You must think about it, Zoja Akusa Ormea," he said.

She winced at this reminder of her position.

"There is also your son, Ferco, to think of," Balanji said. "He will be safer hidden. You must protect his life so someday he may be able to take his rightful place."

She gave an impatient shake of her head and rose. "He will be safer here," she said and turned again to the window.

Balanji's lips tightened at her turning her back to him in front of his subjects. "Very well, Zoja," he said. "We can discuss this when you feel more yourself." He strode abruptly across the room, and the startled servant leaped to open the door for him.

In the hall a small crowd of men straightened suddenly, then bowed more or less profoundly depending on what they considered their rank or how much they wanted from him this time. Balanji surveyed them silently, the cool damp air in the hall soothing his nostrils. In front stood his two bodyguards. Behind them waited Viti Nalama and Viti Dervi. Behind them stood his page and the tutor of his oldest son, and last of all, Familo, an impoverished relative of Malenga. Everyone but the person he needed to see.

"My Zoji," began Viti Nalama, stepping forward.

The bells of the palace temple began to ring, and Balanji suddenly knew where Nikilo Vitujak would be found. "Ah, the bells," he interrupted gently. "My Vitis, let us together pay homage to our Creator and High Zoji." Laughing inside at their startled expressions and sidelong glances, he led them to the chapel.

The room was fuller than he remembered it being in the past, and the service had already begun. The Massadaran priest faltered in mid-sentence as they filed in, then went on with no other acknowledgment. Vitujak, sitting near the back as appropriate for a Pakajan and a kali, looked around, raising an ironic eyebrow as he took in the latecomers.

Still laughing silently, Balanji went straight to the gold-tasseled row reserved for his family. There he knelt, hearing behind him the creaking and popping of knees as his reluctant subjects followed. In sudden vivid comparison, Balanji again remembered his grandfather kneeling in pounding rain, the entire city and army also kneeling to give fervent thanks to the Creator. Today seemed a farcical imitation of that solemn moment. Balanji snorted and directed upward a silent ironic comment to Zojikam: *Will this do?* Yet the contrast displeased him.

The service wound gently on in ancient Massadaran. They all vaguely understood it for it was the language of their education, and many of the men had visited Massadara for polishing. But even the most Massadaran of viti in the palace increasingly spoke the vigorous Illigan Pakajan of the city. Despite their high Massadaran airs, Balanji thought, his viti encountered almost as much scorn from true Massadarans as they themselves heaped on Pakajans.

Pity us, he added to himself, rising absently to his feet with the others. *We will never again be Massadaran, yet we are afraid to let go and become what the Pakajan Peninsula will make of us.* Perhaps that was the source of the *Sadra* Laws—fear.

The laws were designed to hold back the strange, the new, the Pakajan. But Pakajans would not be held back for long. They were energetic, canny, industrious. Somehow in the years when his father bickered and fought with Perijo and formed and broke alliances with other Massadaran outposts, the wealth of the land began to pass more and more into the hands of a Pakajan middle class: merchants, mine owners, shipping masters. The results, when the Massadaran newcomers became nervous, were new and stiffer *Sadra* Laws, higher taxes, and a seething discontent in the city. All of which Balanji had inherited.

He'd heard a rumor that together the guilds planned to bring him a petition. They wanted a city council where they could have a voice. Well, they had the money, and with their merchants' inter-city networks, Balanji had to admit they had increasing power. So why not allow them their city council? Put some of that money to work. The viti would hate it. They barely approved of the guild system. But some would see reason. Viti Nalama would.

Balanji considered it gravely. It would mean opening the door a little wider to the strange, the new, the Pakajan, with who knows what result. Yet after generations of colonization the Pakajan should no longer be strange and new. In fact, two of the three men he trusted most were Pakajans—old Kintupaquat, and Vitujak.

He glanced back at his secretary as he rose for the Confession. He'd known vaguely of Vitujak before, from his poetry, essays and critiques, many written in the scorned Pakajan language. But Balanji's attention had rapidly focused when the man went to Vosa as secretary for the ambassador. The ambassador's reports arrived inked in a dark, up-and-down hand, often with Nikilo Vitujak's personal postscript added. His comments often politely disagreed with the ambassador, and Balanji found himself relying more and more on them. The next time the ambassador returned to Illiga, Balanji had spent a long time closeted with Vitujak. The result was two reports coming to him from Vosa—the second quite secret. Vitujak knew Soza as well as anyone could.

As soon as the service ended, Balanji caught his secretary's eye and jerked his chin. He exchanged quick pleasantries with the priest, avoided the reproachful eyes of the men clustered behind him, then whisked the waiting Vitujak off to his office.

The office felt stuffy and smelt of ink. Balanji opened a casement and sucked in a deep breath of cool air. "Did you read the reports?"

Vitujak pulled a sheaf of papers from his surcoat.

"Quite carefully. Soza took Ormea almost exactly the way he took Vosa. Down to the same mistakes, even."

Balanji took the papers—Akusa's story and the stories of each of the men who accompanied her. "Do they match?"

"Yes. And . . ."

"And?"

Vitujak's lips thinned with distaste. "And yes, it is a Bcacmat pattern."

"But no way to prove it."

"Nothing but circumstantial evidence. Such as the Black Eagle, on Soza's coat of arms. According to these reports the viti began seeing signs of the Black Eagle *ikiji* in Ormea a little before its fall. And, My Zoji, one of my nephews tells me he's seen the claw symbol here. There's also these pamphlets."

Balanji took the muddy pamphlet his secretary held out. " 'Zojikam is uncaring,' " he read, " 'but *mahigas* will help you if you worship and appease them correctly.' Who published this?"

Nikilo Vitujak shrugged. "They appear. There's worse." He held out another pamphlet. This one elaborated the misrule of the zoji's, particularly himself, and proclaimed that Pakajans should revolt and rule themselves once more. That the Black Eagle would help them.

"Sedition. Do you have any more?" asked Balanji, holding himself under careful control.

"No."

Balanji let go and paced the sparsely furnished room, down to the desk at the far end, back to the windows, down again. He'd have to crush this fast, he thought. Get Kintupaquat to shut down every press in town. Were the students involved, perhaps? He'd make the dean sweat over this.

He spun on his heel and caught Vitujak blowing on his hands to warm them. "Shut the window," he conceded. And when Vitujak had done it he added, "I have two tasks for you, Kali. Any day now I will send you out to find me a vidyen hidden in the hills where

I can hide Zoja Akusa. I want you to do it because her safety depends on the utmost secrecy."

"When would you like me to go?"

"I'd *like* you to go today. However the zoja has not yet agreed to the plan and I have a more urgent matter at hand. But I want you ready to go on slight notice."

Vitujak's face registered no emotion. "I will do my best. What is this other matter?"

"We have found our traitor: Viti Malenga."

"I'm not surprised," Vitujak said. "But I thought there would be more involved."

"There are. That's where I need you. Somewhere in the city is a merchant supplying money to Soza." Vitujak merely nodded and Balanji realized he'd already reached that conclusion. "You have contacts among the merchant class," he continued. "I want you to find me this man. I will make an example of him and his entire family. *Find him for me.*"

"Oh, yes," Vitujak said grimly. "I will find him."

Chapter 11

Marita

"I don't understand why this rug is more expensive than the larger one," complained the fat viti lounging among the pillows.

"This one," said Marita mysteriously, "is very rare. Bcacmat. I bought it at great expense, and consider it an important investment."

"Hnff," sniffed the viti, but he leaned over his own paunch to pull the silken rug closer, fingering it meditatively. Marita hid her satisfaction—she had him. At a soft step behind her she turned her head. Taverik slid past the waiting servants and quietly seated himself in the corner. She met his eyes but immediately turned her attention back to the buyer.

"It is so small," the viti complained.

"It is rare and precious. I have seen only one other of its kind in the city. Search for yourself and see."

The viti stroked his several chins. "Four hundred and eighty, then."

Marita bowed respectfully. "My Viti, you honor me with your patronage. However this rug I could not let go for less than 500."

The viti smiled whimsically. "I will tell you what. If you make it 490, I will still be able to tell my vita that I bargained you down, and your money-grubbing merchant soul will also be satisfied."

Marita's answering smile was thin. "Done. Your vita will love the soft pastel colors which the northern rugs never achieve."

The viti heaved himself off the cushion and nodded to a servant, who counted out the money. Marita bowed them out of the shop, the money heavy in her hand. They could eat! They could pay the year's guild fee. She could get Whitey's saddle out of the pawn shop.

"Nice rug," Taverik said from his corner when the viti had gone. "You have a talent for picking the unusual ones."

"Yes," she said, "I'm almost sorry he took a fancy to it. Almost." She slipped the coins into her purse and grinned at him. "You're looking better since I last saw you, a week ago."

"Eight days," he amended. He stood up and his eyes lost their usual glint, becoming softly bright. "You're looking better yourself."

She hesitated, confused by his sudden warmth. "Stay to eat," she said to cover the awkwardness. "Then we'll go to the guild meeting."

"Thanks," he said.

She'd missed him. Ever since her escapade the week before, Sahra had buried herself in books and responded in monosyllables to Marita's remarks. She'd asked nothing about the riot, and had provided no comfort or support in the ensuing days of slight depression when Marita's shoulder reknit. The publisher had returned Sahra's manuscript with a note saying he and all other presses had been closed down by order of the zoji, and he could not foresee any change in the immediate future. Sahra had reacted oddly, refusing to talk about it with Marita, but obviously more frustrated than disappointed. She buried herself even deeper into her books. Last night she'd even brought a book to supper, propped it on the salt cellar, and read while she ate.

Marita had eaten in stiff silence, glowering across the table at her. Bibi tiptoed around them, her eyes apprehensive. Finally Marita slammed down her goblet. "What's wrong with you these days?"

"Nothing is wrong," Sahra said into her book.

"All you do is read."

"I balanced the ledger yesterday; that's not just reading."

Marita tilted her head back and regarded her through half-closed eyes. "You're upset about something. About the riot?"

"Why should that bother me? That sort of thing puts zest in your life."

Marita could tell from her monotone she'd get nothing more from her. She'd flung away her napkin and scraped back her chair. "Enjoy your books then," she growled and stalked from the room.

She hadn't seen her since last night. Perhaps Taverik's presence would break the stalemate. She hoped. The disharmony preyed on her mind.

"Actually," said Taverik, helping her roll up the rugs she'd displayed, "I have an ulterior motive in coming. I want to see you throw a knife. Who taught you?"

"Ot taught me. He said it was safer for me than letting anyone get close."

"Show me," he said, the light kindling in his eyes.

She laughed in response. "All right. Come on." She locked the shop and led him through the inner door. "Set another place for lunch, Bibi," she called. Then she took him to the stable where Whitey brayed an earsplitting greeting.

Her second day in the house she'd drawn a target on the far wall. The boards around it had splintered raw by now from her practicing. "Look," she said, and flipped a knife upward from her boot. It hit the center and quivered. Satisfying.

Taverik whistled. "Our little viti-boy doesn't know how lucky he is."

"Viti-boy! Don't let the authorities hear you say that. And luck has nothing to do with it. Not with the amount of practice I put in."

"Let me try," Taverik said. She handed him the knife she kept in her sleeve and he raised his eyebrows. "You're a walking cutlery shop."

She laughed. "When we lived in the cart in the slums I made a point of practicing out in the open. Made a nice deterrent and I rarely had trouble. Didn't help much last Friday though," she added soberly. The memory of the student chanting to that Black Eagle charm had left a chill darkness within her.

"You did fine," he said. "You just didn't dare risk killing a viti. When he closed with you, you needed to hold it like this." He pressed the knife into her hand, his fingers warm around her wrist. "So. I come at you. Don't raise your hand so high."

"Reflex."

"He'll aim at your face to bring your arms up, then slide in underneath. Come out here. More room. Now!"

Marita concentrated, her world narrowing down to the two knives and Taverik's voice. Back and forth they trampled until her breath came in deep gulps. Suddenly Taverik stepped back and lowered his knife. "You're hurting."

"I'm fine," she said. "Let's keep going. This is wonderful."

Taverik shook his head. "I can tell when you hurt. You're favoring that arm." He handed her back the slim throwing knife and flopped into the wild thyme under the apple tree.

A slight movement above her caught Marita's eye. She looked up in time to see the curtain fall across the second story window. Sahra had been watching. Odd, the strange guilt she felt. She shrugged it off and sat down on the weathered gray bench under the tree. "Wonder when it will snow," she said. "Queer winter. Did you come just to teach me how to use a knife?"

Taverik rolled to his side and propped himself up on his elbow. "Partly. I also came to ask you three questions."

"Questions three, for a fee," she quoted. "Do I get a wish if I answer them correctly?"

He gave her a quick look. "Perhaps. First, uh, you know the reputation of the Zandro family. Why don't you mind me for a friend? I know of at least one case where I was bad for your business."

He spoke casually, as if he didn't care anything about her answer, but she wasn't fooled. Never before had he brought up this subject, and she answered him carefully. "My first day at the guild," she said, "I came up the steps, nervous at what might happen in this men's stronghold. And sure enough, right away, a gang of youths surrounded another, shouting at him, wanting to beat him up. That was you."

Taverik nodded and his eyes crinkled. He actually seemed to find it funny. "They wanted Chado, but thought I'd do since I was at hand."

"I remember admiring the way you talked them around, made them laugh and went off with them for beer. You were laughing too, but when you looked at me I saw the hurt in your eyes."

"Oh hogwash," he said. "I was used to that kind of stuff by then."

"No, I saw it," Marita insisted. "Later, when all the older men kept warning me against associating with you and your family I weighed what they said against that look. And then you took me on that first caravan and helped me get started, with no strings attached. I've always been grateful. Wondered in turn why you bothered."

"Huh," he said. "You were thin as a nail. Obviously starving to death. Someone had to help you."

"Apparently no one else in the guild thought so."

"Second question," he said firmly, and lowered his voice. "Do you ever wish you could return to skirts and be a woman again?"

She blinked at the suddenness of his transition. "No. I value my freedom too much."

"Freedom," he repeated, sounding disappointed.

She gave him a cheeky grin. "Well, would you trade?"

"No, I guess not," he said slowly. After he'd remained silent for a bit she nudged him. "What was your third question?"

"Oh, ah, will you—ah, are you sure your father was no one particular in Vosa?"

"Are you still on that?" Marita could have sworn that wasn't what he'd intended to ask but she answered anyway. "No one in particular that I know. In those days I minded my lessons and little else. He was a well-to-do merchant and we lived quite comfortably. But he was, we have always assumed, a bastard from a Massadaran family. I suspect that his family cast him off for marrying a Pakajan merchant's daughter, and her family cast her off for marrying him. So they declared they'd make their own way, and never spoke to their relatives again. It was understandably a forbidden subject among us."

"So why would Soza go after him?"

Blood drained from her face so rapidly she felt sick. "Who said anything about Soza?" she managed.

Taverik's fingers curled around her booted ankle. "Sorry. I guessed it. What had your father done to cross him?"

"We don't know it was Soza for sure," she croaked. She cleared her throat. "But I think Papa went to Zoji Vos and tried to warn him about Soza. He was humiliated and kicked out of the palace—who listens to a merchant? I know for sure he spoke in his guild and got them well riled about Soza. We were attacked that very night. Soza killed all the Vos family next day."

"Your father didn't tell you anything more? How'd he find out about Soza?"

"I don't know." Marita frowned, thinking back. "I wonder, though," she said slowly, "if he might have expected reprisals, because he made a point of showing me where he hid his strong box."

She could remember that night as vividly as if she were again living it. With the sounds of destructive plundering overhead, Bibi had pulled her away from her father's body. "Hurry, hurry!" she'd whispered. Sahra had already gotten through the library window, but Marita had something to do first. Struggling free of Bibi's clutching hands, she ran to the bookcase and threw book after book to the floor, searching for the catch. Bibi had flurried after her, supposing her hysterical, but understood when the hidden panel swung open at last. They dragged the heavy box from its secret den and struggled out the window together, barefoot across the dewy garden to where Ot waited at the back gate. Only when they'd collapsed in the alley had Marita realized she'd left the panel wide open for that evil man to see.

"Marko? You all right?"

Her eyes focused on Taverik again. He knelt before her, gripping her elbows hard enough to hurt. "You turned green," he said. "Like you did before you fainted."

"Sorry," she said, getting strict hold of herself. "I'm stupid to let that man do this to me. Even the mention of his name turned me cold. So stupid."

"Not stupid," Taverik said. "That Black Eagle *ikiji* is damn weird. Listen, Marko, at the temple last Friday, the priest prophesied, right in the middle of the service. And the words were the same as the Pakajan priest's dream. 'An eagle chased a hawk, the hawk fled, but—' "

She pulled away, shaken. "But there's no place to hide."

"Zojikam will help."

"When has he bothered?" Marita snapped.

"When have you asked?"

She hadn't, but she wouldn't admit it. She turned away stubbornly and hugged her knees to herself.

"Wouldn't you like to be free of this business? You live in bondage to a shadow. Maybe it's time to stop and face it."

"And get killed?" Anger, or fear, gave her voice a sarcastic edge.

"I have an uncle with access to all sorts of information," Taverik pressed. "Suppose I ask him to find out more about your father. Maybe that would shed light on why Soza is chasing you."

"No," she said firmly. "I want nothing to do with Soza. I'll stay as far from him as possible and remain unnoticed, thank you."

She stood up. "It must be time for lunch. Let's go." Struggling to compose herself she strode to the house without looking back. Behind her she heard a sigh as Taverik got up and followed, and that irritated her too. Why did he have to keep poking around?

At the head of the stairs she found Sahra just closing the door to the study. Her sister had changed from her patched, green gown to the dark blue one she wore to the temple. She'd even pulled her hair under a fresh cap. Marita blinked. "Why'd you change?"

Sahra ignored her and smiled at Taverik, who had just topped the stairs. "Good morning, Kali Taverik."

"Hello, Kala Oma," he said. "It's been a long time."

"Too long," she said, her face blushing pink. "You must come more often."

A pulse of unfamiliar emotion brought color to Marita's face as well. She hid it by opening the dining room door. "Enter, Kali, Kala. We'll have to hurry to make the guild meeting."

"Guild meeting?" Sahra said as Taverik seated her. "Odd time to have a guild meeting."

Bibi set plates of bread and cheese on the table then stood off expectantly. Recalled to her duty, Marita prayed Zojikam to bless the meal, raising her head in time to see Taverik laughing at her. She ruefully remembered her bitter words to him about Zojikam, and couldn't help a sheepish grin in return. Somehow

Taverik always managed to nudge her off her high horse.

He offered Sahra a plate of bread and returned to her comment. "Most certainly, Kala Kastazi, an odd time for a guild meeting. You see, a petition has been drafted asking the zoji to establish a city council composed of merchants, lawyers and other respectable kali. It's the Textile Guild's turn to debate whether to endorse it. But I'd have thought Marko would have told you that."

"Oma and I haven't had much chance to talk lately," said Marita.

"Do you think, Taverik," said Sahra leaning toward him, "that Zoji Balanji will agree to it?"

"Not in a thousand years. What do you think, Marko? How come you're not eating?"

Marita hastily picked up the cheese knife. "They are afraid of us. We have the money and connections, therefore much of the power."

"That's right," Taverik said. "But we still can't ride horses or carry a sword."

"Or own too much property outside the city or wear more than four rings," Marita recited.

"Or," said Taverik daintily, "eat grapes with a fork." He speared a purple globe with his cheese knife and sank his teeth into it.

"Then why bother?"

Marita snorted. Sahra knew why bother as well as she herself did, and had in fact written satiric poetry that bothered indeed. One more good reason to hide behind the "Humble Kali." Why was she suddenly asking Taverik all these naive questions?

"Why bother?" The dickens had descended upon Taverik as it often did when the guild was in discussion. "We bother in order to give the honorable President Kali Frez Ittato something to keep his mind off his gout. It's an act of charity to prevent him wasting more money on doctors."

Sahra smiled her rare smile, showing dimples that Marita seldom saw these days. She *was* pretty, Marita thought. Always prettier than Marita had ever been.

And Taverik seemed to bring out the best in her, though she hid her intellect from him. Why shouldn't she attract him? If they married, Marita and Taverik could remain friends, and Sahra would have the security she needed so badly. It would be a good idea.

Still she felt wretched, but put it down to Taverik's persistent snooping into her past. His three questions were oddly unrelated. Weren't they?

She came out of her abstraction and found Sahra quoting poetry to Taverik. Marita almost laughed aloud at Taverik's politely poleaxed expression. "I don't know much about that stuff," he told Sahra apologetically. "I ought to introduce you to my uncle. You two would get along like bacon and eggs."

Marita did laugh aloud at that, and felt instant contrition when Sahra turned crimson. "We'd better get going," Marita said, hastily getting up. She let Taverik proceed her, then turned back to apologize. She found Sahra crying silently, her face crumpled like a child's with the effort to keep quiet.

Marita sprang to her side. "Sahra, I'm sorry," she whispered. "I didn't mean—"

"Go away," Sahra said, averting her face. "Go do whatever you do out there. I don't want to hear about it."

Marita knelt beside her chair but Sahra struggled up and went to the window. "Go!"

She went. Anger battled with contrition all the way up the city. Taverik, after a few tries at conversation, lapsed into silence. Nor did the city improve her mood—the streets were jammed with Ormean refugees, the crowds on edge and discontent. The gentle peace of Illiga had evaporated and it was all Soza's fault.

The Textile Guild hall, with its famous dome, faced the square. Whitey, by long habit, turned down the long alley beside it which led to the stables in back. Marita gave his warm neck a pat and gave the reins to a stable boy. Taverik joined her and together they pushed through the bustle of merchants, clerks and servants at the back entrance.

Inside she paused to loosen her cloak. "What next!"

roared a man to her right—he stood in a cluster of merchants all staring at something she couldn't see. The air bristled with their indignation.

Sanisman was one of them. "Somebody ought to do something about it!"

"Who?" ridiculed Gunnar Chisokachi, a loose-jawed young man with freckles and pure Pakajan features. "Who's going to pass a *Sadra* Law prohibiting kali classes to bare their buns in public?"

Curious, Marita inched closer to the group and followed their outraged glares. She stared in astonishment. Several youths loitered around the door to the meeting chamber, trying their best to look at ease in surcoats so short they barely covered their buttocks. Instead of sensible, warm knit hose, they wore flamboyantly colored silk which must have cost their merchant fathers many a vidla.

Beside her, Taverik choked with laughter, more, Marita thought, at the indignation of the merchants, than at the youths. Fat Ulmo folded his hands over his black-draped potbelly. "It's all those Ormeans causing riots in the city that's doing it."

"Ormeans?" Sanisman said. "Ulmo, that style's pure Massadaran. They wear those silly *hamas* in Massadara now."

Gunnar struck a feminine pose. "The Massadaran look ith all the rage."

The others roared with laughter. "Well, I think it's disgusting," complained Fat Ulmo.

Taverik patted the man's paunch. "On you it would be." He snatched his hand away as Ulmo glared and swatted at it.

Gunnar chuckled. "It takes good buns to get away with it. Like young Marko here."

His hand descended on her shoulder and her heart gave a great lurch. "Not I," she declared, her heart racing. "You wear it, Gunnar. Run over and ask them who their tailors are."

"Let's try you out for size, Gunnar!" whooped Echin, an abrasive young man Marita didn't like. He grabbed Gunnar and tried to pull off his surcoat. Gunnar struggled like a fish on a hook but several others helped Echin. Laughing, they wrestled him to the floor and tore off his belt and surcoat, leaving him in his baggy woolen hose, shirt tail and purse dangling. The crowd laughed uproariously. Sanisman snatched up the surcoat and tossed it to Fat Ulmo.

At the first sign of the rough house, Marita backed away. But the crowd had tightened to hold Gunnar in the circle, and she couldn't get through. She tried to escape notice by blending into the line next to Sanisman. But Sanisman caught her shoulders. "What about you, youngster!" he shouted. With a two-handed shove he thrust her into the circle.

Chapter 12

Marita

"I'll tailor you, boy!" crowed Echin, grabbing her surcoat.

Marita twisted free. "I'll choose my own tailor, thank you," she said. Scowling, Echin came at her again, and she straight-armed him right under the breastbone. With a loud wheeze, the wind went out of him. She left him doubled up, and stalked to the edge of the circle.

The crowd roared with laughter. "That's telling 'em, lad," hooted Ulmo. Still on the floor, Gunnar threw back his head and gulped with laughter. Suddenly they gasped and quieted. Marita spun around.

Echin had drawn a knife. "No one does that to me," he said softly.

"You started it, Echin," she said.

Echin lunged at her. Marita sidestepped, sliding up the knife from her boot. She'd get him in the leg and stop this nonsense at the start. She drew back her arm, then hesitated. Taverik had leaped into the circle right behind Echin. Before Echin could turn, Taverik pulled his surcoat high, exposing Echin's toothpick legs and mended underhose. "The Massadaran look!" Taverik announced.

The crowd laughed with released tension. With an outraged snarl Echin slapped his coat down. He started after Taverik with his knife, but instead of defending himself, Taverik lifted his own surcoat to his knees and smiled innocently at Echin. "A nice style," he said, "but perhaps a bit drafty?"

Echin glared at him foolishly, then thrust his knife back into his belt. Relieved, Marita slid her own knife away and pushed back against the crowd. Sanisman unrepentantly slapped her on the back. "Hoped you were going to demonstrate the new look for us, lad!"

Ha, ha, she growled to herself, but she forced a smile in return and nodded at the circle. "I'll let that one do it."

"Aye, Taverik the clown, the black sheep of the guild. He'll be wearing it for real tomorrow."

Gunnar waltzed up to Taverik and fluttered his eyelashes. "Ooh, Kali, your knees are so manly!"

Taverik responded with a ribald comment on Gunnar's buns. Beside Marita Fat Ulmo cackled, and the crowd hooted. Taverik offered his elbow to Echin. "My dear?" he said.

"Get lost!" Echin tried to leave but the crowd tightened around him, just as willing to laugh at him as at Gunnar. As they shifted, Marita found an opening and backed out quick as a crab. Ruffled and angry, she leaned against the wall, willing her knees to stop shaking.

"So you don't like the *hama* style?" asked a quizzical voice behind her.

She found herself next to Frez Ittato, president of the Textile Guild. He leaned on his cane, his bandaged foot propped before him, a tall morose Pakajan looking over his shoulder—his latest quack doctor, she supposed. Marita bowed respectfully. "Kali, I mistrust their ability to create it," she said.

Ittato gave a dry chuckle. "Just wait until they start wearing Pakajan beards. You'll have to work hard to catch up. How old are you anyway?"

Adrenaline pulsed in her veins. "Old enough," she said. She found herself fingering her downy cheek and dropped her hand.

"Young Marko Kastazi, is it? You seem quite young to set out on your own. Do you have a father in the business? Who *was* your father?"

Strange resonance with Taverik's question. Who *was* her father? Why was he suddenly important to everyone? She didn't like questions, she didn't like attention, she didn't like Ittato's curious, sharp blue eyes. "My family wasn't from here," she said evasively.

"Not from here? Don't you have any relatives in Illiga?"

"No," Marita said. "Dead. They're all dead. We're starting out anew."

He raised a grizzled eyebrow. "We? I thought you said you didn't have any relatives."

"I meant, *we* didn't. We, my sister and I."

"Ah. And where did you live before, lad?"

"Vosa," Marita said reluctantly, feeling as if she were on trial.

"Vosa!" Ittato's brows snapped together. "Riots there. Temple closed. Rumors of citizens sold to Bcacma as slaves. Foolish rumor, Soza's a Peninsula man, wouldn't have truck with Bcacma. So you're from Vosa. Before its fall or after—"

The crowd convulsed with laughter as Taverik and Gunnar minced a circle about Echin. "They call it the *hama* style because it exposes your hams, Echin," Taverik said. He patted Gunnar's rear. "And it makes you the *butt* of every joke." Echin tried to get through the circle but Sanisman pushed him back.

Ittato watched and thumped his cane. "Those Zandros. The curse of the guild. If I could find an excuse to expel that one, I'd be a happy man."

"Taverik's not like the rest of his family, Kali Ittato,"

Marita said earnestly. "He's straight in his dealings. That's why he took over the textile work completely."

"A lot you know, lad. Just the other day I had a complaint about Zandro textiles. A rotten wool. Aye, I've noticed you with Zandro a lot. You watch your step, lad, or he'll lead you into the same unsavory reputation."

"That wool was Chado's fault. He did that while Taverik was on caravan."

"Chado, Taverik—those Zandros are all alike. Count your fingers after you've shaken hands with them. And *you* watch your step." Ittato hobbled off, growling to himself, the doctor drifting silently behind.

With his going the crowd began to loosen up. Echin pushed through and took himself off. Marita waited while Taverik and Gunnar gave each other gallant bows.

Taverik stiffened suddenly, then straightened and dropped the hem of his surcoat. A huge man in a padded purple velvet surcoat blocked Marita's view, standing hands on hips, feet apart. Taverik's brother Chado slouched behind, smirking around his bulk. "My son, the buffoon," the huge man growled.

Gunnar backed away, hastily picking up his scattered clothes. "Meeting's started," he mumbled, and escaped past Marita. Sanisman suddenly found Fat Ulmo to be a great friend and draped his arm around his shoulder. They strolled after Gunnar. The back hall quickly cleared.

"Hello, Father," Taverik's voice said calmly.

Donato Zandro lowered his head like a bull about to charge. "Why is it," he announced, "that whenever I come upon you I find that the firm is once again being disgraced? *Why!*" He thundered the last word. Marita burned at the injustice of it.

"Just not your lucky day, Father," Taverik said moving back into view. He gave his father an ironic, elaborate bow. "Shall we attend the meeting like respectable guild members?"

"Idiot," Zandro said. He stalked past Marita to the stairs leading to the second level.

Taverik and Chado followed. "Ooh, Taverik," Chado was drawling as they drew level with Marita. "What pretty knees, you have."

"Oh shut up, Chado," Taverik said cheerfully. His eyes met Marita's and rolled toward the ceiling, then he was gone.

Marita exhaled, feeling disappointed somehow, and went to take her seat.

The tiny, exquisitely proportioned dome of Illiga's Textile Guild was considered one of the architectural triumphs of the city. Commissioned and paid for by merchants, it was also a point of bitter contention because of the several *Sadra* Laws stretched by it, and the new law made because of it. But the dome remained, one of the landmarks of the city's skyline.

Afternoon sun filled its beveled windows, pouring down into the assembly hall like golden water, flooding the soberly clad merchants with light and rainbows. The entire guild must have turned out for this meeting, Marita thought. The bustle and noise on the main floor reminded her of the inside of a bee hive, and in the semi-circular balcony above, men shouted back and forth from the coveted private boxes. Marita glanced up at the box belonging to the Zandro firm but saw only Chado, balancing out at a dangerous angle to talk to the man in the next box.

As a newcomer to Illiga, she still sat on the backless benches of the general seating. She squeezed in next to a white-haired, trembling man just as Ittato limped across the dais and thumped his cane for silence. The room quieted slowly. Ittato thumped again. Finally he nodded to the clerk and retired to the table where he presided. The clerk, a pear-shaped man, stepped forward on skinny calves and read the Prayers of Convocation.

As soon as he finished, Ittato cleared his throat. "This unusual meeting has convened over a matter of great import. Most of you are aware of the petition drafted by our brothers in the Silver Worker's Guild, requesting Zoji Balanji to form a governing body for this city composed of the respectable kali residents here.

"We are the first of the city's guilds to meet to consider this petition and decide if we wish to endorse this matter and join our brothers in signing it."

A roar greeted his words, rising around Marita like a small ocean. Ittato pounded his cane again. "Kali, kali!" he shouted. "Let us discuss this with order!"

The fleshy-faced man whose name Marita could never remember stood and Ittato recognized him. "How can we even consider such a disgraceful proposal?" he spluttered.

Someone shouted from the balcony. "Same way we consider anything!" A wave of derisive laughter spread across the hall.

"Kali!" shouted Ittato. He glared up at the balcony, reminding Marita of Taverik's prank years ago, tethering a goat in the president's chair. Or was it a pig? She chuckled softly.

The old man beside her used her knee to push himself to his feet. "We are trying to usurp authority from our rightful Massadaran rulers. It isn't proper. In my day the guilds had more respect!" Choruses of hoots drowned out the few who agreed with him. He plumped down again, the bench bouncing from his weight. "In my day they had more respect," he growled at Marita. She wasn't sure if he referred to the guilds or the hooters, but she gave him a sympathetic grin before turning her attention back to the argument.

"Before we talk of respect or lack thereof," said a stoop-shouldered importer who had warehouses in Perijo, "we need to hear the petition."

"Very well," said Ittato. He signalled the clerk who brought him a large piece of vellum. Ittato peered at it, squinted, held it at arm's length, then finally handed it back to the clerk with an annoyed gesture. As the clerk read, Marita found herself admiring the simple logic of the request, and the dignity of the wording. The petition called for a council of six, who would take responsibility for the civic functions of the city, bring order to an increasingly chaotic situation, as well as give a growing part of the population a chance to gain the ear of the zoji.

When the clerk finished everyone talked at once. Ittato pounded impatiently. One of the rainbows had crept across his face, coloring it alternately green and red as he moved. At last Sanisman took the floor. "Suggest we alter the wording of the last paragraph to include a subtle hint of remuneration to the zoji from the arrangement. No promises, just enough to give him an interest in it."

"Will you be more specific?" Ittato said, signaling the clerk, who picked up his pen. Marita nodded as Sanisman tried a phrasing. A sound idea. Others suggested rephrasing, but in the end Sanisman's original stood.

The afternoon wore on. One person suggested seven, not six members, in case of tied votes. Another went on too long, demanding a clause that would guarantee a Textile Guild member would always be on the council. One person kept interrupting angrily, but Marita couldn't make out what his point was. The sunlight crept up the wall and its gold deepened to orange.

Finally a silk man stood in the balcony box three to the left of the Zandros. Twisting around to hear him, Marita could see Taverik and Chado and their father all looking to their right. Taverik had folded his arms along the rail. "I suggest it would be inadequate to merely write an addendum to our fellow guild's excellent petition," the silk man said. "I move we draft our own petition which will express our interests more directly and reinforce this one as well."

"No," Marita muttered. The impact might be lost if each guild seemed to merely be seeking its own advantage. But no one else seemed to agree with her.

"Second the motion!" yelled Gunnar, several benches ahead. She suspected he was merely bored and wanted to end the meeting.

"All in favor," said Ittato. A sea of hands went up.

"Opposed?" Marita took a quick breath. She shouldn't bring attention to herself. Foolish. But dammit, she *was* opposed. She shot up her hand, aware she was the only one in the hall to do so. Her cheeks flamed.

"So be it," Ittato said. "Kali, we have continued an hour and a half longer than planned. I propose the Guild Council drafts a petition this evening. We will reconvene tomorrow morning to discuss the results. Dismissed."

The roar of voices immediately rose again. Ittato's thin shout rode above it. "I need to see the Council immediately!"

Marita pried herself off the bench and stretched her stiff back. She froze—across the room Echin had also risen. His heavy brows looked thunderous and he seemed to be searching for somebody. Her? He'd pulled a knife on her in that little tussle and the issue had never resolved. Best leave quickly. She'd survived this long by not taking chances.

She pushed past vehemently arguing men and headed for the deserted east wing which would give her a back door to the stables.

Chapter 13

Taverik

The moment Ittato dismissed the meeting, Taverik shot out of the box. Chado yelled "Wait!" and gabbled something incomprehensible, but Taverik didn't stop. He had to catch Marko before she did her disappearing act.

Thick crowds clogged the downstairs hallway. He pushed doggedly through, ignoring annoyed comments about "those Zandros." Gunnar dragged him back by the sleeve. "Taverik! How come you're protecting that Kastazi boy? You sweet on him?"

"Get out before I beat your nose in!" Taverik looked at Gunnar's loose-jawed faced with loathing. "I just thought it would be an uneven match. Let go."

Gunnar clutched tighter. "Since when are you so altruistic, Tav?"

"I gotta go, Gun." Taverik twisted free and squeezed through the press. Ahead he saw Marko's dark hair among the lighter Pakajans. He ducked around two arguing merchants and grabbed Marko's arm. She whirled, fist clenched.

"You're always picking fights, these days," he complained.

She dropped her hand sheepishly. "Sorry. And thanks."

"Glad to help," he said, falling in beside her. "Echin is not one of my favorite people. Unpleasant sense of humor."

"*No* sense of humor," amended Marko.

They had turned into the deserted east wing and the corridor echoed their footsteps. "Marko," Taverik began, watching her carefully to see how she'd react. "Won't you let me help you shake free of—your problem? Who knows, maybe it isn't Soza who's after you, and you can relax. Or if he is, find out why, then figure out a way to stop him."

He watched her consider it. Zojikam only knew, he thought, he loved her more each time he saw her. If only he could make her safe, take that shadow from her eyes. "How about it?" he urged. "I could ask my uncle to find out whatever he can about your father's murder. We could go on from there."

She chewed her lip, staring blankly at him. He waited, scarcely breathing. Then her face cleared. "All right," she said at last. "But don't let him know anything about *me*."

His heart leaped. "Promised. What was your father's name?"

She started to speak, stopped, then shook her head with a rueful laugh. "It's hard to say it after so many years of being cautious. But it's Kasta. I added the northern suffix when we came here."

Taverik squeezed her shoulder. "I'll be as discreet as an old lady."

She looked amused and worried at the same time. "What have I unleashed?"

"Don't worry!" He opened the door for her and the smell of manure rushed in with the cold, crisp air. Sunset had turned the world to gold. "I'll see you at tomorrow's meeting," he promised.

She'd trusted him! His heart light, Taverik turned back for the cloak he'd forgotten in his rush. Her name was Kasta. That was her *real* name. Kasta. He savored it, comparing it to Kastazi. Liked them both. Maybe someday she'd trust him with her first name.

The hall had emptied fast. He strode through the silent corridors, nodding to an ancient woman kneeling to scrub the marble floor. She looked up from her bucket, her black eyes expressionless above wrinkled cheeks. Wan light shone under the door where the Council still met.

He took the stairs two at a time. In the darkening upper corridor the doors to the private boxes stood ajar like wings; dusk gathered in the secretive depths inside. His family's box was closed. Taverik seized the knob and flung wide the door.

Two men swiveled toward him.

He stopped short. "Excuse me," he said.

His father stepped into the fading light. "Taverik, what are you doing here?" he demanded, his voice waspish with irritation.

"Forgot my cloak," Taverik said apologetically. His eyes slid to the other man. Not Chado. Who?

Donato muttered something and looked behind him. He grabbed the cloak and tossed it at Taverik. Taverik caught it with one hand. "Thanks," he said. He edged over to get a better view of the stranger. "Chado around?"

"No!" said his father. "Now will you . . ."

The other man flung up his hand, checking Donato.

"Please don't bother," he said. "I must be going. This has been quite a profitable chat."

He moved into the light and Taverik's breath caught for a heartbeat. Viti Malenga. Uncle Nik's casual question of last week rang in his ears: *You haven't seen Viti Malenga around the guilds, have you? Talking with merchants?* He'd laughed then at the absurdity of the thought. Well, now he was seeing Malenga talking with a merchant—his father. What of it? With an effort, he gathered his wits and bowed respectfully, then stepped back to allow Malenga to pass.

But Malenga had paused in the doorway and turned again to his father. His voice grew soft and muffled so that Taverik's straining ears picked up only, ". . . by the same method."

Someone topped the stairs and sprinted down the hall. Taverik looked over his shoulder. Chado.

Chado skidded to a halt when he saw Taverik in the dusk, then came on, scowling. "Where'd *you* disappear to, dammit?" he panted. "Been looking all over for you."

Taverik raised an eyebrow. "That's the fastest I've ever seen you move, big brother."

"Well, let me tell you—" Chado began hotly, then broke off and bowed. Malenga had stepped forth. Ignoring Chado, Malenga stopped in front of Taverik and examined him, his eyes like twin probes. Taverik's face instinctively hardened into the familiar non-expression so useful in barter—no thoughts given away.

"So you are the other brother?" Malenga said. "I have not yet met you."

"You honor me, Viti," Taverik said. Behind Malenga his father glared at Chado and Chado shrugged in return. *What was going on?*

"And you are the independent one? The one who does not cooperate?"

"My Viti?" When in doubt, look blank.

"The *spastic*?" Malenga's voice had an edge and Taverik knew immediately the Familos must have been talking to him. He watched Malenga warily. "Tell me, young man," the viti continued, "do you enjoy your work?"

"Very much, Viti."

"Do you never yearn for anything better?"

Dangerous ground. "My Viti?" he asked again, blanker, warier.

"Do you never—chafe—at your station in life? Look for a way to better yourself?"

"My Viti," Taverik said piously, aware of three pairs of eyes intently fixed upon him, "my father has worked hard to provide not only for my needs but for my comfort. Far be it from me to prove so ungrateful as to—chafe—at his generosity."

Malenga's eyes probed. Taverik held tight to his bland expression, using it like a shield against a clever swordsman. Then Malenga gave a short, mirthless laugh. "A well-brought up youth, Zandro," he exclaimed. "Speaks just as he ought."

"Thank you, My Viti," Zandro said, yet his eyes smoldered on Taverik. With no further words Malenga strode into the darkness at the top of the stairs. Perplexed, Taverik stared after him. What had just happened?

He turned in time to catch a significant glance pass between his father and older brother. "What's going on?" he demanded.

"Nothing for you to be concerned about," Zandro growled.

"And the next time you go haring off, Tav," Chado put in, "perhaps you'll let us know where you're going."

"That's enough, Chado," Donato snapped. "It's dark. Let's go home."

Taverik barred his way. "Look, I want to know what's going on! Why were you talking to Malenga? What was he getting at?"

"That's none of your business."

"It *is* my business." Taverik's frustration turned to anger. "It has something to do with the firm, doesn't it? What are you planning?"

Donato planted his feet. "I direct this firm! And I'll do it without help from a buffoon, thank you."

Taverik's vision narrowed. "I have a part share," he spat. "And I say Malenga is bad business. He doesn't have even two vidlas to rub together!"

"Father," Chado warned, putting his hand on Donato's arm. Donato shook him off. His face grew ugly. "Malenga is none of your affair."

"Or maybe you're lending him money?" Taverik saw Chado start and realized his wild guess had gone home. "That's it, isn't it?" he demanded incredulously. "You're lending money to Malenga. Whatever for? I can't believe it!"

Donato gave a strangled, inarticulate roar. Instinct told Taverik to duck, but he was too late. Zandro's fist swung from the darkness and piled into Taverik's cheekbone.

The force of it hurled him against the wall. He slid to the floor, his head pulsing with pain and flashing lights. Through the roar in his ears he heard his father tramp past and down the stairs.

Chado helped him to his feet. "Now, now, little Taverik," he said, laughter edging his words. "You should know better than to make Father mad."

Taverik jerked his arm free of Chado's grasp. "Get out of here," he said thickly.

"Tch, tch. Only trying to help."

"I said, get out!"

"If you say so." Chado swaggered away.

Alone, Taverik leaned his head against the wall and tried to make sense of what had just happened. But his brain seemed as numb as his swelling cheek. At last he pushed himself upright and slogged by instinct to Uncle Nik's.

Chapter 14

Taverik

A metallic clank woke Taverik. He lifted his head from the frayed chairback—damn but his neck was stiff—and peered across the dim, cluttered study. His uncle stood by the desk, fumbling with the lamp. The fire had died down to embers and the room was cold.

"Hello, Nik," Taverik said, pushing himself up in the sag-bottomed chair. "Kala Pardi says you've been away three days. Where on earth have you been?"

"An errand for the zoji," said his uncle curtly. The lamp's glow grew and lit Nikilo's face. His eyes were red-rimmed and dust coated his cloak. "Mano tells me he delivered another poultice to you," he said expressionlessly. "Who was it this time?"

"My father."

Nikilo paused a fraction. "I see," he said at last. "Well, it's not the first time."

"No," Taverik echoed, "not the first." *But it's the last*, he added silently.

Nikilo gave him a long, cool look, eyes moody and impartial, almost, Taverik felt suddenly, as if he were a stranger his uncle had just met. "What's the matter, Nik?" he demanded.

"Have you eaten?"

Taverik shook his head. Uncle Nikilo unwrapped his cloak, revealing muddy boots. "I'll clean up and then we can snatch a bite. Kala Pardi is bringing up something light." Nikilo climbed the ladderlike stairs and soon the ancient floorboards overhead creaked with his footsteps. Taverik stared upward thoughtfully. His uncle seemed reserved tonight, his usual warmth replaced with caution. As if, Taverik felt uneasily, as if his uncle had begun to dislike him intensely. He shook himself; Nikilo was tired, that was all.

He knelt to make up the fire just as Kala Pardi struggled up with a loaded tray. "Your poor face!" she said, continuing her flow from when she'd opened the door to him earlier. "The times we live in! I expect you were caught in another riot?"

Taverik looked over his shoulder with a wry grin. "One way of describing it."

"They do say there have been several riots in the city. Those refugees, I suppose. Though my friend, Kala Ouasi, says she's heard it's all Zoji Balanji's fault. Such rough men in the market place these days—I ask Manokichit to go with me. Mano! Are you bringing the soup?"

"Coming," Mano grumbled from the stairs. He brought in a tray laden with soup and bread, winked at Taverik and stumped out.

"There," said the widow. "Good lamb stew. Eat hearty."

Taverik brushed bark from his hands and stood up. "Thank you, Kala," he said, slipping a coin in her pocket. She patted him on his unbruised cheek and went, bundling up Nikilo's mud-stained cloak on her creeping way.

"Soup's on, Nik," Taverik called up the stairs.

"Coming." Nikilo's voice came over the splash of water.

Taverik seated himself on the wedge-shaped tread where the stairs angled round. "Did you hear about the riots in Vosa? And that Soza closed the temples?"

Nikilo appeared in the soft candlelight at the head of the stairs. "I heard," he said harshly. "I also heard that the arrested rioters and many leading citizens have disappeared. It's rumored they've been transported as slaves."

"Slaves!" said Taverik. "Come on, not even Soza—"

"Not even Soza?" mocked his uncle. He shrugged himself into a brown velvet dressing gown, lifted the candle and started down. "Soza has signed a trade alliance with the Tlath of Bcacma."

Taverik slid to his feet. "He's crazy!"

Nikilo paused on the bottom step, his eyes cool and considering. "Some people may be crazy. But not Soza."

Again uneasiness washed through Taverik. His uncle's words had the same double-edged feel as Malenga's. Oh, nonsense. There must be something on Nikilo's mind, that was all. He had a lot of responsibilities. Which reminded Taverik— "Nik," he said, "now that you're at court, you have access to a lot of information, right?"

Nikilo stiffened. "Some," he said warily. His face had gone tense, as if waiting for a blow to fall. Taverik paused, confused. Perhaps Nikilo was afraid Taverik would want him to abuse his position. "What do you want to know?" Nikilo asked.

Yes, a definite coolness had entered his tone. "Never mind," Taverik said quickly.

"Tell me."

Taverik shrugged. "I just wondered if you could find out for me who besides the zoji family were assassinated when Soza took Vosa."

Nikilo's eyes locked with Taverik's and for the first time in his life, Taverik wondered if he were welcome in his uncle's house. "Yes, I can look for you," Nikilo said smoothly. "Can you be more specific?"

"Kasta. I'm curious about a man named Kasta."

"Kasta. That sounds vaguely familiar. And why do you want to know?"

"For a friend."

Nikilo's eyebrows shot up. "For a friend," he echoed slowly.

This was getting tangled. "A friend—a friend from Vosa." It sounded lame, but Taverik couldn't say much more without bringing in Marko. Why was Nik so touchy?

Nikilo's mouth tightened. "Vosa." He turned to the soup tureen.

"Am I going crazy?" Taverik exploded. He planted

his fists on his hips and glared at his uncle. "What has gotten into you?"

Nikilo gave him a side-long glance. "What do you mean?"

Taverik flung out his hands in frustration. "First my father and then you. There's either something going on I don't understand or else I'm going crazy. Nothing makes sense today!" He ran his fingers through his hair and turned away.

"Why did your father knock you down?"

Taverik laughed bitterly. "I got in his way. I don't know." He turned back and found his uncle leaning against the desk, arms crossed. "I must have poked a tender spot."

He stopped suddenly and stared into space. "In fact," he added slowly, "that's probably it."

"What's probably it?"

"Nik, do you remember a week or so ago when you asked me if I'd seen Malenga with my father?"

Nikilo looked up quickly. "What about it?"

"I have seen him. Today."

"You interest me," Nikilo said. "Tell me about it."

Taverik poured out the entire bewildering conversation in the empty guild hall. "I made a guess," he finished, "and asked Father if he was lending money to Malenga. He floored me and stamped out."

Nikilo took a deep breath and exhaled slowly. "You had no idea Donato was lending money to Malenga?"

"Of course not! Malenga's a lousy risk. Look, what's going on?"

His uncle pinched his lower lip and chewed thoughtfully on it. His brown eyes studied Taverik until Taverik felt he was on trial. "Nephew," he said, at last, "I'm in trouble if I'm wrong. But I think I owe you an apology."

"Well, now we're getting somewhere. What's the apology for?"

"Best have a seat," Nikilo said portentously. He himself sank down in the horsehide chair and massaged his forehead. Taverik stood where he was, watching his uncle warily. Just what was it Nik had held against him?"

"Malenga's a malcontent," Nikilo said, looking up. "An impoverished malcontent. Because of his family heritage he has a right to rooms at the palace and a stipend. But the zoji despises him, and I tend to agree. However I always feared the way Balanji baited him might lead to no good."

"Malenga hates Balanji?"

"Not openly. But certainly. Here's the point. While I was still in Vosa, I caught a brief glimpse of Malenga closeted with Soza."

"Delightful," Taverik growled.

"Indeed. Especially since Malenga tells everyone he has never visited Vosa. Thus when it became apparent that someone in the city was supplying money to finance Soza's campaigns, Balanji immediately suspected Malenga."

"But he's in debt up to his Massadaran nose," Taverik protested.

"Exactly. Someone else had to be involved. Balanji ordered Malenga to be followed, and discovered that a city merchant was actually supplying the money."

Taverik's eyes narrowed and his breathing grew quick and shallow. He had a good idea now what this was leading up to, and a slow rage was kindling within him. "And?" he said softly.

"And . . ." Nikilo hesitated, eyes on Taverik. "Balanji ordered me to discover who. I knew the best merchant for Malenga to go to would be one as dissatisfied as he was. Someone with a complaint. I knew of several. So I watched. Until one day I saw Malenga enter a Zandro warehouse."

"Everyone at court has visited our warehouses," Taverik rasped. "Just what do you imply?"

Nikilo held up his hand. "Wait, let me finish. You're right, I couldn't be sure. But now you've seen Malenga, I—"

"It's all flimsy conjecture." Taverik hit his fist into his palm. "Damn it, you're not even sure in the first place that Malenga *is* supplying Soza."

Nikilo's face grew remote and hard again. "Eyewitnesses saw him leave the warehouse district and pass on money and a map of the palace, fortress and city to a man who headed straight for Ormea."

The news hit Taverik like a blow. He jabbed a forefinger at his uncle. "You're saying my father is a traitor," he snarled. "I don't believe it."

"Then how do you explain this afternoon?" Nikilo snapped.

Taverik glanced at him while his mind sifted frantically through the facts, searching for the loophole. There had to be something that would disprove his uncle's case. But nothing came. Only the remembered words, *by the same method.*

He sat down heavily, fingering his throbbing cheek. "If it's true, then my father's been duped. He doesn't know what the money's for."

Nikilo was implacable. "I wish I could believe it."

"And Chado's in it too."

"Up to now," Nikilo said apologetically, "I couldn't be sure you weren't in it too. Don't glare, I had to be certain. After all, the money is coming from your firm."

"That's why you've been acting so strange tonight?" Taverik demanded.

Nikilo nodded. "I wanted desperately to believe you weren't involved. But—I've been away so long, you could have changed. When I looked into your eyes you seemed the same Taverik, but things I knew . . ."

"Like what?"

"Such as you and Chado both dining with the Famílos, your father entertaining them, the family which sits in Malenga's pocket. Almost certainly Dula was a carrot for your father's cooperation. The priest's strange words and your shutteredness about it—when you want to, you know, you can be about as unreadable as stone. And there was that business about the bad wool. I assumed you'd fallen into your father's ways. And I kept remembering all I'd told you before I realized you might be into it up to your eyebrows."

Taverik shut his eyes; he'd never escape his family. "When you left Illiga," he explained dully, "I took over the textile warehouse and the books and tried to run them straight. I let the family do what they wanted with the rest and concentrated on that and caravans. But while I was away the last time, Chado tried some stinko deals and I had to straighten out the mess he made. That's what you overheard."

He looked up and found Nikilo gazing sympathetically at him. He averted his face, hating it. Inside he felt a roiling, churning mess. He wanted to break bottles, punch a hole in the wall, throw the damn staring owl through the window. "So my father is financing Soza," he said. "My father is a traitor. My father is a murderer."

Nikilo opened his mouth but Taverik cut him off. "Yes, he's a murderer. He's supporting an assassin and a murderer. That makes him one too. For my entire life I have lived with shame, and now he has brought us to *this*!"

Taverik tightened his hands around the arms of the chair as if they were his father's bull-necked throat. "I hate him," he said softly and thickly. He squeezed tighter. "I'll kill him for this."

Nikilo's freckled hands descended over his. "No, Taverik, don't hate."

"Yes, I hate him," Taverik said. "I'll kill him and Chado both before I let them do this thing."

He pulled free. Nikilo seized him by the shoulders instead. "Don't hate!" Nikilo shouted, shaking him. "Don't poison yourself!"

Taverik blinked at Nikilo's startling intensity. Without loosening his grip, his uncle knelt beside him and hurled on, quieter but insistent. "Listen to me, Taverik. All these years I've watched you grow up in that crazy household. I've loved you like a son of my own, sheltered you when I could. Wished I could get you out of there. You were beaten, sworn at and given theft and graft as an example. But you've grown straight. I don't know how or why. It's a miracle. And I love you for it."

Nikilo's grip tightened over Taverik's shoulders until it hurt. Taverik stared up, amazed, into Nikilo's face inches from his, the cheekbones jutting white with strain. "I'd thought I'd lost you to Soza," Nikilo said. "But Zojikam was merciful to me. And so now it breaks my heart to see you wish to destroy yourself with hate and murder, Taverik, my son, my son!"

He broke off abruptly, his dry lips quivering.

Taverik's voice choked. "Oh, Nik," he said, and gently drew his uncle's face closer. They rested, forehead to forehead for a long time.

Chapter 15

Taverik

Nikilo stirred first. He sat back on his heels with a twisted smile. "Forgive a silly old man," he said.

"You're not old," Taverik protested, then added urgently, "Uncle Nik, what did you mean when you called me your son?"

"I've always loved you as a son," Nikilo said, "and wished I could have brought you to live with me."

"Why didn't you?"

"I tried. Not long after your mother died."

Taverik thought back. "I was fourteen. Was that when you and Father had the argument?"

"That's right. Your father had grown rougher and rougher on you boys. And more dishonest, I suspected. I feared for you both, but especially you, Taverik, because I felt Chado's character was already fixed."

Taverik stared at his hands; he didn't want his uncle to see how important his next question was to him. "That was when you stopped visiting, Nik. I always wondered if my father told you— If you were ashamed of me."

"Ashamed of you?" Nikilo looked at him in amazement. "Why should I be ashamed of you? *I* blundered.

I went to Donato and offered to take you off his hands. He grew furious and nearly killed me. Ordered me never to talk to you again. I refused. He said if he caught me in his house that *you* would suffer."

"He said that? Damn him!" How could he *not* hate his father? "He didn't say anything about the river?"

"No. What about the river?"

"Never mind," Taverik said hastily, but he felt like a dark cloud had lifted from his soul. And all these years, he'd thought—

"I didn't want you to suffer," Nikilo said, "so I thought it best to comply and say nothing to you. But my heart ached for you, and when you visited, I tried to make this a refuge."

"It was, Nik." Even the times his father had found out about it afterwards.

Nikilo sighed and got up. "The soup is cold, but I think I could eat anything. You've taken a heavy burden from my shoulders tonight, Nevy."

Taverik took the bowl his uncle handed him. White fat had already begun to congeal on the surface of the stew. He looked away. "What do we do now, Nik?"

His uncle perched one hip on the desk, bowl in hand. He chewed a hunk of lamb, swallowed, and still remained silent, staring thoughtfully into the fire. "I have no choice," he said at last. "I must go to Balanji tomorrow."

Taverik went dead inside. "What will he do?"

"I'm not sure. He may merely have you all watched. But I'm afraid he'll arrest all three of you as an example. Taverik, I think perhaps you should leave the city first thing tomorrow."

"I can't go," Taverik said. "Not first thing. There's someone depending on me."

"Your being imprisoned or hanged is going to help this person?"

"What if we both went to Balanji and explained?"

Nikilo thought about it. "Maybe. Probably not. I don't dare risk you. Taverik, I beg you to leave."

Taverik fingered his bruised cheek. He felt bruised inside, too, and it was hard to think. But he knew he couldn't leave Marko, not without explaining to her.

There had to be a solution, if only he could have time to hit on it. "Uncle Nik," he said finally, "I'm too tired to think. You are too. Why don't we wait until morning to decide?"

"Taverik!" Nikilo exploded. "You don't understand the danger you're in! Balanji is in the mood to hang your entire family outright. And then there's Soza."

"Soza?"

"Yes, Soza. You are a weak link in his little chain. I'm sure they expected to pull you into their plot by now. And you are in a position to discover all."

"I *have* discovered all."

"That's my point!" Nikilo jabbed his finger at him. "One false move on your part and your body will be found in the Giss."

"Surely Father wouldn't go that far."

"*Malenga would. Soza would.*"

Taverik's feet went cold. He was caught between Balanji and Soza, damned by his family's sins. Again he felt exposed, conspicuous, once more the focus of all the unseen beings of the spiritual world. *The hawk fled but the eagle was always there before it, flood and darkness, flood and darkness and fire.* "Zojikam," he breathed.

"Taverik, you must go."

He shook his head slowly, his fingers cold against his hot cheek. "Not tomorrow. I have to do something first." He had to find Marko before he went. Despite his fear a strange elation welled up inside him. They shared an enemy now.

He looked up at his uncle with an affectionate, lopsided smile. "You don't mind if I stay here tonight, do you? I'm a little annoyed with Father right now. And tomorrow you can leave a message at the temple telling me if it's safe or if I should go."

His uncle expelled his breath in an exasperated hiss.

Balanji

The palace had long fallen silent by the time a crescent of moon rose high enough to mingle silver into the glow of Balanji's own lamp. The zoji worked alone in his study, driven by a restlessness he couldn't control. Something bothered him, something on the edge of his mind, that wouldn't come into focus.

In frustration he thumped the desk then lurched to his feet. He prowled the black-and-white tile floor, in and out of the room's shadows. Whatever it was teased him just beyond the edge of consciousness. Once again he unfurled the map and bent over it. There was the Pakajan Peninsula, jutting down to cut off the Sarian Sea from the Great Ocean and the lands to the west. To the east, across the sea, lay Bcacma.

Bcacma, a nation of warriors. A nation whose gods were personifications of its own military might. A nation burning for outlet to the Great Ocean.

To the south lay Massadara, the powerful nation whose common border with Bcacma was a fluid shifting line of fighting. Massadara controlled the Pakajan Strait, and no Bcacmat ship could pass without paying heavy toll. Massadara also controlled the Pakajan Peninsula and no Bcacmat caravan could travel its two trade routes without toll.

To the north lay all but impassable mountains, peopled by fierce barbarians. Bcacma found no exit to the ocean there. The constriction had forced Bcacma into a secondary role in the world, and Balanji could guess how it gnawed the hearts of that fierce, ambitious people. Despite all their worshipped military might, they had found no place to use it. He shuddered.

In his grandfather's time, the Bcacmat army had invaded the Peninsula from the north, pushing down through the mountains. Those were the only times in the colonial history of the Peninsula that the quarrelling city states had united in a single cause. The last major battle had taken place right in the Giss Valley, when his grandfather had broken the back of the invading army. The Bcacmats had been harried north to where the barbarian tribes awaited, angered at the arrogant cruelty of the Bcacmat forces. Rumors said few Bcacmats made it home.

But Balanji held no illusions. Bcacma had by no

means given up. And the Peninsula, with its tiny, quarrelling Massadaran outposts seemed the most vulnerable. Balanji had pushed hard for unity between the city states, pointing out the new Tlath's growing naval fleet. He'd pointed out Massadara's recent slackening of interest in defending the Peninsula as it coped with the intensifying border war with Bcacma. He'd pointed out Soza's bloody expansion. Yet he was laughed at behind his back, and even to his face. For generations the Pakajan cities had muddled along in their petty rivalries. No one saw any reason why they couldn't continue for generations more.

Again he felt that disquietude. Why would Soza sign trade agreements with Bcacma? He didn't even have a direct route to Bcacma. There was a piece missing somehow. Balanji stared into the lamp and willed his mind to find it.

"May I speak with you?" said a woman.

He started. Shading his eyes from the light, he peered into the shadows by the door. "Akusa."

She had begun to withdraw. "I'm sorry," she said. "I didn't realize you were busy."

"No, not at all," he said. "I lost track of time. Please sit down."

She came forward hesitantly as he pulled out the chair from Nikilo Vitujak's desk. "It's just after midnight," she said. "Late, I know, but I wanted to talk to you before I retired."

"You are always welcome." She looked better now, he thought. Still pale and drawn, but she'd make it. She was odd that way, frail and seemingly all emotion, but inwardly hammered steel.

She folded her hands calmly in her lap. "I've decided to take your offer of a hiding place," she said. "It will be safer for my son. And it will free you to move as you see fit."

"Excellent," he said quietly. "Nikilo Vitujak, my secretary, has just returned from the mountains this night, having obtained the very vidyen we need."

She nodded, visibly keeping her emotions in check. "When do I go?"

Balanji hesitated. He hadn't expected her to come around so quickly. "Could you leave before dawn tomorrow?" he asked, watching her face. "Ride out as if for a hunt. But you'll keep on going."

"Whatever you think is best," she said.

"Carry essentials in a saddle bag. We'll supply the rest as soon as possible."

"Then I must prepare immediately," she said and gathered her skirts.

He offered his arm, trying to fathom her thoughts. Her hand was light on his elbow as she rose, but the lace at her wrist trembled. He became intensely aware of her fragrance and her femininity. Balanji felt a moment of pity. She needed something he couldn't, shouldn't give her. For a moment, as his blood stirred, he was tempted to try. Then firmly he put the thought aside. "You are a courageous woman."

Her fingers tightened. "Thank you," she said, and they entered the hall, into the safety of a public place. "But it is not exactly courage."

"It is *exactly* courage."

She looked up at him, startled then gratified. He nodded reassuringly and read in her eyes that he had given her enough.

The two guards outside Ferco's room came to stiff attention as they neared. Balanji opened the door and allowed Akusa to proceed him. Inside, a shaded lamp cast a rosy glow over the drawn curtains of the small bed. The fire had died and the usually overheated room was very cold. Where was the nurse?

Balanji's brows snapped together. Something was wrong. The room was too quiet. He flung out his arm. "Wait."

The door was ripped from his hand. Akusa gasped. A little man in black flung himself on Balanji. Lamp light gleamed on a double-edged blade in his fist. Balanji swerved, the knife searing his ribs even as he seized the man's arm and jabbed him in the throat.

Gagging, the assassin fell heavily. The knife rang on the floor. Balanji stepped on it. Keeping his eyes on the writhing man, he started to pick it up.

The assassin rolled, reaching in his sleeve.

"Back!" Balanji yelled. He kicked just as the assassin's arm flicked. A slim knife hilt appeared between Akusa's breasts just above the bodice of her dress. She cried out and sank in a billow of skirts.

The man sprang for the windows. Balanji swept up the knife at his feet and hurled it. It sank between the assassin's shoulder blades and he fell, skidding forward on the tile floor to fetch up awkwardly against the wall under the window just as the guards reached him.

In two strides Balanji crossed the room. He checked the man and cursed his accurate aim. He'd learn little now. He turned to Akusa.

Her face was calm and peaceful. A thin stream of blood trickled from the wound to puddle in the hollow of her neck. Balanji knelt and touched her wrist gently. No pulse. He shut his eyes, frustration mingling with grief. *One more day* . . .

The two guards bustled about, white-faced and overly busy. "There's a rope here!" exclaimed one. The other industriously searched the assassin's body, trying, Balanji thought sourly, to mask their gross negligence. Balanji crossed to the little bed and flung back the curtains, then turned away. He should have known better than to hope. The nurse, too, in all probability, but he checked the other room anyway. He returned, a cold, detached anger tightening his heart.

The guards awaited him, trembling at his silence. He confronted them, his face rigid. Voices in the hall, the commotion had attracted attention. The captain of the watch burst in and stopped in his tracks. He looked from Akusa to Balanji to the sprawled assassin, his eyes wide with apprehension. Yuot Kintupaquat peered in, his iron gray hair rumpled. He gave a muffled exclamation and ordered someone behind him to get the gates closed and allow no one to pass.

"Just so," Balanji snapped. He turned to the quaking guards. "You will turn yourselves in to the captain of the watch," he said, enjoying in his rage the blanching of their faces, "for gross negligence of your duty. I'll deal with you tomorrow. Get out."

He strode to the assassin's body and kicked it over. The face was lean and swarthy. Massadaran, he thought, puzzled. Kintupaquat came up behind him. "Do you know him?" Balanji asked.

"I've seen him. Around the stables, I think. We'll find out." Kintupaquat leaned out the open casement. "Came down that rope from the roof like a monkey, and right in the window. The knife of course is Bcacmat."

Balanji looked up quickly. "Is he Bcacmat?"

Kintupaquat shook his head. "Who knows? Bcacmat knives are the best in the world. Everyone carries them. That's why I begged you to wear a mail shirt, My Zoji."

Balanji's fingers covered his bleeding ribs. "You are right," he conceded, then nudged the corpse with his foot. "First thing tomorrow, hang him in the square."

"Some of my men may join him," said Kintupaquat, his jaw set hard. "I'll conduct an investigation tonight."

"Call me for it." Balanji turned back to Akusa just as her maid servant pushed through the stunned guards, viti, and servants gawking in the doorway. She fell on her knees beside the body and set up a keening cry. Balanji muttered an impatient oath. "Take care of this," he said to the priest who had just arrived.

He strode away, ignoring the questioning crowd, and slammed the study door. There he prowled up and down like an angry panther, clasping and unclasping his hands behind his back until at last Ela came for him. He rounded on her. "What good is courage against a knife in the dark?" he demanded.

She took him in her arms, and he leaned his cheek on her soft hair. She was crying for Akusa, crying for her son, for the zojis of Ormea and Vosa—*crying for themselves*. He tightened his arms around her as if he could protect her within their circle.

If only he could.

"Before light," he murmured into her hair, his mind already ordering the things he had to get done that night, "you and the children go. Instead of Akusa. Get ready."

Chapter 16

Marita

Marita rolled to her elbow and stared through the darkness. *It* was near, she could feel its presence. Only this time it was actually searching for her. She had to hide, she had to . . .

Familiar outlines took dim shape. Bed curtains. Wardrobe. The chest under the window. "Just a dream," she breathed. "Just a dream." *The* dream.

Wisps of it were slow to clear from her mind. She groped for the flint and steel on the stand beside the bed, her hands shaking as she lit the candle. Its warm glow chased the shadows from the corners and calmed her heart. Pulling her clammy night shirt away from her neck, she sat up to think.

No doubt the dream had been triggered by her giving Taverik her real name. Oh, why had she done that? Him and his insatiable curiosity— "Damn it, Taverik," she growled under her breath. "Why can't you leave well enough alone?"

Her words echoed uncomfortably through her mind. Suddenly she punched the pillow. "Damn it *Soza*, why are *you* ruining my life!"

She found she was clutching the pillow to her chest, staring at the shuttered window as if Soza would burst in to get her. Sheepishly, she loosened her hold. There. She'd said it and survived. She'd been angry at Taverik, angry at Sahra, even angry at Zojikam. All safer targets than Soza, who was actually to blame for her troubles.

Feeling braver, she made a count on her fingers of

the ways Soza had harmed her: murdering her parents, Ot, and Bibi's family, and many of the household servants. He'd turned her out of her comfortable house and forced her to starve, shiver, work beyond exhaustion, worry about her sister and Bibi, endure the slums. He'd chased her from farm to city then even out of Vosa altogether. And now he was threatening Illiga, her adopted city, and the home she'd worked so hard for.

And she'd endured it meekly, running like a little mouse from hole to hole. Marita flushed with shame as she realized how she'd let him invade even her dreams and thoughts. Even at a distance he controlled her through her fears—she who'd taken such pride in her freedom. Why had she never seen it this way before? Tav had, right from the start. "You live in bondage to a shadow," he'd said only this morning. "Maybe it's time to stop and face it."

Her bravado melted. Face it? What could she do against Soza? Her first strategy had been best: get out of the way, remain unnoticed by him. But what about that prophesy of Taverik's—wherever the hawk hid, the eagle was there before it. Well, she was no hawk, and it didn't apply to her, but it did tell her she would find no comfort in hiding. Not any more.

"Zojikam," she said gruffly, "they say you don't care about us anymore. Is that true? Are you stronger than Soza and his Black Eagle? Do you intervene in the matters of men?"

Then, stiffly, since she'd stubbornly done nothing but mouth liturgy since her parents' deaths, she added, "I'm sorry I was angry at you. What should I do now?"

No answer dropped through the ceiling and Marita kicked impatiently at the coverlet. Suddenly she remembered the strong box.

She sat up straighter to consider it. She and Sahra had gone through it many a time, but always trying to find something to pawn to keep hunger away one more day. They had never thought to search it for clues of why their parents had been murdered. Yet she'd told

Taverik just that morning that her father had made a point of showing it to her the morning of his death.

Marita chewed her lower lip. She was wide awake now. Why not go look again? On impulse she flung aside her blankets and thrust her feet into slippers. Swinging her wool cloak around herself and taking up the candle, she silently opened the door.

Outside Sahra's room she hesitated. Perhaps she shouldn't be doing this without her sister's knowledge. She'd even given their real name to Taverik without Sahra's permission. But the memory of Sahra's withdrawal still rankled. Marita shrugged. Sahra didn't care, these days. She would tell her about it in the morning.

Downstairs, the study was dark and chill, with the acrid scent of ashes lingering in the still air. Marita set the lamp on Sahra's table and pushed at the heavy desk. A good heave and the desk scraped across the floorboards. She paused, listening, but no sound came from upstairs or down.

Kneeling, she ran her fingers across the oaken boards until she felt the crack. She dug in with her nails but could get no purchase on the board. She took Sahra's pen knife and pried up the boards, easing them aside one by one. Her fingers closed on the cold handles of the box and she pulled it up.

It wasn't as heavy as it had been the night they'd fled, she thought, opening it. On top lay her father's flattened money pouch. The coins in it had seen them through that first hand-to-mouth year and had brought them as far as Illiga. Marita smoothed its suede then laid it aside.

A second pouch was almost half full—money she herself had saved. She touched it wonderingly. By her own efforts she'd supported three people and still had been able to save this much. It felt good. A sudden, confusing thought took her breath away. If it weren't for Soza she would never have done it, never had her own mule to wander the countryside on, never travelled all over the Peninsula, never bought, sold, never owned her own home, never voted in the guild . . .

For a brief crazy moment, she was actually grateful to Soza!

Confusing. She set the thought aside for when she'd have more time to examine it, and reached back into the box. Next, the bag with her mother's jewels. They'd come close to selling them when they'd first arrived and were living in the filthy tent city near the main gate. Then Bibi had miraculously produced a little money. She wouldn't say from where or how, and Marita, who had learned hard lessons fast, suspected she'd sold herself. Thereafter she refused to accept any more money from Bibi. They'd eaten beans for months until Marita thought she'd throw up if she had to put another spoonful in her mouth. And they'd made it through.

Next, the papers. Marita brought the candle closer and went through them carefully. They mostly recorded a merchant's important transactions, and made a lot more sense to her now than they did the first time she'd examined them. Below, the deeds to the house in Vosa, three warehouses, property in the country, all useless now. Marita sighed and tossed them aside. Odd—

She frowned and picked them up again. Each one was in Mother's name. Why not Papa's name, even if he had assumed his wife's family name? Why had he done that? Was it because he was a bastard and ashamed? Odd, odd, odd. In the last few weeks her elegant, competent father had become a shadowy figure, even to her. Who *was* he?

One last paper remained, a love poem written by her mother, carefully folded and cherished. Marita knew the lines by heart:

My love you gave up all for me
Who little owned to give up on my part.
Instead I receive my all from you
And give in turn a poor thing, though true,
My heart.

Marita read them again. Now she had noticed the deeds, the poem seemed to be carrying undercurrents beyond the mere doggerel she had always supposed it. She read it through again, but any meaning still eluded her. Sahra was cleverer with words. She'd ask her tomorrow.

The box was almost empty. She brought out the medal, a large gold medallion stamped on one side with the falcon of the Vos family, and on the other, their coat of arms. On both sides ran their motto: "I keep my own." Marita turned the medallion over and over, wondering again how it came into her father's possession.

Only the scroll remained. She slipped off its faded red ribbon and unrolled it. It crackled and smelled faintly of oil and ink, a parchment inscribed in a foreign language, probably Bcacmat. Now why had her father kept a letter written in his strong box? He'd dealt in rugs, many of them Bcacmat. He'd even taken several trips to Bcacma. Did this letter have to do with the trips?

"I think," she murmured, her breath misting before her in the cold, "I think it's time to translate you." Her printer was a licensed letter writer, a man who would read, write or translate a letter for a small fee. She'd take it to him during the break in the guild meeting.

She started to roll it up, then hesitated, her fingers rubbing the rough side of the parchment as she thought. Best make a copy of the letter and leave the original here. Safer.

Marita took up the candle and crossed to the table. The Gentle Philosopher's book of essays lay opened atop Sahra's returned manuscript. Sahra had already begun scribbling in the margin. Marita smiled wryly as she sat down. Would this Gentle Philosopher remain gentle if he could poke his nose in one day and discover his worthy opponent was a woman?

She shoved the clutter aside. Wiggling her toes to keep her feet warm, she pulled out a sheet of paper and set about copying the Bcacmat words. Ten minutes later she did her best with the signature then straightened her aching back with a hiss of exasperation. In the guttering candlelight the script had seemed to squirm and twist across the page until she'd had to fight to keep her place amid the alien words. A lot of work for what was probably a letter about a shipment of rugs. Marita tucked her hands under her armpits to warm them, and stood up with a yawn.

Dense fog had crept through the city in the night. By morning when Marita set off for the guild she could barely see across the narrow street. The air felt damp and smelled bad, and she longed to stay home by the fire.

At the edge of the Plaza she pulled up, staring into the thick white murk. She could get lost in that vast square today, she thought with amusement. They'd find her wandering in circles when the cloud cleared. With a snort of laughter, she started Whitey across, guided by the sound of voices. The gallows loomed to her left and she headed that way. The Textile Guild Hall would lie directly beyond.

She was caught in the crowd before she realized its ugly mood. Ragged Ormean refugees jostled against Whitey, shouting in anger at the four guards standing at the corners of the gallows platform. Three men dangled from the cross trees. One wore black, and hung limply. The other two, who wore the uniform of the palace guards, still kicked and swung. Marita's stomach rose to her throat. She hastily turned away her eyes.

"Curse you Illigans!" a woman screamed at the soldiers guarding the platform. She had greasy hair escaping from her cap, and her face was smeared with dirt.

One of the soldiers swung his pike. "Stand off," he ordered. All four wore breastplates and all four looked nervous.

"That for Akusa!" screeched the woman, throwing a handful of mud. The crowd muttered approval and closed in tighter. Marita urged Whitey on but the mule could make no progress without stepping on someone. He snorted and rolled his eyes. A man tried to climb the platform but received the flat of the pike in the chest, sweeping him unhurt onto the people below. The crowd pelted the guards with rocks and filth.

Whitey pranced uneasily, throwing back his clumsy head. Wary of his huge clumsy hooves, the rioters gave him room, and at last Marita won clear of the worst of the mob.

Ahead, a knot of youths had converged around an unfortunate Illigan caught on foot. Marita started to veer wide then recognized the harried man: the president of the Textile Guild. Limping on his bandaged foot, Ittato held off the taunting youths with his cane and shouted for help. One youth grabbed the cane and pulled.

Marita dug in her spurs and Whitey leaped directly at them. "Make way!" she roared in her deepest voice. The youth let go of the cane. Ittato swung it at Marita before he realized who she was. "Help!" he bellowed.

Someone grabbed at Marita's belt. She booted him in the stomach then shook her foot free of the stirrup so Ittato could mount. He nearly pulled her from the saddle as he hauled himself up, then overbalanced and seized her waist to keep from falling off the far side. His flailing cane clipped the already plunging Whitey, and Marita clung unabashedly to the saddle as the mule flattened his ears and crow hopped. Ittato bellowed in her ear, his cane wacked her thigh, then found Whitey's rump. With an outraged squeal, the mule galloped free of the youths into the fog.

Ahead, the pale outline of the Guild Hall solidified in the white. Whitey slowed to a walk and headed straight for the alley leading to the stableyard. Pushing herself off the painful saddle bow, Marita patted his neck. "Good fella," she said. "That's twice in one morning."

Behind her Ittato straightened, transferring his grip from high around her waist to her belt, much to her relief. "You saved my life, young man," he wheezed into her right ear.

"Nonsense, Kali," she said and changed the subject. "What was that all about?"

"Zoja Akusa was assassinated last night."

"No!" cried Marita before she could control herself.

But Ittato didn't seem to notice her suddenly unmasculine voice.

"Her son, too. The Ormeans blame Balanji for not guarding her well enough. Rumors and pamphlets say he allowed it because he wants Ormea for himself. Hence the near riot."

"That's crazy," Marita exploded. "It's obviously Soza who is responsible."

"But how convenient for Soza if Balanji is blamed."

Marita's stomach tightened. Could Soza truly have been behind that riot? And if so, what else would he be able to do within the city? Certainly the contented bustling character of Illiga had soured in the last months. But how could Soza be responsible, she scoffed. He was in Ormea, besieged by Balanji's army. Wasn't he?

Whitey entered the back courtyard where soberly clad merchants stood in gloomy clusters, discussing the morning's news. Their long faces grew even longer with astonishment as they took in the president mounted behind a very junior member of the guild, bandaged foot stuck out and cane jauntily akimbo. Ittato chuckled softly. "We're giving them one more thing to gabble about, the silly fools. That's my new doctor over there, Kastazi. He irritates me and I'll fire him soon, but for now you can put me down beside him."

She headed Whitey towards the tall man, wondering how the town could hold enough doctors for Ittato's needs. Several Council members gathered around, joined by prominent merchants, all wondering loudly what had happened. Ittato ignored them. "Another thing," he said in Marita's ear. "Those youths didn't talk like Ormeans. Nor Illigans neither. Funny accents."

He threw his cane to the doctor and allowed himself to be helped down and borne off by important people. Ignoring the curious glances of bystanders, she dismounted and led Whitey across the muddy cobbles toward the stable. Her thoughts were haunted by those brief seconds a week ago, when her eyes had met Zoja Akusa's.

She stopped dead. Echin blocked the door. His eyes narrowed when he saw her, and his eyebrows lowered. Perhaps she should go around to the other entrance. Avoid trouble. Then her jaw jutted stubbornly. She was tired of ducking people. Sticking her thumb into her belt, she sauntered forward. "Good morning, Echin," she said. "That was fun, yesterday, wasn't it? A good joke, eh?"

His eyes widened. "Fun," he said, almost strangling on the word. But he stepped back. "Uh, yes, joke."

Laughing under her breath, Marita led Whitey past him. The incident almost made the morning worthwhile.

Word about the petition must have spread, Marita thought as she squeezed through the crowd in the back of the hall. Men stood along the aisles and jammed themselves together on the benches. The only bench with room was the last one, under the balcony's overhang where it would be hard to hear. But Marita squeezed in—damned if she would stand throughout what was bound to be a long meeting.

The dome, this morning, let in a murky gray light which flattened surfaces and colors both. Ittato, she noticed as he rose to convene the meeting, hadn't combed his hair since his rescue, and it still flew out in a wild mane about his face.

"Good morning," said Taverik.

She turned with a start. He plunked down beside her, smiling sweetly at the bald man in front who turned to shush him. He wore the same clothes as yesterday, rumpled as if he'd slept in them. His eye was swollen and every color of purple, yellow and green. Marita started to reach for it then dropped her hand. "Your father do that?"

"How'd you guess?"

"I could tell he was itching to yesterday."

"Well, he got around to it."

His voice sounded flat and he acted tired. Marita wondered what had passed between him and his father last night. "Is that why you're sitting down here? Didn't you go home?"

"Correct both times, Mother."

She flushed. Now who was prying? "Sorry, I didn't mean—"

"Shh!" The bald man glared over his shoulder.

Marita turned her attention back to Ittato. He'd begun to orate over the tragic circumstances of Akusa's death, which she'd already heard told with ghoulish relish by the stableboys. She shifted her position impatiently and the paper in her pocket crackled.

"Taverik," she whispered. "Are you in the mood for a little expedition after the meeting?"

He twisted so he could see her with his good eye. "What do you mean?"

Pulling out the transcription, she passed it to him. Before she could explain, Ittato raised his voice. "Marko!" he shouted. "Where is he? Marko!"

Marita looked up in confusion. Ittato stood on the edge of the dais, searching the audience. Successive rows of heads turned until the entire room spotted her in the back. "Stand up, boy," said the bald man with an all-is-forgiven smile. "Don't be modest."

She stood reluctantly, aware of Taverik's surprised face below. Ittato retold the tale of his rescue, embroidering it until it sounded as if she had truly rescued him from certain death. Marita stared straight ahead, cheeks radiating heat until at last Ittato moved on to the first order of business and she could sit down. Damn! So much for keeping a low profile!

"Fighting again?" Taverik whispered.

She glowered at him, but again that disconcerting expression had softened his eyes. She looked away quickly.

Taverik nudged her. "Do you expect me to read this?"

She blinked in bewilderment then remembered the letter. "No," she said. "It's Bcacmat. Belonged to my father."

"Oh ho! So we get it translated today?"

He was quick. She took the letter and tucked it back into her pocket. "Right after the morning session, if you're willing."

"Shh!" said the bald man.

* * *

But after the meeting Marita found it difficult to leave the hall. Men who had never before noticed her clustered around exclaiming their congratulations. One of Ittato's cronies slapped her on the back with a cackle. "Should have left him to the mob, lad!" Gunnar swooped down on her with two other younger men. "Beer on us! We want to hear the *real* story."

"Tonight," she said firmly. "I've got something I've got to get done before the afternoon session." They left her reluctantly and she crossed the damp hall to where Taverik waited, propped against a pillar.

"I was beginning to think," he said, "that I'd have to get the letter from you and go myself."

She punched him lightly on the arm. "Traitor."

His eyes went blank at that, and she wondered what nerve she'd struck. Funny, she didn't remember Taverik having nerves. She looked at him speculatively as she followed him out into the fog. What *had* happened last night?

"There's that miserable little sniveler," Taverik said under his breath.

Marita looked around. Echin stood under one of the granite columns, staring at them. Just staring. A chill crossed her shoulders. "He's still smarting under the humiliation we gave him yesterday," she said softly.

"Not smarting," Taverik said, striding away. "Nothing Echin ever did was smart."

Marita snorted, but when she looked back, Echin still stared.

They'd set out on foot since the printer's shop wasn't far. But when they arrived, Marita looked in dismay on the shuttered windows and padlocked doors. A notice hung limp on a door nail. " 'Closed by order of Zoji Balanji until further notice,' " Taverik read. "I'd heard he'd shut down all the printers, trying to find the source of all these seditious pamphlets."

"I thought he'd still be selling books," Marita said. "Hmm, the tailor by the university quarter has the inkpot and quill symbol on his shop sign."

But the tailor shook his head when Marita asked if

he could translate Bcacmat. Taking his long shears, he snipped a square of white canvas and drew a quick map. "Only place," he said in old Pakajan.

"Thank you," she said, and left a coin. The map led them past the university to the steep cliffs above the River Giss, an ancient neighborhood with narrow winding streets. Alleys darted off into the mist at odd angles and stone stairways led upwards to uneven rows of houses clinging to the rocks.

"Student quarter," Taverik said. "Best wrap your cloak tight around you."

"Yes, one student riot per month is enough." Marita spoke lightly to cover her increasing unease. She squinted down at the soggy map whose ink had begun to blur in the thickening drizzle. Footsteps behind her made her gasp and turn, but it was merely a young man running, head down, to get out of the rain.

She felt sheepish, but noticed Taverik dropping his hand away from his knife. "A bit jumpy, aren't we?" he said. "Don't we turn here?"

"Down this alley," Marita agreed. She peered in and grimaced.

The alley canted so steeply it was actually a series of long steps. It tunneled through grey stone buildings which huddled on each side and nearly met overhead. Part way down, a pawnshop sign gleamed dully in the gloom. Beyond it the alley twisted down into the mist rising from the river.

"Lovely," said Taverik.

"I just hope the tailor knew what he was talking about," Marita said. She stuck her thumb in her belt for courage and plunged in.

The houses looked like fortresses, built in the days of the wars, with tiny high windows barred against intruders and Pakajan raiders. A sewer ran down the middle with a smell that made her gag. Her scalp prickled each time they passed a darkened slit between buildings. Surely this letter wasn't worth the danger. She cleared her throat to suggest turning around.

"Here we are," Taverik said softly.

She looked up. The shop sign bore a faint and peeling inkpot-and-quill painted in the lower corner. On the shop itself, rust stains streaked the flaking stucco, drooling from the iron bars in the two windows. The windows were narrow and set high over the studded oak door. No light shone from them.

"We probably should have left a note," Taverik said, "telling someone where we were going."

Marita looked dubiously to him to see if he was joking. "It's not fair for me to drag you into this."

"You'll probably need me to drag you *out* of this," he said with a reassuring grin.

She laughed softly and opened the door.

Chapter 17

Marita

The smell of mold and incense caught at Marita's throat as she stepped onto creaking floorboards. She peered into the gloom, moving forward only when Taverik gave her a gentle shove in the small of the back so that he could get in too. When he pulled the door shut behind him she almost cried out to stop. Don't be silly, she scolded herself.

Gray light filtering through the encrusted windows began to pick out the tiny shop's incredible clutter. On the wall hung ancient swords and knives beside outmoded armor, ornate helmets and clothing. Marita edged past shadowy, dusty shelves piled with clocks, brasswork, drums and stringed instruments. Another scent touched her nose, oily and familiar, yet she couldn't identify it. Overhead, footsteps creaked, punctuated by periodic muffled thuds.

On the counter stood a porcelain jar, with a lid fastened by a padlock. Decorated with scrolls of blue and gold, it gleamed as if with a light of its own. "Beautiful," Marita breathed, though her unease grew the longer she looked at it. She'd never seen anything like it before, yet the jar felt familiar, like a half-remembered dream on wakening. Its blue and gold glaze shimmered, like satin, like silk . . .

"Don't touch it!" said Taverik sharply.

She dropped her hand and drew back. "Why not?"

"Something's wrong with it. It's . . . *ikiji.*"

The wall slid at her. Marita gasped, then realized sheepishly that a door set flush with the wall was being opened.

"Ah!" said a stooped man in black. "Customers." He shut the door which seemed to disappear into the wall once more, and came to the counter. His skin was yellow and transparent, like beeswax. He looked as if it had been years since he'd seen the sun. Dismissing Taverik with a flick of the eyes, he spoke to Marita. "Young Viti, good day. You come treasure to pawn so pay student debts?"

So, he thought she was a student. Her Massadaran features might give her an advantage here. Marita kept her cloak wrapped tight around her merchant's surcoat and let her eyes assume an eager, inexperienced expression. "No, Kali, I wish to . . ."

He broke in with a knowing wink. "No say no more. You obtained possession of an item you want disappear in turn for money."

Behind her Taverik choked and dropped the shield he'd been twiddling with. He turned it into a coughing fit. Marita kept her face blank. The fellow was a *fence*! "No," she said, "not this time. I'm interested in having a letter translated."

"Ah." His wrinkled face cleared. "I many language know. Charge is twenty pelli a page."

Outrageous, of course. "I hope you will consider a poor student," Marita said. "I'll offer you four."

"Four!" He leaned over and spat. Keeping her amusement out of her eyes Marita looked inquiringly at him. "Not Abado not rich either," he said. "But boys who pay for school can afford my fee which modest is. Eighteen pelli."

"My dear Kali," said Marita, settling into the rhythm and enjoying it. "You have no idea of the taxes the zoji imposes on the university. Five."

Abado smiled gently and subsided onto his stool. They haggled on, Abado interrupting himself to glare at Taverik who was rummaging around and dropping things to distract him. At last Marita volunteered eight and Abado refused. She shook her head and turned away. "Sorry, that was my limit. Come on . . . my friend." For some reason she felt reluctant to give away their names."

"Hasty!" The man leaned over the counter. "Students hasty are. Too young! Eight we agree. Let me letter see."

Marita handed him the page she'd transcribed. Abado glanced at it and scowled. "Bcacmat! Not you not specify in Bcacmat it written!"

"You didn't specify it made a difference," Marita said tartly.

"This more will cost!"

An old trick. Marita took the letter out of his hand. "We made a bargain! I don't like your style of business. Come on . . ."

Abado snatched it back. "All right. Give here, sniveling little boy. And policy I have, children in advance pay."

Laughing inwardly, Marita counted out the pelli with sober courtesy. She'd gotten the best of him, but she'd never let him know she knew it. Abado grumbled and took his time about lighting a lamp and digging out a pen. With a long-suffering sigh he bent over the page.

His eyes widened.

Marita watched intently, wondering at his quickened breathing. He wrote the translation of each word above it, sometimes hesitating at a word she'd apparently transcribed wrong. Finally he stopped, pen hung over the page.

"Are you finished?"

"Where student this get?" he asked.

"Are you finished?" she repeated.

He planted a gnarled finger on the last few words. The signature. "Must word look up."

His yellowed eyes met hers so guilelessly she grew suspicious. Leaning across the counter she snatched the paper from him. "I'll keep this for you in the meantime," she said.

Anger flared in his tawny eyes, quickly suppressed. "I soon return. Wait." Somehow he opened the door in the wall and shut it silently behind him.

Taverik hung up a sword and crossed the room. He leaned close to her ear. "Neatly done," he mouthed, his warm breath tickling her.

She nodded thanks and tilted the page into the lamp light so he could read it too.

> To servant faithful favored Itzil Farasoza Agash. You well have done but I impatient grow. I more by now want. Not I not should questions yours need answer. Why you from I chose path why have veered. Vosa immediately leave. Illiga, Perijo or Novato go. Trade route northern desire my is. Not such plans improvised not continue. Plans these my displeasure incite. At once answer. Noble most, elevated most, adorable most . . .

"Huh?" said Taverik. "This reads crazy! Why didn't he finish it?"

"He said he wanted to look up the last few words."

"The signature? I don't like this. I don't like him, either. I don't like the shop, and I *especially* don't like that." He pointed at the jar, then took her arm. "Let's get out of here."

Maybe her sensibilities had been heightened by the atmosphere in the shop, but the moment he touched her arm she became intensely aware of his warmth, his breathing, the leather, wool and sweat smell of him, of . . . she moved herself firmly aside and suddenly recognized that faint scent that had been bothering her since she'd entered. "Taverik," she said softly, urgently, "that smell. They've got an illegal printing press in operation."

Her eyes met Taverik's as they both realized the implications. "We're going," Taverik said. "Now."

Karaz

Karaz was cleaning his nails with his dagger and didn't bother to look up as Abado shut the door behind him. The inner room here was Karaz's only comfortable sanctum in this damp cold gray city in which his father had required him to live the last few years. Here firelight flickered across luxurious rugs, soft cushions and the bright green parrot chewing on his perch in the corner. The hammered gold goblet beside him held decent wine. Abado served him. He hated going back to his barren room at the university.

"So," he said in Bcacmat, "your customers gone?"

"No, a student and his Pakajan servant wait while I look up a word," Abado said. He added portentously. "The student brought a letter he wants translated from Bcacmat."

Karaz yawned and flicked dirt from his little finger. "And you have forgotten how to read these years?"

Abado scowled satisfyingly. Karaz always enjoyed getting under the skin of his father's servant; Abado thought far too highly of himself. "A letter," Abado said, "from the Tlath to your father."

Karaz straightened with a start. "What! Why didn't you say so? Let's see it."

"I don't have it," Abado admitted, his triumph fading. "The student wouldn't let me bring it in."

"You're getting senile," Karaz sighed. "Let me look." He crossed the carpet to the door and eased aside the cover of the tiny spy hole. He stiffened with a muttered oath. "I know them," he said.

Abado remained where he was, hands folded, head inclined politely. Karaz's smile grew a shade malicious. "Not students at all, my dear Abado. Two of Illiga's most honorable, most estimable *merchants*."

"Merchants!" Abado hissed in anger.

Karaz laughed nastily. "Plucked the wolf himself, did they? You have dung for brains, Abado." He turned back to the hole. If he weren't mistaken, Abado's student was actually a woman. He'd been drunk at the inn, but that scream had been unmistakable. He watched as the blond one—the bastard who'd insulted him and refused him a ride—took hold of her arm. She looked up and her face softened. In that brief moment Karaz was sure. There could be no doubt. A woman dressed as a man.

She moved a few steps toward the edge of his view, her expression already returning to its firm, ambiguous lines. But Karaz had seen enough. He shut the spy hole. "Abado, what is the word you are supposed to be looking up?"

"The Tlath's signatures, Viti."

Karaz rubbed his hands in anticipation. "I'm sure this is the letter for which my father has long searched. He will be very pleased when he arrives tonight. Now I want you to give them a false signature. Anyone, just not the Tlath. Stall them."

Abado bowed and slid silently through the door. Karaz thumped on the trap door in the ceiling. It opened with a rush of ink smell, and a heavy man looked down. "Tlele, come down, I need your help. We must summon the *mahigas* and trap two little birds for the—"

"Viti!" wailed Abado, flinging wide the door. "They've already left!"

Karaz snarled wordlessly, and snatched up his sword. "Get the jar, fools, and come!"

Chapter 18

Marita

Once she started to go, Marita felt an urgency akin to panic. Leaving the door ajar, she leaped after Taverik, half-running up the steep alley until her labored breathing kept time with the tread of her boots on the wet cobbles. Not until they reached the top of the alley did she pause to look back, ebbing adrenaline making her slightly sick. The pawnshop had already hid itself in a shroud of mist.

"I suppose it's foolish of me to want to leave like that," Taverik said. But he also stared down the alley, looking anything but eager to return.

"There was something weird about that place," Marita said.

"Weird, and how about just plain criminal?"

"Oh well," Marita sighed. Now they had gotten away, her disappointment surfaced. "I suspected last night the letter might be just merchant business and I was right. But it was worth a try."

"Hold on," Taverik said. "That funny little fellow—Abado he called himself—he practically jumped out of his mummified skin when he saw your letter. He wouldn't do that over just merchant business."

"Perijo, Illiga and Novato are the northern trade route."

"True, but that doesn't necessarily mean merchant business. Let's list what we know for sure."

Marita pulled the paper from her pocket. "A letter which my father kept in his strong box. Written in

Bcacmat by someone we don't know to a man named Farasoza Itzil Agash."

"Or the other way around. They seem to put their words differently. Do you recognize the name?"

Marita strolled on up the road, scowling thoughtfully. "No. Wait! Taverik, Agash isn't a name at all, it's the Bcacmat word for military commander."

"Are you sure?"

"Pretty sure. I've learned some words buying rugs from them in Novato."

"Let me see." Taverik took the limp letter and squinted at it. "A letter to Commander Farasoza Itzil, or the other way around, about trade routes and chosen paths, and, oh rot this translation. Maybe Oma can figure it out. Wonder why your father kept it in his strong box."

Marita's thoughts soured suddenly. "Taverik, you don't think it was written by my father, do you?"

"No. Why would he still have it? In that case, it was probably written *to* your father. Not that it's likely."

"Then my father was Commander Farasoza Itzil."

"That's crazy!"

"It's not," she insisted, though her world was turning upside down. "Why else would he have the letter? Who is he? I have no idea where he came from. He took my mother's name, and even the warehouse deeds are in her name. Why was he murdered and the house searched? That's got to be the connection."

Taverik gave her back the letter. "A connection there may be, but don't go leaping to conclusions about it. Did your father go around calling himself most noble, most elevated, most adorable?"

"Especially adorable," she said, relaxing enough to chuckle. Even if her father was Commander Whatever, she still trusted him. She started forward, then checked. Fog closed them in. The houses towering over them looked unfamiliar and grim. "Taverik, where are we?"

"Oh, we are—huh. Just keep going uphill."

Uphill looked unfamiliar. With her first step she felt

a presence behind her. "Someone's following us," she said softly.

Taverik looked back. "Keep going."

A heavy set man leaped into the road ahead, sword in hand. Behind them two other men moved out of the mist, closing them in. Marita backed away. A low drumming filled her head. She thought it must be the blood pulsing in her ears except it went faster and faster until her heart raced to keep pace. The fog darkened and blotted out the houses on the far side of the road.

An alley yawned to her left. "Taverik," she said, "this way." She plunged into the mist, Taverik right behind her. The pounding in her ears grew until she couldn't think, but merely fled before it.

The alley ended in a wall. Marita slammed her hands against it in frustration. Taverik's breathing sounded hoarse.

A dark tendril brushed her thoughts, a new presence. She knew it, the dark being which haunted her dreams. She pushed it away but it returned, stronger. Stalking her. Bidding her to come.

"No!" She gathered strength and shoved it away again.

"Marita!" Taverik shook her. She started awake and realized she had begun to walk back down the alley. "Come on," he said, "we can get through here."

She followed him through a narrow slot between two houses, unsure anymore if this was real or if she were asleep and dreaming. The fog darkened until they both stumbled over garbage, steps and something soft that twisted away. Behind them, on each side, Marita felt the leering mind and realized it was driving them like sheep where it wanted them to go.

Taverik stumbled and she collided with him. "Damn, what *is* that thing?" he breathed.

So he felt it, too. "You're in my nightmare," she explained. "Look—that's a doorway. Try the door."

Slow footsteps closed in on each side of them. Taverik fumbled for the knob and pushed. It gave suddenly and they stumbled inside. Marita gasped, paralyzed.

They stood in the pawnshop. At the counter the wizened man looked up and smiled. "Give me the letter," he said.

"Zoji!" swore Taverik. He yanked open the door again and Marita, propelled out by his broad hand, found herself facing the wizened yellow man in the street. Behind him stood a man with a sword. Marita recognized him and wasn't surprised—Viti Karaz. He carried the eagle claw talisman in his hand. On the uphill side the heavy man with the sword materialized from the mist, trapping the two of them. "Give me the letter," Abado said.

"No," said Marita. She shifted so that she stood back to back with Taverik, and slid her hand into her sleeve, her fingers curling around her knife. The pounding in her ears increased to a roar, and her senses were drowning in blackness.

"Give me the letter," said Karaz. The eagle's claw enlarged until it gleamed in the darkness.

That was when Taverik seemed to go quietly crazy and actually began to sing aloud in a thin, strangled tenor. Marita recognized the wobbly tune: part of the litany of the temple service. The words of praise were ancient, given they said, by Zojikam himself.

The three attackers stepped back a pace, the student's eyebrows lowering into a thick line straight across his face. He raised the claw and began to chant his own litany, louder and harsher. The darkness thickened until Marita's thoughts groped for air. Through it Taverik's voice sounded, like a gold thread, or a filament of light, reminding Marita of her delirium. That night such a thread had led her to safety. Perhaps it would now. She began to whisper the words too, then gradually found strength to sing them.

The student took another step backwards, raising his voice. The pounding in Marita's ears roared until she could only tell she was singing by the vibration of her throat. She closed her eyes and pictured a filament of light driving back the darkness. The light brightened and brightened until it seemed to explode, searing brighter and whiter until it pierced her eyelids. She opened her eyes, shielding them with her hands, to find the fog swirling, coruscating with white light, flowing, rushing outward. She was staring into the face of a man, no a Being, with terrible eyes locked onto her own.

She cried out and fell against the wall, trying to escape inward.

Silence. She felt a touch on her arm and cringed. "Don't be afraid," came a curiously light voice which sounded more inside her mind than her ears. "I am sent by Zojikam, not by that other."

From Zojikam. She numbly watched as the Being leaned close to her. He breathed on her until warmth spread from the center of her soul into her cold fingers and feet.

The Being looked more like a man now, though she could see the outline of the pawn shop door through him. He didn't seem to stand on the pavement either, but be fixed on some other plane. Beyond him, their three attackers sprawled, senseless on the pavement.

Taverik was kneeling to her right, shielding his eyes against the light. "Are you an *ihiga*?" he whispered, using the Pakajan term for the spiritual beings said to serve Zojikam.

The creature turned its eyes on him, to Marita's relief. "Not exactly, but you may call me so, for there is no human word for me. Zojikam sent me with a message for you. There is a great war at present in the unseen world, and now it has spilled into yours. You must remember that though the result may be physical, the cause is spiritual and it is there this battle must be fought."

"Viti," Marita ventured humbly and flinched as the white fire in those eyes was turned once more on her. "Why doesn't Zojikam just stop it? Isn't he powerful enough?"

The fire blazed suddenly, searing her, then slowly faded. "Young woman, Zojikam has chosen to work through his creatures. He has a task for the two of you to do, just as he is fighting the otherworldly battle through me, my brothers and cousins." For a moment the *ihiga*'s face seemed to become more human, and more tired, or rather more scarred, Marita thought, though she could see no mark upon it.

"A task?" Taverik asked and she found time to be amused at the dismay in his voice, though she felt it herself.

The light returned to the Being's face. "Yes, a task, and at the right time you will know what to do. And I am sent with these instructions for you. Young man, you must not be afraid of flood, nor darkness, nor fire."

"That's what the priest said," Taverik croaked. "What does it mean?"

The creature seemed to look inward. "The answer is not given to me. You will know. And you, young woman . . ."

Marita's heart lurched in her chest. The *ihiga* drew close. "You are bitter at Zojikam, and the Dark One has gotten holds in your mind. I've asked Zojikam why he entrusts important things to such as you, but he tells me you can do it. You must never give in to these evil *mahiga*. And remember that if the abode of a *mahiga* is broken, it will disperse and be of no use to the foolish ones who try to use them to their own ends. Do it now."

"Now?" Marita echoed, bewildered.

The *ihiga* gestured to the jar lying on its side just beyond Abado's outstretched hand. With shaking fingers, Marita lifted it and looked inquiringly at the *ihiga* and received a nod. She smashed it on the pavement.

With a screaming noise the darkness rolled back, and suddenly the alley returned to early afternoon on a misty day. "Remember," the *ihiga* said. "Use all the tools Zojikam gives you. Now you must go."

Taverik got to his feet and looked down at the three still men. "What about them?"

"Poor fools," said the *ihiga*. "They worship a creature and ignore the one who created it. But their time is not yet up. You must go whilst I hold back your enemy. Go."

Taverik took a step away, and reluctantly, Marita joined him. Suddenly she hated to leave this powerful creature who seemed to know so much and who could disperse the evil that had closed them in. "Stay! Please stay," she cried and leaped forward to seize his arm. Her hands closed on air. The *ihiga* was gone. The world seemed flat and dead, the alley cold and sordid, with fog creeping in once more.

The student stirred and half sat up.

"Marko, come on!" Taverik said.

"Go!" insisted the voice inside her head.

Marita turned and ran.

Chapter 19

Donato Zandro

"Absolutely not!" said Donato Zandro. Despite the cold fog, perspiration dripped from his chin. He glared up at Malenga—so damned smug on his huge bay horse. "I told you, I've done all I'm going to do."

Malenga's voice hardened. "Perhaps you don't fully understand the position you are in. Your behavior affects the safety of you, your business, your two sons."

"You leave them out of it!"

"They are in it already."

Zandro ground his teeth in fury. He'd always been proud of his ability to get his own way—it showed strength. But now his anger beat impotently against Malenga's smooth marble surface, and Zandro had no other resources to fall back on. He saw his own folly with a clarity that made him want to throw up. He hated Malenga. He hated himself for a fool. He hated his family because soon they'd realize he'd been a fool.

The bay arched his neck and pawed elegantly, as if impatient to hurry on to more important things. Beyond Malenga the donkey stood patiently in the cloaking fog, its saddlebags full of gold, the last, Zandro had hoped, that he'd give Soza.

"Look," said Malenga soothingly, "it is, after all, such a little thing. Just house your master for a few days and ask no questions. That's not hard, is it?"

Zandro felt like a tongue-tied Pakajan bumpkin and hated that too.

"I'm asking you. Is it?"

"No," he muttered.

"You must, of course, prevent questions from your sons and household." Malenga's voice grew edged. "For their own safety, of course."

Zandro thought feverishly: Chado knew and would cooperate. But Taverik. Taverik would ask questions. He'd have to get him out of the house. Damn him—how was it you could despise someone and love him desperately at the same time?

Malenga smiled as winningly as he used to in the early days before Zandro had swallowed the hook. "Come, friend, you still have doubts," he said sweetly. "Put them at ease. Your reward comes soon. Soza will remember it was you who provided the means for his glory. I must remind you that when he has the city you shall have money, you will be a viti with your choice of high-born maids for your sons to wed. Perhaps even for you."

"For me?" asked Zandro despite his determination to remain sullenly silent.

"Certainly for you. Soza soon, very soon, will be able to look on your case with personal consideration. He is most generous. True, Dula Familo rejected both your sons, but perhaps my niece, a lovely girl . . ."

"Your niece—" Zandro's breathing quickened as he considered the heady possibility. For Chado? No, perhaps for Taverik. He should try higher than Malenga for Chado, who was more cooperative. "Well, all right," he said grudgingly. "But this is the last thing I'll do."

"We'll see," said Malenga. "Expect him late tonight then. I'll be there tomorrow morning for a meeting with him. We'll need a private room. What about that son of yours?"

"Which one?" Zandro said, though he knew full well.

"The one who doesn't share your ambitions. The one who made fools of the Familos. Make sure he isn't around or I will have to take matters into my own hands."

"He won't be," Zandro snapped. This last irritated him more than all the others. Taverik was Donato Zandro's own business, and if the boy didn't want any part of this affair he didn't have to be involved. Hog swill, all of Malenga's promises. Well, he was forced into this one, but he'd find a way out of the next. Without another word he jerked the mule's head around and kicked him toward the road.

Taverik

Flood, darkness and fire, Taverik thought, his forehead pressed against the hard wood of the prayer bench. If only he could return to the safety of his former materialistic world.

When he and Marko had won free of the alley, Taverik had headed straight to the temple to sort it all out. He was slightly surprised when Marko had come, too, but it did make sense—one doesn't face both a *mahiga* and an *ihiga* in one hour then merely go home to dinner. He'd been relieved to find the sanctuary empty, and dropping onto the nearest bench he'd pleaded silently, in the most unprayerlike language, for Zojikam to leave him alone. He hated this constant awareness of the other world he'd been experiencing lately, and the thought of taking part in some kind of spirit world battle made his insides twist.

And yet . . . the face of the messenger had sent quivering longings through him. Longings for what he didn't know, perhaps a kind of rightness, but that word didn't explain it well either. When the *ihiga* had appeared, he'd fallen to his knees without knowing what he was doing, just drinking in the terrifying, beautiful face of the messenger. A messenger for which there was no word in his language; at that thought alone the hair on his arms stood up, and he again felt that wave of yearning. Perhaps Marko could explain it. She and Oma were both clever with words.

Marko knelt to his right, her face buried in her hands. Her black hair had fallen forward off her neck so that her skin looked creamy white by contrast. His fingers longed to touch her, to see if that smooth skin felt as soft as it looked, to see what her hair felt like, to pull her against him so he could comfort her, and she him.

Like a kick in the stomach, he remembered. He had to leave Illiga. Where he'd go he had no idea. Novato, he supposed. But now came the time he'd been putting off. He had to ask Marko to go with him, or perhaps lose her forever. He broke into a cold sweat at the thought and squeezed shut his eyes. Right now, he should ask her to marry him. He'd put it off all day long because once he asked her and she refused, that would be it.

"Young Zandro," said the priest behind him.

Taverik looked around. Marko lifted her head from her hands and gave the priest an owlish, wary look.

"I have a message here for you. I told the boy that this is the last place to look for any of the Zandros, but he insisted you'd come."

The priest held up a wrinkled slip of paper. Seeing his gnarled hand, Taverik had a sudden, vivid memory of how those callused fingers felt as they curled over his cheekbones a week ago, when the priest had touched him to bless him and had instead received prophetic words—words which the *ihiga* had repeated identically. A shiver rippled across his stomach.

"I apologize for my behavior that Friday night," the priest said, somehow knowing his thoughts. "Later I realized I'd tasted no evil coming from you, despite the odd nature of the prophesy. I will bless you now."

"But no more prophesies," Taverik growled, only half-joking.

The old man's eyes twinkled. "They *are* rather uncomfortable, are they not? However, I do not seem to have much control over them." But his blessing, which included Marko, remained safely unremarkable, and he at last gave Taverik the note before busying himself at the altar. Taverik ripped it open eagerly. *B. not in Illiga today,* Nikilo had written. *Leave tomorrow morning. See me first.*

Marko was still watching the priest. "What was he talking about?"

"A long story," Taverik said. "Do you remember asking me what had happened last night?"

She gave him a quick look. "Yes."

"After I left you, I went back up into the balcony to get my cloak, and I found my father talking with Viti Malenga."

"Malenga? At a guild?"

"Yes. And—"

Two women entered and began mopping the floors and dusting the benches. He couldn't tell her now. "Look," he said urgently, "what are you going to do now, Marko?"

"Go back to the guild, get Whitey and go home."

"I'll go with you. I have something really important to say."

"All right," Marko said and got up. He went with her, turning over and over in his mind how to phrase it.

"Taverik!"

His father's bull roar. Taverik looked over his shoulder and saw his father riding up the hill behind them. Oh, rot, he didn't want Marko entangled with his father if he could help it. "Marko," he said quickly, "you go ahead. I don't know how long this will take. I'll come to your house when I can. But listen, it will be tonight. It's got to be tonight. Wait for me."

She gave him a long, considering look from those gray eyes. "What's the matter?"

"Taverik, you stop when I talk to you!" yelled his father.

"Go. I'll explain tonight."

With a last glance at his father she shrugged and walked on across the plaza. Taverik headed back to his father, anger thickening his face. He clenched his teeth against reckless words which fought to get out, but which might spoil everything.

Mud coated the legs and belly of his father's mule, and sweat roughened its winter coat. Taverik noted its rolling eyes and flattened ears with distaste. "Taking out your frustrations on the animals again?" he asked.

"None of your mouth." His father dropped his reins and crossed his arms. Mud stained the hem of his surcoat. "I want to talk to you."

"Wish I could say the same."

His father's face purpled, then oddly, achieved a smile. "About yesterday," Zandro said, gaze lingering on Taverik's black eye. "I'm sorry. I overreacted."

"What do you want from me this time?" Taverik asked.

"I have your future at heart and you give me lip. What I want is for you to obey me for once, so that I can secure a good life for you. Do you wish always to be a despised merchant, catering to the viti, marrying another little despised woman from your class? Don't you want to rise in the world? Don't you want money, power, status? What if you could take your pick from any woman in Illiga? Malenga's niece?"

"Never saw her," Taverik said sourly.

"Me neither," Zandro admitted. "But just think about it!"

Taverik thought instead about Marko, wondering what she would look like in a dress, with her hair pulled back to expose that white neck and her delicate ears.

His father's voice changed to a rare coaxing tone which brought all Taverik's suspicions alert. "If you would just listen to me and not ask questions for once, you could have all these things."

"And prison, too. I told you years ago I wanted nothing of your crooked schemes."

"You throw away every opportunity I give you. I worked hard and spent money so Familo would consider you or Chado for Dula. Marriage with her was handed to you on a platter. And she suddenly rejects you! Malenga says she called you a horrid twitch. *What* did you do?"

"I went to dinner, just like you said, Father," Taverik said innocently.

"Malenga is suspicious!" roared Donato. "He's met you now and knows you aren't!"

"Father, please don't volunteer our private business to the entire street." Taverik stopped and looked him straight in the eye. "Tell me what Malenga has to do with it."

His father's mouth opened and shut, opened and shut. "Never mind," he said at last. "I'm sending you on a buyer's trip. To, ah, um, to Perijo."

"To Perijo," Taverik echoed. "Are you crazy? It's *winter*!"

"I don't care when it is. I need, ah, spices. Yes, spices. The more the better. Get a head start on the trade this spring."

"No. No one tries to cross the passes in winter."

"There's no snow yet. Leave tomorrow morning. No, leave tonight. I want you to come with me now and pack. You can get halfway to the foothills before dark."

Taverik scowled. "Why are you trying to get rid of me?"

"Don't ask questions. Just do what I say."

"I've heard that one all my life." And, he thought bitterly, Nikilo must be right in his suspicions. His father was a traitor to Illiga. He nearly choked on the rage and disgust that clogged his throat. Don't hate, Nikilo had said. How could he not hate?

If his father wanted him out of the way so badly, it must mean some part of his scheming would take place tonight. Well, he was going to discover exactly what it was. He'd pack all right—everything he owned. He'd leave the mules with Nikilo for the night, then slip home to discover just what his father was up to. He'd tell Nikilo in the morning, collect the mules and leave. For good.

Would Marko go with him?

"Well?" demanded his father.

Taverik looked up blankly. "Well what?"

"I'm cursed with a fool! Go home and pack!"

"All right, Father," he said with a sweet smile that made Zandro scowl with his own suspicions. "I'll pack."

Abado

Raw early dusk had fallen by the time the knock sounded on the back door of the pawnshop. "Late," Abado said, straightening from the overcooked meal at the fireplace. Karaz, who had sulked ever since the fiasco in the alley, jerked his head irritably at the door.

Abado opened it, feeling the same quickening of his blood he always got whenever the agash came. He stepped back and prostrated himself on the carpet. "Good evening, Abado," said the agash. "Karaz, is everything ready?"

"Yes, Father," said Karaz.

"Abado?"

Abado looked up in time to see Karaz scowling at him. The boy hated it whenever the agash seemed to prefer Abado's opinions. Jealousy. Abado had served Farasoza Itzil since before the boy was born, before Itzil had become agash, and even before the Black Eagle had entered him. They knew each other well and trusted each other. And this, Abado knew: the boy would never be the equal of his father.

"All is ready," Abado said, climbing smoothly to his feet and venturing to look into the agash's face. His master's eyes were his own just now, and merely showed guarded approval. Behind him stood one of his wesh-agashes, the one who had built the army in the pass this year—an ugly brute with a huge black beard and rings in his ears like a barbaric Pakajan.

The agash noticed Abado's glance. He gestured to the wesh-agash who brought out a small jar. Abado took it reverently, feeling his skin crawl as usual when handling the abode of powerful *mahigas*. How could the Pakajans think them *ikiji*? And how strong the agash must be to be able to control such beings. He placed it on the shelf where the other jar should have been, wondering what the agash would say when he learned about this afternoon. "Will you eat, my master?" he said softly.

"Immediately." The agash reclined on a cushion and gestured the wesh-agash to another. Tlele brought them water to wash with while Abado served up plates of his spicy food, silently listening to their talk.

"Now, Karaz," said the agash, "tell me about the so tragic demise of Akusa Ormea."

Karaz smiled wolfishly. "The Ormean refuges, helped on of course by our people, rioted this morning. Tlele's pamphlets gave them a wonderfully muddled idea that Balanji himself is to blame for her death."

The agash chuckled. "What could be better?"

"I'll tell you what was better," Karaz said. "When our man did in the Ormean woman, he very nearly got Balanji at the same time. Wounded him in the side!"

At that the agash threw back his head and gave a great bark of laughter. "Bring me this fellow," he cried. "I wish to reward him!"

Karaz shook his head. "He was killed in the attempt."

"Pity. But no matter. Abado, is this not a good sign?"

"Excellent, my agash," said Abado, proud to be remembered. "Will you take wine?"

"Thank you. The pamphlets worked then, Karaz?"

"Father, they were an important key. When I first came here, the city was happy and loyal. The university students were fat, silly Massadarans with no reason to be discontent. I could do nothing there. But the pamphlets reached the others, the Pakajans, the Massadaran lower classes, chafing against *Sadra* Laws, unable to get ahead. The pamphlets even stirred up those disgusting merchants to an extent."

Abado knew it useless to expect Karaz to give credit to anyone else. He cleared his throat, then said, "I had the idea for the pamphlets when I saw how much every class in the city reads. They are always going mad for this poet or that philosopher. They even hold dinners to discuss them."

"Excellent, Abado."

Abado smiled blandly into the boy's narrow-eyed look. "But," Karaz said nastily, "Balanji caught on. He's closed down all the presses trying to find us."

The agash lifted his hand. "You can stop now anyway. We will have the city in a week."

Karaz straightened. "A week!"

"My wesh-agash here has troops a day's ride from the city. Karaz, how many of our men are in the city now?"

"More than we ever hoped. They fill the slums and streets. Who will slay Balanji?"

"The man is here already, and just awaits the signal. I will take a day or two to inspect the city and position the men. When I give the signal, the wesh-agash will attack both river gates, the men inside will attack from here. Balanji's death will enable us to take the fortress. He thinks me still penned in Ormea."

"Yes, what about Balanji's army besieging Ormea?" asked Abado.

"My wesh-agash will see that none return."

The wesh-agash bared his teeth.

"Father," said Karaz hesitantly. Abado stiffened; here it came. "Two merchants brought a letter to Abado to translate from Bcacmat today. A letter from the Tlath to you."

"What?" The agash's eyes pinned Abado to the wall.

"Yes, master," he said trembling. "I think it was the missing letter."

"What did it say?"

"The Tlath was pleased with Vosa, but wanted the northern trade route instead. Asked you to get a northern city immediately."

"And you translated it!"

"Master, I didn't know what to do, so I stalled, said I had to look up a word, then I came in here and asked the young master what to do. He said he'd take care of it."

To his relief those blazing eyes shifted to Karaz. "Well?" the agash said.

"Father, they left before we could trap them in the shop. So we took the jar, summoned the Black Eagle and the *mahigas* and stalked them. We trapped them in the alley in front of the pawn shop, but they got away."

"*They got away?*"

Karaz's throat bobbed and Abado almost laughed aloud to watch him squirm. "They, ah, called on Zojikam, Viti, and there was something like a million lightning bolts, and the next thing I knew I was just lying there and they were all gone. And—the jar was broken."

"The jar was broken," repeated the agash, and Karaz gathered his feet under himself, ready to duck. "Who were they?"

"That's the funny thing," Karaz said. "I'll swear the one with the letter was a woman disguised as a man."

The agash hissed. Abado shrank back; the agash's eyes had changed again. The Black Eagle glared unwinkingly out and the agash's movements had gotten jerky and random as they always did when *it* was there. "A woman disguised as a man?"

"I'm sure of it."

"At long last. A piece of unfinished business shall be closed."

"What's this all about?"

The agash was back in his eyes again. "Long ago a letter was stolen from me. Its contents have the power to ruin me, make it obvious I am Bcacmat, unite this squabbling peninsula against me. Yes, I have had great success, but while this letter was at large I could not rest easy, and I could not let anyone who knew its contents survive. But two of these people escaped me, two women. I've sought them these years. Brooded over them. And at times I could sense one and draw her. I almost had her, but she escaped and the trail grew dim. But lately, oh, lately, I've felt I could almost reach out and pluck her. And now I know what this afternoon was all about."

"You knew about this afternoon?" Karaz faltered.

"I felt the Black Eagle's power go out, and I went with it until I could almost see this woman. I'm certain I shall know her when I face her."

Abado felt admiration mingled with fear. What a man his master had become! Perhaps greater even than the Tlath himself. "Master, how long will you stay with us?"

"I won't stay here. Malenga has arranged for me to live with one of our Illigan supporters in the center of the city. He will be very useful to me this next week. Karaz!"

The boy started. "Yes, Father?"

"That letter must not become public. Find it, and find that woman." His voice sharpened. "This time do not blunder."

Chapter 20

Marita

From the crowded stables Marita knew the guild still met, but she ordered Whitey saddled anyway. Too much had happened; she needed quiet to sort it out. But first the task she dreaded: telling Sahra all she'd done without her sister's knowledge. She wasn't looking forward to that at all.

The wind began to rise as she rode home, blowing off the fog with colder air. In the courtyard behind the house the long branches of the apple tree whipped and rattled. She settled Whitey in his stall then went upstairs with the firm resolute tread of someone with an unpleasant duty to discharge.

Sahra, wearing a shapeless black wool surcoat over her dress, sat at her table, tilting the Gentle Philosopher's book toward the lamp. She looked up as Marita came in and her face paled. "What's wrong?"

"I think," Marita said, crossing to the fire and

unwinding her cloak, "I think I made a mistake in judgment."

Sahra stilled. "What do you mean?"

"I copied the Bcacmat letter last night." Sahra looked blank and Marita added, "The one in Papa's strong box, remember? Taverik and I took it to be translated."

"You never told me about this."

Marita shrugged. "I didn't think you would mind. You never seem to care about anything these days."

"Try *asking* me if I mind!" Sahra shut the book and scraped back her chair. "You think you run everything, don't you?"

"I wish I wasn't forced to."

"You're the one who makes the plans. You always say, 'We'll do this, we'll do that.' No, better yet," Sahra amended, snapping her fingers with each phrase. "You say, 'I did this, I did that, now what do you think, Sahra?' "

Marita's vision narrowed with anger. "If you didn't bury your nose in a book all day, I might be able to ask you what you think."

"Much you care what I think or feel!"

"Well, what about you? Do you ever ask *me* what I've been doing? Care if I've had a rough time? I need support, too!"

"Ah, so that's it," Sahra said. "You're the breadwinner. We must all drop everything to attend your every whim."

It was like old times in Papa's house, when the two of them had fought, screeched and pulled each other's hair, then turned as one on anyone foolish enough to try to separate them. Marita caught Sahra's arm. "You selfish pig! I need help, not your sulky silence. It's hard for me out there, and it's dangerous, too. But what I'm doing is keeping us afloat. We'd be in the slums still, begging, if not for me. Or dying a slow death scrubbing rich men's floors. So before you start sneering about my behavior you better think of the benefits!"

"Be grateful to you, you mean?" Sahra stamped her foot. "I'll tell you how you are. You're all dressed up just like a man, then you come home and expect service just like a man."

"That's not true!"

Sahra grabbed the Gentle Philosopher's book and shook it under Marita's nose. "And maybe you bring me a little gift, just like Papa used to do."

"Shut up!"

"No, I won't shut up!" Sahra threw the book at Marita, who caught it automatically. "Papa's dead," she shouted. "Dead! And I don't want you for a father!"

She ran out, slamming the door. "Dammit!" Marita cried and hurled the book after her. It hit the door and clattered to the floor. Marita spun on her heel, shaking with rage.

A timid knock. "What!" she snapped.

Bibi peeked in, her pink face screwed up with the courage it took her to interrupt at that moment. Marita controlled her irritation. "What is it Bibi?"

"Taverik's below," she gasped. "He wants to see you."

"Tell him to go away—" She stopped; Taverik had said he wanted to tell her something important that night. "Oh, damn, tell him to come up."

Her face felt unpleasantly swollen. Fighting for control, she rested her burning forehead on the cold glass of the window. Damn Sahra! And yet, she admitted wryly, she'd wanted Sahra to talk. Well, now she'd gotten an earful, and perhaps rightly so. Perhaps she had been patronizing. At least they were talking now. Gradually her breathing slowed.

Recognizing Taverik's step at the study door, she turned and found he'd stooped to pick up the book. "Poor Uncle Nik," he said, and tossed it to the table.

She ignored the cryptic comment. "You look cold," she said, and pushed wearily off the window sill. "Stir up the fire, would you?"

Taverik merely nodded and pulled a log from the box. He seemed more abstracted than usual, Marita thought as she bent to drag a bottle of brandy from the chest. She straightened with a groan. "Curse that pawn broker, anyway," she grumbled.

Taverik brushed bark off his hands and sank into a chair. "We," he said, "act like a pair of battle-scarred old veterans."

"We *are* battle-scarred veterans," she said as she poured the brandy. "Considering the last month or so."

She handed him a glass and sat down, enjoying the easy comradeship between them. Taverik studied her with an intensity that made her shift uneasily. "What were you going to tell me?" she asked.

His eyes slid away to the fire, and he gathered himself as if for some task. "Marko," he said, "I have to leave Illiga."

"Leave?" she echoed, dismayed.

"Tomorrow morning," he said. He cleared his throat and went on in a rush. "It makes me realize how much you've come to mean to me, and what my life would be like if you weren't in it and, oh damn, I love you and want you to marry me."

She stared at him, stunned. "Me? Marry you?"

He leaned forward and took her hand. "It would solve everything. We could go to a new city and start again. You wouldn't have to hide anymore."

She pulled her hand away. "No, it's impossible."

"Why?"

"Oma, Bibi."

"They could live with us. They'd be safer."

"I never thought, I never imagined—" Marita felt suddenly trapped and her heart began to thud. "I had no idea you felt this way."

"I was afraid you'd run like a rabbit if you knew."

Marita retreated a safe distance to the window and sat on the sill. "All this time I thought you were attracted to Sah—to Oma."

"She's very pretty, and very smart. But you are you." He gave her the crooked grin he used when he wanted people to think he didn't care a hoot. Her heart tightened. He was serious, then.

"I've seen the women you've been attracted to," she said slowly. "I'm nothing like them. You don't really want to marry me. You've never even seen me in a dress."

"True," he acknowledged. His eyes gleamed suddenly. "Go try on one of Oma's dresses and we'll see how I like it."

She snorted. "Go jump in the Giss!"

"As I observed," he said with a rueful laugh, "you are you."

Marita stared down at her boots trying to sort herself out. Might as well try to sort out a whirlpool though. Her thoughts were a jumble of half-finished impulses with emotions seething underneath, making her want to cry and laugh at the same time. This was too much, coming right after being chased by a *mahiga*, rescued by an *ihiga*, and a passionate argument with her sister. She rubbed her forehead with the palm of her hand trying to think what to do or say.

Taverik got up and stood in front of her. "Let me put it an easier way. Do you love me?"

She searched his familiar face—the wide cheekbones, faint freckles, anxious blue eyes—could she bear it if he went away? If she never saw him again? She shivered inwardly at the thought. It was like peering down a long, empty corridor going nowhere. "Yes," she said. "I think I love you. But . . ."

"But?"

She frowned, trying to word the gnawing reservation she felt inside. "But, if I marry you, I shall have to wear skirts once more. That means I could no longer go where I please and do what I please. I couldn't go riding without an escort. I bought this house with money I earned myself; how can I tell you what that means to me? And I could no longer belong to the guild. My opinions will be gently dismissed. I'll lose my freedom and a good part of my hard-won respect."

Taverik's cheekbones stood out in his white face. "I would always respect you."

She held out her hands. "Don't you see," she said, "what you like in me now is a companion to gallop across the countryside with, visit taverns with, to get into scrapes with. But Illiga's women don't do those things. So you'll do them by yourself, and when you come home, you won't have a fragile feminine beauty to make up the difference. You'll just have me, and that's . . ." She swallowed and gestured down at the muddy surcoat she hadn't had time to change.

Seizing her by the shoulders, he said roughly, "You're what I want."

She gave a disbelieving gesture. "There's another thing."

"Not *another*!" He let her go, his face registering comic dismay.

"Soza. If I marry you I will only be dragging someone I love into danger."

"No problem. I'm already in trouble with Soza."

The shadow had returned to his eyes. "What do you mean?" she asked. "Is that what you started to tell me? Is that why you're leaving?"

"I found out last night. My father has been financing Soza." His voice turned bitter. "He's a traitor who will lead my family straight to the gallows. Both my father and my uncle beg me to leave town, though for different reasons."

Marita inhaled. "So that was it. I was sure something had happened. I'm sorry."

He shook his head and paced away. "I'm the one who's insane," he said. "I'm asking you to marry me when it will soon be a race between Balanji and Soza for my hide. And *you* say you don't want to get me in trouble!"

"Where is Soza?" she asked sharply, controlling the impulse to look over her shoulder. Funny the power even of his name to set her heart to pounding uncomfortably.

"Still besieged in Ormea, I suppose. Tomorrow, Uncle Nikilo must inform Balanji of my father's, uh, activities, and he wants me to leave town first."

Marita suddenly felt ill with fear. Balanji would have no mercy to traitors, and he'd never believe Taverik had nothing to do with Soza. "Yes, you've got to leave. Soon."

But life without him would be so hard, so lonely, so laughterless. Then marry him and go too. She couldn't. She must. Oh, what should she do?

Taverik had been watching her face. "Look," he said gently. "You're tired, and this took you by surprise. I'll come back in the morning before I leave. We can talk then. I'll tell you where I'm heading, so you can join me later if you need more time."

"All right," she said, gratefully. "Did you manage to get a letter of transferal?"

He laughed ruefully and shook his head. "Don't want my father to know what I'm doing. I think I can make it without. Besides, I'm going to change my name to Tazur."

"I'll go to the guild extra early and get one," Marita said, and when his face lit up, warned, "Just in case. I know what it's like to try to join a strange guild without one."

Taverik nodded, accepting it. She was thankful for his backing off, though she could tell from the way he was looking at her, how much it cost him. She knew, too, how hard he found it to talk about things that really mattered to him. Long ago he'd learned to hide them. Marita stretched out her hand. "Thank you."

He caught it and stepped close, looking at her face as if to memorize it. Again, as in the pawn shop, her senses flooded with his broad-shouldered presence and the quickening sound of his breathing. The scent of his perspiration mingled with that of leather and wet wool, making her heart hammer for some crazy reason. She stared, transfixed, at him.

His lips landed lopsidedly beside her nose. Marita stiffened—she'd never been kissed before—but he pulled her closer and found her lips, the stubble of his beard scraping her cheek. It wouldn't hurt to respond this once, she thought, then gradually didn't think at all.

After a timeless space he released her. She backed up, encountered the window sill, and sat down hard. "I'll be back tomorrow morning," he said, and was gone. Cold wind rattled the window.

Chapter 21

Marita

Marita watched from the window until Taverik was out of sight, then flung herself into the carved chair. "Oh, blast," she said shakily to the ceiling. "Now what do I do?"

She scowled and tried to make sense of her roiling emotions, but found she could barely define them, let alone make sense of them. What would it be like to link her fate to another person? Frightening, the loss of control. But the other person was Taverik, who she admitted she loved. Yet how could she just up and leave, with her business at last supporting her. And did she really want to be linked to the Zandros, always fighting the machinations of Donato and Chado? Look where it had brought Taverik. Even if he did begin anew in another city, she doubted he would ever totally be free of his family. Besides, she didn't *want* to leave. She looked around the low-beamed room and felt her throat thicken. She'd bought the house with money she'd earned herself, and furnished each room with money she'd earned herself . . . how could she abandon it now?

But Soza. He had spies in the city, therefore he might just be coming here. Better to leave in good order than to have to flee once more with nothing. And yet—

Bibi knocked and entered. "Dinner is on the table, Kali," she said.

Marita's stomach clenched. "I'm not hungry. Eat without me."

"Kali?"

"Eat without me, I said!"

Bibi backed out hastily. Marita groaned and rubbed her forehead. Why did she have to decide tonight? What would Sahra say? If only she'd be reasonable so they could talk it over.

She liked her freedom. To go back to skirts and a constricted life seemed agony to her. But she might never see Taverik again. And that also seemed agony. Soza—Taverik now had a link with Soza that made her profoundly uneasy. It brought her enemy too close for her to relax. So, leave. Ah, she couldn't! If only she didn't have to decide by tomorrow.

Marita sank lower in the chair, distantly aware of the sounds of dinner, Sahra's murmurs and Bibi's monosyllabic replies. Later she heard Sahra's step on the stairs, then directly overhead. Downstairs, Bibi rattled plates and glasses. Marita felt lonely, irritable, and, she had to admit, frightened. Her thoughts churned like the Ao in flood. At her elbow the brandy bottle still sat. She poured a glass and drank it quickly, shuddering as it went down.

Get up, she told herself. Think this through rationally. Instead she poured another glass. The house grew silent and still she sat.

The chiming of the temple clock roused her—midnight already. The door opened quietly and a glimmering light filled the room. Marita looked up wearily. Sahra.

"Your fire's out," Sahra said. She wore a brown wool shawl over her nightgown, the same gown that Marita had been put in the night they called in that doctor. Lifting her candle higher, Sahra stared in dismay at the nearly empty brandy bottle. Marita glowered back.

"Bibi says you refused to eat," Sahra said. "She told me you've been here all evening." She shivered and set down the candle. "I'll make up the fire."

Go away, Marita thought. This sudden bustling around irritated her. But the fire, she conceded as Sahra stood up, did feel good. The room had gotten steadily colder. Sahra went to the door. Marita heard her talking to Bibi. Something about meat and bread. A conspiracy then, this visit. Her shoulders hunched defensively. "Don't bother," she called, feeling the full force of her earlier hurt feelings. "I don't expect service just like a man."

Her sister made a soft noise in her throat. "Oh, Mari, I'm sorry. I'm a pig for saying those things, and I've come to apologize."

Marita suddenly heard and despised the sulkiness dripping from her voice. She'd made a mistake drinking all that brandy; she could barely think, but her troubles still sat on her shoulders. She made an effort: "Just like old times, wasn't it?"

Sahra laughed sheepishly. "Yes, it was, and it felt good, too. Guess we're both tense." She curled up on the padded couch and wrapped the shawl around herself. "When I stopped being mad, I thought about everything we said, and I want to explain. You're right, I do read all the time. I can forget our troubles in a book."

She twisted the fringe of the shawl into tight knots. "Marita," she blurted. "I'm terrified something will happen to you! What would I do then? How would I live? When Taverik brought you home almost dead, I thought I'd go crazy. And you've been involved in three other incidents since then."

"Four," Marita said mechanically.

"I can't take it any more!" Sahra buried her face in the brown wool and sobbed.

"Oh, Sahra, I'm sorry." Marita moved to the couch and put her arms around her sister. "I didn't know. When you'd be silent for days at a time, I thought that you were just trying to irritate me."

"I *was* trying to irritate you. It's all so complicated." Sahra laughed wryly through her tears. "I wanted to know what was going on, but afraid to know at the same time. I felt so useless. I resented you for it. I guess it was because I'm afraid."

"Afraid?"

"You wouldn't understand because you are so brave and able to cope."

"But I'm afraid, too," Marita said.

"Oh, go on."

"No, really. I only have to hear Soza's name to start trembling like a fool, and you know my nightmares. I keep trying to make us invisible, hide us, move us on, run away. And it doesn't work."

Sahra looked thunderstruck. "I had no idea. I thought you *liked* this life."

"Well, I do. Usually. Oh, like you said, it's complicated. But I'm frightened, and I suppose that even this—" Marita pointed at the brandy bottle, feeling insecure at all this self-exposure "—even this was an attempt to run away. And it didn't work. *The eagle chased the hawk, but wherever the hawk fled, the eagle was there before it.*"

"Maybe," Sahra said thoughtfully, "maybe the time has come to stop running away. Face Soza."

She broke off as Bibi came in carrying a tray with cold meat and fruit. Bibi set out the plates, her face growing troubled as she moved the brandy bottle away from Marita's elbow. Marita's eyes met Sahra's and they smiled, and when Bibi had gone, Sahra hoisted a slab of chicken. "Let's start over, Marita. I'll carry my share of the load."

"And I'll try not to patronize. And I'll not act without consulting you anymore." Marita took a deep breath. "Which means I have something else to confess."

"What was that?"

"I told Taverik our true last name."

Sahra's eyes widened. "Why? Are you sure that was safe?"

Suddenly Marita wasn't sure. "He said he'd make quiet inquiries and find out who Papa was."

"Papa was Papa. Wasn't he?"

"Don't you ever wonder why all the deeds were in Mother's name? And why he took Mother's name? And why we knew who Mother's relatives were but not his? And why someone hated him enough to massacre his household and chase us?"

"I suppose I must have. But there was no answer, and I put it away. I don't like to think of that time.

But you're right, it's odd. Did Taverik bring the answer this afternoon?"

"No. He asked me to marry him."

Sahra drew back. "Marry you," she faltered.

Cursing her tactlessness, Marita nodded. She told Sahra all Taverik had said about his father, adding, "He has to leave Illiga tomorrow morning and asked me—all of us—to go with him."

"Did you say yes, then?"

Marita saw the dismay in her sister's face. "I said I didn't know."

Sahra looked relieved. With reason, Marita told herself. Crazy to think it would work. All the same, a small knot of unhappiness tightened in her stomach.

"Just in case," she said, "I think I will go to the guild first thing tomorrow and get a letter of transferal, so we can join the Textile Guild in another city without a year's waiting period."

"Oh, please, let's not move again. Not unless we have to."

"It's just in case, Sahra." Marita clenched her hands together wondering if she were acting now out of fear. "What Taverik said about Soza and the Bcacmat translation makes me uneasy."

"I meant to ask, what did it say?"

Marita pulled it out, crumpled and limp, from her pocket. Sahra took it and frowned at it. "Word for word," she said in disgust. "Let's see if we can make it more legible."

In her own element now, she went to the table and rummaged for paper. Marita watched over her shoulder, grateful to have the old Sahra back again. "Bcacmat must have a different word order than Massadaran or Pakajan," she said.

"Let's see," said Sahra. " 'To my faithful favored servant—' "

"Agash means commander, I think."

"Good. *To my faithful favored servant Commander Itzil Farasoza. You have done well but I grow impatient. I want more*—no, it must be, *I wanted more by now. I should not*—double negative there—*need to answer your questions. Why have*, hmm, double interrogatives, too, *why have you veered from the path I chose? Leave Vosa immediately. Go to Illiga, Perijo or Novato. The northern trade route is my desire. Do not continue improvising plans. These plans incite my displeasure. Answer me at once. The most noble, most elevated most*—adorable? He sounds anything but adorable. Why are you smiling, Mar?"

"Because that's what Taverik said. Must mean worshipped."

Sahra shuddered. "*Ikiji*. Who is he? Why no signature?"

"Because," Marita said, remembering with a grimace. She told Sahra everything that had happened that afternoon. Everything. Sahra listened, her mouth open. "You saw an *ihiga*?"

"It said we could call it that because human language as yet had no word for it. It said there is a battle going on in the unseen world and it's spilling over to our world. And it said Zojikam had a task for us but we'd only know what it would be at the right time. It told Taverik not to be afraid of flood, darkness or fire, and it told me that if the abode of evil *mahigas* is broken they disperse and are no more use. And it said to use all the tools Zojikam had given me, and then it told me to break that jar."

Sahra looked rapturous. "I wish I could have seen it. Marita, aren't you afraid?"

"Yes, I'm afraid!" she said indignantly. "I just haven't had time to think about it. Listen, Sahra, do you suppose that Papa could have been the Agash Itzil Farasoza? Or that he wrote the letter?"

"It's possible, I suppose. But this I know: Papa was good. He loved Zojikam, and I trust him. Maybe Taverik will find out for us."

"If he has time." Despite Sahra's positiveness, Marita wasn't sure she wanted to know who Papa was. And that, she supposed, was again running away.

The tower clock chimed two. Sahra yawned. "We'll think better in the morning. Good night." She picked up her candle and drifted out.

And that was that. Marita sighed wearily. Behind her eyes she felt the faint beginnings of the headache to come. Damn the brandy! She shoved aside the desk and hid the translation in the strong box, then trudged upstairs.

The wind rattled the closed shutters. So sharply cold had her room become she could see the cloud of her breath against the yellow candlelight. Marry Taverik, she thought, pulling off her surcoat. Could he really love her? Would he love her even in a woman's dress and role? A small mirror in a red-painted frame hung by the window. She took it down, brought it to the candle and looked. Really looked.

Her eyes stared back, gray and troubled. How, she wondered, could a person be in such turmoil inside, yet so quiet on the outside. She glanced down her shivering, lean, small-breasted length and shook her head. "Fool. You're a fool, and so is he. It would never work. Tell him so tomorrow."

She nodded her head in agreement with herself then slammed her fist against the wall. "Damn Taverik and his kisses!" She prowled the room restlessly. He'd awakened something in her with that kiss, an unaccustomed stirring of a part of her, denied and dormant all these years.

And, she acknowledged, the thought of living without Taverik made her desperately unhappy. "Zojikam," she said aloud. "What should I do? Should I go?"

The wind roared and the shutter slammed back. Marita whirled and gasped, then laughed weakly. She went to close it, then paused to look out, fingers curled around the cold latch. The cypresses at the top of the garden tossed fretfully in the wind's blasts. Behind a scrim of clouds the moon shone pale. Surrounding it wavered a halo of watery luminescence. "Ring around the moon," she murmured. "Storm coming."

Wrapping a blanket around herself, she sat on the chest and stared out into the wild night. In only a few hours Taverik would come by on his way out of town, possibly forever. Should she go with him?

The sky gradually turned from black to gray, and still she sat.

Chapter 22

Taverik

Shivering the dank early morning, Taverik slid the saddlebags from his shoulder and bent his ear closer to Chado's keyhole. He still couldn't make out the words.

When he'd returned last night he had prowled the house, waiting and watching. But all had remained silent and empty. No sign of his father, or Chado either. The servants huddled in the kitchen, not answering his bell until he went down there himself. He paced and paced, until the chimes struck three. Any meeting, he decided at last, must have been held elsewhere. He'd fallen onto his bed fully clothed, and slept.

Raw cold had awakened him to a grim, gray morning. He lumbered to the window and flung back the shutter. Heavy clouds sat low over the city. Rain, he thought, then as his breath misted, changed his mind. Snow. It *would* come the day he had to travel. He turned away, shuddering inside from grinding tiredness and the knowledge that Marko wouldn't go with him. He had seen it in her eyes.

Shouldering his packed saddlebags, he'd opened his door, started down the hall, then stopped. Chado's door was closed. Now when, Taverik wondered, had Chado gotten in? Sometime between three and dawn. And just where had he been? Taverik softly tried the knob. Locked.

About to knock, he'd paused with his fist still raised. Low voices sounded within, one confident, the other answering and servile. Neither one Chado's. He bent lower to hear better.

A step behind him. Before he could straighten he was thrown against the wall, his father's dockworker fists locked about his neck. "What are you doing here?" whispered Donato.

"I'm—"

"Shut up!" his father hissed, giving him an urgent shake. His usually florid face looked gray. "I told you to leave last night."

"I had to pack," Taverik whispered. "Where's Chado?"

His father pulled him away from the wall. "Leave now. Don't stop. Cross the Ao. I'll send a servant with what you need."

"Father, what crooked trick are you pulling this time?"

"When will you just do what I say?" He shoved Taverik toward the stair. "Go!"

The door behind them opened. "Stay."

The man in the doorway wore a merchant's black wool mantle, plain leather belt and boots, but he'd never been a merchant, Taverik knew instantly. He stood proud like a soldier, and arrogantly assured, as if he owned this house and the Zandros were his servants. His face, with its aquiline nose and heavy brows looked vaguely familiar, and despite the polite smile curving the lips, the eyes held a glitter that Taverik found disturbing. Without quite knowing why, he remembered that panic-stricken scramble through the fog, chased by three men and something else, something not human. The blood began to drain from his face and his vision narrowed.

"So, Zandro, this is the other son?" the man was saying.

"My youngest," grated Donato. "A poor retard who doesn't know the time of day."

Taverik stiffened at the insult, then checked his retort. Deep currents ran beneath the surface of this conversation. Best listen until he understood. He forced himself to meet the stranger's intense gaze guilelessly. "A retard," the man said gently. Unbelievingly.

"A retard," Donato repeated, "who was to go to Perijo for me yesterday, but who lazily put it off."

Again a rakeover with the eyes. "Retarded and lazy. You, boy—you don't look lazy."

"I put it off," Taverik said, "having other business." The moment he spoke he heard a quick movement from someone inside the door.

"Other business?"

"The guild." Watch it—he was letting this man put him on the defensive. He took firmer hold of himself and settled into his best dull, blank expression.

"I've wanted to visit the guilds myself. Part of my tour of the city. You will come with us?"

Donato's face squeezed up with alarm. "Certainly," Taverik said, "Viti . . . uh, Viti . . ."

"Kali," the stranger supplied smoothly. "Kali Fara."

Fara. Taverik bowed respectfully. Fara, he thought as he straightened. He'd heard that name before. It stuck in the back of his mind, just as the stranger's face had.

Fara turned to his father. "I would like you both to show me your lovely city," he said, all charm. "I would like to see everything, oh, the guilds, the fortress, the gates, the walls."

Donato murmured something Taverik couldn't catch. Fara, Fara, he thought.

Farasoza. Agash Itzil Farasoza.

Soza.

It hit him like the kick of a mule. This was Soza himself. And now he knew where he'd seen that face before. It was an older, cannier version of the student in the alley. Karaz, who wore the Black Eagle. Taverik knew then with certainty. This was Soza, actually standing before him.

Surely the man must see how Taverik's face was stiffening, turning white, sense how his heart had begun to pound, his vision narrow. But no, he was merely questioning Donato, complaining gently about something, Taverik didn't know what—their words blurred together. He had to warn Balanji. Marko! If Soza were going to the guild he might find Marko!

Taverik forced a clear space into his mind. He'd go to Nikilo. Nikilo would have access to Balanji and Balanji would believe him. Then he had to get Marko to safety, and get out of town himself before Balanji swept down and arrested Soza, his father and Chado (wherever he was) and executed them all.

He backed away. Both his father and Soza stopped talking and looked at him. Meeting their gaze squarely and innocently was as hard as wading against the Ao's strong current. Taverik bowed low once more. "Excuse me, Kali, excuse me, Father. If I'm to go to the guild instead of to Perijo, I must change first, and unpack my mule."

Soza's eyes narrowed. Taverik's heart lurched so hard his chest hurt. His mouth dried.

"We're leaving in a few minutes, Taverik," Donato said peevishly.

"Yes, of course," he said. He started down the stairs, walking stiffly, willing himself not to break into a run. At the landing he looked up. Both men still watched him, Soza thoughtfully, hands on hips, his father a little behind, his lips shaping the word, Go. Taverik gave a faint wave, turned the corner and ran.

Abado

Despite the bulk of the two men, Abado managed to get a look at that other son as he went down the stairs. It *was* him—the one with the yellow hair and the eyes that mocked. Abado knew he shouldn't speak before the red-faced fool, but time fled. If only he could talk in Bcacmat he could explain everything. But the agash had strictly forbidden any hint of Bcacma, and had already punished Abado for his side business of translations. Abado timidly spoke up in Massadaran. "Master, that one already I met."

The agash swung around, not seeming to mind the impertinence. "Where?"

"He came to my shop," Abado said with significance, "with a young woman and a letter to translate."

The agash's brows snapped together as he understood. "This son of yours is not one of us?" he demanded of the father, who had been looking puzzled and now looked frightened.

"He's just a retard, O Zoji," the red-faced one bleated. "I thought it better he not know. I am sending him away. He's too much under the influence of his uncle."

"Is his uncle living here, too?"

The other drew himself up with ludicrous offended dignity. "Nikilo Vitujak and I are no longer on speaking terms."

Abado sucked in his breath at the name. The agash's anger coiled like a whiplash. "Nikilo Vitujak! You hobnob with Vitujak!"

"I just told you I don't. He is no longer welcome in this house."

"But your son goes to his?"

"Despite my orders not to. What is the problem?"

"The problem, you ass, is that Vitujak is secretary and advisor to Balanji himself, and seems to have made himself quite the little expert on my movements."

The grain-fed fool looked like he'd been poleaxed. "Nikilo Vitujak is nothing more than a tutor of kalis, and sometimes a secretary to traveling vitis."

"He is Balanji's personal secretary! For your sake I hope you are truly as stupid as you say. If I find out you have betrayed me . . ."

"No, Zoji," Zandro pleaded. "I assure you, I never knew. If Taverik knew he never told me. I'll strangle him for not telling me!"

"Get him and bring him to me."

"Vitujak?"

"No, idiot, your son, Taverik."

"Zoji, he is a nice boy, and knows nothing of this. Leave him alone, he's going away."

"He will betray us."

"No, he knows nothing of this. He's the best of our family, leave him alone."

"Get him."

The merchant drew himself up, his face paling until the little red veins showed across his nose and cheeks. "No. I won't."

Abado held his breath with anticipation, for his master had gone still with that inner stillness which meant this fool had said his last no. Then suddenly, disappointingly, the agash relaxed. "No need to fear, no harm will come to him. We will merely keep him safe until the city is ours and he cannot betray us. Are you still stubborn? Let me add some incentive. Perhaps you have wondered where your other son is?"

"Chado! What have you done with him?"

"Nothing. Yet. We will do some very nasty things to him indeed unless you cooperate with us. On the other hand, if you cooperate, both your sons will be kept safe and afterwards you shall all be rewarded."

Zandro deflated like a pricked bladder. "Very well, I'll bring Taverik back."

"That's better. All will be well. You have my word. Hurry."

"Master," Abado said in Bcacmat the moment he'd left, "that son has seen that letter to you from the Tlath. Let me get rid of him for you."

"He knows where the girl is. When Zandro fetches him I will make him tell me."

"He's not one of us, that young one," Abado said. "He's not our kind. I don't like his eyes."

"Well, just in case, I will also visit this guild, the Textile Guild you said? There I may possibly find the girl and her sister, who have eluded me so long."

"Here comes Zandro again."

Heavy breathing and muttering preceded Zandro up the stairs. His pig-eyed face ran sweat though it was cold, even in the house. "Zoji, he has already left," he wheezed. "I couldn't catch him. Please spare him, it couldn't be helped."

Ha, Abado thought gleefully, a far drop from his earlier arrogant pomposity. And he'd drop farther yet. But oddly enough, the master reacted with serene indifference. "He is probably still in the city. I'm sure we'll find him in time. And now, I wish my tour. Prepare mules for my servant and myself. Remember, the safety of your sons depends on your cooperation. Abado!"

"Yes, Master?"

The agash nodded toward the room, and Abado followed him in. The moment he shut the door, the agash shed his indifference and paced with short agitated steps, muttering to himself, his eyes flickering. "The son must have recognized us."

"Let me kill him."

"It may be too late. Find out where this Nikilo Vitujak lives."

"I know already."

"Send people there. Shut him up. This Taverik Zandro may show up there too—tell them to wait and take him alive. He'll tell me where to find the girl and her sister, and we need him to put pressure on the father."

"Yes, master."

"Damn! It may be ruined already. We should pull out immediately."

Abado's scalp crawled as he met the agash's eyes and saw that other looking out. The *mahiga* inside him seemed to be stirring him up, controlling him, putting him in a dangerous mood. Sometimes Abado wished his master had never gone through the Black Eagle's initiation.

"Are our people in place at the palace?"

"Yes, Viti Malenga is hiding your assassins and the soldiers."

"And Karaz?"

"He's greatly increased the forces hidden within the city. They are ready."

"My wesh-agash?"

"He can bring his men in four hours."

"It's only seven in the morning." The agash chewed his lip. "We can do it! We'll attack the moment the clocks strike one. Notify Karaz and my wesh-agash. Send a man to Malenga. And don't forget Vitujak. Go, my faithful! We will do it!"

"Yes, my master," cried Abado, catching his eagerness.

"And Abado—"

"Master?"

"Tell them to get rid of the entire zoji family at once this time. I don't want a repeat of the messes made at Vosa and Ormea."

Chapter 23

Marita

"So, young Marko, you plan to expand?" The guild president sat back in his desk chair and thrust his bandaged foot before him. On the desk lay the printed transfer paper bearing the sheep and flax logo of Illiga's Textile Guild. Beyond the closed door sounded the earliest stirrings of the guild staff preparing for a day of meetings.

"Yes, Kali," Marita said. *Just sign it,* she thought. Her whole body ached from lack of sleep and too much brandy. What an idiot she'd been to drink so much.

"Are you sure that is wise, right now?"

"What do you mean?"

"These are turbulent times. War. Bandits preying on caravans. You are young and inexperienced; perhaps you don't understand the amount of work that goes into keeping business in two far-removed locations. Are you prepared for the amount of travel you'll be forced to do?"

"Yes, Kali."

"Ask yourself if this is something your father would have done."

She caught the inquiring look. Ittato was still curious about her background. She said nothing, and the guild president at last picked up the quill. "Well, then," he sighed, "what city shall I inscribe?"

"I haven't decided yet."

He put down the pen. "Not decided yet? My dear young man, I dislike seeing you so impulsive. For your own sake . . ."

"Does it matter what city?" she asked earnestly. "Would it make any difference to you?"

"I suppose not."

"Then why not leave it blank and let me fill it in when I've decided."

"That would be most unusual."

"But not illegal?"

He brushed his chin with the pen. "No," he said reluctantly, "not illegal. But so irregular. Are you sure you must do this?"

"Yes, Kali."

He settled his spectacles on his nose, dipped his pen in the ink pot again and began his careful, neat handwriting. A knock sounded from the hall. Ittato suspended his pen again, to Marita's agony. "That will be my new doctor," he confided to her. "I found him yesterday after the meeting, and dismissed that other long-faced cloud of gloom. This one says he can work wonders with the gout, though I'm not sure I like the amulets he uses. Too *ikiji* for my taste. Come in!"

Marita looked curiously at the tortoise-faced old man who entered, and snapped awake. *This was the one.*

"Dr. Efila," Ittato said, struggling to rise, "I'd like you to meet Marko Kastazi, one of Illiga's promising younger merchants. If you need a rug, he's the one to visit. Has a special talent for them. Marko, Dr. Efila."

"How do you do, Doctor," she said, steadying herself as she extended her hand. She'd be out of context to him; he'd never recognize her.

The touch of the doctor's dry fingers felt familiar. His black piercing eyes, remembered so well from that pain-filled night, searched hers. "You look familiar," he said, dashing her hopes. "Have I treated you in the past?"

"No." Marita turned firmly back to Ittato.

Ittato reseated himself by thrusting forth his bandaged foot and failing back heavily into the chair. "I'll be with you in a moment, Doctor. Please make yourself comfortable."

The old man bowed and withdrew to the windows. Marita let out her breath and tried to relax. It had been hard to think quickly. Mind and body ran sluggish this morning.

"Now what day is it?" Ittato wondered aloud. Marita told him, curbing her impatience. Ittato inked the pen again and wrote in the date with a flourish.

"Are you sure I've never treated you?" asked the doctor suddenly.

"Me?" Marita spoke without turning. "Yes."

"Perhaps your sister? That must be it. Do you have a sister?"

Ittato looked over his spectacles with interest. "You've got a sister, haven't you Kastazi? Has she ever been treated by Dr. Efila?"

"No," Marita said. She'd begun to sweat despite the chill rawness of the early morning. "Is that all?" she asked Ittato.

"Uh, not quite." He bent over the page and began her name.

"I treated a woman who looked just like you, for a sword wound in the left shoulder. Damaged the pectoral quite a bit, with a good amount of blood loss."

Ittato looked up again. "What a coincidence. Marko just recovered from a wound in the left shoulder, didn't you, lad?"

"This was right in the beginning of winter."

"Funny. That's when that raid hit your caravan. Last caravan of the season, too."

"Funny coincidence," Marita agreed. She peered across the desk. He'd finished her name. All that remained was his signature and hers.

The doctor came closer, his eyes fixed on her face. Marita retreated, realized she was doing it, and forced herself to stand. "If I didn't know any better," Efila said, "I'd say you *were* the person I treated."

"Nonsense," said Marita.

"Thought you said you treated a woman," Ittato said. He'd at last begun his signature.

"I did. And this is she."

Ittato looked up sharply. "What are you saying?"

"He's crazy," Marita said. The page was done except for her signature. The sooner she could get out of there the better. She reached for the pen.

"I'm not crazy," the doctor declared. "And I say this is a woman. She even paid for my services with a rug."

"I don't have to put up with this," Marita snapped. She stuck her thumb in her belt and glared at the doctor, though her heart thundered.

"Kalis, Kalis," Ittato soothed, pulling off his glasses and sitting back with a quirky smile on his face. "Young Kastazi's manhood is easily enough proved. I'm sure he won't mind disrobing. Would you Marko?"

Marita's vision narrowed. Ittato was looking at her—really looking at her this time. Doubt crept across his face. She drew herself up. "Yes, I mind," she blustered. "I will not accept the absurd accusations and whims of a stranger."

She reached for the paper but Ittato pulled it away. "You were equally resistant the other day when the men were clowning about the new short *hama* style. And now that I think of it, when I sat behind you on your mule and had my arms around your waist . . ."

"This is ridiculous," Marita insisted. "I refuse to be insulted like this."

"She's a woman," said the doctor. "I should know."

"Young Kastazi, or whoever you are," said Ittato, "I really must insist you open your shirt if you wish to prove the good doctor's accusations absurd. Your refusal to do so merely compounds the suspicion."

"And I refuse to be subjected to such indignities," Marita shouted. "Kali Ittato, you've known me longer than you've known this fly-by-night fool."

"Call in a few strong men," the doctor suggested. "They can help you prove me right, and afterwards throw the hussy in prison for you."

"Kastazi," said Ittato, "which shall it be?"

Marita gave up on the transfer paper. She'd be lucky

to merely get away. "I won't stay where I've been so insulted," she said and started for the door.

The doctor seized her wrist. She hit him in the face and he fell backwards. "Help!" shouted Ittato. "Help! Help!" Snatching the transfer paper from his hand, Marita spun away to the door, kicking over a chair in the path of the doctor, who was scrambling to his feet. Down the hall she pelted, followed by Ittato's cries for help.

"What's wrong?" gasped a pale, skinny clerk, skidding from the office next door.

"Ittato needs help!" she cried, pointing back. "Hurry!"

He rushed past her. Behind her a tumult grew. She made it to the stairs and clattered down, past startled merchants who did not yet realize anything was amiss. This was the east wing, she thought. Good, closest to the stables.

She brushed past the stable boys, her chest aching and hot fire searing her sides. "Where's my mule?"

At her voice Whitey pulled his head from the manger, still chewing a mouthful of hay. His bridle hadn't been removed, she saw with relief. She hurried to him, backing him out of the stall with hands clumsy from panic.

"What are you doing!" cried the boys. "Here, that's for us! Don't you want your saddle?"

No time for the saddle. She clambered onto Whitey's bony back. "You owe us!" one of the boys shrieked. "Pay for the day!"

"Get out of the way!" she thundered. They squeezed against a stall as she kicked Whitey forward. She ducked as he burst through the stable door, already at a canter.

"Stop him!" someone shouted from an upper window. The men on the steps of the hall scattered, some running towards her, others running to block the narrow alley. Marita leaned low over Whitey's neck, clinging precariously to his steep withers and painfully sharp backbone. One man reached the alley first and jumped in front of her, waving arms and shouting. Whitey's pace faltered and his long ears went up. She dug her thumbs into his neck. "Go, go, go!"

"Halt!" shouted the man, Echin, she saw now. She drummed Whitey's sides with her heels and Whitey obediently lengthened his stride. Echin thrust out his hands, then flung himself to the side.

Whitey skittered into the alley, the racket of his hooves resounding from the stonework on each side. Then the sound fell away as they broke free of the walls and she headed down the hill toward home.

Chapter 24

Taverik

Kala Pardi opened the door, flustered by his pounding. "Gracious, Taverik, I thought you were—"

"Where's Nikilo?" Taverik demanded.

"Why upstairs, of course, whatever is going on?"

Taverik thrust the reins in her knobby hands. "Here, take care of the mule for me, all right?" He took the stairs two at a time and burst through the door at the top. "Nik!"

His uncle met him at the study door, map in hand. "What's wrong, Taverik?"

"Listen, Nik, Soza's in the city. He stayed the night at our house, and I met him there this morning."

Nikilo's freckled face sharpened. "How do you know? Did he introduce himself?"

"Yes, as Kali Fara."

"Then how can you be sure?"

"It's too long to explain." Taverik flung out his hands in frustration. So much had happened since he last talked to his uncle. "He's the same as the Agash something or other Farasoza. I've seen a letter written to him from the Tlath—and it was nearly stolen by that student with the black eagle."

"The Tlath? What letter? Taverik, you are not making sense."

"Not only that," Taverik plowed on, "but yesterday afternoon Father ordered me to go to Perijo."

"In the winter?"

"That's what I thought. It's crazy. Don't you see?" Taverik shook his uncle's arm. "He wanted to get rid of me, that's the only explanation. And this morning I find a stranger in the house, who wants a tour of the city—and I can *feel* who he is. You've got to believe me, I'm sure it's Soza."

"Nothing you've said makes sense to me, Taverik." Nikilo tossed the map on the table and tore off his dressing gown. "But I'm going to trust your judgment."

"You've got to hurry to the palace. Warn the zoji!"

Nikilo brushed past him, buttoning his surcoat. "He's not even in the city."

Taverik stared, aghast. "Not in the city?"

"He's taken the zoja and tet-zojis to a safe place. I'm the only one who knows where he is!" Nikilo slammed back the shutter in the salon and stuck his head out the window. "Mano! My mule—fast!"

He pulled in his head. "What did he look like, Tav?"

Taverik followed him downstairs. "Dressed like a merchant, but military. Hook nose, graying black hair. Looks Massadaran. You get an odd feeling from him, but ordinary otherwise. Even handsome."

"That's him," Nikilo said grimly as he rounded the newel post. "One would expect him to have a green face." They strode through the kitchen where Kala Pardi was setting out bowls of dough to rise. "Mano!" Nikilo shouted, pulling open the back door.

"You need your cloak and hat, Kali Nikilo," cried the widow. "It looks like snow."

"No time, woman! Mano!"

"Coming," Mano yelled from the tiny stable at the rear of the yard.

"Hurry up!" Nikilo paused at the top of the back

stairs to let Taverik catch up with him. "By the way," he said. "I found out that piece of information I promised you."

"What information?"

"About the fate of one Kasta, assassinated in Vosa, presumably by Soza."

Taverik faced him eagerly. "Who was he?"

Mano led out Nikilo's cream-colored mule and flung on the saddle. "Almost ready, Kali," he said.

"Good," said Nikilo. He jumped down the back steps. "I thought his name familiar when you mentioned it. Kasta was none other than the fourth son of Zoji Vos."

Taverik frowned, then followed his uncle through the grassy yard, Kala Pardi's chickens scattering and clucking ahead of them. "Hold on! There were only three tet-zojis in Vosa. And their names were Vos, not Kasta."

Nikilo took the reins from Mano and mounted. "The fourth was the youngest. He fell in love with the daughter of a Pakajan merchant, and humiliated the family by marrying her. Vosa, you know, is even more rigid than Illiga about the *Sadra* Laws. Old Vos disinherited him, he took her family name, and further insulted the Voses by remaining in the city and becoming quite rich and powerful on his own."

The mule sidled restlessly. Taverik caught the bridle. "He was assassinated?"

"He and his wife, and a day later, the entire Vos family. The end of the dynasty. Except, perhaps, for Kasta's two daughters who disappeared without trace. They are presumed dead."

He bent toward Taverik and gripped his shoulder. "I must know how it is you are asking these questions, Taverik. And furthermore, I want you here when I get back—your explanations are needed. I hope to Zojikam you are not just imagining things."

"I only wish I were." Taverik stood back to let the mule past. Suddenly he remembered. "What were the daughters' names?" he shouted after his uncle.

Nikilo turned as he trotted out of the courtyard. "Marita and Sahra."

Taverik stared after him. Marita and Sahra. Marko and Oma, of course. Did they know who they were? Probably not. Almost certainly not. Marita. He liked that, it suited her. Not that it mattered. He'd just asked a zoja, one of the last of the Vos dynasty, to marry him. He laughed softly. "And I thought my father was ambitious," he said to the lowering sky.

"Here, you young gawk," said Mano, poking him in the ribs with a gnarled finger. "You going to stand in the cold all day?"

Taverik focused suddenly. Marko had said she was going to the guild this morning. He had to get to her before Soza did. "Where's my mule?"

Mano chuckled and tilted his thumb towards the mule grazing placidly in the frost-withered garden. "Don't trip over him. Not to mention the three you brung last night. Get on now. I got my work."

The old man held the stirrup as Taverik mounted, then gave him an affectionate pat on the knee. "Take care," he said.

Taverik shook his callused hand. "Take care, yourself, you old codger," he said and stirred the mule into its tooth-jarring trot.

The courtyard of the Textile Guild roiled with unusual bustle as Taverik trotted in. Everyone in the guild seemed to be out there, standing around in clumps, talking and waving their hands. A large knot of people entwined around Ittato who was just stumping from the hall. Taverik waited on Frez's back for the stable boys to finish saddling a large number of mules.

Gunnar Chisokachi and Echin came out the stable door. "What's going on?" Taverik asked.

Gunnar squinted up at him. "Suppose *you* tell us, Taverik."

"What do you mean?"

"You were best cronies with Marko—you going to tell us you never knew?"

Taverik's hands went cold. "Knew what?"

"That he's a woman!" Gunnar roared. "He's—she's

bilked us all these years. Walked around cool as you please, drank with us, told stories with us, did everything with us. And all the time she was a woman! I'd like to wring her neck. And I'll wring yours if you knew and didn't tell anyone. Did you?"

"That's idiotic, Gunnar." Taverik looked nervously at the men closing around him, listening. "How do you know?"

"Ittato's new doctor swears he is a woman in disguise," Echin put in. "Swears he treated her for a chest wound."

"He's crazy," Taverik protested, but his heart sank.

"If the doctor's crazy," Echin said, "why did Marko refuse to undress? Positive proof. And he wouldn't do it the other day either."

"Neither would you," Taverik reminded him.

Gunnar snickered and Echin shot him a sullen look. "Anyway," Gunnar said, "Ittato and the council members are going to Marko's house to face him with it. And, Taverik, Ittato said he wanted to see *you* the moment you arrived."

So now he was in trouble with just about everyone.

"All this time we thought you liked boys, Tav," smirked Echin. "And instead you're stealing a march on us."

"Shut up, fatmouth," Taverik said. "It wasn't like that."

"So you did know, eh, Zandro?" demanded one of the men who drifted near.

"He knew all right," said another. "Fetch him down off that mule and let's find out what those Zandros are trying to pull this time."

Hands grabbed at him. Taverik flashed his knife. "Don't touch me," he warned, his mule sidling nervously. "Let go of the reins." Most of the men backed off, leery of his knife, but he could make no other move. Now what?

Over the heads of the gathering crowd he saw Ittato limping toward him. The crowd parted respectfully and in a moment Taverik found himself looking down into the grim face of the guild president.

"Put the knife away, Zandro," he said. "Just answer me truthfully. Is Marko Kastazi a woman?"

Taverik sheaved the knife. "That's a long story," he said.

"It is not. Is Marko Kastazi a woman?"

The crowd hushed, listening. "Ask Marko Kastazi," Taverik said.

The doctor shoved his way next to Ittato. "I know him," the old man said, "He's the one called me to the injured woman, stayed there all night, and paid me to do it."

And also paid extra for discretion, Taverik thought. What a waste. He kept his eyes on Ittato so he wouldn't have to see the disgust and anger on the faces of the merchants, all too ready to use a Zandro for a scapegoat. "I think, Taverik Zandro," said Ittato, "that you will go with myself and the guild's council members to visit this Marko Kastazi. We will sift this matter immediately. Bring my mule. The rest of you go home. The guild will meet tomorrow."

The way through the narrow streets to Marko's villa never seemed longer. Breaths misting in the chill air, the four soberly-clad council members and the doctor closed about Taverik to keep him from escaping. It was, he thought ironically, the last thing he wanted to do. He planned to make sure Marko had every chance of getting away whatever the cost to himself. He would call out the moment he saw her, warn her, then hold back the committee while she bundled Sahra and Bibi out the back door. His heart squeezed into a leaden lump as he realized the pitiful inadequacy of his plan. "Zojikam," he pleaded inarticulately as they arrived at Marko's gates and one of the four council members dismounted to knock on them.

No answer. The doctor raised his Black Eagle amulet. "Come out in the name . . ."

"Put that disgusting thing away," snapped Ittato. "We'll have no *ikiji* here."

The doctor scowled, but put it away. "More powerful," he said.

"She's hiding," broke in the shivering council member beside Taverik. "Break down the gates."

The man on foot put his shoulder to the gate and heaved. The gates flew wide, tumbling the council member to the frozen ground. They'd been unlocked the whole time.

"Marko!" Taverik yelled.

"Shut up, Zandro!" snapped Ittato.

"Marko, look out!"

No response came from the house and Taverik shut up, hope beginning to quicken his breathing. The committee crowded into the tiny yard until the mules could barely turn. "Nothing in the stable," reported the doctor. "Try the house," Ittato commanded.

But Taverik, exultant, knew they'd find nothing. If Whitey and the cart were gone, Marko had gotten away. Now for his own escape. Leaving these stolid businessmen was as simple as backing his mule out the gate. "Ho! Zandro!" cried the nearest council member. But Taverik laughed and waved good-bye, trotting down the cobbled street. No one pursued.

He'd reached the square, bright with market tents, before he wondered what he should do. Soza was after him. The guild was after him. His father and Balanji were probably after him. And Marko was gone without a word. He laughed a short mirthless laugh. "I'm not as popular as I used to be," he told the mule. "Not that that's saying much."

Best dismount so he'd be hidden by the crowd. Leading Frez, he worked his way through the market, squeezing past baskets, livestock, carts. He chewed his chapped lips and warmed his hands in his armpits, trying to think through a plan. He might still catch Marko if he hurried. Yet he wasn't sure where she'd gone. How in the wide world could he ever find her again? And his uncle had said he wanted Taverik to be at his house by the time he returned. The safety of the city might depend on information Taverik could supply. On the far side of the square he stopped to decide. One snowflake fell, then another.

His father came up the side street. He saw Taverik

and whipped his mule. "Taverik!" he called in a low voice. "Wait, thank Zojikam I've found you!"

The novelty of his words surprised Taverik into listening. "What?"

"I was afraid they'd find you first." Donato's face looked gray and his shoulders slumped uncharacteristically. He dismounted and talked urgently under the noise of the market. "Listen, that wasn't a visiting merchant you met this morning. It was Soza himself."

"I know," Taverik said. His voice turned bitter. "I thought you were going to give him his tour of the city so he could better take it."

Donato Zandro went even grayer. "You *did* know then. He swore you knew. Listen, he has taken Chado hostage."

"What!"

"He's going to kill him, he says, if I don't do exactly what he says. He wants me to find you and bring you to him. Quick now, you've got to get out of here." He shook Taverik. "If only you had left when I told you. Why won't you ever cooperate? You've brought this on yourself!"

"No!" Taverik backed out of arm's reach. "You've brought this on yourself, you traitor. The blood of every person in this city will be on your head."

His father raised his fist, eyes locked with Taverik's. Then he dropped his hand and licked his lips. "You've got to move fast. I think Soza had you followed this morning when you left."

"Followed? Oh, no, Uncle Nikilo!" Taverik flung himself into the saddle.

Donato grabbed the reins. "Tav, don't go there!"

"Let go."

"Get out of the city. Soza is going to take it today—I heard them." His father thrust a purse into his hands.

Taverik hurled it back at him. "You traitor!"

"I thought it was best," Donato cried. "Forgive me, Taverik!"

Taverik turned the mule and lashed it into a gallop.

Chapter 25

Taverik

No one answered his pounding. Taverik stepped back and cupped his hands. "Mano!" No answering shout. With deep unease he dismounted and led the mule to the back himself.

Crash! Taverik jumped, but it was only the back door swinging in the wind and thickening snowflakes. "Kala Pardi!" he shouted. The door banged again against the house. Taverik left the mule standing and ran to the steps.

"Anyone home?" he called, entering the kitchen. The table and floor were white with flour from an overturned jar. Huge footprints tracked the flour every which way. Upright in the middle of the mess sat a bowl of rising dough. Beyond it Kala Pardi lay face down on the flagstones, her black dress gray with flour.

With a wordless cry, Taverik knelt beside her, gently turning her over. He drew back in horror, staring at his fingers. The damp bodice of her dress had stained his hands sticky red, and a darkening pool of blood lay on the flagstone under her. Gingerly he fingered the long rips across her dress. She'd been knifed.

Her faded eyes stared sightlessly in her flour-dusted face. Swallowing hard against his gorge he clasped her doughy hand and shut her eyes, noticing as he did so the tear streaks traced through the flour on her cheeks.

He threw a glance over his shoulder, his first impulse to run. But no, Nikilo might be here. He might need his help—or he also might be dead. At any rate, Taverik thought, he had to know for sure.

Stilling his breathing, he listened. Footsteps! No, just his pulse surging in his ears. He drew his knife and on second thought also picked up the fire poker. Stepping around the flour mess he catfooted into the hall.

The pantry empty. Kala Pardi's sparse chamber empty. He crouched and checked under the sagging bed. Nothing.

He turned his eyes up the stairs, to the door closed in the dusk at the top. Perhaps he should get help. From whom? And meanwhile, Nikilo might be up there, needing him. He crept up the dark stairs, skipping the fourth step which always creaked. He paused at the top, then silently opened the door.

The sitting room empty, tidy. He eased in, the pounding of his heart now tangling with the slower, even tick of the study clock. The entire house seemed to be listening.

He noticed the smell next. The strong odor of human waste. Taverik moved to the study.

Mano. He'd been on his way to empty the slop jar lying cracked on the floor beside him, its contents soaking into the floor. He must have been caught by surprise. Taverik could see no signs of struggle.

Taverik leaned against the door jamb, almost panting from fear. The stuffed owl on the mantle glared over his head. *Get out of here*, his good sense told him. But no, he thought stubbornly, Nikilo might be upstairs. And anyway, the assassins had probably left by now.

He inched between Mano and the clock, forcing back memories which threatened to undo him. He'd grieve later. Using both hands, he silently climbed the almost vertical stairs.

Nikilo's room. Taverik's hands shook as he pushed open the door. Nothing. He took a second look half expecting Nikilo's corpse to suddenly appear on the floor. The bed's coverlet lay as smooth as only Kala Pardi could make it.

Taverik exhaled, almost sick with relief. Moving quicker now, he passed the ladder leading up to Mano's garret and checked the tiny front chamber he considered his own room. The knee-high windows under the eaves sent weak light across the bare floorboards, highlighting the oak grain. Nothing here.

Now what? Taverik started back down the steps then froze. A sound, gone almost as soon as he heard it. Was it his imagination? Or had the fourth stair creaked?

His heart hammered uncomfortably. He took a deep breath, which didn't help, and silently continued on down to Mano and the slop jar.

The stair door crashed open. Taverik jumped back, colliding with the clock. Two men spilled in, and halted in a crouch as they saw him. Both held slim knives reversed in their hands. Taverik backed away, lifting the poker.

"Not you not move," demanded the heavier of the two, a man with jowls like a guard dog. Taverik recognized him, the other man from the pawn shop. He halted obediently, but kept the poker raised. No help against a thrown knife, he realized, but it made him feel better.

"Not we you not hurt," soothed the other, a slight man seemingly made of wires and steel. Their odd speech rang an alarm inside Taverik which he didn't have time to examine. They'd inched forward past Mano as they spoke and Taverik backed away. The ticking of the clock by his left ear resounded unnaturally loud over his panting breaths. He had reached the stairs.

"Stop!" The heavy one lifted his knife and Taverik stopped. His vision tunneled down to the two men and the knives in their hands.

"Wait, Tlele," said the other. He held out his hand, palm first, speaking low and fast, as if to a frightened horse. "Not we you not hurt," he repeated. "Someone you just want see. Quietly come, not long not take."

Sure, Taverik thought. *Come be tortured by Soza. No thanks. Better to be killed outright.* The realization steadied him.

He grabbed the clock and heaved.

He was already scrambling back up the stairs as it toppled. He heard the thud of knife hitting wood an instant before the crash. Behind him came cursing and banging, then footsteps on the stairs. He scaled Mano's ladder just ahead of them and burst through the trapdoor, slamming it shut, nearly crushing Tlele's fingers. Taverik stood on it and looked wildly around. Mano's small chest stood at the foot of his cot. Taverik shoved it over the trapdoor just as the pounding began from below. "Come!" shouted a muffled voice. "Want you house we want burn?"

The barren garret stretched the two-room length of the house. At the front and back, the roof slanted right to the floor. Small dormer windows overlooking the street and backyard admitted the only light. Taverik could stand upright only in the middle, where the stone chimney, Mano's furniture and the trapdoor took up most of the space. He ducked past the chimney to the back dormer.

It opened outward, and because of the steep angle of the roof, had a small ledge outside. If he could climb out and get up to the rooftop, he might be able to get help. Taverik pushed at the window. It didn't budge.

Behind him, Mano's chest leaped. His pursuers had found something to ram the trapdoor with. With each blow, the door splintered, and the chest edged farther off. The next heave would do it.

Taverik used his shoulder. The window squawked wide on stiff hinges, just as the hatch exploded open behind him. Shifting his knife to his teeth, Taverik squeezed his shoulders through the tiny window, then his hips. Hands caught his legs and pulled. He kicked out, hard. A muffled expletive. He kicked again and squirmed free. Slithering out onto the tiny ledge, he slammed shut the window and wedged his knife into the crack.

He scrambled like a squirrel up the wet cold roof, tiles scattering behind. At the top he threw his leg over the apex and looked about. Across the city, roofs and chimneys formed neat patterns in the light snow, rising up to the fortress on one side, and on the other, falling away to the city gates. For a moment he was absurdly struck by the beauty.

Then he looked down. Vertigo stopped his breath. Paralyzed, he stared down the almost perpendicular roof to the road, four stories below. Two men peered up at him, pointing, all face and shoulder from his high point of view. Snow fell in dizzying patterns, and for a moment he couldn't tell if he were falling or not. His fingers clamped around the tiles and refused to open.

The crash of glass below him brought him to his senses. Tlele had broken the window and began to squeeze his bulk out. Taverik had to get moving.

He pushed himself to his feet, teetered a moment on the single tile of the apex, then inched his way along the roof. His riding boots were clumsy—no time to take them off. At least the snow wasn't sticking yet.

"Halt!" wheezed the thinner man from the window.

Taverik flung a look over his shoulder. The heavy one, Tlele, was already crawling up the roof slope. Taverik broke into an awkward run. The gap between Nikilo's roof and the next was small. He took a breath and leaped. He crossed the next roof quickly, wondering how he'd ever get down. The next gap yawned before him, and he gathered himself and sprang.

A tile broke under his feet as he landed. He flailed his arms for a heart-stopping moment, then fell, sliding foot first down the tiles. Digging in his fingernails, he clung with cold-chapped fingers until he managed to stop himself. When he could think again, he wedged his toes against the tiles and reached up his right hand. His fingers could just reach the apex. He pulled himself up, weak and shaky. He looked back.

Tlele had reached the top of Nikilo's roof and begun to balance himself on the apex. The other crept unhappily up the tiles from the window. No time to rest.

A large stonework chimney now blocked him. He inched past it then stared with dismay. He'd reached the corner house. The gap across the lane below was too great to jump. Trapped.

Footfalls on the next roof got him moving again. He crawled right to the edge and peered over. Dizziness made him pant until he thought he'd pass out, but he did see a possible way down: a small roof protected the jutting block of casement windows overlooking the side street. It ran the entire width of the house.

A thud. "Enough," panted Tlele, squeezing past the chimney. He held a throwing knife loosely in his hand. Another hung in his belt. "You like deer we chase, now enough. I you want to kill, but you alive wanted. Come."

He'd never make it over the edge in time. The only way was to get rid of the men behind him. Ah, Zojikam permit it! "All right," Taverik said reluctantly. He inched back along the slippery tile, wondering if he could get close enough to grapple with him. Even falling would be better than going alive to be questioned by Soza.

Tlele waited until Taverik neared him. "Your hands me show," he demanded.

Taverik held out his empty hands. The man seized him by the surcoat and hauled him the rest of the way. "Want you throw off," he snarled. He half turned and called in another language. Bcacmat, Taverik realized, suddenly recognizing the twisted phrasing of their accents—the same syntax as the translated letter. Even as he thought, he buried his fist in the man's stomach. Flailing, the man hurled Taverik against the chimney. The knife clattered to the tiles and disappeared over the edge. Only Taverik's fingers digging into the chimney's stonework kept Taverik from following it. The man balanced with effort, then drew back his right fist. Taverik lunged forward to free his left hand. He blocked the blow, fought for balance, and sent his right straight upward into one unshaven jowl.

Tlele tripped and fell backwards, hitting his head on the tiles. For a moment his inert body balanced, then began to slither down, head first.

Taverik caught him by the foot.

"You're a fool," he told himself. But he couldn't let the man just drop. He hauled him up by the leg and draped him over the apex of the roof. "At least," he muttered, pulling the other knife from the belt and clambering awkwardly past, "at least he'll be another obstacle."

"Hey!" shouted the other man, one roof back. "Are you all right?"

"If the tiles don't break," Taverik muttered, already crawling down the front roof to lessen the distance to the next floor. Squirming over the edge, he hung his length. His toes felt nothing. He looked down. The roof seemed a mile below him but he had no choice. Counting three, he dropped.

He landed on the ledge and threw himself against the building. Eyes squeezed shut, he hugged the chill plaster wall until his sense of balance returned. When his breathing steadied, he lifted his cheek and turned his head.

He'd worked his way down almost two floors. Not bad. And a few feet to his left was a shuttered window he hadn't seen from the roof. Spirits rising, he inched along spread-eagled until he reached the window. Its huge, louvered shutter was hinged from above. Taverik splayed his right hand against the plaster and pulled at the shutter with his left. It wouldn't budge. He pulled harder and broke a nail.

A shout from below. Taverik looked down. One of the men he'd seen in the street had turned the corner and spotted him. He was pointing at Taverik and shouting up towards the roof, presumably to Tlele's companion. "Damn!" muttered Taverik.

In desperation he lifted his foot and kicked at the shutter. It boomed like a drum but still stuck tight. Taverik hissed through clenched teeth, gave a last spiteful kick, then inched on past it to the back corner of the house. He peered around.

Red tile slanted below him, a roof sheltering an addition. From there, an easy drop to the ground. Snow had begun to stick to the tiles; the surface would be icy. "You've got it now," he whispered. "Just don't slip." Gathering himself, he leaped forward and around.

He landed and sprawled on the tiles, clinging with his whole body.

Voices below. Taverik stayed in that awkward position, cold water seeping into his clothing from top to bottom. Two men had found their way into the yard directly below. But still no shouts. Taverik let out his breath slowly, realizing they couldn't see him from that angle.

"I give up," said one, speaking lower class Illigan Pakajan. "Let's just say he got away."

"No," said the other with exaggerated patience. "He's wanted alive at best, dead at least. No getting away."

"Well, how we going to find him now? He could be anywhere."

"Look next door."

The voices moved back up the row and Taverik inhaled once again.

The shutter on the window above creaked outward. "What the hell?" said an elderly woman. "Thief!"

Taverik looked up, snow clinging to his eyelashes. "Quiet," he begged. Suddenly he recognized the woman glaring at him over two potted geraniums. He'd often seen her gossiping in the kitchen with Kala Pardi. Her name, her name . . . "Kala Ouasi!"

The old lady shifted a flower pot and leaned out to look closer. "Why, Taverik. Whatever are you doing?"

"Those men," Taverik said, "murdered Kala Pardi. Mano too. Probably my uncle. Now they're after me."

Her nostrils flared. "Come up at once."

A hail sound from below. Taverik tensed. "You! Old woman!"

"You! Thieves!" yelled Kala Ouasi. "Get out of here or I'll old woman *you*."

"We're not thieves, woman." The speaker stood directly below Taverik. "Have you seen a yellow-haired rascal?"

"He jumped the fence and ran that way."

"Go look," muttered the man.

A small piece of terra-cotta broke off from above. Taverik stretched and trapped it silently with his finger tips. It crumbled beneath them and the pieces clattered down each row of tiles, reached the edge and disappeared. "What the . . ." said the man below. "There he is!"

Taverik twisted around, lost his grip and slid. He

grabbed a tile but it merely came loose in his hand. He grabbed at the eves, then fell.

He landed hard and rolled in damp snow, still clutching the tile. "That's him!" someone shouted, looming over him. Taverik hurled the tile into the man's face and clambered to his feet, drawing Tlele's knife from his belt. He slashed out with it, and the man backed away.

He was a burly man, dressed like a dockworker. "Hurry up!" he bawled over his shoulder and an answering shout came from the next yard. Taverik backed toward the fence, knife held before him. The man followed.

"Look out, Taverik!" Kala Ouasi shouted. She hurled a flowerpot. It exploded between them, dirt flying in every direction. The dockworker ducked and Taverik sprinted for the fence.

Crash! Another flowerpot. Clods of dirt skittered under his feet. Taverik leaped, caught the top of the fence and hauled himself over. He tumbled down the other side, heedless of his scraped-raw hands, and plunged down an alley, running until his breath seared his lungs.

When he could push himself no further, he found a stone stairway and collapsed in its shelter, sobbing for air. His shaking fingers searched out the discomfort in his side: a long scratch, more bloody than serious. But it stung.

He pressed it tightly and looked about him. The snow had thickened. A steady traffic of market wagons made slushy ruts in the steep street, drivers and passengers huddled against the driving flakes, snow collecting on their shoulders and hoods. He had made it to one of the roads coming up into the city from the Ao Bridge. Good. If he could cross the river he might escape Soza's men. Then he'd have time to figure out what in the world to do next.

Lurching up, he joined the slow stream of carts leaving the city. Damn, but he was cold—surcoat soaked through, feet numb from trudging through the slush. He was also exhausted and hungry. Hardly an auspicous way to begin a journey. It was getting colder, too; the flakes had become smaller and faster.

At the bridge the street leveled out, joining the square before the guardhouse. The little square seemed busier than usual, filled with more men than normally had time to idle on a market day. Taverik's tired brain considered that, wondering why it seemed significant. The guards looked edgy, watching the crowd nervously.

Taverik passed the stone defense of the bridge and started across, regretting now that he threw his father's purse back at him. Below him, the Ao gushed, swollen and roaring. A man leaned against the wall, watching the plunging waters. He straightened as Taverik passed and too late Taverik realized who he was.

"Not do not move," said the wiry man who had been in Nikilo's house. A knife flashed in his hand and Taverik felt another in his back as someone moved up behind him. The wiry Bcacmat cautiously removed Tlele's knife from his belt. "I thought you bridge go."

Above the noise of the river the temple tower struck one.

The wiry man laughed. "The hour now is!"

A blood-curdling yell drowned the rest of the clock's chime. Before Taverik's horrified eyes the guard tower was overwhelmed in a surging mass of attacking men. On the bridge, farmers yelled, women screamed, and people began running. The knife dug deeper into Taverik's back. "Don't move," said the man behind him, the Pakajan dockworker.

"What's going on?" Taverik said.

The wiry man smiled again. "One o'clock! Agash—I mean, Soza, reaches forth city to pluck!"

Taverik clenched his fist to hit that smug face but the knife in his back pricked a warning and he let his hand drop. Cries arose from the far end of the bridge as Soza's men attacked the outer defense. Frantic civilians jostled past but Taverik's captors stubbornly stood their ground. "Over soon," said the wiry one. "We stay put."

Balanji's men began to retreat toward the city, squeezing the bridge traffic between them. A two-wheeled cart backed toward Taverik, propelled by a panicking mule. The farmer stood in his seat and lashed out with his whip. The mule brayed and plunged. "Look out!" shouted the Pakajan angrily, then jumped aside as the cart tipped up on its near wheel.

Taverik twisted free. "Stop him!" shouted the Bcacmat. The mule reared. Taverik darted under his hooves, collided with a screaming woman who had a basket of cabbages on either arm, then scrambled onto the parapet.

His breath stopped.

Below, the Ao River raged, gorged with rain water, sweeping in a roaring muddy flow. Standing waves and eddies dashed against each other, constantly gushing, never changing.

"Stop him!" shouted the Bcacmat again. Both he and the Pakajan struggled through the crowd after Taverik. On either side, Soza's men overwhelmed the bridge guards.. The fighting had reached him. The farmer screamed—Taverik whirled in time to see him fall from the cart seat, one of Soza's men pulling a pike from his chest. The soldier leaped over the body, raising his pike in a sweep that would take off Taverik's legs at the knee.

Taverik jumped. His long, breath-robbing fall ended in the shock of cold violent water.

Part II

Chapter 1

Taverik

For some time the voice had risen above the unceasing roar of the world, bothering Taverik like a fly brushed off only to land again. Now it sharpened, insistent, irritating, and pure Pakajan. "Come *on*, young feller, I can't do it unless you help me."

"Lemme alone," Taverik mumbled.

"That's the way," approved the voice, located just behind Taverik's right ear. "Move your feet."

Taverik couldn't even feel his feet. He opened his eyes into blinding snow and found himself knee-deep in icy water. The constriction around his chest was the locked arms of a man determined to drag him out of the roaring, churning river. "Come on, you lazy mule," the man grunted. "Try!"

Taverik obediently lurched forward, nearly plunging them both into the rocky water. "Good," panted the man. "Again."

He floundered against the swift current, his boots filled with water. His cloak was gone and his belt too. His surcoat clung to his shuddering torso, the wool saturated with cold water and weighing an unbelievable amount. He longed to drape himself over a boulder and sleep but every time he faltered the man swore.

They stumbled out of the shallows, rocks turning under feet Taverik could hardly feel. The man shifted to clamp Taverik under the left arm, pulling his right arm over muscled shoulders. He had red hair, and red fuzz on the fingers pointing into the snow. "See that willow thicket up there? Just gotta make it that far."

Taverik couldn't see it, but he bent his head and concentrated. The exertion of walking wore off the numbness of his feet but that, he grumbled to himself, was no gift; now they burned and tingled. He forced himself to keep at it, half-carried up the bank where freezing mud crunched under ankle-deep snow, and through endless willow thickets to a vidyen in a clearing.

The house was Pakajan, and probably ancient. Quite a number of round rooms had grown from the main circle, and each conical roof blossomed with sweet-smelling smoke. Taverik's rescuer threw open the unpainted board door. "Pour some hot, Kaja!" he shouted cheerfully. "Look at the fish I pulled from the river."

In the dim, rosy light of the central hearth, a crowd of people suddenly leaped into commotion, converging on Taverik with loud clucks and exclamations. Overwhelmed, he sagged against his host and lost track of what was going on.

When he began noticing again he found himself staring at oak beams carved into the vigorous twisting animals and plants so loved by the Pakajans of old. He lay on a high-backed wooden bench by the fire, under a heavy load of blankets. His surcoat and underlinen were piled in a sodden heap beside him.

"His poor feet must be cold as ice," a woman was saying.

A red-haired teenager tugged on Taverik's right foot. "Aye, we'll probably have to cut them off."

Horrified, Taverik struggled up. "Don't cut them off!"

A roar of laughter resounded on all sides. "Shush, don't laugh at him," the woman said. "He thinks you mean his feet. We're talking about your boots, dear. We can't get them off you. Drink this."

She held out a steaming crockery mug, her apple-cheeked face wrinkled with concern and sympathy.

Taverik reached for it but his hand shook so much that it sloshed all over him. "Sorry."

"He's as bad as me!" chortled a quavery old man across the fire from him.

"Aw, no one could be that bad," said another young man from somewhere behind the bench back.

The woman helped Taverik sit up some and guided the cup to his mouth. The hot liquid scalded his tongue and stomach and felt wonderful. He reached for more, but a violent tug on his foot spilled it down his neck. "Let him drink, Little Skaj!" the woman said.

The red-haired man came in again with a blast of snow and an armful of wood. "Lucky for you I came along," he said, feeding the already blazing fire. "Found you out in the Giss, clinging so hard to a rock I could barely pry up your fingers. What happened?"

Taverik swallowed hard, remembering. "What time is it? How long have I been in the river?"

"Almost two o'clock, now," said the man. "How'd you fall in?"

"I jumped—"

The teenager let go of Taverik's boot. "Jumped!"

"Suicide," said the old man knowingly. "Lovesick."

"Poor dear," said Kaja. "Drink some more."

Taverik pushed the mug aside. "Soza attacked Illiga at one o'clock."

"Soza!" exclaimed Skaj.

"It's true." Taverik forced his muzzy thoughts into coherence. "I found out he was in the city and tried to warn Zoji Balanji, and Soza's men were chasing me to prevent it. I only escaped by jumping off the Ao Bridge. But the attack had already begun. Started when the clocks struck one."

The woman turned frightened eyes to her husband. "Skaj," she began.

"Don't worry, Kaja," he said easily. "Balanji, Soza, who cares? Tell me the difference between Massadaran rulers."

"I'll tell you the difference," Taverik said sitting up until the blankets slipped off his naked shoulders. "Soza's not Massadaran. He's Bcacmat."

"Bcacmat!" cried the woman, turning pale.

"Them murdering fiends!" declared the old man.

"Quiet, Father," said Skaj.

"I was a boy when they came from the north, but I remember their raping and pillaging and slavery and—"

"Quiet, I said!" The old man folded his lips sulkily over his gums but subsided. Skaj turned his open freckled face to Taverik. "How do ya know?"

"They talk Bcacmat. And there's a letter to him from the Tlath telling him to leave Vosa and take the northern trade route instead."

Skaj pondered this, chewing his lip. "Sounds iffy. But just in case: Boy, you take the livestock up to the hiding place."

"Yes, Pa." The teenager behind the bench went to the door, a shorter replica of his father and brother.

"And boy," said Skaj, "I don't have to tell you to erase your tracks. Alka!"

Two girls, blossoming in handmade lace caps and embroidered skirts peeked in from the room where, Taverik guessed, they'd been banished when his clothes had been stripped off him. "Yes, Papa?" said the older.

"Put on your cloak and watch the approach. Same as always."

"Yes, Papa." She crossed the room, glancing at Taverik out of the corners of her eyes and blushing. Her mother followed her glance and firmly pushed Taverik back onto the bench and pulled the blankets up to his neck. "Drink some more of this," she said.

"Let's get those boots off first," said Skaj. Between him and his older son, they worked off the boots, Taverik clinging to the sides of the bench. Then they stripped off his hose, exposing his white and wrinkled feet. "Kaja, do you get a hot stone to his toes, and I'll get him some clothes."

The door burst open. "Papa!" cried Alka, whirling in with the snow. "Horsemen crossing the brook!"

"Too soon," cried Skaj. "Girls, into the back room. Kaja, help me get the lad into the cellars."

"Oh, Skaj, it's so cold down there."

"Do as I say," he said stripping the blankets from Taverik. "They's maybe looking for this one, why else come down here?" He propped Taverik on his shaky legs and propelled him toward the hole in the floor that Kaja had just uncovered. Taverik descended the ladder clumsily and stood shivering at its foot, looking up wistfully at the square of light above him. "We'll get you out as soon as we can, lad," said Skaj. He heaved, and Taverik's soggy clothes splatted down, along with the blankets. "Wrap yourself up."

"Pa, they're coming!"

"Zojikam, keep the boy in the woods!" cried Kaja. The heavy door thudded shut and Taverik stood alone in the black.

He shook with cold, finding it a strangely difficult business to get the blankets around him. As his eyes became a little accustomed to the dark the hulking shapes of casks and bales began to solidify around him. He stared at them, puzzled, until suddenly he understood—Skaj was a smuggler. The vidyen was in a perfect position to hide goods smuggled downriver. He snorted with the wry thought: now he himself had become smuggled goods.

Subsiding onto the last rung of the ladder, Taverik pulled the blankets tighter with clumsy fingers. He could hear nothing from above, and his thoughts turned inward, grieving at last over Kala Pardi and Mano. Nikilo? Where were Nikilo? Most likely dead as well, and beautiful Illiga now under the thumb of Soza. And Marko—Taverik's throat swelled painfully. In one day everyone whom he loved had been taken away, as well as his home and his city.

Tired. He curled up on the floor, feeling the cold seeping up from the flagstones. Perhaps Marko had escaped the city before Soza attacked. If so, he was glad for her. But he'd never see her again. He had no idea where she'd gone. Taverik tried to shake off his misery and couldn't. Throughout his life he'd been able to laugh off embarrassments, beatings, ill will, and somehow keep going. But now his resilience was gone for good. He would never be happy again. Gradually his thoughts unraveled like string and became hard to follow until at last he gave up and didn't think at all.

Time stretched into an unhappy infinity, filled with nightmares, discomfort and tossing. He surfaced from a semi-delirium and found himself in a warm bed, woke again only to realize he'd dreamed it and was still in the cellars, though unaccountably dressed in a thick nightrobe. His father often stood beside him, saying, "I thought it was best, forgive me, Taverik," and Taverik tried to tell him exactly why he was unforgivable.

After a seeming eternity Taverik woke. He lay in a warm bed near a hearth, and he felt good. His head had cleared, his muscles no longer ached, and the nightmares had receded. Stretching out, he luxuriated in the simple comfort of the absence of pain. White morning sunlight squeezed through the shutters into the small, round room. Muffled sounds outdoors told him it had probably snowed all night. Hard for travel, but he should get going. Where? He propped his head on his arms and stared up at the carved beams, mulling it over.

"Ah, you're awake," said Skaj, poking his head in the door. He disappeared to yell to Kaja about soup, then came back into the room. "You must be starving after so many days."

"So many days?" Taverik repeated warily.

"Well, four or five. You've been a little delirious." He scratched his grizzled hair sheepishly. "S'pose we shouldn't have left you in the cellar so long. The cold got you."

"And," said Kaja, bustling in with soup, "you go and dump him in again."

"Had to, Kala Kaja, love. Here feller, you let her feed you. You're limp as a worm."

Taverik gave up and opened his mouth for the spoon. "So it wasn't a dream, I was in the cellar twice."

"And you hollering you'd never forgive me. But I had to do it or them soldiers you say are Bcacmat woulda took ya. See, when they come to the house, they search the whole place like they own it, the barns too. Took everything our boy hadn't gotten up to the woods. We keep everything up there now, cause they're always prowling around.

"Anyways, they ask in particular for two people, and one of the ones they describe sounds just like you. Oh don't worry, we played good and dumb, but here they stay around all night, sitting out of the snow so their captain won't know."

"And we having to feed them," put in Kaja, jamming another spoonful into Taverik's mouth as if he were one of the soldiers himself.

"So they takes off in the morning, and we get you out of the cellar, but we thought we'd lost you. Wasn't till that night we breathed easier though you was in a high fever. And we'd just gotten you coming along when Little Skaj runs in 'cause them damned soldiers are coming back. So down you goes again, with Kaja here threatening to skewer the lot of them if you don't last.

"They were still asking for two people, and beating the hillsides for them. So I'm wondering, feller, if you are actually Zoji Balanji in disguise."

Taverik's jaw gaped, then he burst out laughing. "I ought to say yes. Maybe I'd get special treatment."

"You're already getting it. And if you ain't Zoji Balanji, I guess you are Taverik Zandro."

Taverik stopped laughing. "They were searching for—him—by name?"

"Yep. Are you related to Donato Zandro?"

He gave up pretense. "I'm his son."

"The old bastard," said Skaj fondly. "Didn't know he had another son. How come I never met you?"

"I just worked the river," Taverik said. Best not add he'd refused to have anything to do with smuggling for the last six years. Figured, he thought sourly, that he'd be pulled from the river by one of his father's smuggling cronies. He'd never escape Donato's shadow.

Skaj had whistled, new respect in his eyes. "Dangerous work. You must be good. Anyway, after Soza's men left we hauled you out and started all over again, and here we are."

"Now eat," insisted Kaja.

"Can't," Taverik said, tired already. But when Kaja nodded and stood, he caught her skirt. "Yes, you are giving me special treatment," he said, including Skaj with his eyes. "Thank you. I know I'm a danger for you. I'll get going as soon as I can."

"Oh, don't worry about that," said Skaj. "We're used to smuggled goods."

When next he woke, the only light came from the central hearth. He pushed back the blankets and climbed shakily to his feet. The flagstones were cold, but he forced himself to walk. Alka found him clinging to the window, trying to summon strength to return. She called her mother who scolded mightily and hustled him back to bed. He mollified her by requesting more of her good broth, then eating it all. His stomach protested, but he didn't listen. The sooner he got out of there the more chance he had of finding Marko, and the less chance of his bringing ruin to his hosts.

The next morning Skaj brought a pair of woven slippers and news. "Soza controls the city. He attacked from within the palace, and apparently had an easy job of it because both Balanji and the marshal, that Kintupaquat fellow, were unaccountably absent. Murdered probably."

Taverik thrust on the slippers and made a determined circuit around the room. "What about Illiga's army, at Ormea? Are they doing anything?"

"Not a thing—they ain't no more. As soon as they got word, they came roaring back, only to get wiped out in the pass at the rapids."

"So easy," Taverik said. "How the Bcacmats must scorn us."

"You say they're Bcacmats. I don't believe it. I say, let the Massadarans fight it out and leave us in peace."

"They won't leave you in peace! You've heard what Soza did to Vosa. He just hasn't gotten around to you yet. Besides, I've met Soza, and he gives me the creeps."

Skaj nodded skeptically. "Well, Taverik Zandro, all is not lost. Your precious Zoji Balanji apparently escaped

Soza's clutches along with his wife and children. Soza is dividing the countryside for him, but the snow has slowed him down."

"So he did escape." Taverik gave a satisfied smile. "Good luck to him, wherever he is."

The news put heart into him and he doubled his efforts to get back on his feet. Though his grief still sat heavily within, his returning strength brought back the resilience he'd thought had left forever. He began wading out through the knee-deep snow to the barn to help Skaj with the chores. He'd return white and exhausted and Kaja would scold. But by the fourth day he found he still felt energy after supper when the family gathered around the hearth in the main room. He fished a bridle out of the pile of tack Skaj had brought in and dipped his fingers in the pot of grease Little Skaj nudged toward him. "Guess I'll move on tomorrow."

"Move on!" exclaimed Kaja. "You're hardly out of bed."

"We thought you'd spend the winter with us," said Alka shyly.

"Why are you so all fire determined to leave?" asked Skaj. "You know you're welcome to stay here."

"Thank you," Taverik said, deeply warmed. "I owe you my life, and even the clothes on my back."

"Pooh. Why are you going?"

"Because I love a woman who fled the city just before it fell. I asked her to marry me and she was to tell me her answer that very morning. I don't know where she's gone, but if I don't find her soon, I'll never know the answer."

Kaja's eyes moistened. "And her to be your wife."

"Knew there was a woman!" crowed the old man.

"So sad," whispered the younger daughter, dabbing at her eyes, but Alka looked steadily at her hands.

Skaj was more practical. "How you going to find her?"

"Been thinking about that," Taverik said. "She wouldn't go south to Vosa or Ormea. That leaves Perijo to the west, Yassa to the north, and Novato to the east."

"That narrows it jes' fine," said Skaj.

Taverik's fingers smoothed the grease in gentle circles. "I don't think she'd go to Yassa. She's never been there for one thing, and it would be too strange for her."

"You mean, too Pakajan for her," growled the old man.

Taverik let it pass. "She's been to Perijo once, and Novato twice."

"I never heard of a woman traveling so much," marvelled Kaja. "I'd like to see those cities myself."

"Foolish notion," snapped her husband.

Taverik met her wistful eyes and thought with a painful twist of the stomach how much he treasured Marko. "So I think she'd have gone to Novato, and that's where I'm going."

"Doubt she could have gotten there in that snowstorm," said Skaj. "And the passes are closed for the winter now."

"I'll get through."

"Soza's men are searching the countryside. Looking for *you* in case you forgot."

"I'll get through," Taverik repeated stubbornly.

"No you won't," Skaj said and held up his hand when Taverik glared at him. "Not without I show you the way."

"What! I couldn't let you. As you said yourself, Soza is looking for me. If he found you helping me—and besides, you can't leave your family."

"I can take you one day's journey to my partner's place. From there I'll tell you the way from Ervyn and the secret path up the pass. Then I'll come home. That's only one night away. You'll never make it otherwise."

He would know. Taverik swallowed. "Why are you doing so much for me?"

"Let's just say," said Skaj with a mischievous grin, "I wouldn't mind if your father owed me one."

Chapter 2

Taverik

"Don't look at them, lad," whispered Skaj from behind his tree. "Don't even think about them. You'll draw their eyes."

Taverik obediently moved his gaze from the ten horsemen filing along the trail almost directly below. Instead he looked northeast to where the Pale Lady and the Dark Lady blazed brilliant white against the cobalt sky. All that morning they'd struggled towards those peaks, Skaj leading him deftly through knee-deep snow past the Pakajan vidyens and Massadaran manors of the Giss Valley. At noon they were working themselves along a steep, pine-wooded hillside above a trail when they heard a horse sigh and the chink of hoof against rock.

Without a word Skaj dove behind a pine. Taverik dropped to his knees in a clump of broad-leafed evergreens just as the first horseman rounded the bend. Taverik recognized him immediately—the black-bearded bandit who had clubbed him from his mule when the caravan had been attacked. He rode arrogantly, hand on hip, eyes searching right and left. Blazoned on the saddle blanket was the taloned circle of the Black Eagle.

Behind him rode nine others of the same cut. Any of them looking up could have spotted the two men hiding above them. Taverik's legs trembled from the strain of holding still, but not until the last hoof beats died away did he sprawl into the cold snow. "So that's how Soza hid his men," he said. "They're the bandits that have plagued the pass for the last year."

Skaj's freckled face puckered. "That so? They'll know the pass like home then. You watch out, lad."

"Well, they haven't caught us yet."

"Yet. But I don't like that damn trail of footprints we're laying across the countryside. If they stumble across that it'll lead them right to us. Let's get going. It's a long way yet to Achicha's."

Taverik stood up and brushed snow from his mantle. "I'm grateful to them at least for the rest. I'll admit I'm not as fit as I thought."

"Ahh, see?" said Skaj, but nevertheless he started out briskly. Soon Taverik had to concentrate to keep up, and by mid-afternoon Skaj was forced to slow the pace for him. But not until the two guardian mountains glowed pink and apricot in the setting sun did Skaj stop.

"Just over this rise, lad," he said and started vigorously up the slope. Taverik toiled doggedly in his wake. Skaj reached the top, a black silhouette against the sunset, then threw himself flat in the snow. Curious, Taverik crept up beside the smuggler, shivering as snow slid between his mitt and sleeve.

Below them stood a stone vidyen composed of only one round. The door hung crazily on one hinge and no smoke came from the central chimney. The snow around was trampled and dirtied, the wood pile scattered every which way. A great trail of hoof prints lead away to the west.

"No sign of Achicha," said Taverik.

"No." Skaj's freckled face wore no expression. He stood, snow coating his entire front, and edged down the hill into the blue twilight below. Taverik came after him, pulling back his hood as he crossed the churned up yard, listening to the screaming silence beyond the crunch of his boots. Skaj shouldered back the broken door and slid inside. "The bastards tore it apart," he said softly.

Taverik didn't relish the idea of sleeping in the snow. "Is it safe to stay here tonight?"

At once a hand slammed across Taverik's mouth and a knife blazed cold against his throat. "Not safe at all. Tell your pal to get out of my house."

The hand eased enough so Taverik could talk. "Achicha?" he said.

The knife bit. "Who are you?"

"Did you say something, lad?" Skaj looked out and his eyes widened. Then his face broke into a quick grin. "Knew you'd escape."

Taverik was released. He turned, wiping his throat, to find a tall, skinny Pakajan calmly returning his knife to his belt. "Who's this, Skaj?" said the man.

"Zandro's son."

"No he ain't."

"The other one."

"There's another one?" Achicha looked him up and down. "Not named Taverik by chance?"

"Yes," said Taverik warily. There was something ferrety about Achicha's long face.

"Huh."

"What do you mean, 'Huh?' "

Achicha limped past him. "Got a price on your head. I'm going up in the woods for the meat I got hid."

A price on his head. Taverik stared after Achicha's hobbling figure until Skaj's ungentle elbow recalled him. With deep disquiet he helped Skaj gather the scattered firewood and start a fire. He'd blocked a broken window and pounded in the hinge of the door with a broken chair leg by the time Achicha came back with a frozen haunch of venison over his shoulder.

Skaj and Achicha ate jovially, exchanging insults and reminiscing past adventures. Taverik stayed silent, sitting a little back from the others on the rush matting that served in place of the ruined chairs. He hadn't liked Achicha from the start and he liked him less the more he heard him talk. How could Skaj, a decent cheerful fellow at heart, be so blind to Achicha's basic viciousness? Then again, Skaj seemed to like Donato Zandro just fine, too. Maybe he liked everyone just fine. Taverik felt a little less warmed by Skaj's befriending of him, though he was no less grateful.

At last Skaj belched and sat back. "Achicha, you're the one with the famous cat feet," he said lazily. "How come Soza's soldier's are taking you by surprise?"

"Didn't. Sprained my ankle last week and couldn't run. Only managed to slip away when they began trashing the place. They was asking me if I'd seen one Zoji Balanji, one Taverik Zandro, and a young merchant and his sister." Achicha gave Taverik a slantwise look that stopped his breath. "Offered money for information about any of them."

"They'll be back," said Skaj. "Achicha, best you come down and live with me and Kaja. Could use another strong arm these days, and you won't be busy up here until trade gets back to normal."

"Kaja don't like me."

"She has nothing to say about it."

Achicha jerked his head at Taverik. "What about him?"

"I'll be all right," Taverik said, reluctant to reveal his plans to Achicha.

"He's going to Novato," put in Skaj.

"Novato, eh? They'll get you for sure the moment you try the pass. Stay and hide."

Taverik shook his head.

"You'll never make it," Achicha said, seeming to relish the thought. "You look pretty sickly to me."

"I'll be all right," Taverik repeated stubbornly.

"You're crazy!"

"Of course he is, ain't he a Zandro?" said Skaj. He added with seeming irrelevance, "Taverik here says Soza's a Bcacmat."

Taverik flushed under Achicha's derisive gaze. He got up and went to the door. "I've got to take a leak," he said.

The cold air felt good after the smoke-filled room. Taverik peed into the snow, then walked a little way into the night. He was tired right to his backbone. Achicha was right, he might not make it.

But that didn't mean he wouldn't try. He had to find Marko and make sure she was all right. And tell her that she and her sister were the last zojas of Vosa.

Maybe help her come into her inheritance, if she had any. After that, well, he didn't know. For a Pakajan merchant of disreputable family could not hope to marry even an exiled zoja. Perhaps he could be content with making sure she survived. Perhaps.

Provided Achicha didn't turn him in for the money. Disturbing, the thought of soldiers going to every farm asking for him, greedy people on the look out for him. He felt exposed, yes, the same way as when he'd felt every spiritual being in the Peninsula was watching him.

He stilled, thinking of the prophesy—uncanny how it seemed to be coming true. Both the priest and the *ihiga* in the alley had mentioned flood, darkness and fire. Taverik had already survived a flood. Did darkness and fire lie ahead? His stomach clenched.

The *ihiga* had also said that Zojikam had a task for him. Taverik scowled up at the stars. "I want to find Marko," he insisted. "I'm going to Novato."

Crazy to demand his own way when he needed Zojikam's protection more than ever. Yet every fiber of his being had lined up to go to Novato. A thought suddenly struck him: maybe that was what Zojikam wanted too. Funny how he assumed that Zojikam's wishes must inevitably clash with his. He gave a quick look at the vidyen, then softly said aloud, "Zojikam, zoji, please help me find Marko, and I will do any task you want. Only you've got to help."

Rising sun crept across Taverik's face as he bent over Skaj's map drawn in the snow with a stick. "Now that's how you get to Ervyn," said Skaj, looking up at him, his breath a curling plume. "Got it?"

Taverik nodded. "About the same as yesterday."

"Right. You should make it easily unless you lag again." Skaj erased the map and dug in the stick. "This is the Pale Lady, and here's the Dark Lady. Tomorrow, go northeast out of Ervyn angling so you can't see the Pale Lady any more. You'll find a glen, and that's the start of the secret way."

"Secret no longer," growled Achicha. He appeared

in the doorway, stuffing his bedding into a feed sack. "Why don't you tell him how to find our gold as well?"

"Shut up, Achicha," said Skaj. "This is Zandro's son."

"How come I never heard of him?"

Skaj ignored him and drew a line straight east. "Follow the glen. At the top, look for a tree bent to the ground and still growing. It'll have a blaze and the blaze will tell you which direction to go, and how far. You go from bent tree to bent tree all the way up. Got it?"

"Got it."

"It's easy until you get towards the top. Then you gotta cross the trail back and forth. Hide your footprints same as I taught you yesterday. The trail ends at the top, and after that you're on your own. Now here are the blazes and what they mean. Memorize them."

Taverik bent closer, absorbing the abstract shapes. After his first panic he found they had an order that made sense, and soon he knew he wouldn't forget.

"You've got it," said Skaj, satisfied. "You'll do fine, boy. Didn't we pull you out of the river?"

"Thank you." Taverik touched the small purse Skaj had given him, and the winter cloak and mitts. "How can I repay?"

Skaj's freckled face broke into a grin. "Just mention me to your father."

At that, Achicha burst into laughter. Skaj joined him and neither would tell Taverik why it was funny. Taverik set out ruffled, wondering just what his father had done.

He soon let it go and enjoyed the day. The sky's blue deepened in intensity as the sun rose, and the air warmed to nearly melting. Above him the Guardion Ladies towered, watching his approach. Taverik swung along, determined to make as much distance as he could while he still felt good.

His way soon led him up into the foothills, laboring along deer trails just beyond the limit of farmland. Hard going, but safe; brush, brambles and vines clustered so thick a horseman would have a hard time getting through.

When he began to flag he pushed himself, but still the sun was getting low by the time he reached a vast open area. Taverik stopped, panting, still under the last scrubby pines.

Immediately to his right, black cliffs rose sheer into the blue. To his left, open farmland stretched down into the heart of the Giss Valley. Skaj had told him about it. "You'll have to cross it, lad," he'd said. "Your most dangerous bit today. But Ervyn is only an hour's brisk walk after that."

Taverik rested a moment, watching and listening. Nothing moved except a hawk circling lazily in the azure sky. Still, he felt reluctant to leave cover; the dark fringe of brush and woods ahead seemed miles away. But the sun sank lower and he wouldn't get to Ervyn without crossing, so, taking a deep breath, he strode out into the open.

Instantly the hawk let out a sharp cry and wheeled towards him. Taverik gave it a startled glance and went cold. Not a hawk. It was a huge eagle, bigger than he'd ever seen.

It circled directly overhead. Taverik broke into a run. His scalp prickled and he glanced up to see the eagle fold its wings and drop, talons outstretched. Its dark body grew larger and larger.

Taverik dove into the snow just as its weight smashed his shoulder. Cloth ripped and heavy wings beat the drifts on either side of him. The eagle screamed and lifted above Taverik. A spray of fine snow chilled his neck.

He scrambled to his feet and ran. When he ventured another look the eagle was gone. Sobbing for air, he pushed forward again. Two huge rents gashed his cloak at his shoulder.

A faint cry brought him around again. He spotted the eagle, tiny now, circling out over the valley floor. Below it—a column of horsemen. As he watched, the eagle screamed once more and rounded in his direction. The column turned and galloped after it.

"Oh dear Zojikam!" breathed Taverik. The eagle was showing them where he was. Perhaps he should go back—but no, he'd already gotten halfway across the meadow. If he could just make that dense brush on the other side he could outrun any horseman.

He plunged forward, hearing a distant shout when they spotted him. The woods were nearer; he could make out individual trees. Suddenly the eagle screamed directly above him. A rock-like weight hit him between the shoulder blades, throwing him headlong. He staggered up, shielding his head with his arms. The eagle hit him again and he fell.

The horsemen entered the lower end of the meadow. One shouted in Massadaran, commanding Taverik to stop. Taverik drew his knife and slashed at the eagle, and ran.

Bramble canes now poked above the snow. The brush grew thicker and crunched under Taverik's feet as he ran. Taverik tore through, heedless of the thorns snagging his cloak. He made it to dense cover. Above him the eagle screamed with rage, and screamed again. The cries reverberated in Taverik's ears, tensing his stomach with fear. He wasn't safe yet.

Hoofbeats and angry shouts resounded along the edge of the briars. Taverik dropped flat and muffled the sound of his hoarse breathing in his sleeve. The sun was setting, turning the treetops a rosy orange. Blue twilight crept through the brambles. Taverik's spirits rose a little. Night would favor him. When his heart and breathing steadied he squirmed on until he found a rabbit run. Grateful for his thick mitts, he followed it under the arching canes bristling with dagger-like thorns. He'd reached the trees now, and the shouts and thud of hooves faded behind him.

A shadow fell over him, travelling slowly across his back and bringing a paralyzing chill with it. Taverik sensed a presence, seeking him, calling him. He crawled faster. It was hard to see; twilight was deepening awfully fast.

Taverik collided with a thornbush. He jerked back and swore softly, cradling his cheek. Lucky it wasn't his eye. Blood darkened the leather of his mitt, but even as he looked, his sight misted over. He glanced up. The thornbush blurred and dimmed. Suddenly Taverik understood and his blood went cold. He'd felt that same presence in the alley behind the pawnshop; the *mahiga* of the Black Eagle.

As if in answer to his recognition, he felt a voice inside his head. "Come."

"No," he said aloud. Shielding his face with one hand, he pushed blindly through the thorns. The darkness thickened to more than night blackness. It pressed in on him, hindered him, clouded his mind. The Black Eagle stalked him, voices whispered on either side of him.

"This way," he heard, and he turned toward the voice only to sense the *mahiga*, close and approving.

"No," he said again and crawled in the opposite direction. The rage of the *mahiga* crackled inside his head. He cowered in the snow until it eased, then stubbornly, blindly, crawled forward again. His mitts and surcoat were soon soaked through, and his exhaustion drained him. He couldn't go much farther.

"Come and rest," he instantly felt in his mind. He pushed the thought away and in the tiny clear moment that followed realized he was being herded always west. West, out of cover.

At that moment he heard the horsemen moving along to his left. He fell flat and listened. "Spread out, you fools," said the black-bearded bandit. "He'll be flushed out of those damn brambles anywhere along here."

"I'm not staying alone with that thing loose," said another.

"You just better get used to it," said the chieftain. "You'll be worshipping it for the rest of your life."

A third warned, "Don't make it angry with you."

Other voices echoed inside Taverik's head. "Go to them," they whispered, louder and louder until he couldn't be sure they weren't audible. They pulled at him as if they'd planted hooks in his thoughts. The darkness pushed. Taverik buried his face in the snow. "No," he whispered, and added with the simplicity born of desperation, "Zojikam, don't let them get me!"

The pressure in his mind suddenly eased. In its place

came the memory of the stern, sad face of the *ihiga*, the eye-blinding brightness of his presence, and the sweet scent of his love for the High Lord, Zojikam. "They worship a creature," the *ihiga* had said, "ignoring the Creator."

Taverik inhaled deep with the memory. To him personally, the *ihiga* had said, "Fear not flood nor darkness nor fire . . ." Sure enough, he'd found flood. Well, now he'd found darkness. *Fear not?* he thought, and laughed grimly. Then he pushed himself up and crawled deliberately into the thickest darkness.

The anger of the Black Eagle snapped and burned inside his head. Taverik closed his eyes and set his face as if into a high wind. Brambles tore at his clothes but he kept going until his arms trembled so badly he collapsed.

Instantly the cloying darkness thickened around him until he could hardly breath. It clogged his thoughts, dulled his will. "Come, come," urged the presence.

Taverik could resist no longer. He sat up, then blinked. Had he seen a light? There. A brief spark.

"Come!" Taverik rubbed his forehead with the pain of the command, but continued to watch for the spark. Two of them appeared, then another, spinning crazily in tightening circles until it seemed two, no three eyes looked at him. They reminded him of the terrible eyes of the *ihiga*.

"This way, human," a voice said. It was the *ihiga*. Taverik plunged gratefully towards the tiny points.

An eagle's scream shivered the silence. The lights blinked out abruptly as snow flurried in a mad gust of wind. Everywhere he looked now he could see light, sometimes pinpoints, sometimes a rolling glowing ball, sometimes fiery wheels he could see even with his eyes closed. Against their light he could see thick blackness, like a fog with tendrils, smothering them, extinguishing them. His eardrums shivered with unheard concussions. Taverik panted with terror. He'd never dreamed he could be so frightened.

The *ihiga*'s voice again. "Stand up," it cried. "You're out of the brambles." Taverik stood up, thrust his hands in front of himself, and stumbled forward. Light intensified around him until he could make out faint black trunks of trees. Then the darkness surged back, like the waves of a river, knocking him off his feet. He waited until he saw pinpoints of light once more, then staggered up and followed them.

"Up here, human." The *ihiga* spoke to his right. "Hurry!"

Taverik veered in that direction. Instantly all lights went out. Blackness surrounded him. Too late he realized he'd listened to the wrong voice.

He closed his mind to it and pushed through darkness as thick as water. Tendrils caught at his ankles, hair and cloak. He was released so suddenly he tumbled forward once more into the snow. A spark spun beside him, tighter and tighter until a single white eye blinked at him. "Test the spirits, human," its voice urged.

"How?" Taverik cried, but the spark blinked out. Tentatively he experimented, reaching out his mind to the presences crowding around him. To his amazement he *could* tell the difference. He could almost taste it, first savoring Zojikam then comparing the flavor. The skill added little comfort. He now realized that not all the sparks of light tasted of Zojikam. They tasted foul, disquieting, revolting. And now so intensely aware of the evil around him, Taverik found it harder to hold back his panic. To fall into their hands was unthinkable. But he did make faster progress and the *ihiga* had to call him less frequently. When it did, its voice showed terrible strain.

How long had it been? He'd drop in his tracks soon. The battle intensified. Great gusts of wind whipped up the fallen snow into fury that beat against Taverik's chapped face.

A flash of light burst before his eyes. "Look out!" it cried. Suddenly Taverik tasted evil all around him. The ground shook. With a keening wail the light shrank to a point and went out. Darkness engulfed him, drowned him. The triumphant scream of the Black Eagle resounded in his ears. Taverik struggled but could not move.

The Black Eagle spoke, the words so loud he thought they were spoken aloud. *Back or he dies!*

The air began to glow, and Taverik sensed an *ihiga*'s presence. As if in response, Taverik's breath involuntarily expelled from him. He couldn't breathe. He doubled over, his consciousness beginning to darken.

"Help us, human." The words came faintly, just as he hovered on the edge of not understanding anymore. "Add your strength."

What strength? "Zojikam!" Taverik croaked from an airless throat. It was enough. The hold broke and he drew in a long, shuddering breath. Now he remembered what had helped him twice before. In a creaking monotone he began to sing the Call to Worship.

Two things happened at once. The Black Eagle's reaction whiplashed his mind, and an incredible blaze of white light hurt his dark-sensitive eyes. "Run, human!" cried the *ihiga.*

Taverik ran. He broke from the woods into crystalline moonlight as bright as sunlight, though silver. Down across a long sloping field gleamed the roofs of Ervyn. And immediately before him stood a tall, burly man.

Taverik could summon no strength with which to escape. Instead he fell in the snow at the man's feet. Vise-like hands closed on his collar.

Chapter 3

Soza

Furious at the interruption, Itzil Farasoza was dragged back into his body. Someone was shaking him, gibbering, "Zoji, Zoji, are you all right?" and that made him even angrier; he hated being looked at when the Black Eagle pulled him out of himself.

He'd gone unwillingly this time, for the city still seethed with unrest. But the *mahiga's* command was sharp and he'd had no time to even lock the door before he'd found himself riding a thermal near the eastern pass, examining the hills below through the eyes of the eagle form the *mahiga* assumed as one of its physical manifestations. The sun was slipping behind the western mountains.

Taverik Zandro stepped from the forest. Farasoza's blood heated, and in response to the Black Eagle's question he answered, "Yes, that's one of them."

Simple to stop the young man, hold him up until his wesh-agash arrived. And oh, he wanted this one badly. Zandro held many of the missing keys and had escaped him too long. And he wore the mark of Zojikam. The eagle claws dug deep into Zandro's shoulders as he ran.

The soldiers closed in. The eagle had just circled high for another pass at the struggling figure below. Then this! Worried voices crying, "Zoji, Zoji! Are you ill, shall I call a doctor?" Fingers touching him, shaking him from the Black Eagle's grip, sliding him back into his body.

He blinked balefully at the three people before him. Regaining control over his physical shell, cross-legged on the floor, took time. Meanwhile he was helpless and he hated having anyone see him so. Where was Abado? Abado would have guarded his master better than that white-faced Malenga. But he'd sent Abado with Karaz to Novato, to keep watch in case Balanji surfaced there.

Sensation returned. He felt nauseated as he always did after such prolonged contact with the Black Eagle. He hadn't realized, when he'd offered his body to the *mahiga* in exchange for power, that he would be so completely taken over. If only someone had warned him back then. Ambitious but middle-aged, he'd seen the Black Eagle cult as a quick path to the top. But gradually the *mahiga* dominated him until, powerless, he'd done acts he himself considered foolish or disgusting. The Black Eagle had its own ends. It wanted worship, and was bent on wrenching the world from Zojikam, whom it hated savagely. Itzil Farasoza would give anything to be his own person again. And he would warn others too, except the *mahiga* would not allow it.

Farasoza could now recognize the three before him. The Pakajan mercenary, second in command under his wesh-agash, bent over him to check his pulse. Beyond, the young priest wrung his foolish hands, pleading with the commander to come away and try again later. Worst of all: Donato Zandro, backing toward the door, staring at him with undisguised horror and disgust.

Itzil Farasoza closed his mouth. He'd drooled as usual, curse Malenga for letting them in to look at him. He pulled his wrist from the commander's grasp, though it would be some time before he could stand. "Why," he croaked, "have you disturbed me?"

"Zoji, do you want a doctor?" bleated the priest. His former god, Zojikam, had never pulled him from his body. It frightened the man.

"A doctor is not needed when serving as the Black Eagle's eyes," said Farasoza. "You yourself will soon learn the powers of the *mahiga* you now serve."

The priest looked anguished, and for a moment Farasoza thought he'd take back his recantation. But the trembling man merely swallowed and looked doubtfully at the Pakajan mercenary.

"My Zoji," said the commander, his expression neutral. "We have caught a number of citizens conducting a secret worship service for Zojikam."

"So," said Farasoza, wishing he could stand. "You have arrested them?"

"As you ordered, Zoji."

Farasoza looked at the priest. "Tell them they must serve the Black Eagle now. Tell them all the advantages of doing so. Promise that any who will swear allegiance will go free as you did. The others will join your stubborn fellow priests rotting at the city gates. March them past to look at the carcasses, if it would help. Commander, you will arrange it."

Trembling, the priest started to speak, but Farasoza was sick of him. "Go!" The commander shepherded the man away and Zandro made to join them. "Zandro," said Farasoza. "What did you want?"

"My Zoji," said Zandro, kneeling before him. "I only wanted to ask about the tax on registered merchants. Please Zoji, since the looting, they have so little, and to take seventy-five percent—and they hate *me* for it. Could we make it sixty percent? They will praise you for your generosity."

"You'll do as I say," snapped Farasoza. And because the man's disgust and horror still rankled, and because the Black Eagle had been pushing him for human sacrifice and he was finding it harder to resist, he added, "So you don't like the looks of a trance, do you? Obey or I will feed you to the Black Eagle and leave you forever so, as a lesson to others."

Zandro's red face turned gray, but Farasoza felt not one whit better yet. "But first," he added, "I will show you how it works with your son. Now, will you do as I say?"

"Zoji, your wish is my order," bleated Zandro.

"Then get out!"

Left alone, Farasoza sat still in the dusk-filled room. Taverik Zandro had not yet been caught, he sensed that. He could also sense the resistance the Black Eagle was experiencing in stalking him. Zojikam's creatures had entered the fight on the human's behalf and an enormous battle had shaped in those woods.

Taverik

"Stop struggling so, brother," said the man. "I'm trying to help you."

He'd spoken old Pakajan. Taverik stilled and reached out his mind as he'd learned in the woods, and met a spirit strong with the love of Zojikam. In a strange, silent greeting, the man's spirit responded with joy and recognition. "So," he said aloud, helping Taverik to his feet, "*you're* the reason Zojikam sent me out into the snow."

Taverik recognized him, though moonlight cast black shadows slantwise across the bearded face. "You're the priest of Ervyn," he said, also in old Pakajan. "You helped me and my friend after the caravan was attacked."

The white head inclined. "I remember well. I also remember a certain disturbing dream about an eagle and a hawk which I felt had much to do with you two. Ikatabalcha is my name. Children and tongue-tied Massadarans call me Ika. And you?"

Taverik was prepared by now. "Tazur," he said.

"Just Tazur? Falcon in the old tongue, which you speak fairly well for a city merchant. But then I know you are more than just a city merchant, just as I know that Tazur isn't your real name. Though in a sense, it is more your real name than your real name. Ah, you say, trust a priest to blather on about useless paradoxes when the woods are uncannily alight and the earth is shaking."

Taverik spun around. The trees stood silent and dark.

"Whatever was there is gone now," said Ikatabalcha. "Ever since dinner I felt Zojikam calling me to come out to the woods. I resisted, thinking it merely the result of a spicy sausage, but at last the command burned like fire in my bones and out I come only to find strange lights in the woods and an unearthly battle. Then I heard a most earthly voice singing the service, so I joined in, giving it my best, and behold, here you are."

"It was the Black Eagle," Taverik said. "And Soza's men."

"Then you may rest easy. Soza's men have already reached Ervyn. They have battened themselves into the inn, to forget with drink that which they don't want to remember. And the Black Eagle is, simply, gone. For now."

"You're right," Taverik said, reaching out his mind. "I don't sense them."

"All that remains is for me to hide you. Will you follow?"

The priest started off, not toward Ervyn, but upwards to the woods on the mountainside above the town. Taverik gave a last look at the line of trees and tried to project his thanks to the *ihiga* who had helped him. No answer seemed forthcoming so he thanked Zojikam instead, and that seemed more right. He crossed the road and trudged after Ikatabalcha.

By the light of the almost-full moon the priest led him deep into the woods. There he stopped before a half-vidyen so cunningly built into the rocky slope that Taverik would have walked right past it. "I built this long ago for my wife," Ikatabalcha said, unlocking the door. "Now she is dead, I use it for a retreat—and certain other things, Massadaran tyranny being what it is."

Ikatabalcha lit a lamp on a log table. Taverik found himself in a round room, tiny enough to cross in six paces. Besides the table, it held only a chest, a cot and a chair. The priest opened the chest and brought out a pot. "Fill this with snow, will you?" he said, thrusting it into Taverik's hands.

By moonlight Taverik found a smooth stretch of snow. Pulling off his mitts he packed the pot and brought it in. The sweet scent of a newly lit fire greeted him. Ikatabalcha still rummaged in the chest. "Hang the pot over the fire, will you?" his muffled voice said.

"Then have a seat. I'm looking for my snowshoes. Ever wear them?"

"No," said Taverik, sitting gratefully on the one chair and stretching his wet, cold feet to the hearth. A deep peace filled the air, and with each breath, found its way into Taverik's being.

The priest emerged from the chest with a loaf of bread and cheese. "Stale, I know. But better than nothing. Must have left the snowshoes in town. Eat."

Taverik ate. The bread tasted fine and the cheese very passable. Ikatabalcha sat on the chest and stared into the fire, humming and twirling strands of his beard. Only when Taverik finished and sighed contentedly did the priest speak. "I am agog," he said, "to hear what happened."

Taverik told him, awkwardly at first, because the whole thing sounded preposterous. Then to explain, he had to add the whole business in the alley, and about the *ihiga* and the prophesies, which sounded even weirder. But the priest listened, head inclined, nodding now and then as if what Taverik said made sense. "I always wondered what happened to you two," he said at last. "How gratifying. I knew you would have some part in Zojikam's plans."

"Ika, how is it I now have this power to sense good and evil?"

"*You* don't have the power. It is given you by Zojikam. Do not grow proud—for Zojikam can take it again. All powers are given us by Zojikam to be used in his service."

"But the ones who worship the Black Eagle have powers."

"Not in themselves. The *mahiga* gives powers, and human fools think they can use them to their own ends. Instead, the Black Eagle controls them for its own purposes. In the end, the two are inseparable."

Taverik thought this over, fingering the bramble scratches on his face. "Soza," he said slowly, "must be under the power of the Black Eagle, then. I've met him, and he feels, no, he tastes, just like the thing that came after me in the woods."

"Some peoples, such as certain Bcacmat military castes," said the priest with a grimace, "purposely *invite* the Black Eagle to control them. Gives them great powers for a while, but they do have a history of rapacity and madness."

"I've proof that Soza's a Bcacmat."

The priest did not scoff. "That explains much indeed," he said. "I shall tell my people. It will stiffen their resistance. And now I understand why I must help you."

"I don't like being involved in all this spirit stuff," Taverik said.

Ikatabalcha smiled gently. "Materialism is so much safer, is it not? Or at least it gives the appearance of being so. But wearing a blindfold will not make danger go away."

"If Zojikam is so powerful," Taverik said, "why didn't he just rescue me instead of putting me through all that?"

"Zojikam works through his creatures. He gave you what you needed to win through, and you are a stronger person because of it." The priest leaned both arms on his knees and looked Taverik in the eye. "Tell me, my falcon, if it were possible, would you erase tonight from your life?"

"No," Taverik said slowly. "I guess I wouldn't."

"Ah! Just remember, the power comes from Zojikam. Look, your snow water is hot. I shall steep dried healall in it and bless the water, and you may wash the bramble scratches on your face."

Fragrant steam rose from the wooden bowl Ikatabalcha set before Taverik. Taverik plunged his chapped hands into the warm water and sighed with the relief. He splashed his stinging face. Tense muscles around his eyes relaxed, and though he still felt exhausted, the grimness faded. He knew his sleep would be sweet.

"Best have no fire to betray you tonight," Ikatabalcha said, throwing blankets on the cot. "These will keep you warm. I'll be back tomorrow to set you on your way."

"Thank you," Taverik said. "Thank you for everything." The priest gave a final wave, shut the door and locked it. Rolling into the blankets, Taverik stretched out on the cot. He sighed, then slept.

He woke stiff and groggy, morning sun in his eyes. It must be almost noon. Where was Ikatabalcha? Why hadn't he come? He ate more of the bread and cheese, paced, unlocked the door and looked, paced some more. Should he go? But the priest had promised to come. How long should he wait?

Not until the sun was westering did Taverik hear footsteps. He peered from the window then stiffened. A middle-aged woman, bundle over her shoulder, struggled up the hill through the knee-deep snow. She looked behind her, then turned and floundered on, straight toward the vidyen.

Taverik locked the door and stood against it so she wouldn't see him if she looked through the window. He heard her heavy breathing outside, then the scrape of metal; she had a key. The bolt fell back and the door opened slowly. "Kali Tazur?" she said softly.

He pulled her in and shut the door. "Who are you?"

"Ikatabalcha's housekeeper," she said, her old Pakajan strongly countrified. "They're taking him to Illiga. He told me to bring you this."

Taverik caught the bulky sack she swung toward him. "I've got to stop them," he said. "They'll execute him."

"You leave that to us Ervyns," the woman said, pushing her brown hair under her cap with thick, competent fingers. "We will get our own back. I must go. Only five soldiers took him. The other five are camped in my master's house, making me cook for them. Ikatabalcha says they're Bcacmat. I say they're pigs!"

She opened the door and marched into the snow, hurrying through the flickering gold and purple tree shadows. Taverik watched her out of sight then shut the door, feeling oddly alone.

The sack. He hoisted it to the table and opened it. Inside were two large wooden circlets with stout leather webbing. Snowshoes, he guessed, though he'd never seen a pair before. A torn piece of paper fluttered to the floor and Taverik picked it up. Its spidery handwriting said, "You need these for the pass. Soldiers demanded I lead worship for their disgusting Black Eagle. Do not try to follow me—you have your work and I have mine. Zojikam's blessings and protection on you."

"And also on you, Ikatabalcha," Taverik murmured. Cold fury shook him: one more score lay against Soza.

In the bottom of the sack he found a small amount of food and a bottle of blessed water. Taverik added two blankets and tied it to his back. He removed all traces of his presence in the room, then swung out into the last rays of the sun. To the north a line of hemlocks marched up the mountain, dark green against bare oak branches. He labored toward them, guessing they marked the glen Skaj had told him about. At last he stood beneath the first huge hemlock, his panting breath a mist in the gathering cold. Below him lay a deep cleft in the mountainside, silent, dark and mysterious.

The snow deepened here. He'd have to wear the snowshoes now or he'd never make it. Dragging them from the sack, he sat on a log to bind them on. Then he grabbed a low branch to pull himself to his feet, and ended up dumping a cold rush of snow down his neck in the process. Laughing ruefully, he shook it off as the sun slipped beyond the far mountains. Then he took his first step into the blue dusk of the glen.

He floundered awkwardly down the slope to where the brook gurgled under snow and ice. The snowshoes kept stepping on each other or tangling with brush. Worse, the bindings loosened until his boots sloshed within them. He was climbing over a fallen hemlock when his left foot flew free. Exasperated, he pulled off the other snowshoe, only to sink into thigh-deep snow. Damn! He'd *have* to wear them.

Precious minutes fled as he put them back on, but this time he bound them tighter. Gradually he found a rolling walk that kept the snowshoes from crossing, and soon even his breathing kept rhythm. Moonlight now filtered through the hemlock branches. Black and silver flashed confusingly as the mighty trees stirred in the wind. The chuckle of the brook and crunch of his snowshoes kept him company.

The path became steeper and more difficult as he neared the head of the glen. Finally he was forced to climb an almost vertical slope beside a frozen waterfall. A tree leaned out like a friendly hand, and he grasped it, pulling himself up until he was seated on its odd, bent knee. He'd reached the top.

Taverik started to get up then sank back. *A tree bent to the ground and still growing.* He'd found his first sign. He brushed snow away and examined the blaze, two circles with numbers. North two hundred, west one hundred.

Spirits rising, Taverik set out, counting as he went. After the dark of the glen, the moonlight in the open was bright enough to read by, reflecting off blue-white snow between sparse birch and pine. He easily found the next tree and its blaze. Higher and deeper into the mountains he labored, falling into a contented, dreamlike state. Overhead, the white peaks of the Pale Lady and the Dark Lady glimmered against the night sky. The lopsided moon became a silent companion, casting Taverik's shadow before then behind, as he followed the twisting trail.

When the moon set, the stars sharpened, but Taverik could no longer make out the blazes. He cut spruce bows and made a shelter under a jutting rock, welcoming the relief from the wind as he crawled in. Oddly contented and at peace, he ate frozen bread and cheese until his body heat warmed the blankets enough for him to doze.

He woke with a start and stared in confusion at spruce needles inches from his cold nose, remembering and discarding the various places he'd been, until at last his mind clicked into place. He was halfway up the pass. Maybe only a day's trek below the top. Pushing aside a spruce bow, he peered out, screwing up his face against snow spicules hurled by the wind. A gray sky pressed low upon him, the clouds heavy and portentous. He lay in the arms of the Pale Lady, and from across the pass, the Dark Lady peered serenely down at him, mist crossing her black and white face.

Taverik ate again, though slowly; the cold sapped his strength. Odd the way he felt, as if his past had detached and drifted away, as if Taverik Zandro, son of the notorious Donato Zandro was gone. Instead he was Tazur, the falcon, beloved of the mountains, beloved of the moon, beloved of Zojikam. Peace filled him like water in a glass.

He slid out, shaking with cold. Even simple tasks took an age, but at last he got the shelter down and the branches scattered. Lacing on the snowshoes, he started out. Three strides later he turned back and took up one of the spruce bows; today he would be crossing the trail several times, and he would have to disguise his path.

Slow going—dimly he knew cold and exhaustion were rapidly taking their tax, but his head was filled with one driving thought: to get to Novato. If only the wind weren't so blustery. He clung to a bent pine tree and fingered its blaze, which pointed him directly across the trail. No sign of life in either direction. Go.

Crossing the trail, he started up the far bank, eyes on the bent tree above. Voices behind him. Taverik turned his head and stiffened. Around the switchback below came five horsemen, bent low against the wind. Wind roared up the pass, whirling snow into a great funnel. For a moment the five soldiers were blotted out, and Taverik managed to slip behind the trees before the snow hissed back to earth and the air cleared. He watched tensely as the men approached his crossing. They did not pause. Taverik breathed again. The wind had filled in his tracks.

But now he followed the blazes with a nagging worry. The higher he climbed, the more open areas he had to cross. Soon it would be hard to keep out of sight. From behind a boulder he listened to the horsemen travel back down, passing not ten yards away from him. Their persistence warned him they had somehow guessed he was in the pass. When the next blaze pointed him across the trail he listened for a long moment, summoning nerve to move out of cover. At last he rolled forward, quickening the snowshoe rhythm and sweeping behind him. He was back in cover and paralleling the road before the horsemen returned. Once more the gusting wind had removed all trace of his passing. Tazur, beloved of the wind, he thought groggily. Though the wind was a difficult friend, whose fingers found every chink in his clothes.

He crossed several more times, that long day, before they spotted him. The cold was making it harder and harder to think and he'd lost track of where the soldiers were. He took a chance, moving out in a huge flurry whipped by the wind. The snow-covered rocks on the other side made hard going, and when he was only halfway up the exposed slope he heard them shout.

They stood in a cluster on the road, pointing at the sweeping marks his spruce bow had made. One man followed the marks off the road and called out when he found where Taverik had ceased sweeping and the snowshoe prints became obvious. Their eyes followed it upwards until their excited gesturing and pointing told Taverik when they spotted him. The soldier off the trail urged his horse upward, but the tired animal half-reared and refused in the belly-deep snow. One of the other men shot his crossbow but the arrow struck far down the slope.

No use trying to hide. Taverik got up and trudged on, ignoring their loud demands to surrender. Two riders then went down the pass, and three moved up. They'd be waiting for him next time he crossed.

Softly, snow began to fall. Taverik groaned at the added difficulty. Flakes clung to his eyelashes, and made it hard to breathe, and danced dizzily before his eyes. But the snow would also help conceal him, he realized. Really, he should be thankful, not sorry. In fact, the snow was a gift. With a confused notion that the Guardian Ladies had provided the snow at Zojikam's request, Taverik floundered on to the next tree.

The terrain was flattening now. He must be near the top where the secret trail would end. Taverik threw away the spruce bow, relieved to be rid of its burden.

His pack was a burden, too. He pulled it off, tossed it under a tree and kept going. After a while he threw off his mitts, as well. His wool cloak and surcoat chafed and grew heavier. He'd have to get rid of them. He loosened the cloak to pull it off, but it tangled with the bottle of blessed water he'd hung around his neck. He pulled the cork and drank some.

The liquid coursed down his parched throat, tingling, warming. His head cleared. Suddenly Taverik was horrified. What could he have been thinking of, throwing off his clothes that way? The cold had unhinged his mind. He backtracked and found his mitts. The pack was long gone. He'd have to let it go.

Sobered, he took a small swallow of the water every little while after that. Its energy somehow kept him going until he reached the flat top of the pass and the secret trail ended. Now he could hide and build a shelter.

He stepped forward and found himself surrounded by horsemen and a bristling wall of pikes.

Chapter 4

Taverik

Taverik swore under his breath. To make it this far only to be snatched a few miles from safety . . . And better dead than in Soza's hands. He eyed the huge dappled horse to his left, wondering if he could fling himself under the pike, roll under the horse's belly, and escape to the deep snow of the woods.

"Who are you?" demanded the leader in Illigan Pakajan. The Massadaran borrowings sounded familiar-strange after weeks of pure Pakajan.

"My name is Tazur," said Taverik.

"He's the one," said the man on the dappled horse. "This is the very hare hunted up and down the pass by Soza's buffoons. We've watched you all day."

Taverik looked up, confused. "You aren't Soza's—?"

"Don't be insulting," the leader said. "We are the loyal First Mounted Corps of Zoji Balanji. Who is, alas, no more, so we are without master."

"But Balanji isn't dead," Taverik said.

"You lie!" The lances converged toward him.

"I do not," he said, drawing himself up. "Soza has been conducting house to house searches and combing the valley looking for him. He got away."

The men whooped for joy until their leader shushed them. The wall of lances broke at last and the leader dismounted to stand beside Taverik. He wore a shabby jumble of poorly mended clothing, but his captain's insignia gleamed on his chest, and his penetrating eyes looked Taverik over sharply.

"Who are you, then?"

"I was the one, I think, who warned Balanji," Taverik said. He got no further. The eight men crowded around him, shaking his hand, clapping him on the back.

"Come on, Pemintinuchi," said the man with the dapple gray. "Can't you see he's perishing of cold? And Soza's men will find us if we stand around. Let's take him to camp and pry his story out of him there."

The one called Pemintinuchi gave Taverik a look that silently promised ill if he betrayed them. "All right," he said. "He'll have to ride with you. That monster of yours can carry two."

The other brought the dapple forward. Taverik put his hand reverently on the warm moist flank. "I've always dreamed of someday riding a horse."

Pemintinuchi cursed fluently. "Damn *Sadra* Laws," he said.

"Should have joined the army, lad," said another. "Only way a Pakajan can ride a horse or carry a sword. You want a sword?"

"Wouldn't know how to use it," Taverik said, trying to tie the snowshoes to the saddle. His fingers wouldn't work well, so one of the men slid off his horse to help, then gave Taverik a boost to sit behind the big Pakajan. After riding steep-withered mules all his life, Taverik found it hard to grip the horse's round barrel. He clung, lightheaded, as the troop wound their way through the forest and up into a hidden cleft.

Pickets challenged their arrival long before Taverik saw the myriad fires of the camp through the trees. Almost a thousand men had gathered on this shoulder between the Guardian Ladies. And though the camp was rough, the men maintained strict military order. Pemintinuchi, Taverik gathered as the captain escorted him to a fire, must be in charge. The rest of the patrol, who seemed to have adopted Taverik, circulated through the camp with his news. Great jubilation arose, and Taverik, given dinner under Pemintinuchi's grim eyes, fervently hoped Balanji actually had escaped.

"Now," said Pemintinuchi. "Who are you, and why is Soza after you?"

"He thinks I know where Balanji and certain other people are," Taverik said. "I don't," he added looking around at the circle of hopeful faces orange-lit by the fire. "I also have information that Soza desperately wants suppressed."

"What's that?" asked Pemintinuchi.

"Soza's a Bcacmat. He's an agash of the Tlath."

In the silence that followed, Taverik could hear snow hiss into the fire. Then everyone talked at once. Pemintinuchi quelled them and gave Taverik a skeptical look. "How do you know?"

"A letter written in Bcacmat, addressed to Agash Itzil Farasoza."

"Farasoza!" Pemintinuchi nodded his head as if he'd heard of him. "Who was it from? What did it say?"

"From the Tlath, complaining about the agash's lingering in Vosa when he should be taking the northern trade route."

The captain's next look was friendlier. "Soza, Farasoza. Black Eagles—makes sense. And Balanji is alive?"

"Last I heard."

"This changes everything," Pemintinuchi said softly. His eyes shifted from Taverik to the men crowding round. "We've just been existing, demoralized, discipline breaking down. Now we know Balanji is alive, we have new purpose. Every day new stragglers find us—now we will purposely search for them. We will gather an army for Balanji, and hold the pass for him until he needs us."

"Hear, hear!" roared the men, their eyes gleaming in the flickering firelight.

"Join us, Tazur," urged one of the men who had been on the patrol. "We watched you all day today. Soza's men riding up and down, and you just going where you pleased. They'd walk right past you in the snow squalls. I never saw such a thing."

"Aye, you're a clever one all right," said another. "Stranger, you bring welcome news, you turn our sorrow into rejoicing. Why don't you join us?"

"Yes," agreed Pemintinuchi surprisingly. "Join us."

"Thank you," Taverik said gruffly. "But I seek someone in Novato. If that person is dead, then I'll gladly join you. I have a high score against Soza."

"We'll kick his butt all the way back to Bcacma!"

"Don't underestimate him," Taverik warned. "He uses the power of the Black Eagle. We must depend on Zojikam if we are to defeat him." He stopped, embarrassed at sounding like a priest, but a mutter of agreement went around the circle.

"Another thing," Taverik added, "one of his leaders is that bandit chieftain that hid up here last year. He knows the pass well."

"Not as well as me," said a man. "I grew up here."

"Me too," said another. "We'll fix the bastard."

Pemintinuchi put out his hand, his eyes speaking friendship as strongly as before they spoke suspicion. Taverik shook hands with him gladly. "We'll see you on the road tomorrow, Kali Tazur," the captain said. "And if you ever need us, we'll be here."

Marita

The hunchback ran ahead of Marita to open the door of the print shop. He bowed her through saying, "I tell you Novato is crazy about the Humble Kali and the Gentle Philosopher debate."

He lowered his voice and Marita came back up a step to hear him. "Just between you and me: I've started a rumor that both are Novatans, not Illigans. That's made the city sit up!"

"Wicked man!" Marita exclaimed, laughing. "I've heard that rumor."

The intelligent eyes twinkled in the printer's ugly face. "Call me wicked when your royalties mount. My boy will deliver another advance of paper to your address. You'll see the Humble Kali gets it. Sure it's not yourself?"

Marita held up her hands. "Do you see ink?" She waved and ran down the steps more lighthearted than she'd felt since she fled Illiga. In her purse lay a nice advance against royalties, pushing back for another few weeks, complete destitution. Ironically it was Sahra who now kept the small family from starving, and the twinge that gave Marita's pride told her she had indeed patronized her sister. Worth it to see Sahra's eyes sparkle again.

Whitey drowsed, one hip cocked, in Novato's brilliant morning sunshine. "Won't have to sell you this time, old dear," she said, giving him a pat. Scrambling onto the blanket that now served as saddle, she tucked the proofs of the first few chapters in her pocket, then headed for Novato's Textile Guild.

Maybe they *would* make it, she thought as Whitey slouched past the gleaming whitewashed buildings of Novato. It was the first she'd found hope, though with Sahra and Bibi she always pretended calm confidence. But anxiety for the future kept her awake at night, anger at Zojikam seared her, and loneliness for Taverik twisted her heart. The memory of Taverik, her best and dearest friend—gone for good—had become a dull pain accompanying all her waking thoughts. How, she sometimes wondered, could anything non-physical hurt so badly?

The white marble of the Textile Guild gleamed above Novato's blue-green harbor. Columns soared into the cobalt sky, supporting the magnificent portico that had nearly been torn down by Novato's jealous Massadaran viti. Even yet, whenever the viti felt pressure from the surging, energetic Pakajans, there'd be new talk about leveling the overly magnificent guild halls. Novato's columns, Illiga's dome—*Sadra* Laws were the same everywhere.

And though Novatan merchants might wave their arms more than Illigans when they talked, Marita thought as she reached the guild, they had the same tendency to gather in worried clusters when the news was bad. Today they crowded under the portico, staring out to sea as if they could make out the Bcacmat fleet hovering just beyond the horizon.

"Take your mule, Kali Namina?" said a stable lad.

Namina. That was her now. Belatedly she dismounted and gave him the reins and a small tip. Hard to get used to being Namina instead of Kastazi, but she didn't dare use her Illigan name here. News about the woman merchant dressed as a man would travel fast. Even with her new name, her risks had tripled. Ironic that the document she'd risked and lost everything for was now completely useless to her. Once again she'd been forced to start over from practically nothing. And she'd done it. The knowledge felt good.

She threw back her shoulders and mounted the marble steps, ragged but proud among the well-clad merchants. The beggars sunning on the steps and sleeping under the portico never bothered to thrust out their palms to such a half-starved young man, and Marita passed them without looking; their presence always reawakened her nagging fear of being reduced to such straits herself.

Suddenly she stopped. She frowned, started forward again, then turned to look back along the line of beggars, wondering what had caught her eye. A one-legged veteran stared back, the old man next to him tentatively extended his hand. Beside him a dirty, ragged young one slumped, sound asleep, the next two argued with each other. Her eyes came back to the sleeping one. She took a step forward. "Taverik?"

Foolish. She'd seen Taverik everywhere at first, her heart skipping a beat until she'd realize it was someone else. She started to go on now, but the old beggar had seen her interest and shaken the sleeper. "Wake up, the kali wants you."

The young man pushed him away and sat up. "Taverik!" Marita shouted. She leaped forward and pulled him to his feet.

"Marko!" He started to hug her then pounded her back instead. "I found you."

"I thought you were dead!"

"I hoped you'd be here!"

Interested beggars peered past each other at them, and merchants were craning their necks to see the commotion. "My name is Kali Namina now," she said in a low quick voice, and added, "Old friend, you look gaunt and worn out, dirty, unshaven, and you smell."

"Always so flattering," he murmured.

"When did you last eat?"

He squinted, thinking.

"Forget the guild meeting," Marita said. "I'm taking you home."

She got Whitey from the puzzled stable boy. "You ride," she told Taverik.

"I'll be all right," he protested, but let her bully him up onto Whitey's ever bonier back. "You don't look so fat yourself, Kali Whatever," he said as they started. "What happened that morning?"

"I went for transfer papers, and Ittato's new doctor was you know who. He recognized me, I nipped home, threw everything into the cart and took off."

"Just as easy as that?" he said dryly. "Did it snow?"

"Funny thing," she said, remembering. "It's almost as if we travelled five steps ahead of the snow the entire trip. Anyone pursuing us would have bogged down in it. Amazing luck. How'd you get out?"

"Jumped off the bridge and walked."

Marita laughed. "Just as easy as that?" she quoted.

He laughed too, the new lines on each side of his nose easing. She'd get the rest of the story out of him later, she thought, falling into companionable silence as the mule began to climb.

Like Illiga, much of Novato perched precariously on steep cliffs. But instead of granite quarried from the hills, the houses were built of whitewashed limestone, glowing so brilliantly in the sun they hurt the eyes. Between them sparkled glimpses of the blue-green sea. Marita liked it, but she also found herself longing for the soft misty grays, mossy roofs, and moist gardens of Illiga.

Unlike the self-contained Illigans, Novatans carried their business into the street. They shouted from house to house, sat talking on their front stairs, gossiped from upstairs windows. Raucous children ran, shrieking and laughing practically under the mules's hooves. As the neighborhoods grew poorer, Marita slid her hand to her purse. A man leaped into the street right under Whitey's nose. Broken crockery and a torrent of female abuse followed.

"Lovely neighborhood," said Taverik.

"This neighborhood is home," she said, pulling up at the house next door. Taverik dismounted and looked up without comment at the tiny house, unpainted, ramshackle and jammed between its neighbors. Marita, fumbling for her key, felt defensive. "Better than the tent city."

"Looks fine to me after the last few weeks," Taverik said mildly.

She unlocked a low heavy door. "The stable and the kitchen are here on the ground floor," she said. "Upstairs, there's just one room and a balcony looking on the garden. We sleep in the attic. On warm days, we can smell ol' Whitey clear to the top. Watch your head."

Inside the musty dimness she tied Whitey to a ring bolt to keep him from the hay bin; the stall partition had long ago fallen from dry rot. Taverik picked it up and let it drop again. "You should fix that," he suggested.

Marita's fingers clenched suddenly. Repairs, food, clothing, guild fees—all the pressures that kept her staring at the ceiling each night. "I can't do everything!"

Instantly he took the saddle blanket from her and engulfed her in a hug. "You're doing just fine," he said.

His strong arms were comforting. She relaxed into them, feeling not so alone and knowing suddenly that when he asked her again to marry him she would say yes. She wondered what it would be like to wear a skirt again and not have the freedom she loved, but she didn't fear the change. Life with Taverik was better than freedom without him.

He smiled down at her in the dim light and bent closer. She lifted her face to be kissed, but Taverik's expression changed quite suddenly and he drew back. She searched his face, wondering what was wrong. He sighed and released her reluctantly. "You will come into your own, someday," he said.

"What do you mean?" she demanded.

But he merely touched her cheek and turned away.

She wondered about it as she led him up the rickety outside staircase to the living room. Sahra sat in the wooden armchair by the one window, picking threads from a scrap of black wool to use in mending their clothes. Marita held the door wide. "Look who's here."

Sahra peered against the light. "Taverik!" She jumped to her feet, small rolls of thread scattering from her lap. "You're alive; I'm so glad."

"The feeling," said Taverik, giving an oddly formal bow, "is mutual."

Marita held up the proofs the printer had given her. "These are for you, Sah—Oma," she said.

Sahra seized them and opened one. Then she resolutely put them on the cluttered table. "Come in, Taverik, and shut the door. But, are you ill?"

"Just a little tired," he said.

"Sit here." Sahra gestured to the armchair with a shy smile. "This chair's our most comfortable. Of course it's the *only* chair, but that doesn't alter the fact."

Taverik laughed and shot Sahra a surprised glance. He'd probably never seen her so lighthearted, Marita thought. Sahra without pressure was fun to be with.

"Yes, do sit, Taverik," Marita said. "But watch the wobbles. The back leg has a tendency to fall off."

"Wobbles I can cope with," he said easing himself gingerly into the chair. In the direct light of the window his face looked haggard. "I found out who your father was."

Marita stilled. She'd forgotten she'd told Taverik her real name. Years ago, it seemed. And now she wasn't sure she wanted the answer.

"Zoji Vos had four sons."

"Three," Marita amended.

Taverik shook his head. "Four."

Sahra's eyes widened. She took a step closer to Taverik. "Are you saying Papa was . . . ?"

"The fourth."

"That's absurd!" Marita exclaimed.

"Maybe not," said Sahra. "Remember our last night in Illiga, Mari? We wondered who Papa was, the mysteries around him. I'd never thought about it before, but since then I've been thinking." She turned to Taverik, face intent. "He abdicated?"

"Not by choice. When he married your mother, the daughter of a Pakajan merchant, old Vos completely disinherited him."

"Ridiculous," Marita said. Desperately she didn't want this to be true. "He never said anything to us about it."

"No," Sahra said slowly, "but remember it was a forbidden subject."

"That's because he was a *bastard*!"

"Perhaps that's why we thought he was a bastard. You yourself wondered why Papa changed his name, and why all the property was in Mama's name. Remember Mama's love poem? 'My love you gave up all for me, who little had to give up on her part.' "

"Oh come," Marita scoffed. "Someone would have talked about it to us."

"Remember," Sahra said, "Bibi used to call us her little tet-zojas?"

"Just a pet name!"

"Remarks mother made, such as calling Papa 'his

high zojiness' whenever he got angry. It was all there. We just missed the clues because we weren't expecting them."

Marita thumped the table. "No one would miss that big a clue."

"What about you?" Taverik suddenly put in. She looked at him and he left off massaging his forehead and met her eyes. "You spent more than three years walking around dressed as a man. No one noticed. Yet once I found out it was so obvious to me I couldn't believe you escaped detection. Which are you, by the way? Marita or Sahra?"

"Marita."

"Thought so," he said, satisfied. "The name suits you."

"Just make sure you don't use it." Marita felt ruffled and grumpy. Why was this bothering her so?

"If that's who we are," said Sahra, "then no wonder Soza was, ah, interested in us. And that explains how Papa might have come across that letter. He tried to warn Zoji Vos and got kicked out, warned the guild, and that night was assassinated."

"No!" Marita paced the room, letting her boots thud across the bare floorboards. "I refuse to believe it. People don't just suddenly become zojas. Absurd."

"Ask Bibi," Taverik suggested.

"I'll get her," said Sahra. She went into the tiny hallway.

"Marko-Marita," said Taverik when they were alone, "why are you so afraid to become Marita Vos?"

She faced him, trying to sort her feelings. "All I want is a quiet peaceful life pursuing my own business. If I become a Vos I will be involved in the affairs of a family which means nothing to me, and who rejected my father. I've grown up a merchant, I don't want to be caught between two worlds."

"You haven't—" Taverik began but broke off as Sahra returned. Behind her came Bibi, drying her hands on her apron.

"Kali Taverik," she said, a slow smile crossing her pink face.

"Thank you, Bibi," he said, replying, Marita noticed, to the unspoken rather than the spoken words. "Is your name really Bibi?"

Her eyes flew wide and she shot a questioning look at Marita. "Yes," Marita said, "her name really is Bibi. It was too hard for her to remember another."

Sahra seated herself on the stool, her darned and stained skirts billowing around her. "Bibi, are Marita and myself the daughters of an abdicated Vosa tet-zoji?"

Bibi's jaw dropped, closed as she licked her lips, then dropped again. She looked nervously at Taverik, then appealed to Marita. "Abdicated?"

"Was our father a tet-zoji of Vosa?" Marita explained gently.

"Yes, Kala. I mean Kali."

Sahra leaned forward. "Are you sure?"

"Yes. I . . . thought you knew."

In the stunned silence that followed, Marita heard voices in the street below. Then heavy footsteps shook the wooden outside stair. Several people were coming up. "You expecting anyone?" Taverik asked.

Marita shook her head. Quickly she loosened her knife in its sheaf, and placed herself beside the door. Taverik had no knife—no purse nor anything, Marita suddenly noticed—but when he stood up the back leg of the chair fell off again and he grasped that. He circled to behind the door. Marita glanced at Sahra and found her calm, though green around the mouth.

The first feet stopped outside and a heavy rap resounded. Marita nodded at Bibi. "Open it," she said. "But not too wide."

Chapter 5

Balanji

Balanji prowled the pink salon in the back wing of Novato's palace. What was taking Nikilo Vitujak so long? Perhaps Zoji Oblatta had merely kicked him out—a despised Pakajan with an absurd story. What then? Fretted, Balanji clasped and unclasped his hands, his enormous energy driving him with nowhere to go. Show him how to get his city back and he'd do it. But this waiting ate him up.

Where was Vitujak?

His bodyguard, a Massadaran named Rinatto, stayed by the door, plainly uncomfortable with the room's fussy pastels and delicate furniture. The room looked just like Zoji Oblatta, and just like the city itself. Balanji suspected he wouldn't find the help he needed, but he had to try.

The door opened. Quickly, Balanji drew his hood further over his face and took his stand with his back to the light. Rinatto grasped his sword hilt.

Three soldiers entered, peering suspiciously about. Vitujak followed, and last, Oblatta. Balanji gave his uncle-by-marriage the humble bow of viti to zoji. Oblatta looked down his aesthetic nose at him. "Well, my man? You say you have important information about Zoji Balanji? It had better be worth this interruption or I'll have all three of you flogged."

"For your ears alone," Balanji said.

Oblatta sighed with exasperation. He turned to Vitujak and Rinatto. "Leave the room. Guards, leave, but keep the door open." Balanji waited as Vitujak, his freckled face tight and inscrutable, followed Rinatto and the guards from the room. "Now then," said Oblatta impatiently, "what is it?"

Balanji pulled back his hood. Oblatta's eyes widened, then a thin smile creased his face. "Balanji," he said quietly. He shut the door then stepped forward to enfold Balanji in a perfumed embrace. "I'd heard you were dead."

"Not yet, Uncle," Balanji said. "Just thirsting for revenge and my city."

Oblatta's face went expressionless. "Yes, I've heard. Your army wiped out, your court executed or imprisoned. I'm sorry. Ela?"

"Safe." As far as he knew. He and Marshal Kintupaquat had been returning from hiding her when Vitujak had caught him on the road and warned him. Balanji had raged at being out of the city when it fell. But during the ensuing weeks of being hunted like deer, Kintupaquat and Vitujak convinced him of Zojikam's grace: he would not have survived if he'd been at the palace. Now he could work to free his city from the outside.

Zoji Oblatta shook his head. "A tragedy. My dear Balanji, I open my palace to you. You are welcome to take refuge in Novato. I treat you as my honored nephew."

Balanji bowed politely. "Your generosity overwhelms me. Yet I would not put you to so much trouble. Only lend me your army for six months, and funds to pay them, and I will soon be lodged in my own palace once more."

"Ah, my nephew," Oblatta said gently. "You are optimistic. Your beloved city will not succumb that soon. Your walls are built on a most fortunate site. Fortunate once for you. Fortunate now for Soza."

"There is another way," Balanji said.

"How?"

Balanji paused, reluctant to disclose it yet. "Only lend me the army. Think of the disadvantage of Soza at your back."

"I have a greater disadvantage right now," Oblatta

said dryly. "You must be aware that even now a Bcacmat fleet lies off the coast. Yesterday they raided a merchant convoy. Took the goods, carried off into slavery the men, then burned the ships. Few ships escaped. So you'll surely see why Novato's army must remain here."

"Tomorrow you'll have Soza sneaking in your back door!"

"We'll deal with the Bcacmats first," said Oblatta. "Then we can deal with Soza."

"Are you blind?" Balanji exploded. "Can't you see the way Soza works? You don't have time to deal with him at your leisure! You'll be assassinated in your sleep."

"Come, come, Balanji. Surely your situation clouds your thoughts."

"So? He's already got Vosa, Ormea and Illiga. Next will be you or Perijo. Don't you see? The trade routes. You're on his list."

Oblatta stared at him. "Perhaps," he said slowly. "Yet we have first to deal with the Bcacmat menace."

Balanji clamped down tight on his temper. "You assume they're separate menaces. What if they're not?"

"What do you mean?"

"Suppose Soza is somehow in the pay of, or allied to Bcacma?"

"Nonsense!" The zoji's lower lip protruded in indignation.

"Tell me then," Balanji said, "who is Soza?"

"Why, he was marshal under Vos. Who grew ambitious on his own."

"That's right. *But who was he?* Where did he come from? What's his family?"

Oblatta's thin mouth worked slightly. Balanji held his eyes. "Well?"

"All right," Oblatta conceded. "We don't know where he comes from. But he's probably just a rogue who fled Massadara. There's no reason to link him with Bcacma."

"The Bcacmats have wanted the Peninsula for years. They have no exit to the Great Sea without it. They tried once to invade from above, and it almost worked until we banded together to stop them. The last time their fleet attacked Novato, I sent you men, Vos sent you men, and Perijo, too."

Balanji paused to let this reminder of obligations sink in, then added, "They know now an open attack doesn't work. What better way than to take the cities, one by one, from the inside? Keep them quarreling, prevent them from helping each other? And look at the methods Soza uses, assassination, traitors, spies. That's Bcacmat, not Massadaran. And he's supposed to be involved in Bcacmat's Black Eagle cult as well. *Ikiji,* as my Pakajan subjects would say."

"Then let *them* say," Oblatta said. "*You* don't have to use their crude, ugly language. You're letting Illiga go barbarian, I've always said it. You allow too many of them around you."

Balanji's anger broke loose. "That's not the point! I'm telling you Soza and your Bcacmat fleet are connected!"

"Poosh," said Oblatta, flapping his hands. "Come back when you have proof."

They stared at each other, Oblatta detached and kindly, Balanji fighting to regain his temper. "My dear Balanji, you are tired," Oblatta said. "Come, let me find some decent clothes for you. You need sleep. We can discuss this further, of course, but I'm sure you see my position. You and Ela are welcome to make your home with us for as long as you wish."

"And make an excellent target, as Akusa Ormea did? No thank you."

"Surely your trials have strained your imagination?"

Balanji gave up. "Then will you indulge my strained imagination, Uncle? Please keep my presence here in Novato a complete secret."

"You have my word," Oblatta said, openly relieved to have at least one request he could grant.

Only when the crowds on the quay made progress difficult, did Balanji try to control his pacing. He found a quiet corner by a pile of crates and allowed his attendants to catch up. "Were we followed, Rinatto?"

"Not that I could see, My Zo—I mean, My Viti."

"Keep watch. Vitujak, what time is it?"

"Lacks more than two hours until noon, Viti."

He'd been pacing Novato for an hour and a half, then, his pent energy overflowing in frustration. Inactivity would drive him mad yet. He looked at Vitujak. "We have almost three hours before we meet Kintupaquat. How shall we spend the time, patient secretary? You suggest."

A Massadaran would have said, "As *you* please, Zoji," but then Nikilo Vitujak was not Massadaran. "If you mean that indeed," he said, "I do have a suggestion. I've engaged for some time in an anonymous philosophic debate with a man calling himself 'The Humble Kali.' "

"Oh ho," said Balanji, delighted. "So *you* are the Gentle Philosopher! I might have known."

Vitujak bowed. "I'm honored that you have read my books."

"Yours and the Not-So-Humble-Kali's. Enjoyed them."

Vitujak smiled. "I could never pry the Humble Kali's identity from his Illigan publisher," he said. "But this morning I learned that the Humble Kali fled here to Novato when Illiga fell. Perhaps it would be amusing to get his address from the publisher and look him up."

Laughing inwardly at Rinatto's horrified expression, Balanji nodded. "Lead the way, then, Gentle Philosopher. Only keep our identity a secret, and make sure we meet Kintupaquat on time."

But Balanji had second thoughts when the well-bribed printer's lad led them down a narrow road in a rough neighborhood and pointed at a tumble-down, unpainted house. Surely no educated man would live there—though the boy had said this was the agent's address, not the author's.

Rinatto glanced down the alley at their backs and grimaced. "Viti," he began, "I don't think . . ."

"A bodyguard's nightmare, isn't it, Rinatto?" said Balanji. He shrugged. "Pay the boy, Vitujak, and lead on. It's your adventure."

The door opened to Vitujak's knock, and a round-faced old woman peered out. Balanji thought she looked unduly frightened.

"Good morning, Kala," Vitujak said in Pakajan, with the same abstracted courtesy he gave the highest vita at court. "Is this the residence of a philosopher known as The Humble Kali?"

The woman's pink mouth shaped into a surprised O and she slammed the door. Vitujak cast an exasperated look at Balanji, and knocked again. Balanji chuckled and folded his arms, prepared to enjoy himself. The door opened again, this time by a dark-haired youth with stormy eyes.

"Good afternoon," said Vitujak, undaunted. "Are you by chance the Humble Kali?"

Humble Kali? thought Balanji, *he looks more like a young hawk.*

"You are mistaken," the youth told Vitujak curtly.

He made to close the door, but it unaccountably stuck open. Balanji leaned forward. Ah yes, Vitujak's foot. The youth's hand closed around a slim knife in his belt and Vitujak hurriedly added, "I was mistakenly told the Humble Kali lived here. Could you by chance direct me to him? My name is Vitujak, Nikilo Vitujak and—"

Crash! That sounded like a large piece of wood hitting the floor inside. The youth—such a haughty youth for all his stained merchant's clothes—looked questioningly over his shoulder. Suddenly the door was flung wide. Vitujak blinked and stepped back.

"Nik!" shouted a second young man, even more ragged, with tangled dirty yellow hair and several days growth of beard. The young man swooped on Vitujak before Rinatto could defend him.

"Taverik!" Vitujak exclaimed. The two of them pounded each other's back, each exclaiming in Pakajan too torrential to follow.

Taverik, Balanji wondered. Not the nephew? The one who had recognized Soza, the one who had warned him, *the son of the traitor?* His interest sharpened.

The nephew pulled Nikilo Vitujak into the house.

Balanji followed, appalled by the barrenness of the room. It held only a severely listing wooden armchair, a stool and a table piled high with books and papers. At his feet lay the missing chair leg.

The dark-haired youth placed himself silently—defensively—next to a young woman with a pale face and clenched hands. Brother and sister, he judged, from the same high cheekbones and finely chiseled mouths. Certainly not Pakajan. In fact, they looked as Massadaran as the emperor of Massadara himself. The serving woman hovered in the shadows of the hall beyond.

Vitujak held his nephew by the shoulders and looked at him. "Damn, boy, but you stink," he said in Pakajan slow enough for Balanji to follow. Balanji made note of the deep love in his voice. "At least you're safe, though not, I see, without cost."

"Sticky at times," Zandro admitted, his eyes sliding questioningly to Balanji, Rinatto, then, narrowing, back to Balanji.

Vitujak switched to Massadaran. "I beg your pardon," he said. "May I present my nephew, Taverik Zandro. Taverik, the—"

Balanji thrust out his hand to stop him. Too late. The nephew placed him suddenly. "Zoji Balanji!" he breathed, and pulling off his soft cap, he sank to his knees. The brother and sister gave Balanji startled looks and also knelt. Behind them the servant creaked to her knees.

Balanji sighed inwardly; soon everyone in Novato would know he was here. But aloud he said, "Thank you. Please be at ease."

They got up, looking anything but at ease. Vitujak broke the awkward silence. "Taverik, perhaps you'll do the honor of presenting your companions?"

Zandro flushed but spoke excellent Massadaran. "May I present Oma Kas—"

"Namina," broke in the dark-haired youth smoothly and also in excellent Massadaran. "Kala Oma Namina, Zoji. And I am Ali Namina. Please, Zoji, will you do us the honor of eating dinner with us?"

Namina gestured to the armchair, realized the missing leg lay at Balanji's feet and turned a dark red. Balanji picked it up and gave it to him. "Yes, I do thank you," he said easily. "I'm famished."

Instantly he regretted it, for the servant's mouth pulled again into a distressed O. They probably had little to spare, but too late now, Namina had motioned with his head and the servant disappeared. The sister gave a graceful curtsey and also started to withdraw. Balanji stopped her. "Please, be seated," he said, gesturing to the armchair which her brother was fixing. She chose the stool instead. Just so she stayed. He didn't want people loose who knew his identity.

Balanji sat in the armchair, himself. A lot of undercurrents, here, he thought, glancing around. Rinatto's lips curled whenever he glanced at Vitujak's unshaven, disheveled nephew, but he stared boldly at the young woman, who sat with her back straight, her dress darned and redarned. She was pretty in a pale, aesthetic way, and her manners, refined, as were those of her brother. How would poor merchants learn such manners? Or learn such beautiful Massadaran?

Young Zandro, for that matter, spoke well and had good manners. His uncle's influence, probably. Quite a coincidence, Vitujak finding his nephew here. Except Balanji didn't believe in coincidences.

That awkward silence again. Vitujak broke it. "Look," he said, picking up a wad of printed papers from the table. "Here's the Humble Kali's new book. And here are my books too! The Humble Kali *must* live here."

Balanji watched their reactions. Zandro looked puzzled, Namina carefully blank, his sister . . . ah, *she's* the one, he thought incredulously.

"I assure you, young Kali," Vitujak said with a bow to Kali Namina, "I have nothing but the highest regard for my anonymous critic and would be happy to meet him at last. You need not fear to admit your work."

Balanji intervened. "If I'm not mistaken, my dear Vitujak, you are addressing the wrong Namina." He nodded at the young woman eagerly staring up at his secretary. "Humble, perhaps, but certainly not a kali."

Nikilo looked directly at her for apparently the first time, and his face glowed as if the sun had risen within. "My dear kala," he said, "you?" He seized one of his volumes and found a page. "Then I must tell you, you completely missed the point of my argument here."

"Say rather," she said with spirit, "you failed to express yourself plainly."

The arrival of the servant with a steaming pot interrupted the literary discussion. She ladled soup into three bowls, and gave Balanji the first. He received it with a polite thank you, looked in vain for a spoon, then sipped, striving to act as if he always drank his soup that way. From the brick red faces of his hosts he knew they felt the lack. "This is delicious," he said, though it had been thinned to the point of flavorlessness in order to feed everyone. Balanji felt ashamed and grateful at the same time, and didn't like the sensation.

Even before the meal had been cleared away, Vitujak and the Namina woman had plunged back into the book. Under the hum of their conversation, Balanji turned to Zandro. "Tell me, Zandro," he said in his fairly fluent Pakajan, chuckling inwardly at the young man's surprise, "how is it you are hobnobbing with philosophers? Do you take after your uncle?"

Zandro gave Vitujak an affectionate glance. "Not in that way."

"Then how is it you happened to be here when we arrived?"

Zandro's face went maddeningly blank and hard to read. "I am a friend of—of Namina's, so I sought him out when I escaped Illiga."

Balanji found Namina's eyes on him. The youth was leaning against the wall trying to follow both conversations. Balanji turned back to Zandro. "You are the one who recognized Soza and passed on the warning."

Zandro visibly steeled himself. "I was at my father's house, and met a man whom my father seemed to be hiding. He introduced himself as Kali Fara. It sounded familiar to me, and I put Fara together with Soza and realized he must be Agash Itzil Farasoza."

"Farasoza!" Balanji sat forward. "He was one of the old Tlath's most trusted generals. But he dropped out of sight when the son assumed power. How do you know of him?"

"From a letter. Then—"

"What letter?"

Zandro's face again assumed that damned impenetrable blankness. "Just a letter I found," he said.

"Just a letter you found?"

Namina stepped forward. "My letter. I found it in my father's things. A scroll written in Bcacmat."

Balanji forced back his excitement. "Go on."

"I copied part of it, and we took it to be translated, Taverik and I."

"Let me see it."

Namina shook his head. "It's in my house in Illiga."

"Do you remember any of it?" Balanji watched him curiously. Now who would this youth's father be? Another mystery.

Shutting his eyes, Namina recited, " 'To my faithful servant Agash Itzil Farasoza, you have done well but I grow impatient. I want more, I . . .' uh—"

" 'I shouldn't have to answer your question,' " supplied Oma Namina, looking up from her conversation.

"That's right," said her brother. " 'Leave Vosa immediately, go to Illiga, Perijo or Novato. I want the northern trade route.' Then something like, 'Don't keep improvising, you're making me angry. Answer at once, the most elevated, most noble,' then a signature."

"You forgot adorable," put in Zandro. "He calls himself adorable."

Vitujak gave him a repressive frown, then turned to Balanji. "There you are," he said. "Proof."

"Proof?" asked Namina uneasily.

"That Soza is a Bcacmat, acting secretly on behalf of the Tlath. The Peninsula is being brought covertly under the dominion of Bcacma. If they attacked openly we'd unite against them and drive them off."

"That's right," Taverik Zandro said. "People are saying, 'Balanji, Soza, what difference between Massadaran zojis?' " He met Balanji's eye and broke off.

"No, go on," Balanji told him. "The information is useful."

"When I'd say Soza was a Bcacmat, first they'd be afraid, then they'd scoff. Except for your men up in the mountains. They said it figured."

"What men?" Balanji demanded.

"I met them in the pass," Zandro said. "They thought you were dead, but I told them you weren't because Soza was conducting house to house searches for you."

"Yes, he was, wasn't he," Balanji said, remembering. "Uh, how did the news affect them?"

"They cheered enough to start an avalanche. They're going to hold the pass for you until you need them."

Vitujak laughed. Balanji smiled, his spirits lifting. "Thank you, Taverik Zandro. You have done me great service. Now, Namina, how did your father—"

The clock struck. "Zoji," said Vitujak, "your appointment."

Damn! But he didn't dare miss Kintupaquat. He drew his secretary aside. "You stay here. Don't let any of them leave, not even the servant woman. Rinatto and I will go, and return as soon as we can. Something here doesn't tally."

Chapter 6

Abado

"He's here," Abado said.

Karaz looked up from his third cup of wine. "Where?"

"The waterfront. I caught a quick glimpse of him, and managed to get closer. He had two people with him. One of them is Vitujak."

"Where is he now?"

"I followed him to a house, Master, then returned here immediately."

"They may leave at any moment."

Abado bowed his head to hide his scorn. Of course they might leave at any moment. Karaz's father would have taken action immediately, not sat around, tapping teeth and looking uncertain.

"Where's Tlele?"

"Still watching the palace."

"It'll take too long to reach him. I'll have to come with you. But mind you, don't miss this time."

"*I* will not miss, Master."

Balanji

Novato's brash sun poured full into the upper chamber of the inn, picking out each discouraged line in Kintupaquat's face. The marshal sat back, shaking his head. "That is all I could discover, Zoji."

Balanji concealed his own dismay. "You did well, my Ironbiter. What about Commander Lomar?"

"Dead. Killed in the ambush. Because of his carelessness the army was wiped out. Completely."

"Not completely," corrected Balanji.

Kintupaquat raised an eyebrow. "How so?"

"Do you know a Captain Pemununtin—something Pakajan?"

"Pemintinuchi?" Kintupaquat looked interested. "A good man. Did he survive? How do you know?"

"Taverik Zandro told me he met him."

"Zandro!"

"Why yes," said Balanji, enjoying the situation. "I ate the noon meal with him. He says that this Pemintinuchi and—"

"You *ate* with him?" Kintupaquat exploded. "That traitor!"

"Son of a traitor."

"Small difference!"

"Keep your voice down. A big difference in this case.

You won't forget that he warned us in time to escape. And that he shares with me the dubious distinction of a price on his head."

"Along with some other merchant and his sister. I still don't trust him."

"Some other merchant and his sister!" Balanji said. "Of course! Bless you, Ironbiter, I'd forgotten all about that. I knew there was a connection between them! Now what are they hiding?"

Kintupaquat looked bewildered. "Who? What?"

"I'll explain in a moment. Zandro says Pemintinuchi is gathering an army of survivors, and will hold the pass for us. You say Soza's force in Illiga is relatively small?"

"So far. But you know well, it doesn't take many to hold the fortress."

"From the outside. But from the inside . . ."

"Inside!"

Balanji waved his hand with more confidence than he felt. "I can get men inside. It's a long family secret, passed from zoji to zoji. But I think this is the time to reveal it."

"How will you do it?"

"A passage from the palace cellars into the rocks. One branch surfaces under the pavement in the temple, the other goes down to the river."

Kintupaquat whistled, his face brightening like the dawn. "Given the surprise and enough men—it's a long chance."

"It's our only chance. If we lose this one I'll retire to Massadara in disgrace. But there's one problem."

"What's that?"

"The entrance can only be reached by boat, thus at night, and only a few men at a time. At that rate it will take weeks to accumulate enough men. I have no idea how many men the passage will hold, and how long."

"They could be hidden somewhere in the city." Kintupaquat pulled his long nose thoughtfully. "Raises the risks of discovery."

"Who's left in Illiga?"

"No one. I told you, the viti have been killed, imprisoned, shipped away or are under close scrutiny."

"The city is empty?"

Kintupaquat shrugged. "Merchants, laborers. Soza's left them. He needs money and he's taxing the life out of the merchants but the little money grubbers don't care as long as they make some of their own."

"Soza allows them movement?"

"Curfew, registry, papers. Anyone caught disobeying is hanged."

"There's our contact," said Balanji.

Kintupaquat wrinkled his nose. "Merchants?"

"Look clearly, Kintupaquat, the old ways are changing. The vitis' hold on power is slipping. They have allowed the money and the worldwide contacts to pass into the hands of the merchants you so despise. Even in my palace, the young viti speak Illigan Pakajan, not Massadaran, when they play with each other. *Sadra* Laws are like trying to dam the Ao with silk. I'd like to repeal them."

"You'd have armed rebellion from your viti," said Kintupaquat.

"Yes. But I had been seriously considering the guilds' demands for a city council. Now they can earn the right to one."

Kintupaquat cleared his throat. "I would like to see my people freed from the bondage of *Sadra*," he said softly. "But I'm not sure that merchants as a class can help you regain power. I'm willing to give it a try, however. Now our only problem is to find us a merchant."

"I've found two."

"Two?"

"Taverik Zandro, and one merchant travelling with his sister. All we have to do is persuade them to cooperate."

"*If* you can trust them."

Balanji frowned. "Yes. If I can trust them."

He rose and Kintupaquat with him. "Good work, Ironbiter. We shall do. Now, come meet my merchants. I want your opinion of them. Oh, and how much money do you have?"

Kintupaquat grimaced. "Not much."

Balanji brought out the purse Oblatta had given him. "Leave the rest of your men here. Send Rinatto for food—plenty of it. He'll know where to bring it. Wish I could risk buying a few chairs."

"Chairs? What do you mean?"

Balanji laughed. "You'll soon see, old friend, you'll soon see."

Marita

Dung thudded to the sledge. Caught in the rhythm, Marita swung up another shovelful. Here's Vosa's lost tet-zoja cleaning a stable, she thought, and laughed aloud. No doubt what Taverik had discovered was the truth, but it meant nothing to her. Truly, her layers of identity deepened all the time. Vos, Kasta, Kastazi, Namina, female, male. What had any of these to do with this actual person standing ankle deep in dirty straw?

What would Balanji say if he knew? It had made no difference to Taverik, still deep asleep upstairs. She tossed another load to the sledge and paused, shovel in air.

Yes, it had made a difference.

She'd wanted him to kiss her and he'd pulled back, she'd wanted him to ask her again to marry him, and he'd been silent, she'd wanted the old companionship, and he'd been remote. Sour disquietude washed over her. Taverik would never ask even an exiled, unacknowledged tet-zoja to marry him. Instead he would do all he could to restore her to her position, then bow low and go off to live his own life.

"Damn!" Savagely, she thrust her shovel into the manure.

"Let it live!" Taverik said.

She whirled. He stood in the gathering dusk rubbing his scruffy beard sleepily. "May I borrow your razor, Kali Namina?" he asked.

Marita's anger dissolved. She'd just have to do something about the situation, that was all. "Steal your uncle's. Where is he by the way?"

"Discussing absolutes with Oma. Let me shovel."

She shook her head because he still looked tired, but he pulled the shovel out of her hands. "Why," he said, taking a good load, "were you so angry when I came in?"

"The night you asked me to marry you," she started, "I prayed to Zojikam, and put everything into his hands. Nothing but disaster has resulted."

"Oh, I don't know about that," Taverik said. "What went wrong?"

"The very next day I was discovered, we had to flee with almost nothing, in a snowstorm, Illiga fell and . . ." She broke off, unable to say, *and now you think I'm above you.*

"Look at it this way," Taverik said. "If you hadn't been discovered, you'd have been in the city when Soza took it. Zojikam got you out just in the nick of time. The snowstorm foiled pursuit and gave you time to get over the pass. Illiga fell, but I had time to warn my uncle, and that got him out of town and safe, too, as well as Balanji. Soza's men chased me around, and I had to jump in the river, but that got me out of the city in time, too. So even that worked out."

"And," he added slowly, not looking at her, "as I went up the pass, it was like I became different, like I was, hmm, well, different. Like the son of the mountain . . . I don't know. Different. It was good."

He gave a frustrated gesture and took another shovelful—whatever had happened apparently was beyond his ability to express. Marita cleared her throat. "I hadn't thought of it that way," she admitted gruffly. "I'd rather hate Zojikam. Then I don't have to remember the *ihiga* said we had a task to do."

"I agree," said Taverik fervently. "By the way, I met the *ihiga* again."

"What!"

She listened with wonder while he told her of the Black Eagle, his horrible blind flight through brambles, the sparks of light and the *ihiga* who helped him, and his escape. "It was the same as your nightmare thing that stalked us before," he finished. "Somehow, Marko-Marita, we've gotten ourselves thoroughly involved in the unseen world."

"We do have a knack," she said, "for getting ourselves in trouble."

His eyes lit. "I love you," he said.

"Then why—"

"Hello! Anyone home?"

With a grunt of annoyance, Marita squeezed past the sledge and peered out the cobwebby door. Zoji Balanji stood in the dusk outside, hand on Whitey's rump, as calmly at home as he might be in his own palace. With him stood a tall military-looking Pakajan whose grizzled brows lowered as he took in her manure-stained boots and dirty hands. She lifted her chin and stubbornly stepped forth. "You are welcome, viti."

Taverik followed. "Your servant," he said.

Balanji had just begun to acknowledge when two men sprang from the alley behind him. "Look out!" Marita shouted. A blade flashed and the zoji fell, his attacker running past without stopping. The other had flung himself on Balanji's military companion, who blocked his thrust and threw him to the ground almost at Marita's feet.

She knew him—the student who twice now had threatened her. Karaz rolled to his feet and ran. Taverik hurled the shovel at his legs. It caught him behind the knees and he staggered. Without conscious thought Marita drew her knife from her boot and flung it. Easy as hitting the target in her stable—but less noise. Karaz flopped to his face and did not move.

Taverik bent over him. "Nice shot," he said, pulling her knife and wiping it on Karaz's pants.

She swallowed and passed her hand over her stomach, not sure how she felt about it. Taverik squeezed her shoulder. "You're never taken a life before," he said.

"Oh yes," she said and sighed. "Yes, I have."

He gave her a quick look but to her relief all he said

was, "Well, we should'a killed the nasty little bastard the first time."

The Pakajan helped Balanji to his feet. "You know him?" the zoji asked.

"A student. Viti Karaz," Marita said. She looked around. Two men watched with interest from the steps of a house a few doors down, and a small boy leaned from a window just above them. "What do we do now?"

Balanji turned to the Pakajan. "What do we do now, my Ironbiter?"

The tall Pakajan scowled. "About time you thought of that. Get him off the street at least. We'll stick him in the stable until we can report his death to the authorities."

"No authorities," said Balanji firmly. "We'll give him a private burial."

The scowl deepened, but the tall man merely pointed to Marita. "You. You killed him, you move him."

Marita took the student's feet and waited while the Pakajan heaved up the shoulders. She backed toward the stable, the Pakajan muttering, "Never thought I'd see the day I'd help hide bodies . . ."

Marita laughed softly. She looked up at Balanji and their eyes met with shared merriment. "He'll growl about that for a week," Balanji said, following. "There'll be no repercussion?"

"Not here. This neighborhood is the equivalent of the west side in Illiga. But there is the one who got away."

"You knew him too?"

Marita nodded. "He had a pawn shop in Illiga, but he actually fenced stolen goods."

"And," added Taverik, bringing up the rear with the shovel, "he ran an illicit press."

"So ho," said Balanji.

"That's where we took the Bcacmat letter to be translated," Marita said. "Afterwards, he and this one chased us and demanded it from us. They're part of the Black Eagle *ikiji*. I thought he'd killed you, Viti."

"Mail shirt," Balanji said shortly. His mood had

quickly changed, and without so much as a by-your-leave, he turned and went up the rickety wooden steps to where Taverik's uncle and Sahra waited. He said something to Vitujak then went into Marita's house.

Marita sighed. Having an exiled zoji use her house as headquarters would rapidly get old. She helped Balanji's tall friend lay the body down, then stepped back to let him pass. Taverik squatted in the corner beside Karaz, fingers searching his pockets. "Need a cloak?" he said. "And yes, how about a small bag of money?"

She steeled herself. "Count it. Maybe we could buy some dinner for the zoji." The search turned up little else beside a pen knife and Taverik helped her finish cleaning the stall. But not until he'd hauled the sledge to the dung pile and she had reinstalled Whitey did she speak the worry which had been churning around inside her. "Know what I'm thinking?"

"Yes," said Taverik, taking down the lantern. "That somewhere out there lurks Karaz's ugly little friend, who knows exactly where to find us and Balanji as well."

Marita built the fire that night with Whitey's stall partition, throwing the boards on the flames with a vague feeling of burning bridges behind her. Brushing off her hands, she squeezed past Kintupaquat and Nikilo who were discussing Illiga's bridge defenses, and joined Sahra in the corner. Her belly felt like a hard knot. Too much rich food too suddenly. Balanji, a wealthy man, had no idea how humiliating his overwhelming gift of meats, breads, cheeses, wines and fruit had been to his poverty-stricken hosts. But Marita had put aside her embarrassment and eaten her fill with the others.

As the flames rose, Balanji called for attention, and the company sorted itself along the walls to listen. Marita had offered him the armchair, but his energy soon drove him out of it. He paced back and forth before the fire, graphically describing the fate of Illiga. Orange light gleamed on his black hair, unstylishly longer than his shoulders now, just as his boots and surcoat looked shabby. But he stood proud, his presence solid and commanding respect, even reverence.

Marita watched his shadow cross and recross the opposite wall where the Massadaran bodyguard leaned arrogantly. The fellow's eyes constantly followed Sahra, and Marita didn't like his leer. He'd also taken an instant dislike to Taverik and had jostled him provokingly several times. The sooner Balanji took himself off, and his bodyguard with him, the better.

Bibi hovered in the doorway, requested to stay, but obviously uncomfortable with all these grand vitis. Marita gave her a reassuring smile. Beyond her, Taverik sat on the floor with his uncle and Marita felt a quick stab of jealousy at their belonging together. She suppressed it, fighting to regain her old independent spirit.

Marshal Kintupaquat sat with one hip on the table, his eyebrows lowered, his keen eyes watching first Taverik, then Sahra then her, then back to Taverik and around again. His scrutiny made her edgy. So? What did it matter what the old curmudgeon thought of her? He'd be gone soon and she could get back to normal life.

No, she couldn't. Downstairs lay the body of her enemy, and another enemy knew where she lived, and that she and Taverik had killed his friend. And surely those two were connected somehow with Soza.

She and Sahra would have to leave again. Should go tonight. They should be packing up right now, not listening to an exiled zoji's recital of who was left inside his ex-city. Tomorrow might be too late.

No money. Oh Zojikam, what to do?

Damn Soza!

"The only people who are given passes and somewhat free movement," Balanji was saying, "are the merchants."

Marita snapped awake. "Soza is encouraging trade," Balanji said, "and rumor has it he might allow intercity trade once the snow melts in the passes." He turned to Kintupaquat. "Is that the sum?"

The old Pakajan pulled his eyes away from Marita. "The rivers are open already, and he's allowing some boat trade, but he watches it tight."

Balanji looked at Taverik, then met Marita's eyes. "That is where you come in. I can take my city back with your help."

Blood drained from Marita's face leaving it stiff and cold. Go *back* to Illiga? Return to Soza? She felt Sahra's quick glance. Taverik's uncle looked astonished then grim. Taverik, damn him, looked interested. "How can *we* help?" he asked.

"I can get men into the walls," Balanji said. "But if the only people allowed movement inside are merchants and other lower classes, I will need help from them. It will be dangerous, I warn you, though I will not involve you in the fighting."

The zoji threw back his dark head and regarded Taverik with hooded eyes. "I do not know your loyalties to me. However, if Soza is indeed Bcacmat as you say, and if he has brought the Black Eagle to Illiga, I appeal to you, please, help me free my beloved city." It may have been the firelight, but it seemed to Marita that Balanji colored from his neck to his forehead.

Taverik cleared his throat. "I'll help."

Balanji looked at Marita and her stomach clenched. "And you, Kali Namina?"

Chapter 7

Marita

Her heart thudded great beats against her chest. Balanji held her eyes. "We need that letter of yours," he said. "It could make all the difference. If people had proof that Soza was Bcacmat they would band together to drive him from the Peninsula."

"What if the house has been ransacked?" she asked. "Or if someone lives there?"

"We'll decide then what to do."

Marita looked down at her fingers. Sahra, Bibi? How could she put them back in Soza's hands?

"Marko," Taverik said softly. "I can get the letter. You stay here."

"Stay here? With Soza's man knowing where we are?"

"We will hide you."

Her heart lifted. If they could stay hidden, they could wait in safety while Taverik returned to Soza's hands and fought against him and the Black Eagle and its *mahigas* and maybe came back to her in triumph . . . she shook her head.

That prophesy, what had it said? *The hawk fled, but wherever it hid, the eagle was there before it.* Truly, no matter where she went, Soza had found her. For some crazy reason, Zojikam had given her this task and she couldn't seem to hide from that either. Her father had risked and lost his life, she realized suddenly, trying to stop Soza. Had he known, when he told her about the strong box, that he was passing on the task to her? If she didn't deal with Soza and the Black Eagle someone else would have to. At least, she thought, with grim humor, she'd already had a little practice.

She looked up at Sahra. Her sister's eyes had gone dark, her face pale, but to Marita's surprise she nodded a firm yes. Marita looked at Bibi. Her pink face screwed into a tight twist, but she also ducked her head yes. They'd had far less problem committing themselves than she, Marita realized with a twinge of shame. Marita turned back to Balanji, a mood of desperate resignation settling over her like a cloak. "Zoji, we will go with you."

"Excellent!" said Balanji.

But Kintupaquat scowled. "What do you mean, we?"

"My sister and I, and our servant."

"We can't take women."

"I cannot leave them alone here."

"A woman," said Balanji politely, "will be inappropriate at this time. We will of course provide for their safety."

"I will not be separated from her."

Balanji's face darkened dangerously. "You must."

Marita stood up and met his eyes squarely. He wasn't her zoji anymore, they were both exiles in this city. "If she does not go, nor do I."

"I told you!" Kintupaquat exploded. "Merchants! No discipline. You can't win a city with such damned insubordination."

"Zoji," Taverik said. "Forgive my interrupting, but I have an idea."

"What is it?"

"There'd be others in the city who have comparative freedom of movement—women for example. Who would pay attention to two women with market baskets? A woman scrubbing a dooryard? They could give you much information as well as bring you food."

Kintupaquat and Balanji both stared at him. Marita held her breath. "Well, Ironbiter?" Balanji said.

"I don't like it."

"Vitujak?"

Taverik's uncle raised a red-gold eyebrow. "I have high respect for the intelligence of Kala Namina," he said. "Of course, 'twould be irregular, but so is the entire plan as far as I can see. Perhaps the irregular will give us the advantage against Soza."

"Kintupaquat?"

The marshal shrugged. "I give up. But don't blame me."

"They come," said Balanji with an impatient gesture. He flung back his head and the room suddenly seemed smaller. "I would have you all swear fealty," he said. "All of you. Fealty to me, and fealty to Zojikam since this battle is not for Illiga alone. Will you swear?"

"Yes," cried Kintupaquat, straightening his back.

Vitujak scrambled to his feet and bowed low. "My Zoji," he murmured. More awkwardly, Marita and the others followed his example.

Balanji sat on the armchair; Kintupaquat knelt before him, placed his left hand under the zoji's thigh, raised his right hand and repeated his oath. Vitujak followed, kneeling gracefully. Marita suddenly realized where Taverik had inherited his lean frame and broad shoulders, so different from his father.

Taverik knelt before Balanji. "Taverik Zandro," the zoji said, "your father is a traitor."

Taverik's spine stiffened visibly. "I am not my father."

"Do you swear by Zojikam you had no part in any traitorous activities?"

"By Zojikam I swear it."

"I will accept that. But do not cross me." Balanji proceeded with the oath, and then it was Marita's turn. She went down on one knee and tentatively slid her left hand under the zoji's warm, muscular thigh. "Namina," he said, "you are hiding something."

Her vision narrowed, and her brain stopped dead.

"I will allow you your secrets," he said, "if you can swear that not one of them will affect what we are about to attempt, or affect your loyalty to me."

Marita dropped her eyes. Yes, some of her secrets affected the operation directly. She felt trapped, but it was a trap she would knowingly walk into. She met Balanji's keen stare. "Zoji, my name is not Ali Namina. In Illiga I am known as Marko Kastazi. I have had other names. I am not in favor with my guild. Soza is searching for me to kill me."

"Is that the sum of your secrets?" he said sternly.

"No," she said. She hesitated long, but could not bring herself to say more. "But I do not think they will affect what we are about to do."

"You will swear complete loyalty?"

"Yes."

"I will accept that."

She raised her right hand and completed the oath. The moment she finished his fingers circled her wrist. Tight. "Marko Kastazi," he said, his eyes hooded. "You are now a sworn subject. You will not balk me again."

Her mouth tightened—would he now take back his decision? He released her and she rose, stubbornly not rubbing her throbbing right wrist. Suddenly Balanji smiled. "My humble hawk," he said. "So. Let us now have the ladies, who will do our spying for us."

When Sahra and Bibi had sworn, and Rinatto as well, Balanji stood and delivered his own oath, a promise of wisdom, protection and reward. Then he looked around the room, meeting each of their eyes. "We shall do," he said, satisfied. "Now, Kali Kastazi, you are not the only one to reveal secrets tonight, here is one of mine. There is a secret passage under the rock of the fortress. We can bring men in and surprise Soza from the inside.

"Problem: the passage will not contain many men for any long period of time. To accumulate enough, they will have to be hidden in the city, and I will rely on you, Zandro and Kastazi, to contact loyal merchants who will help. You perceive the trust I will put in you."

Marita exchanged a glance with Taverik and knew instantly what he was thinking. Balanji was trusting in a discredited merchant woman disguised as a man, and in the youngest son of a despised and traitorous family. What guild member would listen?

"The second problem," Balanji continued, "I don't yet have a solution for. The tunnel entrance is right at the tip of the confluence of the Giss and Ao. It can be reached only by boat. How do we bring in men and still escape detection? Ideas?"

"The moon wanes," said Kintupaquat. "The night will aid us."

"We'd have to start up river," mused Taverik's uncle, squinting as if he looked at a map in his mind. "Can't very well load up right at the bridge, and spring floods make it hard to row upstream."

"What about the bridge?" said Kintupaquat. "Soza's got a guard on it. Can't very well float a few boat loads of men right past."

"True." Nikilo Vitujak pinched his lip. "Could we get a rope across and have the men pull themselves over?"

The marshal considered it. "Best possibility."

Taverik shifted uneasily. Marita touched his knee and looked a question at him. His eyes held the same expression they'd had the day after he'd found out his father was a traitor. "Vitis," he rasped, "I can get you down the river without Soza seeing you."

Balanji swung around eagerly. "How?"

"I know a safe path for a small boat at night, which, ah, utilizes the blind spots of the lookout points."

Kintupaquat's ferocious eyebrows bristled. "So you are nothing more than a smuggler!"

"If you are nothing more than a jumper to conclusions," snapped Taverik.

"As marshal of Illiga, I am accustomed to hanging smugglers."

"Taverik," said Nikilo Vitujak, his face rigid with anger, "did Donato Zandro force you to smuggle for him?"

Taverik turned to him. "I'd always thought you'd known!"

"How would I know?"

"I thought Father told you that night when—" He looked around suddenly and went on in a quieter voice. "I haven't done it since I was fourteen."

"I should never have left."

"I made out all right," Taverik growled.

"Kali Zandro," Balanji interposed firmly, "in the interest of Illiga, Marshal Kintupaquat and I will ask no more questions about how you learned this skill. Isn't that right, Kintupaquat, my official hider of bodies? We shall merely bless Zojikam for bringing the young man to us."

Amusement narrowed the zoji's eyes. "We shall leave the questions to the young man's uncle. And later, I beg. Now, Zandro, how many men can you ferry in a night?"

"Three trips at the most, two probably, considering the cargo is alive. Five men per boat besides me. That's ten men a night."

"Too slow. I don't know how many men Soza has, but we need more than that ourselves. Can you teach others your skill?"

Taverik considered it. "Took me years to learn. I'd say no."

"We'll see," Balanji said.

"Zoji," Marita said tentatively, then flushed when all eyes turned to her. "Could we bleed off a number of Soza's men with a diversion? Riots in Ormea, perhaps?"

"Kintupaquat?"

"Yes, a good idea." The marshal gave a grudging nod. "Another good idea: Soza's man has discovered where we are. The sooner we move the better. I suggest we leave immediately. We can work out details when we are better hidden."

"Yes," said Balanji, and Marita's stomach tightened. "We go. Nikilo Vitujak, will you petition Zojikam for us and place our cause in his hands?"

And just like that the zoji knelt. Impressed, Marita shifted to her knees and bowed her head, hearing a rustle as the others followed. *Zojikam help us,* she thought as Taverik's uncle began to speak. *We'll need it.*

Chapter 8

Marita

Cold rain poured out of the black night. Shielding her eyes, Marita crouched in the bow of the bucking boat, staring past the zoji into the dark. "Rocks on the right," she said as loud as she dared.

"Get ready," Taverik gasped, straining muffled oars against the current. She could hardly hear him over the roar of the Giss in flood. Spray from the confluence of the two rivers made it hard to get a full breath. Driving sheets of rain hid Rinatto and another bodyguard, Barsatta, clinging to the stern.

The boat shuddered against a hidden shelf. Bracing himself against Marita's thigh, Balanji played a thin beam of the shuttered lantern across the rocks. Marita glanced nervously upward at the great black cliff, rain pelting her face and streaming down her neck.

"There!" said Balanji.

An iron ring. In a flash she threaded the rope through. Balanji shut the lantern and grabbed the rope end, belaying it around the thwart. The little boat swung outward, wallowing sickeningly. Water sloshed over Marita's boots. They'd capsize for sure. She couldn't swim. "Pull us in!" Taverik urged. "Hurry!"

She released the thwart and helped Balanji pull on the line. The stern came around too—Rinatto must have gotten his rope around a rock. Taverik dragged in the oars. "Here we are, My Zoji," he said as calmly as if they were all taking a walk in a garden.

"Well done," Balanji said. "Zandro and Barsatta, you stay with the boat. Kastazi, and Rinatto, come with me." He thrust the lantern into Marita's hands, grabbed a wet rock and sprang. The boat rebounded wildly. Marita steadied herself, then followed, determinedly blotting the black water from her thoughts. Rinatto crept past Taverik but she had no time to wait for him. Balanji had already disappeared in the rain and blackness.

Marita scrambled after, her fingers wearing raw from rough stone dimly seen. Above her, up a great sloping slab, she could hear Balanji. Her foot slipped out from under her and she fell with a grunt of pain. Glass tinkled—the lantern had broken. She only stopped her slide backward by jamming her left boot into a crack. Swearing under her breath, she doggedly crawled up on hands and knees.

The roar of the river faded here. "That you, Kastazi?" whispered Balanji. "Give me a light. Can't find the crevice."

She opened a slat of the lantern, relieved to find it still burning. The tiny light showed her Balanji crouched on a ledge, hands splayed across the rock face. Rinatto had reached the slab. Marita offered a hand. He ignored it and hauled himself up just as Balanji gave a satisfied "Ha," under his breath. "Here's the opening," he said. "Bring the lantern. Follow me closely."

She followed him up an almost vertical crevice, hampered by the lantern. Balanji showed her how to brace her feet and shoulders against the rock walls when no handholds offered. Behind, Rinatto easily maneuvered, silently scornful. At last Balanji stopped. "Lantern."

Marita lifted it. Balanji took hold of a metal ring in the rocks. Bracing his feet on either side of it, he heaved. Rock slid against rock. "Watch out, Kastazi," he grunted. She moved back as he settled a heavy slab into the crevice. A round black hole the size of a barrel mouth gaped in the wall. "Give me the lantern," Balanji said. He pushed it in, inserted his head and shoulders and disappeared, leaving Marita in the dark.

She swallowed hard and followed. Wriggling on her belly, she followed Balanji up what seemed to be a smooth streambed, her fingers mashed every so often by Balanji's boots. By Rinatto's muttered curses, she was probably doing the same to him. The passage darkened suddenly. "You can get up, now, Kastazi," Balanji said from directly above her. She reached up and he tried to help her, his hands grasping her under her shoulders, too close to her breasts. In quick reflex she shook him off and scrambled up on her own. He made no comment, merely bending to help Rinatto. Ruffled, Marita opened all the shutters on the lantern and found the glass had broken on only one side. Soft light now filled the darkness, and she looked around.

They stood in a round room at the bottom of stairs carved into black, dripping rock. Dark hid the ceiling. Rinatto shuddered. "Think of all that mountain above us," he said, "houses, people sleeping, the rain."

"Don't think about it," said Balanji, taking the lantern. A streak of mud crossed his aristocratic nose and his black hair hung in rattails, dripping water onto his black cloak. His eyes glowed. At times like this, in the last two weeks, Marita had found it hard to remember he was the zoji of Illiga. He seemed more like a good comrade to whom she would willingly entrust her life. Then, at other times he could become so unapproachable that even Kintupaquat and Vitujak tiptoed. He led off up the stairs now, bending slightly to protect his head, his shadow growing and shrinking grotesquely with each swing of the lantern. Marita gave a last glance at the black hole at her feet, and hurried after him. The dark fled ahead and chased them behind. The stairs were slippery with moss and each carved at a different height, making it hard to find an energy-saving rhythm. Soon Marita's legs ached and her buttocks trembled. Rinatto's breath grew heavy.

After an eternity Balanji stopped before a fork in the path. To the right, the tunnel leveled and widened. To the left, the stairs continued up, steep now, and spiraling like a seaweed draped shell.

"These stairs go straight up to the basements of my palace," Balanji said, his voice oddly intense. Against Marita's secret hope he started up the spiral. But they never reached the top. Marita rounded a bend to find Balanji staring in dismay at a wall of rubble that completely blocked the passage. "When was this done?" he said. "My father? My grandfather? It wasn't there when Grandfather showed me the passage."

"How close are we?" Marita asked.

"Doesn't matter," Balanji said. "We'll dig it out. Keep the men busy. Let's try the other passage."

Getting back down was harder than going up. Marita held onto the wall, slime soon coating her hands and face. After the steep spiral, the right-hand fork seemed like a highway. The passage narrowed and widened, but always ran level or even slightly down hill. Marita knew it ended under the temple, and she tried to make the time go faster by picturing herself walking there from the palace by surface streets. To her delight Balanji stopped before she expected. "Here we are," he said, ducking under a low entry and lifting the lantern. They stood in a tiny room with a tiny fireplace. A lamp hung from a chain from the low rounded ceiling, and several lamps clung to the walls. Near the fireplace steady drops of water plopped into a stone basin, whose twisting animal carvings had to be centuries-old Pakajan.

Balanji handed her the lantern. "Light the lamps, Kastazi," he said. He strode across the room to where the blackened chest stood. "Ah ha," he said, lifting the lid. "Oil. Moldy blankets, lovely. What's this?"

Marita, turning from the first lamp, saw him toss something small and hard to the floor. "Petrified cheese, surely," he said. "Chamber pot, anyone?"

A brass pot clanged into the middle of the floor. Rinatto took advantage of it with a flourish. "How about you, merchant?" he mocked. "Use it before those women you insisted on having invade us."

"No thanks," she said.

"The women will stay in one of the other two rooms," said Balanji. "We'll get another chamber pot." He straddled the pot in his turn then tucked himself up and looked at Rinatto. "The wood's damp and old, but see if you can get the fire going. Kastazi, take the lantern and go back to the boat. Tell Zandro to go ahead and bring the others. Show Barsatta the way in. You can rest then, but I want you back down there to meet Zandro when they return. Help them hide the boat for daylight. Oh, and Kastazi, take the chamber pot and empty it."

"Yes, Zoji," she said. She took the pot and left the glow of the chamber for sliding shadows and narrow, wet walls. Dripping water, the echo of her breath and footsteps, the fork in the path—probably they would quickly become familiar.

The sound of pelting rain grew as she slithered, feet first, down the hole. Soon heavy drops pounded her head and back. She pulled her wet surcoat away from her legs and let it fall back clammily against her again. Funny how she'd thought she couldn't get any colder or wetter. Once on the ledge, she inched as far in the other direction as she could go and dumped the chamber pot. She hesitated, then pulled up her coat to relieve herself. Who knew when she'd again get privacy? And what when she menstruated next week? She'd cope. She'd managed on all those long caravans, even though she'd lain awake nights worrying about it. She'd manage again.

She shut the lantern and clambered down in the darkness. "Taverik?" she whispered.

"Here." A tarp rustled, slightly to her left. "Did you find it?"

"Yes. Balanji says you can bring the others now. I'm to take Barsatta in, then meet you, when?"

"Three hours at the least."

Marita steadied the boat while Barsatta scrambled out. Taverik slid the oars into the roaring water. With sudden agony, Marita caught his hand. "Be careful."

"All right," he said absently, his mind already narrowed in on the task ahead. Feeling foolish, Marita released him and threw in the line. The boat caught the current and shot silently into the night.

Taverik

Taverik had forgotten how running the river completely exhausted him. It was the danger as much as anything, he supposed, but by the time he'd walked north, made the tricky second trip, and helped haul the terrified Bibi from the boat, he could barely move. He forced aching arms to help his uncle and Marita drag the boat into cover and then shoulder the bags of supplies.

Marita led the way nimbly up the rocks, and her sister followed her, soaked, bedraggled but determined not to fall behind. Uncle Nikilo came next where he could help both Sahra and Bibi, but mostly, Taverik noticed with amusement, Sahra.

"We'll have to crawl, now," Marita whispered. "It isn't far, and there's a light at the end." So he squirmed up the tunnel, pushing those damned heavy sacks ahead of him, then brought up the half-lit rear as Marita led them up into the mountain. He knew when they'd arrived by the smoke. Heavy and acrid, it filled the dead air of the passage, choking them and making their eyes water. Rinatto's quarrelsome voice sliced through. "I told you not to put that log on it," he said. "You're the one who put it on," said Barsatta, coughing.

Taverik blinked in the doorway, sack on each shoulder. Rinatto and Barsatta stood by the fire, but made way as Bibi went straight for it. Without a word, Bibi rearranged the wood and smoke quickly ceased billowing.

A hand clapped Taverik on the shoulder. "Good work, Zandro," Balanji said. "Man, you're exhausted and small wonder. Put down the sacks and get some sleep. All of you, get some sleep. No watch needed. Kastazi, show the kalas their room. Hang a blanket in the door. Vitujak, bring a lamp up to the third room. I want to talk to you."

Dumping the sacks, Taverik approached the now blazing fire, peeling off his cloak and surcoat. Rinatto edged in front, blocking the heat. "Pakajans sleep in back," he said.

Taverik ignored him. Best begin as you meant to continue, and he didn't mean to continue as second-class. He shook out his cloak, rolled up his damp surcoat for a pillow, and lay down immediately behind Barsatta. Ha, they'd soon find the heat too much and have to move behind him.

"Tell me, Zandro," said Rinatto in a mock chummy tone. "Is smuggling easier than money grubbing?"

He sounded just like Chado. "Shut up, Rinatto," Taverik said and turned his back.

Balanji's voice crossed his dreams. "Eight in the morning."

Taverik groaned and burrowed deeper. Didn't the zoji ever rest?

"Kastazi, tell the kalas to prepare breakfast. They'll cook all meals. And tell them to bring the chamber pot when they come. Zandro, fix the fire."

His orders cracked like a whip. Muscles aching, Taverik groped for his still-clammy clothes, amused to find the two bodyguards curled behind him as he'd predicted. Breakfast was a dour, silent meal of dried meat and a bowl of tea passed round from hand to hand. Sahra and Bibi sat as silent as the rest, Sahra's face pale and determined.

Even Balanji seemed short. He gave instructions for living underground—chamber pots to be used at all times, to avoid odor and illness, emptied only at night into the river. No loud voices in the chamber directly below the temple, no tempers, no horsing around.

"Kalas, you wanted to come, you will earn your keep," he said and gestured around the tiny chamber strewn with damp wrinkled clothes, weapons and supplies. "Clean up in here first. Afterwards I plan to send you into the streets to look around. Can you do it?"

Sahra set her chin, but looked as green to Taverik as Marita had before she'd fainted, centuries ago. "We can do it," she said.

"Excellent." Balanji smiled at her and suddenly Sahra smiled back. Uncle Nikilo patted her shoulder approvingly. "Now," continued Balanji, "Vitujak, Kastazi and Zandro, go up to the chamber under the temple and wait for me. Rinatto and Barsatta, I want to start you on clearing the passage."

Rinatto was looking mutinous, Taverik thought, following his uncle up the passage. The bodyguard probably considered digging an insult. Though, knowing Balanji, ten to one they'd all be digging before this was over.

An iron ring dangled from the ceiling in the temple chamber. Taverik looked at it curiously. "It's a flagstone of the sanctuary floor," Marita said. "Look, if we shutter the lantern you can see light coming through the cracks."

"No wonder Balanji wants us to whisper," Taverik said. "Anyone up there?"

"We can't tell," said Uncle Nikilo.

Marita reopened the lantern shutters. "Will Balanji send us for the letter, do you think?"

"Not by daylight," Nikilo said. "I suspect he'll ask you to make contact with some merchant you trust."

Taverik met Marita's eyes. "Ittato?" he said.

"He'd be loyal," she said. "But he has it in for me."

Uncle Nikilo's mobile eyebrows climbed. "I fell into Kali Frez Ittato's displeasure the last time we met,"

Marita explained. "Taverik has a better chance of being persuasive."

But not much better, Taverik thought. Balanji would never have brought either of them if he'd know all. Zojikam, why *were* they there?

The temple bell boomed nine by the time Taverik stood on the chest and gingerly pressed up the slab. He listened. Nothing. Cautiously he raised it higher and peeked out.

He stared a moment at a wooden surface, inches from his nose, before he realized it was the back of an overturned prayer bench. Morning light outlined thick dust into high relief. No one had been there for a long time. Quietly Taverik pushed aside the stone and pulled himself out, sitting on the edge of the hole.

Three faces tilted up at him. "What's there?" demanded Balanji.

"It's the main aisle of the sanctuary," Taverik whispered, looking around. "The place is a mess, all looted and overturned. But I think no one comes here anymore. The windows are boarded up."

He moved over to let Nikilo through, and together they cautiously inspected the silent temple. The building was empty, and silent with a strange, almost knowing hush, as if, Taverik thought, the walls themselves watched them. Odd. The doors indeed had been boarded over except one: a side chapel, which had been hidden by a rose trellis. Taverik opened it a crack and peered out. Ten feet away, across the winter-killed garden, a yew hedge lined the wall separating the temple grounds from a narrow alley and a stone building beyond. "Look," Taverik whispered. "There's a gate under those overgrown branches."

"Probably locked," Nikilo said. "But try it. Can you get over the wall?"

"Shouldn't be a problem."

"Go, then," said his uncle. "And Tav—be careful."

"Don't worry," Taverik said. He flitted across the open and squeezed among the branches of the yews. The door was indeed locked. He took hold of a crusty yew branch and tested it. Should bear him. Swinging himself up, he climbed into the dark green thicket until he could peer over the wall, the soft needles cold against his cheek.

The alley ran, a narrow slot, between the temple and a massive building which looked like a warehouse. Because of a jut in the wall, the main street was hidden from view, but Taverik could see the back street. Empty. Across the alley was an unpainted door in an alcove of the warehouse. He'd go over, then wait there to see if he'd been spotted. He gathered himself atop the wall and jumped.

The Black Eagle engulfed him.

Chapter 9

Taverik

Taverik reeled into the doorway opposite, pulling in all his senses like a snail shrinking into its shell. For an age he merely pressed against the door, trying to make himself as small as possible.

Gradually he began again to think. Nothing had happened to him; the Black Eagle's presence remained undiminished, but at least not growing any stronger. It must, he realized, lie like a fog over the city.

He straightened and drew a deep breath. His mouth tasted like bitter iron with the presence. Nasty. How could Illigans stand it, he wondered and suddenly understood—most of them couldn't even sense it. Zojikam had given him a special power during that battle in the woods outside of Ervyn, the power of testing the spirits. Perhaps that was why the temple had felt so alive to him—Zojikam's spirit lingered there.

An uncomfortable gift indeed. Would he have to spent his entire time in Illiga weighed down by that miasma of evil and hatred? And, he thought, suddenly chilled, if he could sense the Black Eagle, did that mean the Black Eagle could sense him? Taverik longed to climb back over the wall.

But no, Zojikam hadn't given him a gift like that to keep him safe inside. *Use all the tools Zojikam has given you,* the *ihiga* had said. But first he needed room to work. Taverik shut his eyes and thought of Zojikam, and gradually the heavy darkness withdrew. Even the bitter taste in his mouth began to fade. With a sudden gush his entire being flooded with joy—and refreshment, as if he'd plunged into an entire pool of blessed water. His hand, when he lifted it, sparkled with blue light, like he'd seen in the *ihiga.* Taverik laughed aloud and loved Zojikam.

The light faded, though the joy remained, subdued, tamped down, but flaring if he thought of it. What now, he wondered. He waited. Nothing more happened. A minute crept by. Another. Gradually he began to suspect the next move was up to him. All right, then, time to go. With a deep breath, he walked boldly down the alley to the road.

He'd probably find Ittato in the Guild Hall at this time of day. Not far as the crow flies, only across the square. But for Taverik that would mean a long wandering trek across the heart of the city, avoiding Soza's checkpoints. From local farmers who had ventured to market, Balanji had learned some barricades always guarded the square before the fortress, while others were shifted randomly. Taverik had to get around them, and not attract suspicion at the same time.

He began to work his way in a wide circle around the square, using every side road, short cut and alley he could find. Mano had taught him the underside of the city well in the old days. Back then it had been a lark. Now it might save his life. Funny, less than a month ago, Mano and Kala Pardi had been alive. He wondered briefly if their bodies still lay in the deserted house.

Over everything lay that despairing cloud of the Black Eagle. Taverik kept it at bay though occasionally a blast of it would issue from a passerby. On the other hand, from several other people he could sense strong, stubborn love of Zojikam. Once he passed a small house whose attic windows glowed with that intense, sparkling light. Taverik stopped and stared, the tamped-down joy inside him leaping up in response. In his head he could plainly hear the words of the Promise spoken by many voices—a secret worship service. He glanced at the people hurrying along the street, worried they'd see the light and hear the praise. But they plodded on, somehow blinded to the reality. Their spirits tasted neutral, gray.

Taverik continued on so as not to draw attention to the house, moving over to allow a farmer on a donkey to overtake him. The crusty old man tasted strong of Zojikam, and he gave Taverik a surprised look, as if he in turn could sense Taverik's spirit. Taverik grinned cheekily, and a slow smile dawned on the stern weather-beaten face, but neither spoke. The farmer joined the thin stream of nervous farmers bringing winter vegetables to market. Taverik slipped down an alley.

Sticky crossing the River Road with checkpoints at each end. But a long line occupied the guards' attention, and no one made any comment as he sauntered across and eased down the opposite street. After that Taverik easily reached the back gate of the Textile Guild. In the gate's shelter he hesitated long, chewing his lips. What would be the safest way to get into the Hall? He could think of nothing and at last he merely walked in and climbed the stairs to Ittato's office.

Ittato sat alone at his desk. He looked up and a procession of expressions crossed his face. Taverik shut the door and took his hat humbly in his hand.

"Taverik Zandro!"

"Kali Ittato," Taverik said, "how are you?"

"How am I!" Ittato thumped the desk. "You foist a woman disguised as a man on us, help engineer the downfall of Illiga, disappear with Zoji Soza searching every house and warehouse for you and the woman, then have the gall to calmly walk in here and ask me how I am? How dare you?"

"Kali, I can explain," Taverik began.

The door opened.

Taverik swung around, blood draining from his face. "Gunnar," he said, tentatively.

Gunnar Chisokachi stared, then quickly shut the door. "Taverik. Taverik! Aha, I knew you'd come back. Just like the cat!"

Relief made Taverik feel slightly sick. "Gunnar, President Ittato, I have something to tell you. Did you know Zoji Balanji is alive?"

"After your best effort to get rid of him?"

"I swear," Taverik said, intense, "I had nothing to do with Illiga's fall. I knew nothing about it until too late."

"Oh?" said Ittato neutrally.

"Zoji Balanji has a plan for retaking the city."

Their faces shuttered right up. "Forget it," Gunnar said. "Taverik, are you crazy? Do you know what Zoji Soza will do to you if he catches you talking like that?"

"You'll disappear," Ittato said. "Like all the others. Look, why don't you settle down and accept Soza? Your father's doing well for himself, and Soza does allow trade, even if his taxes are high. We'll soon be back to normal."

"You will not," Taverik said. "Soza's a Bcacmat."

Gunnar's long jaw dropped. "Bcacmat!"

"Nonsense," snapped Ittato.

"I have proof," Taverik insisted. "A letter from the Tlath to Soza, dating from before he took Vosa. The Tlath wanted him to take the east-west trade route—us—not Vosa. Soza is the Agash Itzil Farasoza. He's keeping his identity secret because he knows it's the only way to prevent the Peninsula from banding together against him as we did before. And just think how Soza works, assassinations, traitors, Black Eagle. That's Bcacmat straight through."

He paused for breath, thinking how lame he sounded. And why should they listen to a Zandro anyway?

Ittato shook his head. "Does your father know you're saying these things?"

"What's he got to do with it? Listen, just suppose you believed me. What would you do?"

Ittato rubbed dry-as-paper fingers together. "If, and *only if*, Soza is secretly Bcacmat, I would prefer Balanji."

Gunnar was less cautious. "I'd fight him with my teeth if I had to. Dammit, *Bcacmat*!"

"Show us your proof, Zandro," Ittato challenged.

"I have to get it," he said. "It's in Marko Kastazi's house."

Wrong move. "Listen, she meant no harm," Taverik said. "Soza murdered her parents and went after her just because of that letter. He knew it could destroy his plan. She had to dress as a man to escape, and when she came here, she had to stay that way to make a living and keep hidden. How can I convince you?"

Drumming his fingers on the table, Ittato stared at Taverik. "All right," he said finally. "Bring me the letter in the morning. Not promising anything, but I'll look at it."

"Kali, could you get me a pass?"

Ittato's eyebrows shot up. "You don't have a pass? How'd you get here?"

"Back alleys."

"You're crazy! You know what they'll do if they catch you? Aren't you working for your father and Echin in this?"

"Of course not. I just arrived today. And what's Echin got to do with anything?"

Gunnar and Ittato exchanged glances. "You don't know—" began Gunnar. He broke off, listening. Voices and many footsteps rang in the hall. "Trade inspection," he said.

"I forgot!" wailed Ittato. "Hide him. Hurry!"

"In here!" Gunnar pulled open the door to the oak wardrobe behind Ittato's desk and Taverik pushed in among Ittato's ceremonial robes and damp cloak. Gunnar jammed shut the door just as Ittato spoke. "Good morning, Inspector."

"Why did no one greet me when I arrived?" demanded an angry voice. A bullying voice. A self-important voice. A voice Taverik had heard from childhood.

His father.

Chapter 10

Marita

Time was the hardest thing about the tunnel, Marita thought, leaning tired shoulders against the wall and sliding to the floor. How long had she been hauling rubble out of the blocked passage? Surely Sahra and Bibi should be back by now, and it felt like Taverik had been gone for days. She had no way of telling, for except in the room directly under the temple where the tower chimes penetrated, time stood as still as the rocks.

And a day spent with Rinatto and Barsatta would drag by anywhere.

The two bodyguards were quarrelling over the fire, which belched smoke as it always did when Bibi wasn't there to make it mind. "Quit banging it, Rin," said Barsatta, coughing. "You'll smother us all."

Rinatto gave the fire one last prod with the sword that served as a poker. "Doesn't Vitujak's freckle face look like a spotted handkerchief?"

"We won't need a flag," Barsatta snickered. "Just pop up that red Pakajan head and everyone will cheer."

"Run away, more likely."

Marita leaned her forehead on her muddy knees and massaged her neck with roughened fingers. Balanji had put her and Vitujak to work in the abandoned temple, searching for the key to the gate in the wall. She'd found it in a back office, hanging on a peg behind the door. That done, she had no reason to stay, but she'd been reluctant to go back down. She found the silence in the sanctuary oddly soothing.

With the gate now unlocked, Balanji gave Sahra and Bibi final instructions for their first trip outside. And worse—instructions in case of questioning or arrest. The two had nodded eagerly, but Marita could barely keep from demanding they stay. She watched, silent in the corner as Vitujak and Balanji helped them up into the temple. Balanji, dropping back down, gave her a long look. Marita braced herself for his *told you so*, but he merely said, "Kastazi, go help clear the passage. I'll call for you when they return."

The work *had* helped the time pass faster. But it hadn't taken Rinatto and Barsatta long to notice her lack of strength. They jibed her constantly about it, and Rinatto found subtle ways to make loads heavier. She grit her teeth and doggedly worked. And remembering how Taverik handled things, she jibed them right back. It helped. But Rinatto's laughter was beginning to have a strange edge to it. She didn't trust him.

What time was it? Hard not to worry about Sahra and Bibi, both so unused to danger, betraying every emotion on their faces; how could they keep out of trouble? And yes, she admitted to herself, at last she knew how Sahra had felt each time she herself had left the house. Hours of accumulated anxiety for the ones you loved most in the world wore you out. You had to find ways to cope.

Surely Taverik should be back by now?

"Zojikam, but the mountain feels heavy," said Rinatto, wiping sweat from his forehead. "Even though it's not touching you, all the time it's weighing you down."

"Doesn't bother me," said Barsatta, stretching languidly. He sat up abruptly. "Listen, they're opening the floor."

Marita lifted her head but made no move. She'd learned the hard way not to walk in on Zoji Balanji unless he called for her or she had an important message. In a moment Nikilo Vitujak looked around the door. "Kali Kastazi, would you come on up to the temple chamber?" he asked.

Rinatto made a low-voiced comment, and Barsatta snickered, glancing at Vitujak out of the corners of his eyes. Marita clamped her mouth shut on angry words; Balanji would not welcome quarrelling in the tunnel. But it infuriated her the way they rode both Taverik and Nikilo Vitujak whenever Balanji was safely out of earshot.

"Your sister and servant are back," said Vitujak, leading the way to the temple chamber. "Balanji wants you to hear their report."

Marita heard Sahra's laugh ring out as she entered. Her sister's face was flushed with the success of their venture, and her market basket burgeoned with potatoes, onions and early cabbage. Bibi's basket, even fuller, contained a plucked chicken as well. Balanji poked it with a forefinger. "By the Guardians, I'm glad you kalas came," he said. "My mouth positively waters."

Bibi beamed, and Sahra's eyes sparkled. "We went to all the gates," she said. "They have piles of rocks all along the walls, and armed checkpoints on all the major streets. But they just waved us through. And they have travelling squads of men patrolling."

"Good work," Balanji said.

"Yes, neatly done," said Nikilo. "Did you happen to notice if they've built any anti-siege towers?"

"What do they look like?"

"I'll show you before you go out next," said Balanji. "Now put down the greenery and show me on this map where the checkpoints are. Kastazi, come here and look. You'll be going up there."

Three soft knocks sounded above. "Well, about time," said Nikilo. He sounded as relieved as Marita felt. He clambered up on the chest and lifted the stone. Taverik slid through.

"Zandro, where have you been?" demanded Balanji.

Taverik jumped lightly to the ground and knelt

before him. "Hiding in a closet, Zoji," he said. "Listening to Soza's trade inspectors demand homage."

Nikilo Vitujak raised a sandy eyebrow. "Trade inspectors?"

"Soza has appointed a trade inspector, and an assistant." Taverik rose at a sign from Balanji and Marita watched him suspiciously—he often hid upsets under just that breezy confidence. "The inspector and his assistant," he said, "are in charge of extracting the seventy-five percent tax Soza demands for the privilege of remaining in trade. They have charge of the weekly street passes each city merchant must buy. Any barge coming down river must see them even to pass, let alone to trade. Later, when the caravans begin, the inspector will also extort—I mean extract—fees from them. I'm told he has done well for himself on the side, as well."

"Who is he?" said Balanji. "Do you know him?"

"Oh yes, I know him." Taverik's face went carefully blank. "Donato Zandro."

Marita winced.

"Your father," said Balanji. His half-lidded eyes considered Taverik. "Interesting."

"Who is the assistant?" asked Nikilo.

"A little sniveler named Echin." He met Marita's eyes and grimaced.

"And you," said Balanji, "when not in the closet, did you manage to talk to anyone?"

"I talked to Frez Ittato, president of the Textile Guild. And also another merchant, a friend of mine—I think. Gunnar Chisokachi. They're scared of Soza, but if he's Bcacmat they don't want him. But they didn't half believe me when I told them."

"Will they betray us, do you think?" asked Vitujak.

"I'm not sure. They told me to bring the letter tomorrow as proof. They gave me a forged one-day pass."

"A trap? Will Soza or, ah, the trade inspector be waiting for you?"

"I don't know."

"Hmm." Balanji turned to Marita and her stomach

gave a sudden twist. "Kastazi, tonight you and Zandro go get the lettter."

Only grim resolve brought Marita back to the temple chamber that midnight. But she managed to smile cheerfully at Sahra and tell her not to worry. Sahra hugged her hard, then went to stand beside Nikilo Vitujak. The look Vitujak gave Sahra told Marita much, and her heart swelled with happiness for her sister. Still she couldn't help feeling a little closed out, especially when Nikilo laid his hand briefly on Taverik's heart and Taverik patted it.

Taverik had told them how the Black Eagle oppressively blanketed the city. Sahra had shrugged. "It's not so bad," she said. "The city is depressingly gloomy, that's all." But Bibi had nodded strong agreement with Taverik, and Marita went by that, bracing herself as she followed Taverik into the alley. Still, it was like walking into a cloud. Or her nightmare.

"All right?" whispered Taverik.

"*Ikiji* has to be the grossest understatement in the language," she whispered shakily.

"Not second best at all," he agreed. "Worst, in fact. Odd thing is, most people don't notice it."

How could they not, she wondered. The presence hung over the city like odor from the paper mills upriver when the wind swung around to the north. Gritting her teeth against it, she followed Taverik on a circuitous back alley route across the city, hiding from occasional patrols, flitting across streets. Neither spoke.

Her forebodings intensified as they at last crept down the lane behind her property while the neighbor's dog barked and barked. In the deep shadow of the wall she couldn't see Taverik, but she could feel his warmth and hear his breath as he stopped and leaned closer to her. "Here we are," he whispered. "Put your foot in my hands and I'll boost you."

She did so and was flung skyward. She grabbed the top of the wall and clung, peering down at the silent house below. It looked the same, except the shutters were closed and the back door padlocked, with a sign on it she couldn't make out. But something felt wrong.

Foolish misgivings—she was just afraid, that was all. How could she go back and tell Balanji she hadn't gotten the letter because something *felt* wrong? Go on, she told herself. Up and over.

Instead, she slithered back down and crouched, shivering, against the rough granite. Taverik knelt beside her. "What's wrong?"

"I don't know," she whispered. "Wait a minute."

"Frightened?" His arm circled her shoulder, pulling her close.

"Damn it, of course I'm frightened," she whispered indignantly. "But also . . . uneasy."

She looked inward, sifting through herself for the source of the inquietude. It was her nightmare, she realized, the remembrance of fleeing down dark halls with *it* stalking her. That's why the morbid feeling tonight. Just memories. But even knowing that, she still felt as if she were walking to her doom. Well, she was willing to do it if it would help rid Illiga of Soza, but first there was something she had to know. "Taverik," she said, "you asked me a question more than a month ago and never came back for your answer. I'm telling you now. The answer is yes. If you still want it."

His arm tightened. "You are Massadaran," he said thickly, "a zoja born. You deserve your proper place."

"Half-Pakajan. And my proper place is the place I've carved for myself," she said. "I care nothing for Vosa. But, Taverik, if you've realized that you don't really love me, I understand. I know I'm not any man's ideal woman—"

He made an inarticulate noise at that, and pulled her roughly to him. He kissed her soundly, and she kissed him back, melting against his warm body in the chill, dank night. Her last doubts dissolved. Taverik was going to blather on about her deserving her proper place, but now she knew for sure he loved her. Well, she'd take care of her proper place, she thought, and for a brief moment relaxed into happiness. Not until

Taverik shifted to get more comfortable did the memory of cold duty return. "Taverik, we've got to get the letter."

He released her. She sat up, breathing deeply, trying to refocus her mind to the task at hand. After a moment, his hand found hers. "*Now* will you go over the wall, Marita Marko?"

"Over the moon, even," she said, but wouldn't repeat it when he asked.

Once in the yard she led the way, flitting down the thyme-scented slope under the apple trees. She chose the side of the house away from the gate, where the boundary wall would give them a little protection from prying eyes. Taverik stooped. She climbed shakily to his shoulders and took out her knife. Slipping the shutter's catch took longer and made more noise than she liked—she was working high over her head. Her arms ached. Under her feet Taverik began to tremble from the strain. At last the window released. "Got it," she breathed. "Brace yourself."

She gave a light leap and hauled herself inside.

Dark. The smell of mildew and damp caught her throat; no fire had been lit the whole winter. Marita stepped into the blackness and stumbled against something heavy at knee height. Sahra's table, thrown over. Around her on the floor lay books and papers. The room had been ransacked.

Angry and sad together, she felt her way around the couch, whose cotton padding erupted from long knife slashes. She could see dimly now, enough to find every drawer of her desk had been emptied and flung into the corners of the room. The desk itself had been overturned and lay face down. But she smiled with grim satisfaction; the floorboards remained untouched.

She cleared a path to the desk then pushed and pulled until she'd lugged the monstrous piece aside. Then she pried up the boards and dragged out the strong box. The letter and translation lay on top, just as she'd left them.

Suddenly she stilled, listening. The monotonous barking of the neighbor's dog had increased to hysteria.

Above it she heard the creak of her front gate, and the sound of many horses filling the courtyard below.

Marita seized the letters and stumbled over the mess to the window. Taverik wasn't there. He'd already taken cover. Marita grabbed a large book, shoved the letters into it, and hurled it over the wall into the neighbor's yard. She closed the shutter and relocked it just as horsemen fanned out into the back yard.

The box! She stumbled to it, hurried it under the floorboards and began to shove the desk back over it. A door opened below.

She dropped behind the desk, her heart hammering so loud she could hear it. A stair creaked and a glimmer of light filled the ruined room. Marita went cold; what seemed a good hiding place in the dark became painfully exposed in the light. The orange glow grew and steadied as someone in heavy boots came into the room. "You might as well stand up," said a silky, humorous voice.

Trembling, she stood. A large man waited, a naked sword gleaming in his hand. Soza. She recognized him from when she had hidden behind the curtains in her father's library, watching him murder her father, watching him ransack the room, searching for something. The Black Eagle clung to him—just as in her nightmare. Marita braced her legs against it and hooked her thumb into her belt.

"Unfinished business," he said. "I've looked a long time for you, but I knew I'd get you in the end. The Black Eagle promised. But you have caused me trouble and I don't like that. Where is the other?"

Taverik? No, he must mean Sahra. "She's in Novato," Marita said. Her voice cracked.

"You lie. Where is my letter?"

"What letter?" she said. The sword flashed and her hand went involuntarily to her throat. Blood seeped between her fingers.

"Do not think me a fool. I know you have my letter. That's why I ordered the house watched. I knew you would return."

"The letter's in Novato," she said. "I took it with me

when I fled." The sword arm raised and her hand flew to protect her throat. "I came back for money," she said. "We needed money. I had a lot of it here. That's why I came back. Money."

He watched her, and she stared back. *He has gotten holds in your mind*, the *ihiga* had said. *You must never give in to him, not in your spirit.*

"Very well," he said softly. "And now I will finish a botched job. All the Vos family died that day except two. Now one of them shall go. Which one are you?"

Marita lifted her chin. "Marita Vos."

Again the sword flashed and she involuntarily shut her eyes. Silence. Cautiously she peeked and found Soza frowning at her speculatively. The sword point lowered. "Marita Vos," he said as if to himself. "The city is stubborn. Perhaps I now possess the key to it. It would be foolish to waste it before I find out. Guards!"

Three men with the small, sharp features of most Bcacmats, thundered up the narrow stairs. "Bind her," Soza said. "She's coming with us."

Taverik

Cursing softly and bitterly, Taverik lay on his belly under the cypresses, watching the horsemen mill around the yard.

He'd sensed them even before he heard them, and had called Marita, dammit, called her as loudly as he dared. He'd even thrown a pebble. But she hadn't heard, she hadn't come. At last he could delay no longer, and he'd swarmed over the wall and thrown himself flat in the neighbor's enclosure. The berserk dog charged the length of its chain and strained, forepaws in the air, barking hoarsely.

Something heavy hit the ground by Taverik's head. A book. He squirmed toward it just as the neighbor's shutter opened. Taverik froze. A man thrust out his head, shouted at the dog, then apparently saw the horsemen filling the yard next door, for he broke off in mid-sentence and slammed shut the window. The dog barked on.

Taverik pulled the book to him. The letters were jammed in the back cover. He thrust them inside his surcoat and crept up the hill to the back of the property. Under the thick cover of the cypresses he crawled back into Marita's yard and lay flat. She'd reclosed the shutter. Good. She'd know how to hide in her own house. Once the men left, he'd help her out and they'd get back safely.

A stir in the yard. A big man, Soza himself, strode out of the house. Two soldiers followed—with Marita. Taverik went dead inside. In the flaring torch light her face looked aristocratic and remote, as if she'd become a different person than the one he knew. Soza pointed to a horse and she was bundled onto it. They swept from the gate leaving several horsemen who began systematically to search the property. He had to go.

Uncle Nikilo helped him down the hole, then looked out, puzzled. "Where's Kastazi?"

"Soza got him," Taverik said.

Balanji's eyes narrowed. "What happened?"

Numb, Taverik gave him the letter and told the night's events. Balanji looked at Nikilo. "The house was watched. Have we lost the game, do you think?"

"Possibly," Nikilo said, his freckled face grim. "Taverik, you say he is after that letter. I can't think of any reason why he'd take Kastazi with him except to force him to tell where the letter is."

"Torture?" Taverik said, his mouth dry. "Can't we break into the fortress and rescue him?"

"Out of the question," said Balanji. Taverik found the zoji's dark eyes considering him. "Something doesn't add up. You told me everything that happened tonight, Zandro?"

Taverik hesitated. "Everything I saw," he said. He opened his mouth to tell Marita's secret but Balanji had already turned to Uncle Nikilo. "Well, Vitujak?"

"Kastazi knows the plan, he knows the entrance to the tunnel—he might tell all," Uncle Nikilo said. He shook his head. "We could pull out and try again months later, or proceed cautiously. I'd like to proceed, but perhaps the important thing is to keep you safe."

Balanji paced, chewing his lip. "We'll proceed. Cautiously. Zandro, you did well."

"No." Taverik shook his head in frustration. Not only had he lost Marita, he was beginning to see the enormity of their deception. Sooner or later it would come out, and he'd be finished. The zoji's hands descended heavily on his shoulders. "You did the best you could. You had no idea the house would be watched, and you managed to bring me the letter. Yes, I know you feel grief for your friend. But Kastazi knew the risks when he said he'd come. Right?"

"Yes, Zoji," Taverik said mechanically.

"Then don't throw away his sacrifice by immobilizing yourself. I need you. Tomorrow you must take the letter to your guild president. We have no guarantee that's not a trap either, that you won't be dragged off to join Kastazi. You need your wits. Understand?"

"Yes, My Zoji." He did understand, though he didn't like it.

Balanji released him at last. "You'll do," he said. "Go break the news to the sister, then get some sleep."

Chapter 11

Marita

"It's in Novato," Marita insisted. Sweat soaked her linen, rolled down her face, trickled down the small of her back. For hours now she had sat in that chair in the small room in the base of the tower while Soza asked the same questions over and over. The room was empty except for six jars in a circle around her, each jar exuding the same nauseatingly evil aura as the jar in the pawn shop. Each one, she knew now, confined a *mahiga* which the Black Eagle enabled Soza to control.

She'd stuck stubbornly to her story, but Soza was suspicious. "Balanji sent you here for it," he said once again.

"I didn't know who he was."

"Where is he?"

"Novato."

"You lie. My servant writes the house is empty. Who murdered my son?"

"We killed a man who attacked us."

Soza stepped back, watching her. She stared back, her face sagging with weariness. "I will force the truth," he warned, then laughed at her involuntary reaction. "No, it is not what you think. You may wish it were."

Raising the claw circlet, he began to chant in Bcacmat. The room grew uncomfortably warm; the jars had begun to radiate heat. Before long, Marita could hardly pull the searing air into her lungs. Suddenly flames burst from the top of each jar, licked down the edges and joined to form a circle of fire around her chair. Marita pulled in her feet and clamped her lips together.

Soza's words droned on, their many sibilants piercing her ears into her mind. She could feel the Black Eagle's presence then, surrounding her, demanding the information he sought. Her mouth opened to tell, but instead she gasped, "Zojikam!" *He has gotten holds in your mind. You must never give in to him, not your spirit. Use all the tools Zojikam has given you.* What tools? She had nothing powerful such as these *mahiga* of Soza's. And yet, hadn't the Black Eagle withdrawn when Taverik sang the litany of the temple? Words seemed an impotent, intangible tool. But she had nothing else. Gathering strength, she repulsed Soza and quickly filled the space in her mind with the Promise from the temple service. *Zojikam will not leave you desolate, he will come to you.*

"Where is the letter?" Soza demanded over the

crackle of the flames and the strange, whining hum from the jars.

"In Novato," she said aloud. *He will walk among you and teach you, and . . .* Her mind filled with a sudden picture of a hand cupped over her, hiding and protecting her. The Black Eagle's presence withdrew a step farther. Soza raised his voice and the flames shot high. "Where's Balanji?"

. . . show you his ways. "I don't know. Maybe Novato still."

"Who killed my son?"

"We didn't know he was your son," she gasped, struggling for breath in the searing air. "We killed a man who attacked us."

"What is your name?"

"Marita Vos!"

She could sense his puzzlement, as he dropped the talisman and tried to quell the flames. They gave him a little trouble, Marita noted with amusement, even as she sagged from the chair to the floor. The hot flagstones hurt her hands and face, but she found no strength to do anything about it. Blearily she wondered if that invisible hand was still cupped over her—for she herself hadn't the strength to fight even a mosquito.

Soza stared down at her. "It must be true," he muttered. "No one could have resisted." He strode to one of the two doors in the room and opened it. "Come in now, Malenga," he said.

A Massadaran wearing an elaborate short *hama* court dress slipped in, staying by the door as if ready to flee through it again. "By Zojikam," he gasped, "what on earth was that?"

"Zojikam had nothing to do with it, Malenga," said Soza. "Zojikam is nowhere. What you just experienced was the powerful Black Eagle, your new master. Serve him well and do not anger him!"

Malenga looked at Marita and fastidious lines deepened on each side of his nose. "Who is this boy?"

"Ah." Soza pulled Marita to her feet and held her by her upper arm. "This is no boy. You may bow to the

Zoja Marita Vos. And you will forget you ever saw her in a filthy Pakajan merchant's coat."

"I will forget most willingly." Malenga bowed slightly to Marita. She didn't like his eyes. "Is she real?" he said.

"She's real. Most conveniently real," Soza said. "Through her I will at last bring Vosa under control. Marita Vos, I present Viti Malenga."

Traitor, Marita thought and made no move. Malenga's next bow held more respect.

"In two weeks," Soza continued, "I will wed her. The city of Illiga will rejoice that one of their own will 'rule' them. The city of Vosa will welcome her back, and through her, me. We will gain the loyalities of both cities, and our offspring will be half-Peninsular, half Bcacmat."

"I have heard about the death of your son," Malenga said. "My deepest condolences."

Soza shrugged. "Whoever did it will pay," he said. His fingers caressed Marita's arm. "But this one will beget me more."

Marita pulled away, nauseated. Her father's murderer, this awful man—

"An unwilling bride, it seems," Malenga said.

Soza glared at her, infuriated at the humiliation. Marita's heart lurched; his eyes changed strangely, as if he were suddenly a different person. Beget him children? She'd kill herself first.

Soza shuddered then seemed to return to himself. "Malenga, send a messenger to Abado, who is in Novato. Tell him to return. Tell him to leave Tlele there to search: Balanji apparently still hides there. Next, prepare the fortress, the viti and the people for a special announcement tomorrow. Allow the news to leak—tomorrow at noon we will parade to the square and present the newly found Zoja Marita Vos to the people."

"As you wish, My Zoji," said Malenga.

"Return to my office in an hour. I'll have specific instructions for you." Soza pulled Marita closer. "And you: if you somehow lied to me you will regret it. Now come."

She stumbled along with him, climbing the stairs of the tower into the gold of the sun's first rays. Strange, the sun still rose, the birds still sang.

On one of the landings, Soza opened a door and pushed her before him into a tiny room in the wall. It held only a cot, a chair, and a chamber pot. And a thin woman with sumptuous clothes and a sour face.

The woman rose from the chair and prostrated herself on the floor. "This is the Tet-zoja Marita Vos," Soza said without preamble. "In two weeks she will wed me. This noon I will present her to the city. Clean her up and find her a dress."

The door closed and locked behind him. The woman sat back on her heels and looked Marita over coldly, taking in her tangled, dirty hair and sweat-streaked face, filthy, wrinkled surcoat and muddy boots. "This," she asked in heavily accented Massadaran, "best is Peninsula can provide?"

Marita stared back impassively, then strode to the barred window. It was too high to see out. She shoved the cushioned chair beneath, ignoring the woman's intake of breath as she climbed up into its alcove, muddy boots and all.

The window looked south. The wall of the tower dropped to the narrow cliff edge which overhung the rivers' confluence. Below to her right, the gray-brown Ao roared, distance flattening its turbulence. The Giss ran green and smooth to her left, joined downstream by the Ao's muddy stripe. Above, the sun poured golden on the new day.

"Come down," said the woman. She'd gotten off the floor—odd gesture, that prostration—and now stood, holding up the long spill of fabric in the front of her gown. "They bath water bring. You know how bath to take? I you dress will find, the vita many left. Aye! Who knows if among the vita any such giantesses were. A mask you will need, of course."

Marita slid down at that, and looked closer at the woman. If she needed any more proof that Soza was a

Bcacmat, this was it. Bcacmat women, even the poorest street sweeper, hid their faces behind masks in public. The Bcacmats had an enormous number of odd restrictions, and prostrating oneself, Marita supposed, was one of them.

"Disgusting, unseemly clothes take off," said the woman impatiently. "I now you help, but once you wed, you me must serve."

"Who are you?" Marita said.

"So you *can* talk," said the woman. "I Idbca Farasoza named. I first wife of Soza. You seventh."

Taverik

Taverik held out his pass as he neared the checkpoint. The guard waved it aside. "All citizens must go to the square," he said, barely glancing at Taverik. "Public Announcement. Hey you! Old man! C'mere!"

An old man with a market basket pointed to himself, then came as the guard gestured impatiently. Taverik shrugged and joined the growing stream of people headed toward the square.

The sun warmed his shoulders but his mood stayed somber. Somewhere deep beneath his feet, Sahra Vos still wept, and somewhere in those great granite walls over his head, Marita Vos was a prisoner of her enemy. And he himself might be recognized at any time, Taverik Zandro, son of the new trade inspector.

A great crowd already filled the square. At the gates of the fortress a gaily decorated pavilion stood in front of the grisly row of Soza's enemies, hanged from the walls and left to rot. Taverik edged to the back of the crowd, toward the Textile Guild, just as trumpets blew and the gates of the fortress flew open. Sparkling with colors, jewels and false smiles, a procession of viti marched through the dour Illigans.

The crowd continued silent, watching the procession file into the pavilion. Several viti made speeches promising peace and prosperity. Taverik listened with half an ear, using the precious time to absorb as many details as he could. To Soza's right stood Malenga. That figured. Taverik recognized a few other of Balanji's former viti, though he couldn't put names to them. He wondered what oaths they'd sworn to Soza.

At last Soza stood. He repeated the monotonous promises, but spoke well. Taverik had to admit he could exude charisma when he wanted to. Then, abruptly, he switched gears and talked of the lost tet-zojas of Vosa. Marita. Ignoring the fact that he'd murdered her family, he gave a maudlin, fake account of rescuing her from poverty. Taverik wanted to puke. The people on either side craned their necks trying to see her. "Now," declaimed Soza, "I present to the people of Illiga, the last tet-zoja of Vosa, Marita Vos."

He stepped aside, gently offering his arm to a woman standing behind him. The crowd surged forward against the restraining guards. Elbowing a drayman who got in his way, Taverik stared.

Marita. Even with her hair pulled back under a cap and with a dress on, he knew her. She looked unhurt, though even from the back he could see dark circles under her eyes. Suddenly she stepped forward. "Illigans, beware!" she cried.

Taverik was never sure exactly what happened next. Soza moved quickly behind her, then Malenga was half-carrying her to a seat in the back of the pavilion. Soza turned to the crowd. "Marita Vos begs your indulgence," he called. "The excitement has overcome her."

"Hurrah Marita Vos!" someone cried. Probably paid by Soza, Taverik thought sourly. "Hurrah!" shouted the crowd, picking up the chant. Soon everyone was laughing and shouting for Marita. Soza milked it, smiling and waving as if the cheers were for him. Taverik ground his teeth and pushed his way out of the crowd. At least she was alive.

Gunnar grabbed his belt. "Wait up," he said. Loose-jawed with wonder he fell into step beside Taverik. "That was Kastazi. Right? I'd recognize him anywhere. Did you know who he was back then? Or is this another of your Zandro schemes?"

"Will you shut up?" Taverik said, glancing nervously at a nearby guardsman.

Gunnar subsided and walked along with him to the Textile Guild. "Ittato said to bring you to the back room of the archives. Less chance that Zandro—I mean, your father, will happen on us."

"All right," Taverik said easily, but his stomach tensed. Trap?

The archives smelled of leather-bound volumes, ink, and dust. Gunnar went straight through to the back room, but Taverik lingered, fingers on his knife hilt. He extended his mind, sampling and testing. Did anyone beside Gunnar wait in that back room?

"Taverik Zandro," said Ittato behind him.

Taverik whirled, bringing out his knife. Ittato stood alone in the door, leaning heavily on the cane. "All the same, you Zandros. Good thing *Sadra* Laws forbid swords. Put that knife away and let me sit down. My gout is killing me."

Sheepishly, Taverik checked the empty hall, then shut the door. He followed the stumping Ittato into the back room. High ceilinged and tiny, the room stored a clutter of furniture and junk under draped tarps. Gunnar had dragged out three wooden chairs carved in Pakajan style, and was dusting them with his handkerchief. "Sit here, Kali Ittato," he said.

"Thank you." Ittato sat with a sigh and thrust out his bandaged foot. "Don't stand at the door, Zandro, this isn't a trap. Now tell me, was that Kastazi?"

Taverik sat. "Yes," he said.

"And is Kastazi truly Marita Vos, or is this a trick?"

"She's truly Marita Vos. She fled Vosa disguised as a boy, and found friendship, shelter and a living among us here at Illiga's Textile Guild."

Taverik had chosen his words well. Ittato smiled slightly and said, "We were honored she picked us."

Gunnar laughed. "And to think of the times I clapped a zoja on the back! Taverik, you sly dog, did you know who she was all along?"

"No," said Taverik stiffly. "I discovered she was a woman, of course, when she was wounded in the attack on the caravan. I only figured out who she was the day Illiga fell."

"Taverik," said Gunnar eagerly, "did you, you know, uh, diddle with a zoja?"

"No, Gunnar," said Taverik through clenched teeth. "I did not."

"You knew she was a woman," said Ittato, "but you kept it secret and made fools of us all?"

Taverik stared at him. "You, of course, would have had her arrested?"

"Hmph," grunted Ittato. Then, "You're different, somehow, Zandro. You've changed. Did you know there's a price on your head?"

"Still?" Taverik said calmly, but he couldn't help glancing at the door.

"Let me see the letter."

Taverik pulled out the copy with its awkward translation scribbled over each word. Ittato read it in silence, then started at the top and read it again. "Agash Itzil Farasoza," he said handing it to Gunnar. "I'd heard of him way back. You are saying he is Soza?"

Taverik nodded. Ittato and Gunnar exchanged glances. "I believe him," Gunnar said. "It all fits. Soza's Bcacmat, working secretly for the Tlath. Come *on*, Ittato. You know it's true."

Ittato lowered his white head, hands fisted on his knees. "Yes," he said at last. "I believe it, and I've got to do something about it, though I don't mind telling you both I'm frightened to death. But even if it means my death, I will eject the Bcacmats from my beloved Peninsula."

He raised his head. "What do we do now, Zandro?"

"You swear by Zojikam you are sincere and will not betray Balanji?"

Both Gunnar and Ittato raised their hands. "I swear," they said.

It felt odd, both men looking humbly to him, of all people, for instructions. "You must come with me to meet with Balanji," Taverik said.

Chapter 12

Taverik

"Did you talk to them?" demanded Balanji the moment Taverik returned.

"Yes, Zoji. And they believed me," Taverik said. "Ittato said that if Soza were Bcacmat he'd give his life if necessary to drive him out. They want to know how they can help you."

"Good work," said Balanji. "Did you arrange a meeting?"

"Yes. They're waiting even now in the side chapel of the temple."

"We'll go up immediately," Balanji said. "Zandro, get Rinatto and Barsatta—"

"My Zoji," Taverik said. "There's something else."

His tone stopped Balanji in mid-stride. "What is it, Zandro?"

"Zoji, remember Marko had said Kastazi wasn't his real name?"

"Yes, what is it then?" Balanji's lean face set ominously.

"Kasta."

Uncle Nik's eyes widened with understanding. "Kasta," he said softly. "Vos."

"Vos!" thundered Balanji.

Mouth dry, Taverik told everything; as much as he had pieced together from Marita, and what he knew. He was done for anyway, he thought, so he even told them about the prophesies, being chased through the alley by the Black Eagle, and later in the woods, and all that the *ihiga* had said.

Balanji listened, his black brows closing across his nose. Uncle Nik listened, pale and worried, but fascinated. "Today," Taverik finished, "Soza called all Illiga together and presented her as the lost zoja of Vosa. She shouted, 'Illigans, beware—' but Soza shut her up and told everyone she was overcome. The crowd started cheering her, and Soza urged them on."

He'd finished but neither Balanji nor his uncle said anything. Lamely he added, "Several of the viti were in Soza's party. And Ittato and Gunnar recognized her as Kastazi."

"Is there anything else you haven't told me, Taverik Zandro?" said Balanji.

"No, Zoji."

"Then *I* will tell *you* that your lies, and Kastazi's lies have jeopardized this entire plan," Balanji said. "Do you understand the depth of your fault?"

"Yes, Zoji," Taverik said, but Balanji explained it to him anyway. In detail. The zoji's voice remained low but each word cut sharp as a whiplash. Taverik paled under the unrelenting rain. Sweat prickled on his forehead but he didn't dare wipe it away. His father would have thrown him against the wall, beaten him up, roaring all the time like an angry bull. This was a hundred times worse.

Or perhaps it was worse that Nikilo would not meet his eyes. His uncle stared down at his boots, occasionally licking his lips, occasionally shaking his head. Once more, Taverik thought, he'd disappointed the man who loved him like a father. He'd blown just about everything this time.

At last Balanji curbed himself. "I have a lot more to say to you, Zandro," he said. "But we cannot leave Ittato alone in the side chapel a moment longer. Get Rinatto and Barsatta, then bring me to these merchants."

"Yes, Zoji," said Taverik. All he wanted was to crawl off by himself and regain possession of his soul. But he numbly went down the hall to the first room.

"My, my," said Rinatto when he entered. "You do

seem to have angered the zoji, little merchant. What was that all about?"

Just like Chado. "Balanji wants you both," Taverik said and left without waiting.

Taverik went first to the sun-flooded side chapel. Ittato and Gunnar still sat exactly where he'd left them, but looked uneasy. With any further delay, they'd have been out the door. They may be yet, Taverik thought as he checked the garden one last time. For in some ways, the zoji hardly looked regal anymore. He wore the plainest of black surcoats, by now stained and mended. His raven hair had grown longer than the stylish shoulder length, and far from being coiffed, was gathered in back like that of an ancient Pakajan warrior. Would Ittato and Gunnar believe he actually was Zoji Balanji? How could it be proven if they didn't?

He went to the door of the sanctuary. "All clear," he called, and Balanji came.

Who could doubt he was zoji? He filled the room with his authority, his right. Ittato gasped and clumsily knelt. Gunnar followed him. And later, as the two merchants swore their vows of loyalty, Taverik found his own vows strengthening, despite the raking down he'd just received. In Novato he'd sworn loyalty to get at Soza, to free Illiga, to free Marita. Gradually he'd come to respect Balanji for himself.

He watched from his post at the garden door as Balanji questioned Ittato in detail about the fall of the city and subsequent events. Like most Massadarans, the zoji was not as tall as even Ittato, and his slim figure, dressed in its plain surcoat, was not awe-inspiring. But the incredible surging energy of the man dominated everyone in the room. Tamped down with rigid self-control for the agonizing wait in the tunnel, this intensity burned in Balanji's eyes. His determination was infectious. How, Taverik suddenly wondered, could they lose?

Balanji unrolled a city map, and Ittato's white hair shone in the sunlight as he bent over it, pointing out the location of his warehouses. Gunnar threw himself into the problem, his jaw dropping as it always did when he concentrated. Silver strands gleamed in Balanji's dark hair as he listened and encouraged the two men out of their diffidence. Bit by bit they were hammering out a workable plan for bringing men into Illiga, hiding them until they could be filtered across the city to the temple. They planned for providing food and firewood, and for a network of information. From the door into the temple sanctuary itself, Uncle Nikilo listened and commented, while keeping an eye on Rinatto and Barsatta, who watched the main doors.

"Zandro," Balanji asked suddenly, "tell me again how many men you can bring down the river each night?"

Gunnar let out a great horselaugh. "So that's how you're going to do it! Tav, I knew you must have run the—" He broke off and colored until his freckles disappeared. "I beg your pardon, My Zoji. I forgot myself."

"I will forget the incident," said Balanji gravely, "just as I will forget the false-bottomed wagons you have volunteered, and Zandro's convenient skills. But I will never forget your service to me. Now, Zandro, how many men?"

"Five per trip," Taverik said stiffly. "Two trips per night, maybe three but I strongly doubt it. Perhaps only one, if Soza is patrolling the valley too thickly. I don't know how long it will take me to get back up river. I know someone who may be able to help, though."

"Ten a night," said Uncle Nikilo. "Too slow."

"Perhaps we could bring men in from nearby farms in a vegetable cart," said Gunnar. "I've started selling vegetables—we've all sunk to that sort of thing."

"We'd need more merchants, then," said Ittato. "Zandro, who do you recommend?"

Everyone looked at him, as he ran his mind over everyone in the Textile Guild. Their lives depended on the people they chose at this moment, and he felt reluctant to trust too quickly. "Sanisman," he said slowly.

"Good," said Gunnar. "What about Kittertak? He's clever."

"No," said Taverik.

"Why not?" Gunnar pressed. "You drank with him often enough."

"Not by choice," Taverik said. He tried to put his finger on his misgivings. "He's too impressed by money. I think he'd sell out."

"Zandro's a good judge of people," said Ittato amazingly. "I'll abide by what he says. Besides, I've seen Kittertak with that Echin fellow once too often."

Gunnar whistled. "In that case."

"Fat Ulmo," suggested Taverik.

"Dead," said Ittato. "Died in the takeover."

Taverik ran his mind over the city merchants he knew. Forget the Gem and Jeweler's Guild. Its members were known for their graft, and their president showed them how. In fact, in the entire city there were precious few merchants he'd trust. The metalworkers, the glass, the copper— "Red Kishstash," he said. "He was on the last caravan with me."

"Good man," said Ittato. "Four-square. Religious, too."

"What if," Taverik said slowly, "what if he brought men down river on his barge. They go to an inn to drink. By curfew, they've disappeared into the city. Then the barge moves back up river the next day without them."

"A good idea," said Nikilo Vitujak, "but don't get excited about it until you know for sure that this Kishstash will join us."

"I will talk to him," said Ittato. "Sanisman also. I will think of others we might trust as well. Speaking of Fat Ulmo, I think the building across the alley from where Taverik brought us in was one of his warehouses."

Taverik looked up eagerly. "Can we use it? It has a back door almost opposite the door in the temple wall."

"Perhaps I could buy it," said Ittato.

"Quite convenient," said Balanji. "Use of that building might help disguise any sudden activity around the temple. Look into it. Please proceed cautiously on all these plans, if you will, Kali Ittato. Cautiously. If in doubt, don't. Be extremely careful when you come here. And do not ever go beyond this chapel. Which reminds me. Where are the priests?"

Ittato made a sour face. "Executed," he said. "Soza gave all the priests a public chance to deny Zojikam and serve the Black Eagle. All except one refused. Their bodies still hang at the gates. The one lives in the palace and mouths about the Black Eagle, miserable traitor. This temple was boarded up, but people meet secretly in cellars and warehouses. Sometimes they are caught and executed, and fewer and fewer people are risking it."

Taverik listened, wondering if Ikatabalcha's body hung among them or if the people of Ervyn had indeed gotten their own back. Balanji's lips tightened and his eyes blazed. "Soza has a lot to pay for," he said quietly. "Thank you, Kalis. I depend utterly on you. Zandro, please escort them to the gate, then report to me."

Taverik returned to the tunnel braced for the continuation of Balanji's wrath. But Balanji merely said, "When do you leave tonight, Zandro?"

"Not before nine, Zoji," Taverik said. "There's too much activity before then for safety."

"Please present my compliments to Marshal Kintupaquat when you see him. You may tell him everything that has taken place. Meantime, get some sleep. Let Vitujak know when you leave. You may go, Zandro. Vitujak, will you inform Oma Kastazi that her secret is out, and ask the tet-zoja if she will come up here?"

Tet-zoja. Taverik passed the blanket hung in the doorway, remembering Oma Kastazi of the inkstained fingers and worried face which lit up only when talking of poetry or philosophy. Her world had changed. So had his own.

In the round room, Bibi stirred chicken stew for their dinner. Taverik wrapped a blanket around himself and sat in the corner, at last allowed time to brood about the day's events. Rinatto and Barsatta lounged nearby. "Here's the zoji's little pal," said Rinatto. "What are you doing now, Zandro?"

"Trying to get some sleep."

"Oh yes, you will be the big hero, tonight. Dangerous mission. But oh dear, you don't have a sword, surely you'll need a sword."

"Rinatto," warned Barsatta.

Rinatto's laughter rose too high and lasted a little too long. "Yes, how could I forget? He's only a Pakajan. He's not allowed to carry a sword. So sorry, merchant, how clumsy of me."

Taverik sprang to his feet, fists clenched. Quick joy flared in Rinatto's eyes—a fight was just what he wanted. Taverik clenched his teeth. "Someday, Rinatto, I will beat you to a pulp," he promised. "But not now."

"Oh, go ahead," said Rinatto, thrusting out his chin. "Don't be afraid of me."

"Rinatto," said Barsatta again.

"Look, Rinatto," said Taverik, "neither of us likes the other. But there's too much at stake to brawl in the tunnel."

"Yes, the tunnel makes a fine excuse, doesn't it?"

Taverik turned his back and picked up his blanket. Rinatto swung his fist. Barsatta leaped forward and grabbed it. "Are you crazy?"

"Let go, damn you!" shouted Rinatto. He struggled to get at Taverik and Barsatta wrapped his arms around him and held tight. But nothing could stop his mouth and he rained filth against Pakajans. Bibi threw down her spoon and ran from the room. Taverik's vision narrowed under the abuse, and his face froze. In silence, he took what he'd need for that night, knowing his calm would prick Rinatto the more, and left.

He went on down the tunnel, and had rounded the first bend before he heard Balanji's voice demand sharply, "What's going on here?" Wondering what story they'd give, Taverik tramped on until he reached the tiny chamber at the bottom of the tunnel. There, he wrapped his blanket around himself, turned the lantern low, and settled back. Rinatto sat sour on his mind. Taverik pushed the ugly words away and filled his mind with plans for setting Marita free.

He woke with a start when his uncle said, "Taverik, you haven't eaten."

"What time is it?" he gasped. "Have I overslept?"

"Relax. The bell tower chimed nine a little while ago." Nikilo came down the last few steps and tossed bread and cheese in Taverik's lap. "Here's supper. Everything else burned."

"I'm not surprised." He ate, not hungry but knowing he'd need it.

Nikilo sat on the last step. "I understand a lot now," he said. "I'm sorry I was so dense."

"You weren't dense, Nik," Taverik said. "I deliberately deceived you. I promised Marita I would tell no one. She's deathly afraid of Soza."

"Whom she is now to marry?" said Nikilo dryly. "And of course you've fallen in love with her."

"Oh, Nik, I asked her to marry me," Taverik said. "And she said yes."

Nikilo sighed. "There's another thing you didn't tell Balanji."

"That's because it makes no difference. Not now. Even if Soza hadn't gotten her, what does a Tet-zoja have to do with a Pakajan merchant of stinking reputation?"

"I understand," said Nikilo, and sighed again. "I understand."

"Because you love her sister." Taverik laughed shortly. "What a pair of fools we are. For your sake, Nik, I wish things were different."

"I've never met a woman," Nikilo admitted, "whose mind ran so."

"Nik, what will Balanji do if he wins? About Ormea and Vosa, I mean."

"Rule them, I suppose," Nikilo said. "Possibly the best thing that could happen to the Peninsula."

"What about the tet-zojas of Vosa? Won't they get in his way? What will he do to them?"

"Awkward," Nikilo agreed. "They are heirs, but not raised to rule. Vosa especially will be emotionally attached to them. Balanji is an honorable man, but still a prince governed by practicality. Yet Zojikam has his hand on him. I don't know the answer, Taverik. By the way, I'm so proud of you I could burst."

Taverik eyed him suspiciously. "Proud of me?"

"Given the situation with the exiled tet-zojas, you acted prudently and wisely. You are also handling Rinatto's bigotry well. Even Balanji commented on it to me."

"But I thought Balanji mistrusted me," Taverik said. "Especially after this afternoon."

"The zoji does not entrust the delicate work he's given you to someone he suspects, Taverik. The raking down he gave you was because he thinks you're worth the effort."

"You wouldn't look at me, Nik," Taverik said as casually as he could.

"I merely didn't want to add to your embarrassment. By the way, when you left, Balanji said, 'Doesn't that boy have any nerves? I've seen stone walls show more emotion.' "

Taverik snorted. "I wanted to swear. Or bawl."

"No doubt. When are you leaving?"

"Now." Taverik stood up and threw his blanket at his uncle.

Nikilo caught it and gave Taverik a great bear hug. "Be careful tonight."

Chapter 13

Marita

Even with the fortress gates closed, Marita could still hear the crowd cheering and chanting, "Marita Vos, Marita Vos!"

Soza pulled her from the horse and pinched her throat with iron fingers. "Try anything like that again," he warned, "and you will regret it bitterly." She'd stared at him, empty of emotion, not even sure what she would have said, given the chance. He seemed to sense that, for he released her and ordered her taken back to the cell.

As soon as they left her, Marita stripped off the heavy dress and threw it in the corner. Falling across the bed in her undershift, she slept. Not even the icy voice of that woman, complaining about the crumpled dress and improper sleepwear, could rouse her much.

After that no one bothered her for the rest of the day, and the night as well. She slept and woke, cried, and slept again. Stress brought on her menses earlier than usual, and more painful, beginning just before a Pakajan servant carried in the evening meal. She asked for what she needed, then, repelled by the thought of food, curled on the bed hugging her abdomen. She spent the creeping hours of darkness pacing with pain or dozing lightly. Not until deep night did the cramps ease. She stretched out and slept heavily.

In the gray light before dawn she woke feeling better. She lay drowsily until she heard a door close. The sound came from outside her window.

Curious, she pushed the chair to the window and crawled up into the five-foot-deep niche. Crouched uncomfortably, she jammed her face against the bars and peered down.

The tower perched on the very edge of the promontory. Its ancient Pakajan stonework blended almost imperceptibly with natural rock, leaving only a narrow edge between tower and drop off. As she looked, a metal-studded door opened again, almost directly below her. Soza stepped out into the gloomy light lugging a huge coil of rope. He was alone.

Marita watched as he secured the rope to an iron ring near the cliff edge, then belay it about himself. He stepped to the edge and disappeared. Her fists clenched around the bars. Soza was arranging a private escape route. So that was how he'd gotten out of Ormea. And he'd get out of Illiga, too, unless she could somehow warn Balanji.

From her sketchy knowledge of the tower's plan,

she figured the still-open door below led to the room where Soza kept his *mahiga* jars. She could faintly remember a padlocked door during her interrogation. That would be on the well-guarded ground floor of the tower.

She watched and waited until she thought her back would break from crouching in the niche. At last a hand appeared at the cliff edge, then Soza's head. Pulling himself up, Soza untied the rope, smiling to himself the whole while. Marita growled with anger, then pulled back suddenly as Soza straightened and glanced up at the tower. When she dared look again, he was gone. The door closed below.

Sliding down the wall, Marita sat on the edge of her bed, hands on her knees, to do some serious thinking. Two days ago she would have said that capture by Soza was the worst thing that could have happened to her. Well, the worst had happened, and she'd survived it. She could survive anything. Second, Zojikam had given her a task to do, and she had done nothing as yet. Perhaps he wanted someone inside the fortress. Why? Perhaps to find out things. Perhaps to strengthen resistance within. Perhaps something else which she'd realize later.

Use all the tools Zojikam has given you, the *ihiga* had said. Maybe she should pretend she wanted to be a zoja, and worm her way into Soza's confidence. But the Black Eagle—Soza had told Malenga that the Black Eagle would ensure she was a willing bride. What did he mean by that? Just thinking about it made her hands shake. *He's already gotten holds in your mind.*

"No! Zojikam!" she cried aloud. Shutting her eyes, she tried to remember the feeling of a great hand cupped over her like a protective tent. Gradually, she began to sense a comforting presence in the room with her. As if the words were spoken inside her head, she heard: *The Black Eagle can control you by your fear of him and obsession with him. Trust me, and don't be afraid.*

"I wish I could see you," she said aloud.

I am here.

"What do you want me to do?"

You will see one step at a time.

"I love you," she said quickly, for keys had begun to jingle and scrape in the lock of her heavy door.

The matronly woman entering with a tray looked curiously around the room to see who Marita had been talking to. She wore her hair properly pulled back under her cap, but Marita would have bet it was as red-gold as her eyebrows. Pakajan. Good. Marita smiled encouragingly at her.

The woman put the tray down and knelt before her. "My Zoja," she said in struggling Massadaran. "I am so glad to see you better."

"Thank you," Marita replied in Illigan Pakajan.

The woman's startled blue-gray eyes met hers and she also switched to Pakajan. "You speak my language!"

"I hid here from Soza for almost three years," Marita said. Soza had ordered her to say nothing of her true history, but she guessed she had only to say a few words in this servant's ear and it would be all over the palace by nightfall, and all over the city tomorrow. "He murdered my parents, you know."

"Ah, Vita," said the woman, her face puckering until Marita thought of Bibi. "Such a sadness for you. Eat, My Tet-zoja. You ate nothing all yesterday."

Marita ate hungrily, while the Pakajan woman, Zilvrik, knelt beside her, listening eagerly to each bit of juicy gossip Marita deliberately dropped. "I lived here dressed as a man," she said between mouthfuls, "and supported my sister and myself in trade."

"As a man! Mercy! I never heard of such a thing." Zilvrik's eyes rounded with the scandal of it. "You walked around the city with your hair down?"

"I had to. But Soza found me anyway. He wanted a letter I had which proved he was Bcacmat."

"Bcacmat! No!"

"Oh yes. You didn't know? He's hiding it of course, so Pakajans won't resist him as much. You mustn't tell a soul, you know."

"Of course," Zilvrik breathed, but her lips set, and

she nodded once or twice to herself, as if things made sense.

The guard opened the door for Idbca. Damn! Marita swiftly whispered the last crucial thing—"Balanji is alive."

"Zojikam be praised!" cried Zilvrik.

Idbca's fingers twisted into Zilvrik's neat cap and yanked her head back. "Pakajan forbidden is," she snapped, and slapped her upturned face.

Marita leaped up, overturning the breakfast tray into Zilvrik's lap. She hit Idbca hard enough to stagger her. "You will not treat Pakajan servants so!"

A great red blotch had spread across Idbca's cheek. "Get out," she hissed at Zilvrik. Zilvrik piled the scattered dishes back on the tray and ducked out of the room. The door clanged shut, leaving Marita alone with Idbca, each breathing hard. Idbca stood straight, her hands at her side, scorning to finger her reddened face. "What you her what tell?" she demanded.

Marita shrugged. "I merely corrected her, told her that Balanji was alive."

"You that said! Not you again not say. It forbidden is. Zojikam also forbidden is. Black Eagle now you worship. You example for stubborn underlings set."

"I will not." Marita gave her an underbrowed stare and mimicked her shocked voice. "It forbidden is."

Idbca smiled thinly. "Forbidden by an impotent god. The Black Eagle more powerful has grown."

"We shall see," said Marita.

"Yes, we shall, shan't we." The woman relaxed somewhat. "Hands off hips get. You like a man stand."

"I wish I were a man."

"Dead you'd be."

"I wouldn't have menstrual cramps."

"You cursed now? Yes?" The woman scowled. "Inconvenient."

"Why?" asked Marita surprised at the woman's annoyance.

"Because now you for ten days unclean. No one you may touch without himself filthying. When you to

Bcacma go, proper ways to learn with other wives, you ten days in the isolation room live."

Go to Bcacma—Marita could not conceal the horror she felt and Idbca nodded with satisfaction. "Now maybe you me obey. Servant soon with riding gowns come. You with Soza through city ride so the people you see."

Outside. Marita's heart lifted at that, and when three Pakajan women came with several gowns left behind by Balanji's vita, she meekly endured being turned, measured, and pricked by pins. Idbca stood back and loudly deplored a culture which allowed, even encouraged, a woman to go outside for the express purpose of letting men see her without a mask.

At last the black and red riding gown—Soza's colors, Marita thought sourly—fit and the kalas began to brush her hair back and pin it tightly under a starched cap. Idbca came up behind her and gently strung a pendant around her neck. Marita picked it up and looked at it.

An eagle claw.

With a wordless cry Marita tore it off and flung it across the room. "I won't wear it!"

"You will!" said Idbca. The women backed away nervously, but watched the argument with interest. Idbca picked up the pendant. "Put it on."

"Disgusting *ikiji*! I won't."

Soza entered. The kalas fled, leaving Marita and Idbca once more glaring at each other. Amusement crinkled the corners of his eyes, and Marita realized for the first time Soza could be charming if he wished. "My Vitas," he said. "Quarreling so soon?"

Idbca rounded on him. "She nothing does I tell her, and everything that forbidden is."

"I will tame her for you tonight."

"Not you not will," Idbca spat with sour satisfaction. "She defiled is."

Soza stepped back involuntarily. Truly, Marita thought, the only thing in the world Soza must fear was a menstruating woman. She had ten days of grace, then. Oh, hurry, Balanji.

Idbca opened her hand to show him the claw pendant. "She refuses to wear it. Make her."

Soza looked but did not touch. He gave a quick glance at Marita's truculent scowl. "We will not push our ways on her too quickly," he said. His eyes locked with Idbca's with a message strong enough for Marita to interpret easily. *She will wear it yet.*

He turned back to Marita. "Are you ready now, my fierce little hawk?" He started to offer his arm, then dropped it and stood aside. After a moment, Marita proceeded him from the room. *Hawk.*

"You do know how to ride sidesaddle?" he said.

She knew well, but she considered before answering. Should she be as difficult as possible and pretend she didn't? But then she'd only be dragged around on a box frame. But they might relax their guard enough for her to steal a mule and escape.

"My dear Idbca," Soza said to his first wife, who padded in the rear. "Please mark how Marita Vos questions in her mind which answer might be most advantageous to her. Do not let her trick you into thinking her helpless. She was able to hide from me for more than three years, and made her living. She is subtle. Do not be deceived."

Marita clenched her teeth in anger. Soza laughed, and ordered a sidesaddle prepared.

At first townspeople merely pressed against the wall, silently bowing as the small cavalcade passed. Then a man recognized Marita and shouted. "Vos! Vos!" The cry was taken up and soon a crowd pressed in around Marita, waving and shouting to her.

"Excellent," said Soza, bending near to make himself heard over the roaring din. "They love you, my dear. Your presence reconciles them to this change in leadership. Smile. Wave."

Self-consciously, Marita lifted her fingers. The cheering sharpened. She tried a smile and a real wave and found the people responded. She looked at them, so ragged now after weeks of martial law, the few poor men Soza had spared, the merchants who filled his coffers, the women—all of them starved for security, the promise of peace. One ancient woman reached up to Marita, tears streaming down her face. "Zojikam bless you, my dear."

"And you, mother," Marita called. By the time they arrived at the gates she was earnestly pressing hands, reassuring people, trying to cheer their bleak faces.

Soza waved and smiled herself, turning his surprising charm on the crowd until a few people even cheered him. His face, as they reached the city wall and gate, looked smug and well pleased with his strategy. Marita wondered if she'd done the right thing. Perhaps she should have looked unhappy.

In peace, the area near the wall had been a city of tents, shanties and wagons. What would the cheering crowd think, she wondered, if they knew that she and her sister had lived for a year in a wagon parked just two blocks away. Now Soza had cleared the streets to allow room his anti-siege towers, and stockpiled of boulders and wood. Squads of soldiers in black and red patrolled. Marita took it all in grimly. Balanji's few men had small hope.

Soza's wesh-agash, a burly black-bearded man in red leather, saluted as the zoji dismounted. Marita knew him instantly; he'd led the brigands who had attacked her caravan last fall. He moved to assist her, but Soza said a soft word to him. Abruptly he halted, then backed away.

All right, then, she'd dismount by herself. Humiliated and angry, Marita began to haul up that damn length of velvet of her dress, wondering how a vita ever managed to do anything.

"May I?"

The Pakajan commander who had stood behind the wesh-agash had offered his arm. Soza watched complacently, and Black-beard's lips curled with scorn—let the Pakajan foul himself touching a woman in her curse. Clenching her teeth, she allowed the commander to lift her down and steady her while she arranged the fabric to drape over her arm. "Thank you," she said in Pakajan and enjoyed Soza's quick scowl.

The commander didn't see it. "My honor, Zoja," he

replied, his Vosa Pakajan sending a wave of nostalgia through Marita. She followed the small group of men up the steps to the wall, the wesh-agash talking defenses with Soza, expostulating about too long a line of wall with no tower. Marita let them walk on without her, instead gazing out over the woods and fields beyond, bare of snow but not yet green. If only, she thought wistfully, if only she could jump down, run and hide, get away from Soza. But then, to her surprise, she found that even if she could, she wouldn't. She had a task to do, and the more she saw, the more she was determined to complete it.

She turned to the commander, who waited respectfully several feet away. He puzzled her. He seemed too, well, honorable, to be so involved with Soza. "You are from Vosa, Commander . . ."

"Ucherik," he said, bowing low, his eyes glowing. "Commander Ucherik at your service. And may I say, my zoja, I am most happy you are restored to your rightful position."

"Thank you, Commander." She glanced past him. Soza and Black-beard were still discussing the wall but Soza kept looking back at her. She turned slightly so it looked like she were merely gazing across the city. Below a crowd pointed up at her and stared. Blushing, she strove to appear unconscious of the sensation she was creating. "Tell me Commander, you are a Pakajan from Vosa, yet you serve the man who murdered Zoji Vos and his—my—entire family."

"As a Pakajan," he said gently, "I find one Massadaran ruler the same as another."

Her fingers tightened around her gown. "Soza is not Massadaran. He is the Agash Itzil Farasoza of Bcacma. They are taking by deception now that which they could not win two generations ago."

The commander said nothing. She stole a glance at him. He stood rigidly, staring at Soza and the wesh-agash. Soza looked over his shoulder again, spoke to Black-beard, and started back.

"Prove it." Comander Ucherik said quickly.

"A letter from the Tlath to Agash Itzil Farasoza complaining about his taking Vosa and demanding the northern trade route instead. By the way, did you know Balanji is alive?"

"We search for him constantly."

"Pakajan, Pakajan, Tet-zoja," said Soza, coming near with a smile that touched not his eyes. "Always Pakajan. It is impolite to speak a language not understood by all."

Marita began a bow, remembered herself, and sank instead into a curtsey. "I merely asked him his duties, Zoji."

"Do not speak Pakajan again. You did not know it is forbidden among my men, so I will forgo the commander's punishment this time."

Black-beard looked puzzled and Commander Ucherik, astounded. New rule, Marita thought, her face tight with fear she'd gone too far. "I beg your pardon, Zoji," she said humbly. "I do hope my rudeness will not hurt others."

When at last Marita was returned to her cell, she sank down on the bed with a most unzoja-like gusty sigh. Soza had taken her to each bridge fortification as well, which involved two more passages across the city amidst cheering crowds. But she was pleased with her two contacts that day. She had even talked to Soza, pretending interest in ruling Vosa to get revenge on the family that had disowned her father. Soza seemed to take the conversation at face value, but she wondered what he really thought.

In her absence they'd changed her cell, bringing in a wardrobe for her gowns, and a dressing table with mirror. The narrow cot had been exchanged for a grander bed. But funny how it all made the room seem more oppressive than before. A headache grew and seemed to push at her eyes until it was hard to think of anything but the Black Eagle. Vaguely she remembered Zojikam's warning that her fear and obsession with it would put her in its power, but she couldn't jolt her thoughts free.

And through her mind marched the grim parade of

Soza's fortifications, men, and anti-siege weapons. The troubling thought began to form: what if Balanji failed? *What if Zojikam failed?* What would happen to her then?

Chapter 14

Taverik

The dank smell of wet charcoal filled the darkness. Wrinkling his nose, Taverik approached the clearing cautiously—what ever had Skaj been doing? He made it to the yard before he saw. The comfortable old vidyen was stained with smoke, the roofs gone except for the main round, which had been crudely rethatched.

"Get out," said a hoarse voice behind him. "Get out or I'll kill you."

Taverik came out of his shock. "Skaj?"

"Who's that?"

"Taverik Zandro."

"Well, why didn't you say so?" Footsteps crunched on charcoal and Skaj loomed from the darkness, lowering his crossbow. " 'Sall right, Kaja!"

The door opened and Kaja came out. "Taverik, you came back! Zojikam be praised. Oh, so thin, come in come in, did you get across the mountains? Did you find the path? Did you find your girl?"

Her roughened fingers pulled Taverik inside the smoky room. He answered their questions absently, his mind on how stooped Skaj looked now, how Kaja's apple cheeks had lost color and pulled in tightly; missing the old man behind the fire, the two girls, the boys, and the bright row of pewter on the shelf. "What happened?" he interrupted.

Lines deepened in Skaj's face. "Soza. His men came back while I was still away. The boys had let their guard down. I told them. I told them! I told them a thousand times not to—"

"It is already done, Skaj," said Kaja, putting a gnarled hand on his arm.

Skaj inhaled a long shuddering breath. "They wanted the girls and the livestock, and the boys tried to stop them. I come home to four graves. Kaja buried them all. My father died a day later."

Taverik's face felt like a block of stone. "When?" he croaked.

"Three days after you left us. If only Achicha hadn't talked me into going home the long way!"

"They must have followed our trail back," Taverik said. "They discovered me near Ervyn. I got away, but they'd find the track. I'm responsible for your family's deaths."

"You are not!" sputtered Kaja. "Don't you think that! It's Soza."

"Soza," agreed Skaj. "We are all in this together against him. I'm glad you escaped if only it thwarted him. I could tell you horror stories of what he's done to the people in this valley. And there's rumors, and of course you gotta discount them, but rumors of slavery and human sacrifice. All for that damn Black Eagle. I've never been a religious man, but I'd give anything to have Zojikam back. Listen, boy, you told me once Soza was a Bcacmat. Was that true?"

"Yes," said Taverik.

"Then I'll fight him with everything I got," said Skaj. "But I don't know where to start."

"Do you mean that?" Taverik still felt shaken and sick to his stomach, and he listened to his voice pulling Skaj and Kaja in deeper with an odd sense of hearing someone else. He told them about Balanji, and gave the sketchiest idea of the plan to smuggle men into the city.

Skaj's eyes kindled for the first time. "You can't get

north without me, boy. This valley is crawling with Soza's men. And I can bring a small number of men down safely *if* they obey me."

He frowned suddenly. "I don't know though. This Zoji Balanji is asking a smuggler to help him? Little more than a month ago he'd of hanged me."

"He told me," Taverik said, "that he'd forgive any former crimes, except murder, of anyone who helps him. I swore loyalty to him just to get at Soza, but somehow I've got so I'm loyal to him for himself. And he's talking about doing away with the *Sadra* Laws, and maybe beginning a city council."

Skaj made a rude noise. "Believe *that* when I see it. You don't know what you're getting into when you start messing with Massadarans, boy. They don't think like us. But I'll help you. Kaja?"

She nodded. "Do it."

"So. When you want to start your sneaking around?"

"Now," said Taverik. A sudden doubt hit him. "Where's Achicha?"

"He took himself off," said Kaja scornfully, "when he saw what Soza had done here. Said it was safer in the hills."

"Safer, yes," said Taverik hiding his relief. "If you see him, don't tell him any of this, promise?"

"Oh, Achicha is all right," said Skaj.

"Skaj, you promise," demanded Kaja.

"Women!" Skaj rolled his eyes toward Taverik. "Very well, love, not a word."

With that Taverik had to be content.

A splash and a curse in the dark ahead. Taverik stilled, ready for trouble. "What's wrong?"

Skaj's whisper rode back on the damp spring wind. "Damn mud hole."

Taverik cat footed up to where Skaj floundered, thigh deep in mud. Grabbing Skaj's wet gritty wrist, he heaved him back to solid ground. "Thought you said you knew the way, Skaj."

"Thought you said you knew where they'd be." Skaj bent to scrape off clinging mud, adding bitterly,

"Should have known better than to trust riff-raff claiming personal friendship with Zoji Balanji."

"Not friendship, Skaj." Taverik followed him on, skirting the swampy area. "Not by a—"

"Stand!" shouted a man in Pakajan, adding in Massadaran, "Move and you're dead!"

Faint starlight glinted on a dozen crossbows surrounding them. Taverik raised his hands, his face tightening. Kintupaquat's men or Soza's? Or merely renegades who would murder them for the money, leaving Balanji stranded underground . . . "I'm looking for Pemintinuchi," he said quickly. It was the name of the Pakajan captain who had rescued him in the mountains, and who was now helping Kintupaquat rebuild the army and hide it in the high ranges. Balanji and Kintupaquat had decided between them, in that first council after Taverik had led them to Pemintinuchi's hideout, that the captain's name was to be the password. Balanji had laughed much at the appropriate literal meaning of "a good man."

Light slid across an arrow as a bow lowered. "Come forward. Hands higher. One false move and we'll leave you rotting."

Taverik obediently lifted his hands higher and stepped forward, eyes searching the men for some clue to their loyalties. A ragged man in hunter's leathers took his knife from him.

The circle of arrows parted to allow a man through. Pemintinuchi. He peered at Taverik then sprang forward. "It *is* you, you old bastard!" he said, pounding Taverik's shoulders. "Never thought I'd see you again. He turned to his men. "This is the one Soza chased up and down the pass and still couldn't pin down. Goes anywhere he wants, he does. Who's this?"

"Skaj," said the smuggler for himself. "Just Skaj. As for the brat going wherever he wants—"

But Pemintinuchi had taken Taverik's elbow. "Come on. Old Ironbiter is nearly out of his mind worrying about Balanji."

Kintupaquat didn't look a bit worried, Taverik

thought as he was brought to the marshal. He looked angry. "I expected you last night," he snapped.

"Your pardon," Taverik said in the neutral tone he'd learned deflected wrath. "Unavoidable delay. But all is well."

The weathered face did not relax. He waved his men out of earshot and lowered his voice. "What's going on?"

Taverik recited his message. "The tunnel is open except the branch to the palace. The men are clearing it. I'm to bring five men down by boat tonight. Soza's conscripted most of the boats and registered all the others, so you'll have to get them from up here."

Kintupaquat nodded. "We can do it."

"My friend here can conduct a small party down to a certain farm from whence they will be brought into Illiga by cart. Also, the zoji says to tell you the tunnel requires the utmost discipline and courage. Each man must be handpicked by you, and know the danger he runs."

"It's bad, then," Kintupaquat said.

"It stinks in there," Taverik said frankly. "And after a while you want to scream and pound the walls to get out. There's one more thing."

"Speak."

Taverik controlled his face. "Soza has discovered the whereabouts of Marita Vos and has her imprisoned in the fortress. We don't know yet what he intends."

"I can imagine," said Kintupaquat. "Poor woman. Tell Balanji that we have more than 3,000 men in the hills. We need two days notice to cross the Giss and get down to the land gate. We'll see what we can do about a diversion in Ormea. Not promising anything."

Kintupaquat chewed his lip then added, "Has Balanji said anything about himself returning to safety?"

"No, Viti."

"Fool! You tell him I said so. If he is caught or killed all is lost." Kintupaquat grumbled to himself then turned back to Taverik. "I will not come down to the river again, but will send Captain Pemintinuchi. You can give him any messages for me. When you've rested enough, start your trip down."

"I'll start now, Viti," said Taverik. "Dawn is coming, and even the least amount of light will betray us."

Kintupaquat nodded but didn't move. Suddenly he beat his left fist into his right hand. "Damn you! You're just a merchant. You know nothing of military matters and I'm giving you five, no, ten of my best men. If you lose them . . ."

Taverik clenched his teeth over a hot reply. They glared at each other until suddenly Kintupaquat's eyebrows relaxed. "Your pardon," he said gruffly. "I am out of line. I do have a reputation for turning into a maneater if events are out of my control."

After a moment Taverik took his offered hand. "I can understand, Viti."

Kintupaquat obviously didn't care if Taverik understood or not. "The boat's this way," he said.

Kintupaquat's men opened on either side of Taverik and the marshal, then closed again behind them. Taverik could feel their eyes on him, measuring, judging. His back stiffened and his face hardened into the old defensive response. But at least Kintupaquat gave no public hint of his doubts. "This is Taverik Zandro and his man. They will guide you to the city. While on this trip you will obey immediately any order they give you, with no argument. Understand? Remember you have been handpicked for your discipline and courage. You will need every scrap of it. But I and Captain Pemintinuchi have chosen each of you because we know you can do it. Do not let us down."

A murmur of warm response rippled among the men. "Go with Zojikam," said Kintupaquat and stepped back. "Pemintinuchi?"

"The five travelling by land, stand there," said the captain.

Taverik turned to Skaj. "Keep safe," he said.

"*Taverik Zandro and his man,*" growled Skaj. "I'd like to tell him a thing or two."

"Sorry, Skaj."

Skaj punched him in the ribs hard enough to hurt

and stumped off to the five men waiting beyond. Taverik followed Pemintinuchi to the river where five others waited by a rowboat pulled into the reeds.

They stood in silence watching him come. Four Massadarans, one Pakajan. All bristled with weapons. With a bargainer's skill, Taverik read the ambivalence in their faces. All they knew of him was Pemintinuchi's exaggerated claim that he went wherever he wanted. He'd overheard them discussing Soza's price on his head, trying to figure out what he'd done—Taverik wasn't about to tell them he'd done nothing more than be in the wrong place at the wrong time. Then there was their mistrust of anyone unmilitary. They were, if anything, overarmed—he wore only his knife. And while they also knew Balanji and Kintupaquat seemed to trust him with innermost secrets of the campaign, his ragged merchant's clothes, strongly Pakajan face and accent, and reputation as a smuggler went against all their instincts.

His reputation as a smuggler. For the first time Taverik realized the ruination of his reputation. This campaign would indelibly stamp him smuggler, outlaw, crooked merchant. Son of the traitor, too. It tasted like ashes in his mouth. Then, welling up in him, came the old who-cares mockery, with which he'd long flung off the narrow-eyed stares of respectable merchants. Laughing sardonically, he picked up a smelly handful of black river ooze and smeared it on his face. "Smuggling lesson number one," he said.

Balanji

Balanji looked up from the scrawled message when Sahra Vos entered the tiny chamber. She looked translucently pale, but she'd held up surprisingly well underground. Funny how it took extremity to reveal the hidden depth of a person. Or lack of it, he thought, thinking quickly of the problem of Rinatto.

"I appreciate your coming, Tet-zoja," he said, and

handed her the crumpled paper. "Will you tell me if this means anything to you?"

Her face sharpened. "Marita's handwriting. Where did you get it?"

"Kali Ittato brought it. He found it on his desk this morning. He couldn't think of anyone who would sign just M, and suspected a trap. I wondered if it was your Marita, or Marko, as he would have known her."

" 'Five hundred men in fortress, 4,000 in city,' " Sahra read. "She's well then."

"For now. Kali Ittato informed me that Soza took her on a tour of the city. The people responded enthusiastically to her, and thus to him as well. He's using her for his own purposes, you know."

"She will use him for hers," Sahra said thoughtfully. "Who has the stronger will?"

"I'm afraid Soza will win that contest," Balanji said gently.

"Perhaps," said Sahra noncommittally as she curtseyed and left.

Perhaps nothing, Balanji thought, though he appreciated the bravado. And yet, he'd fully expected the capture of Marita Vos to ruin their entire scheme. Surely Soza must have forced the whole story from her. But somehow she had sidestepped him. Or had she? Perhaps Soza merely waited like a cat at a mouse hole.

Only 500 men housed in the fortress. If the surprise held, they could take it with perhaps 200. Providing they got the gate shut immediately, *and* providing they took the defenders as they poured in confusion from the barracks. And providing Kintupaquat did his part.

As of this morning, Friday, fifty-six men hid in the tunnel, efficiently brought in by the network of merchants Zandro had created. Balanji had been deeply impressed by the merchants' organization, meticulous care and their loyalty. If all continued well, they'd get him enough men by late next week.

If all went well. So much could go wrong.

It went wrong the next day.

Sweating from every pore, and hoarse with worry,

Kali Ittato brought Gunnar to the temple and poured out the news. Sanisman had been caught.

"It was his first trip, and fortunately only one man in his wagon," Ittato said.

"I saw it all," Gunnar put in, forgetting for the moment he was talking to the zoji. "Sanisman was at the bridge checkpoint, showing his papers, and about to be waved through. Then suddenly the place was swarming with soldiers and they're tearing his wagon apart. They drag out the hidden man, but he broke free and ran. He shoulda known he wouldn't make it, but he did it anyway. They shot him down, a million arrows bristling from him." Gunnar began to shake. "He looked like a pincushion."

"Easy," said Balanji, gripping his shoulder. "The man knew what he was doing. What happened next?"

"They dragged Sanisman away. I went straight to his warehouse and got the rest of the men hiding there and brought them with me. They're in the warehouse next door."

"Good work," said Balanji and felt the young man's shakes ease.

"What about Sanisman?" asked Ittato, his face deeply creased. "And what do we do now?"

"That we'll need to discuss," said Balanji because he wasn't quite certain yet himself. "Vitujak, will you go see if your nephew is awake yet? If not, don't disturb him, it's more important he rest. Otherwise bring him."

Vitujak bowed and left the chapel. Balanji paced the narrow aisle as he waited. And when Zandro came and knelt before him, obviously awakened despite orders, Balanji found himself relieved. He depended more and more on Zandro to deal with the merchants. All in all he was pleased with the young man except for that damn Pakajan independence. Though painfully thin now, eyes dark circled, nerve-stretched by the danger he ran every night, he held himself together well. The men in the tunnel obviously respected him, and the merchants always asked his opinion of any new idea.

"Sit there, Zandro," Balanji said. "Now, tell him, Ittato."

Ittato repeated the story of Sanisman's capture, and Zandro's eyes widened as the implications hit him. "They're searching every wagon coming in or going out of the city, Tav," Ittato said. "And still fifteen men at the farm."

"Best lay low," Zandro said, chewing his lip. "But they might be able to backtrack Sanisman to the farm and get the others. Then we're in trouble."

"We're already in trouble," said Vitujak. "Taverik, how much did Sanisman know?"

Zandro turned to Ittato. "You talked to him."

"He knew he was bringing men in for Balanji, that Gunnar and I were in contact with Balanji, that there's a network of merchants doing the same, but no other names. He was to bring them in from the farm, hide them in his warehouse and Gunnar would pick them up, but not where they were to go after that."

"If he gets even half of that out of Sanisman," Balanji said grimly, "Soza will search every warehouse in the city. Kalis, you must be careful then. If Sanisman names you, you will lead them right to us. If Soza picks you up, he'll make you tell everything you know and beg to die. Do you understand?"

They nodded, but they didn't. Not really. One never understood that until he was actually on the rack. Balanji took a pace, scowling. The uncertainty of the situation! He wanted both men off the street immediately, yet both had crucial tasks.

"Didn't you tell me, Kali Ittato," said Zandro, "that everyone had a story prepared?"

"You're right!" Gunnar exclaimed. "Sanisman was to claim the man offered money to bring him in. And that the man refused to say who he was but had a Vosa accent. Met him on the road outside town, needed the money, didn't see any harm . . ."

"If he can stick to that we may yet be safe," Vitujak said. "But we must assume they'll squeeze everything out of him."

"We should do nothing for a few days, until we see what Soza does," said Gunnar.

"Got to warn the men hiding at the farm," Zandro said. "I think we'd better move them up into the woods in case Soza starts searching the countryside. But they can't stay out there long."

"To my thinking," said Ittato, rubbing his eyebrows thoughtfully, "the copper barge worked the best and is least chancy. Perhaps Kishstash could send a barge up river just for them."

"Talk to him," said Balanji. "Arrange it. Zandro, tonight warn them, and also your friend. Ittato and Gunnar, stay out of sight until you know it's safe."

"We must keep moving," warned Vitujak behind him. Balanji nodded but there was one other thing he needed to say. "About the man who died this morning. I had asked Kintupaquat to pick his finest, most self-controlled men, brave but not foolish. What you saw, Kali Gunnar, was a deliberate act of suicide. He would not be the one that betrayed us. Let us honor his sacrifice."

Balanji looked around the room. Vitujak, face grim, stood with his hand on the shoulder of his nephew, who had once more retreated behind a stone face. The old guild president, gouty foot extended, had grown misty-eyed and scowling. Young Gunnar wore an inward look, reliving no doubt, the morning's disaster. His face, which had been unlined and open when Balanji first met him, already wore deepening furrows on each side of the nose.

Balanji loved them suddenly, and the others he hadn't met as well, ordinary citizens risking themselves each day to hide and feed his men. His throat thickened—what was happening to him these days? He was getting as emotional as Akusa. "You may go," he said quickly.

Ittato turned back from the door. "Your pardon, Zoji," he said. "I forgot in the emergency. I found another message like yesterday's. Signed M."

"Thank you."

Balanji waited until they were gone before he read

it. "Zojikam help us," he breathed. Listen, Vitujak: 'Party from Vosa Thursday, large reinforcements. Wedding planned, Vos to Soza. M.' "

Taverik Zandro's fists clenched at that last phrase. Balanji noted the small movement and tucked it away with a number of other observations, to be dealt with later.

Vitujak was staring blankly at him, assessing the news. "So much for the plans we just made."

Balanji nodded. "We've got to strike before they arrive," he said, leading the way back into the temple sanctuary where guards waited. He knocked on the closed paving stone. "We won't have enough men by then, but after Soza's reinforcements arrive we'll never have enough."

"When do you want to attack?"

Balanji knew already. "Tuesday. How many men will we have?"

Vitujak pursed his lips. "*If* we lay low as planned, what we have now. Fifty-six."

"We can't afford to lay low," Balanji said firmly. "How many can we get?"

"If all goes well," Vitujak said. "about 120."

"Not enough," said Balanji. "But we'll do it anyway."

He looked up at Taverik Zandro, standing silent and troubled behind his uncle. "Zandro, tonight, you'll take a message to Kintupaquat. Tell him to attack at dawn on Tuesday. I don't have to tell you how important it is that this message get through."

"I'll get it through," Zandro said grimly.

Balanji scowled and knocked again. "Why isn't this stone opening? Someday we'll be out here when—"

It opened at last, releasing a blast of hoarse screaming.

"What in Zojikam's name is that?" Balanji slipped through and landed lightly on his feet. He strode past the captain who had finally opened the trap door. Just outside the chamber five men clung to a wildly flailing soldier, who screamed some rubbish about the tunnel collapsing.

"It's Rinatto, Zoji," panted the captain. Five parallel

scratches bled down his cheek and his uniform collar hung by a scrap. "He came up here beating the walls and yelling he couldn't breathe."

"Damn and blast," said Balanji. This was his own fault. He should have gotten the young man out sooner. Now Rinatto would remember this failure the rest of his life and possibly never again be as effective. Balanji turned to Taverik Zandro, who was just closing the stone behind them. "You'll take him out with you tonight, Zandro."

Chapter 15

Marita

From Wednesday till Saturday, Marita remained confined in the tower. She saw no one except that horrid woman and the Pakajan servant, Zilvrik. The Black Eagle beat in on her constantly, from all sides, until her sight had darkened and she found it hard to think of anything else. Gradually she'd lost touch with the idea of Zojikam, of goodness and justice, of sunshine and laughter and all things blessed. She'd lived her nightmare, stalked on all sides by the Black Eagle, even as she had talked to her servant, eaten, had her hair brushed, her needs attended to.

She'd held on stubbornly, a tight core of her shouting for Zojikam to help her. She'd even sent three messages through Zilvrik, whose aunt washed floors in the Textile Guild. Two were delivered to Ittato's desk, but Zilvrik returned with the one that warned Balanji about Soza's escape route. Soza had clamped down on the city, and the aunt feared to risk more.

Zilvrik whispered to Marita that the servants hated

Soza and loved her. The news heartened her enough that she even commanded Ibdca to quit her constant crooning praises of Soza and the Black Eagle. Ibdca had looked surprised, and watched her speculatively, but she did shut up the rest of the day. But when Ibdca began once more next morning, Marita lacked the strength to silence her again. Actually, it was nice to talk to someone, even if it was Ibdca.

For the last two nights she'd stayed awake, staring up through the darkness, silently repeating the temple service. It was getting harder to remember the words, and their meanings had faded, becoming mere incantations. She knew she was losing something, something important, but when she tried to focus on what it might be, it slid away.

This morning Marita had no idea what day it was, for time had blurred. Ibdca smiled sweetly when she'd arrived. Marita smiled back, wondering why she'd ever disliked her. She allowed herself to be dressed in Soza's colors and a mask put over her face. The mask bothered her but Ibdca loudly praised her beauty in it. Marita certainly wanted to be pleasing. Two guards then came and led her from her room.

As she passed through the door, she'd silently cried out for help, though she couldn't remember what her problem had been. She knew someone had said he'd help her, but she couldn't remember who. It didn't matter.

Donato Zandro

Soza refused to see him. In deep misery, Donato Zandro trudged back through the tiny courtyard between the palace and the tower. The weak morning sun, hiding in and out of ragged clouds, couldn't warm him.

A few viti had braved the chill spring morning for fresh air, but they turned away as he approached, and never met his eyes. They all knew him as the traitor. Even though they themselves had sworn allegiance to

Soza, and gave at least lip service to his Black Eagle, they despised Donato.

He despised himself. Remorse rode his shoulders with sharp spurs that pierced bitterly, constantly. And to think he'd been proud of his plan. He'd wanted his sons to advance, to rise higher in life than he had, to not be despised merchants, despised Pakajans. Now they were worse off. One was imprisoned, the other had a price on his head, and was eagerly sought by the very ruler Donato himself had helped to power.

Malenga came out of the palace and started in Donato's direction. Donato watched hopefully. Maybe Malenga would help him. But the moment the viti spotted Donato, he spun around and went the other way. Donato's anger rose, then died. He turned his hot face into the blustering wind.

Fellow merchants, even old cronies, spat behind his back. They didn't know he'd tried to help them. He'd tried to lower the tariffs. He always let word leak before an inspection, so they'd have plenty of time to hide most of their goods. He let his eyes slide past hiding spots he could recognize better than anyone. But no, they only knew him as the traitor. The post which should have brought him the power and honor he craved brought him only hard looks and hatred—hatred which focused and intensified the more certain rumors spread through the town.

Rumors! The town was full of them. Rumors that those who had disappeared had been sold into slavery in Bcacma. Of secret ceremonies for the Black Eagle, involving human sacrifce. Sometimes he wondered if Chado—no impossible. Yet he'd never been allowed to see Chado, and the last time he'd asked, a hungry expression had flared in Soza's eyes and he'd never dared ask again.

Other rumors said that Soza was a Bcacmat, and those rumors he believed; he'd seen more of Soza than the zoji had wanted him to see. That was the worst: he, Donato Zandro, had helped bring in Bcacmat dominion. He shrank inside with despair and self-hatred.

The tower door opened. A masked woman came forth, followed by two guards. Suddenly the wind roared, a great cold gust from the mountains. It snatched Donato's breath, pelted him with stinging dust particles and whipped his cloak about his neck. The tower door pulled from the guard's fingers and crashed against the wall, making Donato jump. Then, as abruptly as the wind came, it gentled, settling into a cold steady stream that found its way into his very soul.

The woman pulled off her mask, looked at it, then threw it to the ground. Marita Vos. She stood stock still with her eyes to the sky, gulping deep breaths of air as if she'd been half suffocated. A guard spoke to her, pointing at the mask, but she shook her head and started forward toward Donato. The guards glanced at each other, shrugged and followed.

Unlike Malenga, she did not turn when she saw him, but strode on in her mannish way. Rumors clung to her also, though Soza had denied most of them. She had hidden from Soza in Illiga for three years, walking about dressed as a man. Illigans were proud their city had sheltered her. Those from Vosa loved her. Some servants and townspeople made a V sign with their fingers to give each other courage, and once Donato had even seen two of Soza's soldiers greet each other that way.

The scandalized viti weren't sure how to treat her. She looked pure Massadaran, and spoke Massadaran flawlessly, though her mother had been a Pakajan merchant's daughter. She was tet-zoja, yet had been disinherited by old Vos. She didn't behave as a woman ought, and further, had lived her life as a middle-class merchant, not as a vita. She threw one off balance.

Everyone now knew Soza intended to marry her and she would rule them. But most people disbelieved the unaccountable rumor that Soza not only had several other wives but that the strange, silent woman who chaperoned the Vos woman was actually Soza's first wife.

There was another rumor: that Marita Vos refused to

worship the Black Eagle and that Soza still battled to bend her to his will. Those who secretly worshipped Zojikam, or who had renounced him and regretted it, watched her, silently drawing strength from her own.

She drew near and Donato pulled off his cap and bowed deeply. She stopped. "Good morning, Kali Donato Zandro."

He straightened, startled. She smiled slightly. "Yes, I know you. And you have seen me, no doubt, in the guild."

"I recognize you," he said gruffly. He did too, despite the black and silver dress and the white linen covering every strand of her hair. He had seen her often in Taverik's company. Damn the boy! How much had he known?

She wasn't beautiful, he thought, looking at her. Her aristocratic face was too strong, and already lined around the mouth and eyes. And an ugly scar edged into view above the bodice of her dress. But somehow, she struck the eye and lingered in the mind.

She watched him too, her gaze direct and unpretentious, but said nothing until the guard to her right cleared his throat. Then a shadow came into her eyes and she turned to go.

Donato blurted, "*You*, My Vita, stand strong."

She stopped at that and turned. "And you? Cannot *you* stand strong?"

"Too late for me," he said.

"Who decided that," she said, "you or Zojikam? Or did the Black Eagle decide it for you?"

He turned away from her eyes.

Marita

She watched him go and wanted to cry. Oh Taverik, she thought sadly, even you could find it in you to pity this poor, stooped, broken man. Zojikam help him.

Zojikam. She turned her face full to the frigid wind and inhaled deeply. The cold air wuthered around her ears, buffeting her, waking her. She welcomed it, and laughed suddenly. Zojikam had sent it to her. Her head began to clear of the cobwebs and miasma that had filled it for—how long now? A guard pulled her elbow. She picked up her dress and continued up the stairs to the palace.

Soza waited for her in a long room with north windows. Behind him hovered the turncoat priest, his eyebrows raised in the pleading expression that had become usual with him. Marita balked in the doorway, strongly sensing, after her brief freedom, the presence of the Black Eagle.

Soza gave her a sharp glance and seemed to approve what he saw. "You're looking well my dear," he said.

She said nothing. A hall mirror had told her she looked haggard and haunted, and she was pretty sure he knew the cause. Soza brought forward a chair for her but avoided touching her. Still contaminated, she thought with fierce joy. But she had only two more days of safety, and she still had not found a way to escape. Balanji could never defeat Soza before the wedding. Her stomach churned at the thought.

"I've been very pleased with you these last few days, my dear," Soza soothed in the voice used for a hawk or horse being tamed. He resumed his seat and the priest edged behind him. "Today, I have some tasks for you."

She watched him warily.

"This morning," Soza continued, unbothered by her sullen silence, "my priest will teach you more about your new god—"

"Zojikam is my God," she said.

Soza smiled indulgently. "Zojikam cannot help you, and since the Black Eagle is all about you now, you would do well to appease him and worship him. The priest will also instruct you in your duties at the betrothal banquet tonight."

She blinked. Tonight. So soon.

Soza waved at the priest. "Begin."

The man cleared his throat. "The Black Eagle," he wavered, "is a powerful being who condescends to cooperate with mankind."

Marita looked at Soza. He was watching the priest with a slight smile, and she realized suddenly he was enjoying the man's brokenness. As no doubt he enjoyed the stooped figure of Zandro, and her own hag-ridden appearance. She set her teeth.

The door opened for the Pakajan commander she had talked with at the gate. Commander Ucherik crossed the room, bowed to her, gave her a startled second glance, then bowed to Soza. "My Zoji," he said. "A merchant has been apprehended at the Giss Bridge attempting to smuggle an armed man into the city."

Marita sat up, blood draining from her face. Who?

"I'll come at once," Soza said, springing to his feet. Marita quickly lowered her eyes and let her hands lie limp and indifferent in her lap. He strode past her to the door. "Continue here, until I send word."

She waited until he was gone, then turned to the priest. "How could you," she said, "abandon Zojikam for such an obscene *ikiji*?"

"You don't know what he did to the priests who refused to do it," he pleaded. "I wish I'd been brave but I'm not. I'd give anything not to have done it."

"Do you mean that? Listen, then," said Marita fiercely.

Soza didn't return for two hours. By then the priest had long stopped weeping, and sat with his head down, hands tightly folded. Marita was staring out the window across the city. The fuzziness in her head had cleared steadily since Zojikam had sent the wind, but she wanted to know what had caused it. Had her food been drugged?

Soza's return brought an inward pressure, but her head remained clear. She faced his scowl without flinching. "How dare you," he demanded, "presume to instruct my priest against my wishes?"

She should have known there would be listeners. "I merely," she explained innocently, "asked questions to compare Zojikam, whom I know, to this Black Eagle, whom I don't know."

Soza took two steps and raised his hand. She blinked

but didn't duck. The blow never fell. Still contaminated, she thought. Perhaps the ten-day quarantine of Bcacmat women was all that preserved their lives and sanity.

Soza turned instead to the priest. "I'll deal with you later," he said. "Get out." The man scurried from the room. Marita winced at his indignity. She had wasted breath trying to help him.

"You," Soza said Marita, "will now attend a civil ceremony with me. You will lend your presence and approval to a hanging. I intend this execution to be an example to the city."

She went with mixed feelings. The sun and free air felt wonderful after days in the tower. But she feared the hanging. Who would die? Please Zojikam, not Taverik. Did Soza now know the whole plot? Was he toying with her?

The crowd, already assembled in the square, greeted her with a roar, holding up two fingers in a V for Vos. "They love you," said Soza, smiling and waving to the people as they processed to that hateful pavilion. "Respond. Smile."

Marita lifted her hand in acknowledgment but could not smile. Who would die? Her heart pounded until she counted her footsteps by it. With wobbly legs she followed Soza to the front seats under the silk. Before her the stark gallows awaited. The procession of soldiers now issuing from the fortress would be bringing the prisoner. She searched the ranks anxiously.

There he was in the middle. Black hair. She caught the rail in relief, then tightened her fingers. She knew him.

Sanisman, hands tied behind him, mounted the gallows steps slowly, as if he hurt all over. He turned to face the pavilion. Commander Ucherik stood forth to read the charge. "Your Honorable Zoji has mercifully permitted the citizens of this rebellious city to continue their trade and other such work. Despite this mercy, Amaro Sanisman, member of the Textile Guild, has knowingly and illegally accepted money from an armed stranger and attempted to smuggle him into this city.

This treasonous action shall be duly punished according to the just law . . ."

The man continued, extolling Soza's wisdom and justice and warning citizens against any such temptations. Marita stopped listening. Sanisman stood straight, with his head up, though even from the pavilion she could see he trembled. Almost certainly, she thought, he'd been in on Balanji's plot. Had he talked and spoiled all?

The intensity of her stare must have caught his attention. He smiled slightly even as the hangman put the noose around his neck. She nodded encouragement to him, then found Soza watching her with narrow eyes. "What do you know about this?" he demanded in an undertone.

Her skin shrank with the danger. "I know him," she said. She went on louder, hoping others would hear, glad her words would annoy Soza. "He was a fellow guild member, and we often travelled in the same caravan to—"

"Shut up," Soza interrupted in a whisper. "I told you not to mention that period of your life to anyone."

A roar from the crowd whipped her head around. Sanisman dangled, his neck broken. Startled tears sprang to her eyes, but she fought them back and forced herself to follow Soza from the platform. A quiet sense of triumph filled her—she was pretty sure now that Sanisman had kept his secrets. He'd died without betraying Balanji. *Zojikam avenge you, brave man*, she thought.

And Zojikam defend her, she thought as she was led back up the tower stairs to her room. After what she planned to do tonight at the betrothal banquet, she would need him.

At the doorway of her cell the Black Eagle smote her face like a blow. She stopped dead. "Vita," said one of the guards impatiently, "go on. Please enter."

Clutching the door frame to gain time, she whispered, "I feel faint." She buried her face in the crook of her arm and thought quickly. She'd gotten better *until* she returned to the room. Therefore . . . "Please,

I'd better get some fresh air," she said, heading for the stairs.

"Vita, Tet-zoja," said the guards, taking her by the elbows and practically carrying her back inside. "You must sit down. We'll get you help." They hurriedly locked her door, and she could hear them hastening downstairs, shouting for someone to help the Tet-zoja.

"Damn and blast," she said aloud. She scanned the walls, forcing back the muddy fog already clouding her thoughts. She didn't have much time. Nothing. She looked under the bed. Nothing. She ripped back the blankets, shook them, then felt the mattress. Nothing. The dressing table, despite its pots of lotions, had nothing unusual about it. She turned. The wardrobe.

Instantly a blackness seemed to stream from it, engulfing her. She tried to fight it, but it clung like wet silk. "Zojikam," she shouted and gained room to think. The temple service had helped her in the past; she sang it now, quavering at first, then stronger, as she strode to the wardrobe. The doors felt hot to the touch. She pulled them open and dragged her dresses from their hangers. Nothing. Flinging them to the floor, she burrowed to the bottom, still singing through the increasing roar in her ears.

There it was.

Nestled at the bottom, a small porcelain pot with a locked lid. Marita grabbed it then jerked back with a gasp, sucking burned fingers. Its heat seared into her mind, and she nearly lost consciousness. She shook her head to clear it, and tried to pick up the thread of the litany once more. She'd reached the Promise and she sang it loudly, wrapping her hands in the thick velvet of a dress. The roaring in her ears grew until she could barely hear her own voice. She lifted the jar and held it high. The *ihiga* had told her what to do.

"Stop it! What are you doing?" squawled Idbca from the open doorway.

"For Zojikam!" Marita yelled. She hurled the jar to the stone floor between them.

Porcelain shattered, flames roared high. Flung to her knees, Marita turned her face from the heat and covered her ears against a piercing wail that seemed to go on and on and on. Suddenly it stopped.

Silence. Marita looked up cautiously. The pressure and the fuzziness were gone.

"You wretched little whore!" exclaimed Ibdca, letting go of the door handle. "Look what you've done."

Marita gave her a sweet smile. "I've saved us from some horrible creature, Ibdca."

Ibdca feared no contaminations. She jumped forward and boxed Marita's ear, and would have done it again except for the growing murmur in the hall. They both turned. Guards, servants, and viti male and female peered in, staring at the singed and ruined room, crumpled dresses, scattered shards and a supposed servant striking their kneeling tet-zoja. Marita made the most of it. Lifting her hand to her reddened and throbbing ear, she gave a piteous little sob and heard the murmur rise in pitch.

Ibdca let out a Bcacmat expletive under her breath and shut the door on the people. Marita dropped her hand and got up.

They faced each other in silence. "Not I can not wait," said Ibdca, "until you under my authority are. Not then not merely my hand you will feel. Now we you get ready for this farce of a banquet." She swept away, locking the door behind her.

"Vitis, Vitas," cried the steward. The sparse crowd in the great hall hushed and turned, eyes on Marita who waited behind the man. "The honorable Tet-zoja of Vosa, Marita Risina Esa Vos, betrothed of most elevated, most noble, most adorable Zoji Soza of Illiga, Vosa, and Ormea."

Her cue. Marita took a wobbling step, then steadied. On each side of her, men and women flowed back into bows and curtsies as she advanced. She felt detached from herself, as if she looked down from the ceiling at this strange person, dressed and jeweled in another woman's possessions. The real Marita, if these poor men and women but knew it, was a too-thin, ragged woman dressed as a man, holding her cap humbly in her hand as these very people swept by on important business of their own. Or else, in another life, the happy, indulged daughter of a prosperous Vosa merchant.

Soza waited for her at the top of the hall. Marita watched herself draw near and stand before him, looking up into his face. Abruptly she again inhabited her body. Cold hate gleamed in his eyes, promising retribution for all she had done to thwart him. Her vision narrowed abruptly, and her hands shook as they held her train. She pressed them to her belly.

Surely this must be the strangest betrothal feast ever. Soza pretended no solicitousness. Without touching her, he turned and led the assembly to the banquet table. Marita took her position at the foot as the viti and vita silently found their places according to new precedents set by Soza. Lastly, the kalis and kalas of the court filed in, privileged to stand by the walls and watch the viti celebrate.

Celebrate! The banquet had all the air of a funeral. Marita ate next to nothing. Though the food tasted good, her stomach closed each time she tried to swallow. The viti ate vigorously—this was the first banquet Soza had given since he had taken the city—but they cast curious, covert looks at Marita. Marita looked back at each candlelit face and found a blend of emotions hard to read. How many of them, she wondered, now regretted their oath of allegiance to Soza? How many now knew too much about this Black Eagle and secretly envied those who had made a better, though harder choice? And how many believed the rumor she'd set in motion, that Soza was Bcacmat?

A strange banquet indeed. She watched the entertainment, singers and jugglers, acrobats and dancers, whose acts all fell flat in the increasingly tense atmosphere. At the head of the table Soza brooded, eyes hooded. He was not, Marita thought with a gleam of humor, the best of hosts. To his right sat his weshagash, who seemed to enjoy disgusting the viti by eating loudly and greasily. To Soza's left, the priest sat bolt upright and stared at Marita with wide, unhappy eyes.

Soza jerked his hand upward. Dropping from their toes, the three male Pakajan dancers hurried into the crowd. The zoji stood slowly, his black velvet seeming to suck in the already dim light of the room. His glittering eyes swept down the table past his silent, staring subjects, and locked onto Marita, demanding and deadly. He lifted his wine glass, still watching her. "To our lord and god, the Black Eagle."

She'd been coached and instructed in what was expected of her. Slowly she rose, leaning her left hand on the table to steady her quivering knees. One by one, each face turned to her.

The room seemed to shift and intensify; under her fingers she could feel gouges in the wood, smell the wax of the candles, hear the whistling breathing of the old viti to her right. Her heart pounded so hard she could barely draw breath.

She lifted her wine glass high. Then, deliberately, she poured its contents to the floor. "Zojikam lives!"

A collected gasp from the viti, and the light changed as they turned their faces from her to Soza. Soza's eyes hardened. He looked at his priest, the man who had denied Zojikam for the Black Eagle. "Arrest her," he said.

The man opened and shut his hands several times, cleared his throat. "I will not," he squeaked, nearly in tears. "Zojikam is the one true god. The Black Eagle is *ikiji*."

"And you, Bcacmat," Marita cried out, her voice strange in her ears. "Agash Itzil Farasoza! When will you bring your Tlath to rule our beloved Peninsula?"

She was dead now. Soza went white. The viti gasped, but could no longer pretend they didn't know. From somewhere safe in the crowd a youth shouted "Vos!" The people took it up, chanting "Vos, Vos, Vos!"

"Guards!" shouted Soza. "Take them to the tower!"

Chapter 16

Taverik

River gravel crunched under Taverik's feet as he pulled the boat up the bank. He stared into the darkness uneasily. Where was Skaj? Usually the smuggler was there to meet him, slipping out of the willow thicket to help pull the heavy boats up into hiding.

Taverik gave the boat a final heave, and water sloshed from the stern. Good thing tonight would be his last night on the river—Kintupaquat's boats were getting leakier and leakier. Well, he couldn't wait any longer. Tying the boat under the willows, he squelched up the bank to the vidyen.

Kaja's eyes welcomed Taverik but her mouth looked tight. "I haven't seen Skaj since he went off with you last night. Funny thing, though. Achicha came by this morning looking for him, too.

"Achicha!" Taverik's misgivings deepened to dread.

"Said he had a good business deal for Skaj. Said they'd make good money."

"Look, Kaja," Taverik said, "I think something's wrong. Take enough food and go to a safe place. Stay there until—until this time next week. Or until Skaj or I come after you. Don't even come out for Achicha."

"Especially not for Achicha," she said darkly, her eyes meeting Taverik's.

Taverik started north immediately, feeling as if a great rock sat in his stomach. He wasn't sure he could follow Skaj's secret paths by himself. And last night, he, Skaj and the strangely subdued Rinatto had constantly hidden from crisscrossing patrols. Sanisman's capture had aroused suspicions. Surely the patrols would search again tonight. Furthermore, Achicha was out there somewhere, and Achicha knew the paths even better than Skaj.

One more day before Balanji launched his crazy surprise attack without enough men. Taverik had to succeed tonight.

He encountered the noisy first patrol thudding around the farm. In cold dread, Taverik dropped into tall grass. Thank Zojikam he and Skaj had evacuated everyone last night. What had tipped off the patrol? And what had they discovered? Not until the last hoofbeat was long gone did he get up. Then he began a wide circle around the farmhouse, heading for the woods beyond where the men now hid. He hoped.

A slight movement near the house caught his eye. Something large and heavy swung from the dark oak. Taverik's mouth tightened. He knew instinctively what it was, but he had to be sure.

He approached cautiously, his heart hammering so loud it was hard to listen to the warm spring night. But at last he stood beneath Skaj's body, hanged hours earlier. Another one, he thought sadly, steadying the swinging feet. Perhaps by Tuesday they all would follow. How had they found Skaj? How much did they find out from him?

"Hold it right there," said Achicha. "Back away. Get your hands away from that knife."

Taverik stepped past Skaj's boots, raising his hands. "Hello, Achicha," he said mildly.

"Well, well, it's Taverik Zandro," said Achicha. He loomed from the darkness holding a crossbow, arrow aimed at Taverik's stomach.

Taverik couldn't read his expression but this he knew: Achicha reeked of the *mahiga*. "What," Taverik said, "happened to Skaj?"

"Suppose you tell me, Zandro," Achicha said. "I've been looking for him. Had a great deal. Soza was going to pay us to scout the valley for him. Too bad I didn't find him in time. But they *are* paying me to discover who comes for him. And well, well, well, here's Taverik

Zandro. You're even more money for me, you know, what with the price on your head and—"

The crossbow dipped slightly. Taverik threw himself at Achicha. The arrow sliced the top of his left shoulder, then they both went down in a thrashing tangle. Taverik used his knife without conscious thought, then rolled away from Achicha's suddenly stilled body. Breathing hoarsely, he felt the limp wrist for a pulse. He was dead.

Wiping his shaking hands on his surcoat, Taverik stood up. It had been Achicha or him, he told himself, and twenty men and Balanji depending on him besides. Still he felt sick. His shoulder stung like crazy. He fingered it gingerly. Not too bad a cut, he found to his relief, though it had soaked his surcoat. It shouldn't slow him, at least not much. Best leave Skaj, and not arouse suspicions. Best maybe, but Taverik thought of Kaja, and cut him down. He found a shovel in the shed and got to work.

Twenty men. They stood in a semi-circle around Taverik with grim, set faces, trusting him to know what to do. How on earth was he going to shepherd them all across the countryside without a patrol knowing? If only Skaj . . . He shook himself abruptly. "We're going up river," he said. "A copper barge will meet us beyond the narrows. Half of you will crew it, the other half will hide below. When you reach the city tomorrow you'll go in small groups to a tavern. From there, you'll be led into the warehouse district and so on. Questions?"

No questions. Taverik exhaled. "All right. Let's go."

They formed a long snaking trail across the river valley. Taverik winced as he listened to their thrashing progress. Skaj himself had refused to risk more than five, he had twenty. Snorting wryly at his own folly, he followed Skaj's route as best he could. Once he lost his way and halted the men while he scouted ahead. Good thing, too. Directly ahead a small patrol had been taking a breather. Taverik waited until they mounted and went on. Then he crisscrossed until he found the trail.

By the time he got his straggling file above the narrows to where the barge waited, the moon hung low. Dammit, he thought, almost in a panic, the night was fleeing and he still hadn't reached Kintupaquat's men. At this rate, first light would find him on the river and then he'd be in for it. He hurried the men on board and turned to go, but they surrounded him, shaking his hand and pounding his sore shoulder. The red-haired Copper Guild man gave him a quick salute. "Don't you worry none, Zandro. I'll get 'em in. You keep yourself safe."

Warmed by their goodwill, Taverik pushed the barge into the current and waved. One burden off his shoulders. Now to pick up the last five men and bring them safely to Balanji.

"Where have you been?" demanded Pemintinuchi when Taverik finally found him. "We almost started back."

"Five of you will have to return anyway," Taverik said, still breathing hard from that last stretch he'd covered at a steady run. "Skaj is dead."

Sobered, the men pulled closer. "What happened?"

As briefly as possible, Taverik told them, adding, "We've got to leave now. Or daylight will catch us."

"Right," said Pemintinuchi. "Tell Balanji we'll be knocking at Illiga's gates first light, Tuesday. Now, who's to go down river?"

A low-voiced argument ensued, over the privilege of dying with Balanji instead of Kintupaquat. Skin acrawl with urgency, Taverik strode down to the beached boat and muffled the badly mismatched oars. That done he hitched his belt—he needed another hole in it these days—and paced. He was getting as antsy as Balanji, he thought, and tried to calm himself. It seemed ages before he got the men into the boat and shoved off.

Once in the current he steadied. The danger, even this high on the river, sent his blood pumping until he forgot his stinging shoulder and exhaustion. The men, warned about the slightest noise, lay under the tarps, uncomplaining in the frigid water seeping through the bottom. Zojikam grant, Taverik thought as the first rapids grabbed the boat, that the hull would last until Illiga.

Before long he rowed past the silent copper barge. He was making good time then. He passed two other barges tied alongshore, then the first watchtower showed dark against the sky. He whispered a warning to the men, lined the boat up with the sheltering outcrop of rock and began the nerve-racking run past the city.

He guided the boat down the string of blind spots towards the black bulk of the Giss Bridge. The current stiffened as it approached the six stone arches. Taverik stroked hard and silently, struggling to line up with the eastern arch directly below the sentry tower. This was the one exposed spot on the run, if by bad luck the sentries leaned over the parapet at that moment.

But the night remained silent and the little boat swept safely into the deep blackness under the bridge. Pigeons exploded overhead, the racket of their wings echoing loud in the tunnel-like arch. Taverik cursed their noise, hoping the guards wouldn't alert. He kept tight to the east side of the abutment, for when he emerged, he'd have to hug the shore close enough to scrape bottom for a hundred yards or so.

Faint light gleamed on the water beyond the arch. The last pigeon scrabbled back to its roost and quieted.

Voices.

Taverik clutched the wall, wrestling to hold the boat against the current. His palms skidded in the slime then held, and he strained his ears to hear over the rush of the river.

Splash! A clay jug hit the water a few feet ahead. Thrown from *shore*, Taverik realized with alarm, not from the bridge. The soldier hidden in the stern threw off the tarp and shot his head up to look, rocking the boat and pulling Taverik away from his slippery grip. "Hold still!" Taverik hissed, flinging himself against the abutment and only just managing to stop the boat's stern from moving out in the current. The starboard oar slipped from the gunnel and slapped water.

"What'sh that?" someone mumbled, so close he sounded as if he were in the boat.

"Ha!" said another, "It'sh the captain come to feed you to the Black Eagle."

Muffled gaffaws greeted this great wit. A tenor voice lifted in song and others joined in. Three men, Taverik thought. Probably the bridge sentries, whiling away their watch tippling on the river bank. Ironic that they were more effective sluffing off rather than at their posts—the boat could never get past them unnoticed.

The temple clock chimed quarter past four. The guard wouldn't change until five. Oh help! Would they drink until then? He couldn't hang on much longer; already his arms ached with the strain of holding the boat against the current. Taverik pressed his face against the cold damp stones, inhaling the river scent and willing his exhausted mind to focus.

There were ring bolts in the abutment—they'd help hold the boat. One hung only a little behind him, but he'd have to stand to reach it. The other hung near the waterline, but at the upper end of the arch. Could he back the boat that far against the current?

Someone touched his knee questioningly. Taverik lifted his head and found the soldier who had rocked the boat crouched awkwardly beside him, not daring to move. Taverik could feel him, all of them, looking at him expectantly, waiting for him to get them out of this one. Well, for a start, the starboard oar had swung around against the bow, bobbing in the current. Any moment now they'd lose it, then be stuck for sure. "Get the oar in," Taverik breathed under cover of the raucous song, and added, as the lubber tipped the boat again, "Easy! Slowly."

With the oar safely inboard, he felt for a better hand hold in the slippery slime coating the wall of the abutment. There, one block stuck out slightly more—Taverik planted the heel of his hand against it and pushed, forcing the boat back. Again he heaved, splaying his hands against the abutment, fighting the swift current piling up against the stern. Again! He pushed until his sore shoulder stung and his back muscles cramped under the strain. Collapsing against the wall, he panted as quietly as he could.

The drunken song petered out, and one whining voice rose, complaining about Soza and the Black Eagle and wishing he could just take off to the mountains. The others hushed him ineffectually. Another jug hit the water. The half hour chimed. Only fifteen minutes had passed.

Taverik groped for a new hand just as the boat again rocked him away from the wall. This time it was the short Massadaran captain near the bow, struggling to kneel. "No—stop!" Taverik began in exasperation, then felt the weight of the boat ease as the captain reached out and splayed his fingers against the abutment.

"Try again," whispered the captain.

Encouraged, Taverik pushed. With the two of them now, the boat moved back perceptibly. "Can you hold it alone?" Taverik whispered, and received a faint grunt in reply. He lifted his hands slightly to be sure. The boat held.

Slowly, shakily, he rose to his feet and swept his right arm across the abutment overhead. Nothing. He switched to his left and now his wrist encountered something cold and hard. Triumphant, Taverik closed his fingers around the chill, corroded metal. Now what? His belt. Uncinching it clumsily with his chapped right hand, he strapped it around the ring and sank carefully down again, holding the end.

Easy now to control the boat—providing the worn leather didn't part. And now he had leisure to worry. At this rate, the sun would rise and catch them out in the open. And then? If he were smuggling silk, he'd have slipped into the water and swum away. Smuggled men were different. Especially men who expressly obeyed him because they trusted him to know what to do.

The chimes rang out once more. Less than fifteen minutes until the guard changed. He'd been expected back hours ago. Were Balanji and Nik awake, listening to the bells, worrying?

A deep prolonged belch split the night and a third jug hit the water. Taverik cursed hard heads which could drink so much and not pass out. He shivered in the raw air, and could feel the shudders of the men lying under the tarp in the bitter bilge water.

"I gotta piss," said a drunk.

"You swine! Don't do it here," another exclaimed. "Go under the bridge if you must."

Gravel crunched. Zojikam! The soldier beside Taverik drew his knife.

The clock struck five. From the far side of the bridge a measured tramp resounded. The drunks stopped talking, then scrambled up the bank. Closing his eyes with relief, Taverik listened as muffled exclamations shifted to an angry lecture. Lantern beams flashed along the shore, crossed the water, reflected under the bridge. Taverik hid his face in the crook of his arm. At last silence settled once more, except for the slow steps of the new watch.

Taverik gave them long extra minutes to relax, then let go of the belt. Bent with relief, he rested a precious moment while the boat eased down the river's edge in the blind spot of the bridge abutment. Then once more he put out the muffled oars.

He got them to the landing without further incident and helped the stiffened men to climb out. With a queer shock, Taverik realized he could actually see them in the lightening gloom. They were only just in time.

"Nicely done," whispered the short captain, patting Taverik's shoulder. He looked curiously at his hand, rubbing his fingers together. "When were you hurt?"

No time to think about that yet. "I'm all right," Taverik said. "Help me get the boat under cover."

Hours later Taverik swam up out of sleep to find the same shoulder shaken by the same captain. "What time is it?" he mumbled.

"Just after nine by the tower clock," said the captain. "The zoji wants you."

Taverik groaned and untangled his cloak from his legs. He still lay in the little round chamber, only now men trampled back and forth around him as Bibi and Sahra served breakfast. Blearily he got up and went into the tunnel to find one of the slop buckets. The air smelled of sweat, urine and old cooking, but he usually noticed it only when he'd newly come in. After that his nose numbed.

Men lined the walls of the passage, talking or playing cards. They'd organized shifts for eating, resting, and clearing the blocked passage. Yet only their strict discipline enabled them to survive, with no incidents, a week in such cramped, timeless quarters. Taverik admired them, but was glad he at least got outside.

He'd been out every night, and many days as well. For though Balanji always apologized for disturbing him, the moment a problem arose among the merchants, the zoji would send for Taverik. Taverik had learned to tamp down his strength, portion it out, to sleep at any odd moment. But one of these days, Taverik thought, combing his tangled hair at the mirror Sahra had set up, any one of these days he'd lie down and sleep for a year.

Uncle Nikilo waited for him alone in the tiny room under the temple. "Taverik," he said shortly, "you didn't say you'd been hurt."

"And good morning to you, too, Nik," said Taverik, scratching his stubble and yawning. "Only a cut and Bibi fixed it. I must have fallen asleep on her, but I assume it's all right."

"Young fool," Nikilo said, placing his hand over Taverik's heart, then releasing him. "The captain also reported last night's difficulties. Balanji commended you, though I doubt he'll have the time to tell you personally."

"What's the problem?"

"Ittato's with Balanji in the side chapel," Nikilo said. "His warehouse is to be conscripted today to be used as a barracks, and we have a number of men hidden there. And, by the way, it was your father who warned him."

"My *father* warned him?" Taverik repeated, incredulous. "You heard it right?"

"Go up and hear for yourself."

Ittato and Gunnar both sat by the door. Three soldiers Gunnar had smuggled in with him stood along the wall, and in the near corner, Balanji talked with the captain Taverik had brought last night. The zoji looked up when Taverik knelt before him. "Nicely done last night, Zandro. Sit there. You told him, Vitujak?"

Taverik sat on the bench beside Ittato. "He told me, Zoji. How many men are hidden there, Ittato?"

"Ten," Ittato said. "And twenty at the copper barge, who were supposed to be brought to my warehouse today."

"I must have every one of them here by tonight," said Balanji.

"I'd assumed we had a week to do it," Ittato said. He flung up his hands. "To move thirty men across the city in one day—"

"We can do it," Taverik interposed quickly, seeing Balanji's irritated scowl.

Everyone looked at him. "How?" said Ittato.

How indeed. Taverik thought aloud. "First we have to get the men out of your warehouse. Look, my textile warehouse isn't far."

"But your father—"

"Probably hasn't gone there since the city fell. I'll check. Gunnar, can we bring the copper barge people there?"

"That's the one in the warren? It's even closer than Ittato's," said Gunnar. "But with Sanisman gone and Ittato forced to be at his warehouse, I'm the only wagoneer."

"I'll drive a wagon," Taverik volunteered, though his muscles ached at the thought. Only one more day, he promised himself, then for better or worse it would be over. He hoped. He looked at Balanji. "What do you think of the plan, Zoji?"

"Do it. But take no unneeded chances." The corners

of Balanji's eyes crinkled in that disconcerting way he had of laughing silently at the pageant of people around him. "And Zandro," he added, "shave and get yourself some decent clothes. I don't know about Soza, but I'd arrest you on sight."

Chapter 17

Taverik

He'd been right about his warehouse. Deserted for months. The smell of mold caught in Taverik's nose the moment he slid open the side door.

Gunnar gingerly stepped in after him. "Dust to the ceiling," he said, and sneezed.

"Thought so," Taverik said. "We can bring the wagons right into the loading bay and close the door. You go intercept the copper barge people, and I'll start bringing the men across from Ittato's warehouse."

"Right," said Gunnar. "I'll bring in the small wagon for you. Keep safe, Tav."

"That's very funny, Gunnar," said Taverik, sorting keys, "considering what we are doing."

Gunnar gave a great laugh and left him.

It took but five minutes to reach Ittato's warehouse. But it felt like twenty, pushing through the unseen oppression throughout the city. Zojikam, Taverik thought, will it be like this all day?

Ittato opened the door at his knock, and brought Taverik to the hidden soldiers. He'd disguised them as dock laborers, but they stood, hands twitching, eyes shifting, looking more like ruffians than anything. "Their weapons and armor are in here," Ittato said, proudly thumping one of many barrels with his cane. "They can carry them."

"Good idea," Taverik said. He pointed at the nearest men. "I'll take you three first. And try not to look so desperate."

"You'd be desperate if you had to walk through an occupied city with your sword in a damned barrel," growled a freckled Pakajan. The others guffawed, and Taverik shepherded the first three out followed by a volley of jokes. He wasn't laughing. At any moment Soza's troops would arrive to take up residence in the warehouse. He felt exposed, leading three soldiers right down the street in broad daylight. If only the Giss would send one of its famous fogs to hide them. But the sky remained a lovely blue, the sun gently warm.

Gunnar waited in the bay with two wagons and two of the men from the copper barge. "A woman saw me come in," he said, worried. "Asked what I was doing in the Zandro warehouse. I told her Zandro had leased it to me. She looked like she didn't believe me."

"Was she fat, with a moustache?"

"That's her."

"Delightful," groaned Taverik. "She's an old busybody I wouldn't trust." He chewed his lip, thinking. "We should be all right unless she meets up with my father. Then she'll blab. Here's what we do. One of you must always watch from the upstairs window. Give the alarm if you see anyone coming. I'll show the rest where to hide, but you must clean up the dust in the entire warehouse so your tracks don't give you away. Got it?"

"First a docker, then a charwoman," said the freckled Pakajan, but he obediently nodded, as did the others. An odd feeling, Taverik thought, having orders so instantly accepted. Well, he had some more for them. "Watch for Gunnar and myself too. Two men always be at the loading bay doors, ready to open without our having to wait outside. The sooner the wagons get off the street the better. Switch shifts when you must, and inform the men coming later. Who's in charge?"

"I am," said a captain.

"Will you stay until the last trip, and keep order here?"

The man actually saluted him. "Yes, viti."

Viti. The term merely meant they'd been ordered to obey him implicitly, but it increased Taverik's sense of disconnection. For this short time he'd become a different person, someone in the confidence of a Zoji, commanding a small military operation, someone respected and obeyed. It felt—good.

Taverik saw Gunnar off in the large wagon, pulled by two mismatched mules. He waited a few minutes, then slipped out the side door and headed back to Ittato's warehouse.

The sun had climbed overhead before he brought the last of Ittato's men. A narrow squeak. Soza's officers had just then arrived and Ittato desperately distracted them in front while Taverik hustled the men out the back.

The door of his own warehouse opened for him immediately, and the dust had been cleaned up, but he detected a worsening in mood there. The captain wore a set expression on his face, and three of the men waited with sullen scowls. Taverik's breath hissed between his teeth. The last thing he needed was internal fighting. "All right," he said. "Next lap. Who's the first two in the wagon?"

"Sassan and Okajak," said the captain promptly. Two of the scowlers stood up.

"Let's go," Taverik said, and helped the two men into the false bottom of the smaller wagon. He tamped down the boards again and hid them under sacks heaved up to him by the captain. The captain rolled his eyes eloquently, but said nothing. Taverik gave him a grin and climbed into the driver's seat. "Ready," he said. Two men opened the door, and Taverik guided the mule into the sunlight.

The warm spring day favored them, Taverik thought as the guard at the first checkpoint barely glanced at his papers. All the local farmers and all the city merchants had turned out for this market, clogging the city with wagons and booths. The guards had grown lax in the festive bustle, and Taverik was easily able to blend with the traffic.

As he approached the warehouse next door to the temple, the loading bay doors smoothly opened for him and shut behind. Several soldiers from the tunnel waited there. With few words they helped Taverik move the sacks and open the false bottom. The hidden men untangled themselves and clambered stiffly out. The soldiers would see about filtering them across the alley.

Taverik started out again, careful to choose a different way back. No sense drawing attention to himself by passing the same checkpoints too often. The first of many trips complete.

The number of men waiting for him increased each time he returned—Gunnar's route from the copper barge didn't take as much time, and he could fit more men in his wagon. Taverik wondered how they'd ever get them all to Balanji. Even so, he worked steadily but carefully; the way his father had taught him avoided attention and accidents.

But for all their care, Taverik felt more and more exposed. The brooding presence of the Black Eagle increasingly pressed in on him from all sides until he found it hard to think clearly. The *mahiga* seemed agitated, as if it sensed an enemy at work. Taverik chanted the temple service under his breath, a protective wall about him and the men in his care. He hoped.

As he skirted the marketplace on his way back, the sky darkened. He glanced up. Strange, the sun still shone as before. Uneasily, Taverik looked around. Hard to see. At the same time he sensed the Black Eagle, close. Searching.

Ahead, a new checkpoint had been set up. Taverik squinted, trying to see it better. A soldier waited there, talking to a man on a horse.

A flicker of light caught his eye. He looked left just as a quick spiral glowed and disappeared. He pulled up and searched the air, but it didn't return. But it had been enough—Taverik knew an *ihiga* had passed. The knowledge drove back the dark.

Tentatively he extended his senses, testing, tasting. Evil. Very strong, and coming from the man on the horse, now checking a farmer's papers. The horse shifted restlessly and Taverik now saw the black beard. He drew a quick breath. Soza's wesh-agash.

Quietly Taverik turned the mule and drove the cart down a side street. The back of his neck prickled, expecting at any moment to hear a shout. But he'd gotten away unnoticed.

At the checkpoint on River Road, a line of farmers' carts waited to leave the city. Again he extend his senses and tasted: nothing. Not good, not evil. Gunnar's wagon came through the checkpoint and started up the hill toward him. It was the first he'd passed Gunnar since they'd parted, though the now decreasing numbers of men in the warehouse showed he'd also begun carting up the hill to the temple. Taverik waved at him, and Gunnar drew in close.

"Listen," Taverik said softly, urgently. "There's a bearded man visiting the checkpoints. He reeks of the Black Eagle. Stay away from him if you can, the Black Eagle is looking for us."

Gunnar's long jaw dropped. "What do you mean, looking for us?"

"Haven't you sensed him? It's that oppression we've been wading through all day."

"What oppression? It's a beautiful spring day."

"Gunnar, believe me," Taverik said desperately. "The Black Eagle feels our work, and he's searching for us. I don't think he knows what he's looking for, but he's on the alert. If you run into trouble, call on Zojikam, or say the temple service to yourself. That seems to help. And there are *ihigas* in the city, I saw one."

Gunnar considered him as if he were crazy. "You know, you've really changed, Taverik. You're really different."

"Ho! Move your cart!" shouted a farmer behind Gunnar. Gunnar sat up and picked up the reins.

"Just be careful," Taverik said, but it was to Gunnar's back. He hadn't taken Taverik seriously. In fact, Gunnar plainly thought he was crazy. He *had* changed,

Taverik supposed, but dammit, he didn't want to. It's just that things had happened, and he'd responded to them. He didn't want to be cut off from friends who thought him weird. Damn!

Maybe he *was* crazy. Maybe he'd imagined everything. But the moment he thought that, he rejected it. Gunnar just didn't know, he thought, slapping the reins on the mule's back and moving up to the checkpoint. And given Gunnar had so little sense of good or evil, Zojikam grant he'd be careful.

The sun sank lower until only the towers and west-facing streets reflected its blazing gold. In the early dusk of the warehouse maze, Taverik hurried the mule. Almost curfew, and still several men from the barge to go. They'd have to scramble.

Gunnar opened the bay doors to him. Taverik drove in and found the large room empty, and Gunnar's wagon and mule gone. "What's wrong?" he asked, his heart thundering.

"Nothing," said Gunnar. "We're done. Except for these last few barrels of weapons and provisions."

Taverik climbed stiffly down from the wagon seat and patted the tired mule. "I feel like I've been run over by a caravan."

"Two. Uh, Taverik, you know that bearded man you mentioned?"

"What about him?"

"I saw him. So I tried to feel what you said you felt, but I couldn't. But he gave me the creeps. He rode away before I had to pass him."

A roundabout apology. Taverik accepted it. "He's Soza's wesh-agash, the one leading the bandits in the pass all last year. Come on, let's load these last barrels and get up the hill before curfew. You can drop me off and take the wagon home with you."

They worked in silence, checked the warehouse one last time, then Taverik went to unlatch the loading bay doors. "Wait, Taverik," said Gunnar suddenly. "How come Balanji's got this big push to bring all the men in today? Is he going to make his move soon?"

Taverik paused, hand on the bolt, wondering how much he could say. But his silence had said everything. "He's doing it tomorrow," Gunnar said. "Oh, damn. Where are you going to be?"

"In the tunnel, I suppose," Taverik said. "Help the survivors escape if it should come to that. Gunnar, come in with me tonight."

"I want to," Gunnar said. "Tell you the truth, I'm scared out of my wits. But I've got to stay with my folks."

"Take food enough for a week, bolt your doors, go down into the basement, and stay there. 'Cause I wouldn't put it past either army to sack the city."

Gunnar gripped his hand. "Keep safe, friend."

"Keep safe, Gun. Now, let's go."

They crossed the city one last time, too tired to talk. Gunnar drove, and Taverik slumped beside him, hands limp. Now the emergency was over, his whole frame sagged and protested. He dozed, and woke when the wagon jerked to a stop. The market square checkpoint.

The square looked suddenly empty in the very last rays of the sun. Only litter, and three booths being dismantled, remained from the busy market day. A patrol waited near the checkpoint, and the guards carefully examined the papers Gunnar held down to them. "Almost curfew," said the guard on Taverik's side of the wagon.

"Yes, Kali," Taverik said. "We're hurrying home."

As he spoke, he heard an exclamation behind him. "Who's that?"

The voice was familiar. Taverik looked over his shoulder. Echin! Gunnar slapped the reins on the mule's back and the wagon lurched forward.

"Stop them!" Echin yelled. The patrol closed in. Echin waved and pointed. "Don't let them pass!"

The guard leaped to the mule's head and grabbed the lines. "Go, Taverik!" Gunnar shouted and shoved the reins into Taverik's hands. Before Taverik could react, Gunnar had launched himself at the guard. They went down in a struggling tangle, the guard still hanging onto the reins and almost jerking them out of Taverik's grasp. The mule staggered, head pulled painfully around. Taverik shouted and used the whip. Jerking free, the mule leaned into the harness. But before the wagon could move, the patrol swarmed around it.

Strong hands fastened onto Taverik's surcoat and dragged him from the seat. He struggled as he'd never before, jabbing, knifing, trying to win free. But his exhaustion and stiff left shoulder betrayed him. A heavy blow on his right arm flung his knife from his hand. He was thrown to his face on the cobbles, so many men clinging to him he couldn't move.

He relaxed. Perhaps there was still time to try a break. But when he was dragged upright, still gasping for air, he was held tight. The guards were taking no chances. He'd badly wounded one of them, and several were bleeding and casting murderous glances at him. Echin elbowed his way past and stood directly in front of him, smiling triumphantly.

The captain of the patrol rounded the mule's head, with two men dragging Gunnar's limp body behind them. They flung him at Taverik's feet. Taverik winced as Gunnar's head struck the cobbles, then realized Gunnar would never feel it. In cold anger he looked from the bloodied body to Echin, and Echin took a step back despite the men hanging onto Taverik's arms.

The captain had noticed the mute passage. He scowled at Echin. "What is the meaning of this, you pinheaded merchant?"

Echin stuck up his nose. "This is none other than Taverik Zandro, who your guards almost let slip past your fingers."

The captain turned a pleased, wolfish face to Taverik. "Zandro. There's a price on his head."

"And I claim it," shrilled Echin.

"By the Black Eagle, what do you have to do with it?"

"I spotted him!"

"And *we* caught him."

"Captain," said a man from somewhere over Taverik's head. "This wagon has a false bottom. They've got all kinds of arms in here."

"Take him in," the captain said. "The wagon, too. And if you value your life, don't let him go."

Chapter 18

Balanji

The last man in brought the news to Balanji: Gunnar dead, Taverik arrested, a cache of weapons discovered in the wagon. Balanji's mind went numb with the implications. Why did this have to happen the night before the attack! Beyond doubt, Soza would soon have Zandro telling everything. And Zandro *knew* practically everything. Perhaps they should get out of the tunnel now, before it was too late.

Nikilo Vitujak sat down suddenly on the chest as if his knees had given way. He'd gone so white his freckles stood out like blotches. The young captain who had brought the news looked from Balanji to Vitujak and back again, frightened by his leaders' consternation.

Balanji regained control of the situation. He put his hand on Vitujak's shoulder and squeezed a sympathetic warning, then turned to the young captain. "You've done well. I'm proud of you."

"Thank you, My Zoji."

"Your news may or may not change things for us, but I must request your complete silence about it to the men in the tunnel. I will depend on your honor for that."

The young man straightened. "Zoji, you have my word."

"And you handpicked by the great Kintupaquat,"

Balanji said. "I will count on you tomorrow morning. Go now, rest and eat—tomorrow we attack. Will you request Commander Mamos to come to me here?"

"Yes, Zoji."

When he'd gone, Balanji looked at Vitujak. Vitujak's eyes looked red and his jaw tight as if his teeth were clenched, but he had himself under control. "I beg your pardon, Zoji," Vitujak said.

"No pardon is needed," Balanji said briskly, afraid too much sympathy would again shake his secretary's composure. "And, I have every confidence in Zandro's courage and resourcefulness. Nothing will change: we attack at dawn."

Taverik

Torchlight already lit the fortress bailey as Taverik was marched across it in the wake of the wagon. Despite the knot of fear in his stomach, he almost laughed at Echin's shrill insistence that the prisoner was his and should be brought to the tariff office. Exasperated, the officer gave in with snarling ill grace, and changed course towards a small outbuilding next to the stables. The tariff office.

Taverik was pushed into a tiny room with a board floor. "Stand there," the officer ordered three of the guards. "Don't even take your hands off him. I'm going to get the commander."

Echin, equally determined, gave hurried whispered instructions to a servant. Taverik watched from within the clamped grips of the three guards who were taking their instructions literally. His first numbed shock had worn off and now he felt sick and shaky with reaction.

Dispatching the servant, Echin came back to Taverik. He smirked. "Not so cocky now, eh Zandro? You laughed at me that day. You laughing at me now?"

Any last hope that Echin might help him died. "The whole place is laughing at you, Echin," Taverik replied, and the guards backed him up with loud guffaws of agreement.

Echin's eyes went mean and he swung. Taverik ducked the blow, and prepared for the next. It never came. Echin had glanced toward the door and his expression changed to petulant annoyance.

Curious, Taverik peered around his guard. Donoto Zandro stood in the doorway.

Once robust, seemingly invulnerable, his father now stared feebly across the room at him, deep jowls hanging limp at his throat. "Taverik," he said in a wondering voice. He walked forward, the Taverik grieved at his stooped, flat-footed shuffle.

"Father and son, isn't this nice," said Echin, folding his arms. He was, Taverik realized, enjoying Taverik's shocked dismay. Well, give the sniveler no more satisfaction. He straightened, and smiled pleasantly.

"Hello, Father," he said.

Donato looked him in the eye. His voice strengthened. "You damn fool!"

"Takes one to know one," inserted Echin.

"Why did you come back?" demanded Donato.

"Exactly what Soza will want to know," Echin said.

"I just wanted to visit you, Father."

"So clever, these Zandros," Echin said. "But they've finally tripped over their own feet. And I get the reward. And the promotion."

Echin's insolence got under Taverik's skin. For the first time, Taverik realized how proud he'd been of his father's strength and vitality, even when he'd hated him most. He felt no hate now, only pity. "Father," he said urgently, "why don't you slam the little nosepicker?"

Donato seemed to notice Echin for the first time. "What are you doing here, you yapping puppy!" He aimed a swift backhand at Echin.

Echin yelped and leaped back. "That's the way!" crowed Taverik. The guards roared with laughter.

"What's going on here?"

The room fell silent. In the door stood Soza's weshagash, black beard bristling across his black uniform. The guards snapped to and their hands tightened on Taverik. Blood drained from Taverik's face.

"What is this prisoner doing here?" demanded the

wesh-agash. "Take him to the tower." His very tone expressed angry incredulity that they hadn't done it in the first place.

"He's *my* prisoner!" cried Echin. "I caught him. I get the reward!"

"What!" roared Donato, rounding on him like an enraged bull.

"Move," snapped the wesh-agash. The guards pulled at Taverik. Taverik wanted to balk, shout to his father for help, sit down and refuse to move—but somehow his stiff knees bent and he stumbled, half-supported out the door.

Behind him came a crash. Echin yelled, "Don't leave me! Help!"

Get him, Father, Taverik thought with a faint smile. Strengthened a little, he stood taller and walked on his own, though his smile wilted as they entered the tower. Now it would begin.

Balanji

Balanji held his breath as Commander Mamos crouched below the floor of the palace cellars and spread his fingers against the paving stone. In the predawn hours the zoji had brought his too-few men up the newly cleared stairs. They crouched in the spiral passage, lantern light flickering on their set faces and hands clenching and opening around their weapons.

At the bottom of the tunnel Vitujak and the two women would be waiting, ready to escape if all went ill, Zojikam forbid. Balanji had wanted Zandro there too, the better to facilitate any retreat. Damn, damn, don't think about it.

Vitujak had led the prayers this morning, for they had no priest and Balanji felt strongly that without Zojikam's help this crazy ploy was doomed. He'd insisted on services and prayers as part of the tunnel's discipline. It seemed awkward at first. Balanji wasn't used to consulting anyone but himself and the few men he trusted. But gradually it had come to feel proper, and somehow, well, right.

Mamos lifted the stone a hairline crack. Balanji held his breath. Inch by inch, Mamos eased the heavy flagstone aside, careful not to let it scrape. At last he held out his hand for the lantern. Balanji gave it to him, and allowed himself to hope. Maybe the silence meant Soza hadn't yet had time to make Zandro talk.

Or maybe he merely waited, a spider luring them all into his web.

Noiselessly the file of men passed him. Vitujak and Mamos had made him promise to be the last out of the tunnel—just in case. But he managed to encourage each man as he passed. This time, each man would make a difference.

Finally he himself climbed out into a food storage room in the cellars of the palace. Balanji knew it well. He gathered the men, then moved forth into the gloom of the arched vaults.

Kintupaquat

Kintupaquat had brought his army as close as he dared. Ahead, the city walls took shape in the dark, snaking across the point from Giss to Ao. He knew the strengths and weaknesses of those walls better than anyone, even the zoji. But he'd never suspected that one day he'd be the one attacking from outside. He'd get his city back and kick Soza's butt all the way to Bcacma.

Time to go. Where was Pemintinuchi? Was something wrong? Should he give the order even though the captain hadn't returned? A rustle behind him. He turned irritably. Pemintinuchi crept up beside him. "All ready."

"Excellent," he said. "Give the word."

"With pleasure, Viti!" cried Pemintinuchi. He disappeared into the gray darkness. And minutes later the ancient Pakajan war yell shattered the half-light. The army charged.

Taverik

Taverik woke and stared into the blind darkness, listening. He lay on his back on the chill stone floor of the cell. Damp had soaked into his surcoat until he shuddered with cold. He'd actually fallen asleep from exhaustion—how long? Minutes? Hours? No way to tell.

Voices. They were coming for him, now. As the footsteps and jingly keys neared, he climbed slowly to his feet and stood the length of his ankle chain away from the wall. His legs felt wobbly under him. He hadn't eaten since noon yesterday, that was why, he guessed. That and the fear he'd betray Balanji and his uncle. He had to hang on until dawn. How long would that be? He swallowed. Zojikam help him.

His door opened, and the blinding orange light of a lantern filled his cell. Oh blast it all, he'd begun to shake again.

The jailor, keys hanging from the belt of his black uniform, brought in the lantern and stood aside respectfully for Soza. Behind Soza, came a Pakajan commander. Last, came a bent little man with skin like beeswax. Taverik's heart sank—the pawnbroker. The one who had tried to assassinate Balanji in Novato. Now he was in for it.

The man took one look at Taverik and jabbered excitedly to Soza in Bcacmat.

Soza

"He's one of them, master," Abado said. "He helped kill your son!"

Something flared in Soza's mind, and the next thing he saw was Zandro sprawled on the floor, fingers pressing a split lip. Within him the Black Eagle roared for blood. He struggled against it, though he nearly lost consciousness from the pressure. He couldn't kill Zandro yet. They must extract all the information they could from him. That merchant, Sanisman, must have been lying, there *was* something going on. They must get it from Zandro before it was too late.

The Black Eagle subsided, leaving Soza shaken. He was finding it harder and harder to control its surges, even when its demands went against Soza's interests. He knew bitterly that the Black Eagle cared nothing for him. How he wished there was some way of ridding himself of the *mahiga*.

With the wish came the knowledge that Zojikam could do it. Inside himself he reached eagerly for rescue. Then he remembered. Zojikam also demanded allegiance. Soza, the created, would serve Zojikam, the creator, not the other way around. For a moment Soza longed for it, as something good and right. Then his pride rose. He could withstand both. He'd serve himself.

He opened his eyes. His fist was still clenched, the knuckles throbbing. "Get up," he said in Massadaran, then realized he dealt with a mere merchant. Ucherik repeated it in Pakajan, and Zandro climbed reluctantly to his feet. Soza noted the young man's composure, betrayed only by his quickened, shallow breathing. A little terror would speed his purposes.

He began his questions. Zandro fielded them, but Soza didn't worry. This was just the first step. A little more cold, a little more starvation, and he'd change his tune. They'd shave all the hair from his body tonight. And he'd put a *mahiga* jar in his cell, just out of reach. And he'd describe all this in detail and let Zandro stew about it in the dark some more. They could show him the rack and let him worry about that too. They'd soon know all.

A shout echoed down the stairs. "Who's that?" demanded Soza.

The jailer opened the door and looked out. "What is your business—" he started, then was shoved aside by Malenga.

Malenga's usually precise hair was disheveled, and he panted like a dog in summer. "We're under attack," he gasped. "No one could find you. They've gotten in the fortress. Hurry!"

So that was it! Soza shot a glance at Zandro. The young man looked blank, more interested in his cut lip than the news, but Soza had no doubt he was in it to his ears. Well, if he hoped for rescue, he'd be disappointed.

"Commander Ucherik, Abado, you come with me. Malenga, you stay here." Soza gave Zandro a last, burning look. "Execute him."

When he reached the palace roof, Soza took in the tangled fight broiling in the courtyard. "How did they get past the gate?" he snarled at a hovering aide.

"Zoji, we don't know. Suddenly they fell on the guards there. They were already waiting at the barracks when the men woke."

"They must have found a secret passage in," said Abado.

"Ah," observed Soza, "they've failed to close the gate. We'll have reinforcements from the city soon." Below, Commander Ucherik burst into the courtyard, shouting to the confused men. They rallied around him and renewed their defense. "Good, good," Soza said.

"My Master," said Abado, peering across the city. "Look there."

From the outer walls great billows of smoke rose. Soza stared until the meaning of it came home, then he cursed Balanji back ten generations. "They've attacked the outer wall at the same time," he sputtered. "*How* did they get in?"

Whirling on an aide, Soza snapped, "Get down to Commander Ucherik. Tell him the city walls are also under attack. Bid him keep the gate open. Abado!"

"Yes, master?"

"Go to Idbca's chamber. Tell her what's happening and escort her to the tower chamber with the Vos woman. Give her the key and tell her to lock the door from the inside and not open it until I send word. We may need our emergency exit."

Abado bowed and started away. Suddenly he stopped and shaded his eyes against the sun's early rays. "Look, Master. That's Balanji himself down there!"

"Which one?"

"There."

Soza sighted along Abado's finger and spied a smaller man among a cluster of tall Pakajans in the melee around the still-open gate. Though plainly dressed, the smaller man radiated authority. Undoubtedly Abado was right. "His mistake," Soza said and smiled with satisfaction. "I shall make him sweat before I kill him."

Lifting the eagle claw around his neck, he began to chant, summoning the *mahigas* he'd imprisoned with the Black Eagle's power. In their jars at the base of the tower, the spirit beings stirred and woke from their slumbers. The first licks of their fire flickered along Soza's hand.

Balanji

"Close it!" Balanji roared. "Close the gate!"

His hoarse shout was lost in the furious battle about the guard house. Balanji leaped forward to do it himself. His bodyguard followed, but only when he seized the huge spoked wheel did they understand. They pushed in and did it for him, and he turned to meet the five black-uniformed men converging upon them.

The gate creaked down at last. Balanji's men sent up a roar and renewed their efforts. Balanji pressed into the bloody melee centering now around the barracks. They'd indeed caught Soza's men asleep, and cut them down in the barracks. But now the surprised men had rallied around a leader, still outnumbering Balanji's small force.

A blinding flash of light split the air. For a second both sides fell back, uncertain. Balanji, looking up in shock, saw a figure on the palace roof, hands raised. Soza.

Another flash burst at his feet, throwing him backwards. One of his men screamed and fell, clutching his eyes. His own face blistered with the heat. Balanji rolled away from a third burst, which exploded right where he'd been. Somehow Soza had identified him, and was aiming fire directly at him. *Zojikam!*

Kintupaquat

The surprise worked. Kintupaquat concentrated his first attack on the long stretch of wall west of the gate, where the outpost towers were too far apart. His men stormed the high walls with ladders and catapults. Within an hour of the first alarm they'd breached the wall.

But the defense soon rallied. Soza's forces used rocks, boiling oil and catapults. They shoved the flaming ladders away from the walls. Despite the pressure Kintupaquat applied, his men were gradually pushed back.

The morning wore on. Kintupaquat sent a new attack on another section of wall. Soza's men, forced to scurry cross city, split into two smaller groups now, still held the walls. Kintupaquat persisted, but his worried eyes continually sought out the distant walls of the fortress. Soza's flag still waved.

Chapter 19

Taverik

Execute him. Hope turned to bitter ashes in Taverik's mouth. Balanji would not come in time for him. But at least, he thought, he hadn't betrayed the zoji.

Fastidious lines deepened on each side of Malenga's nose. "Execute how?" he muttered, looking helplessly around the barren cell.

"Viti Malenga," Taverik said softly, "let me go."

"Shut up."

"I will pay you a good sum to—"

Malenga drew his sword. "Close your eyes. I'll make this as quick as I can."

Taverik swallowed convulsively. Backing to the wall on shaking legs, he did shut his eyes. *Hurry,* he thought, *before I humiliate myself and pee or start screaming. Or both.*

A shout, a grunt and a loud ring of metal on pavement. Taverik's eyes flew open. His father and Malenga were locked in a tight embrace, each holding back the other's knife. Donato was the bigger man, but clumsy. Straining and gasping, Malenga twisted suddenly in his grip, kicking the fallen sword closer to Taverik. Taverik got to his knees and reached. His fingers curled around the sharp blade. The two men fell heavily.

Donato landed on top. Both men cried out, fell apart and lay still.

Taverik sat up, staring. Malenga lay on his back, eyes open to the ceiling. Donato lay curled away from him. "Father?" he asked. He stood up to see better. "Father?"

Donato groaned and rolled to his back. In the dim light, Taverik couldn't tell how hurt he was. "Father!"

His father opened his eyes and stared at the ceiling. "I beat that bastard Echin to a pulp," he mumbled.

"Good work," Taverik approved. "How badly are you hurt? Can you get to me?"

His father rolled to his face and lay still a moment. Then he gave a low grunt and crawled to Taverik. Taverik knelt beside him and pulled open the torn, bloody surcoat. His fingers stiffened as he found the wound. Donato Zandro would probably not recover.

He forced an encouraging smile, and Donato scowled. "I know I'm dead," he wheezed. He licked his lips and when he spoke again, Taverik could hardly hear him. He put his ear close and heard something about a horrible mistake, then "Forgive me, Taverik."

"I do, Father," Taverik said. "Forgive me."

Donato lay still for a little while, then spoke stronger. "Best of my sons. Didn't know it until too late."

"Not too late. You saved my life. Father, where is Marita Vos held?"

Two scowl lines appeared between his father's eyebrows. "What does she have to do with me?"

"My life, Father."

"Damn fool. In the tower, of course. Key."

Donato fell silent. Taverik waited for him to regather his strength, then realized he'd died. Taverik shut his eyes and wept.

The deep wrenching sobs bounded back at him, off the damp stone walls. Gradually he realized he cried not from grief so much as hysteria. Between the deaths of Gunnar, his father, even Malenga, and his narrow escape from torture and execution, his insides had wrung themselves into tight twists which release had sent flying. Embarrassed, he gulped and fought for control. At least no one had heard him.

Keys. Taverik searched his father's pockets until he found the jailor's ring of keys. He tried each until his anklecuff flew open. Now to find Marita, he thought, then paused. He'd never get up the tower dressed like this. But if he could find one of Soza's uniforms, he could search with impunity—until Balanji's men found him, but he'd worry about that later. He'd bet his father had picked off the jailor—perhaps he could squeeze into that uniform. Taking up the sword, knives and the lantern, Taverik cat-footed into the silent passage.

Marita

Marita woke at daybreak to distant shouts. She listened, frowning, then rolled from the bed as the possible meaning of the commotion struck her. Had Balanji attacked at last?

Shoving the chair under the window, she pulled herself up into the opening. Now she could hear better, and she identified the noise as men fighting. But still she saw nothing but the serene vista downstream, lit gently golden by the rising sun—the same view she'd gotten her first morning there, when she'd watched Soza create his secret escape route.

Frustrated, she slid down and dressed quickly so she'd be ready for anything. But no one came. She paced, listened at the door, and paced again. The sun flooded her cell, irritatingly normal. No, not normal. She blinked at its arrow-straight rays. They looked cloudy. No, smoky. Something was burning.

She hauled herself back up into the window enclosure. Now she could see billows of black smoke drifting downstream. With it, tinging the edge of her thoughts, came the anger of the Black Eagle. The sound of the battle had changed slightly. What was Soza doing?

Keys jangled in the door. Idbca stalked in, looked at the empty bed, then up the wall to her. The corners of her mouth tightened. "Down," she said, locking the door behind herself. "You woman are, not boy."

Marita stayed, having found it best to disoblige Idbca whenever possible. "What's the smoke? What's happening?"

"Balanji Soza's right defies. They in courtyard battle."

"He got into the courtyard!" Marita exclaimed, and jumped down.

Idbca lifted her chin. "Not he out not get. Soza *mahiga* power uses now. He Balanji to ashes burns."

"Burn?" Marita took a step closer, her mind racing. "Is he using the *mahigas* in the jars in the basement?"

"Of course. Not you their heat not feel? Their power? Not your precious Zojikam not help him now." Idbca turned her back in contempt.

Marita leaped. She landed square on the narrow back, but the woman twisted like a cat. Her fingernails raked Marita's face. Marita caught her hand and dragged it away. She punched hard. Idbca's hand snaked into Marita's hair and pulled her close as Idbca kicked her in the knee. Swerving with the blow, Marita punched once more, in the stomach. This time Idbca folded together, gasping for breath.

Panting, Marita knocked her down and ripped off Idbca's silk belt. She'd tied her hands and feet tight before Idbca got her wind back. "Help!" she croaked. Marita clamped her hand over her mouth. Idbca jerked her head back and bit hard.

"Bitch!" Marita cried, but pressed tighter until she could use Idbca's linen handkerchief for a gag. She sat back, breathing hard and wiping her palm on her skirt. "Your key, now, Idbca, dear," she said, and went through Idbca's pockets while the woman squirmed and glared. She found a small set of keys and a knife as well, a sharp little thing tucked into Idbca's sleeve.

Leaving her kicking, Marita quietly opened the door. The room let onto a landing, with nothing but the stairs spiraling up and down. At the window facing the courtyard a guard leaned out so far only his butt and spindly legs showed. Great bursts of light flashed in the sunlight and with each explosion, Marita heard men screaming. She had to get to those jars.

The guard looked over his shoulder, then back to the battle. Belatedly he registered her identity. "Halt, you!" he demanded. He sprang forward, grabbing her. Marita replied with a slash of the knife. It caught his arm instead of his body as she'd intended. Damn! Two months ago she'd have had him. The guard caught her wrist and pulled her to him. "How'd you get out?" he said.

Footsteps pounded on the stairs as another man ran to assist. Marita's fingers curled gently around the guard's sleeve. Still respectful of a zoja, even an imprisoned one, he wasn't holding her very tight. Just as the second black-clad guard topped the stairs, she swung him around and pushed.

Caught off balance the guard staggered into the other man. "Stop her," he gasped.

"Stop her yourself," the other snapped and punched him in the jaw.

"Taverik!" Marita cried.

In the blinding light of another explosion, the guard staggered back from the blow, then pulled his sword. Taverik blocked the blow with a sword of his own. He handled it clumsily, obviously untrained. Marita looked around for another weapon. The stool in her room! She leaped over the struggling Idbca and snatched it up. She returned just as the guard knocked the sword from Taverik's hand. Sure of himself now, the guard advanced, his back to Marita. Taverik caught Marita's eyes, and leaped sideways. Marita used the stool with all her might.

The guard staggered. Before he could get his knees under him again, Taverik hit him. He fell and lay still.

Taverik straightened and looked at her. Marita felt a shock as she took in his appearance. He looked gaunt and exhausted, eyes dark circled. His upper lip was cut and swollen, and he wore a black uniform.

Many times during her imprisonment Marita had longed to be with Taverik again. Her imagination had created as many meetings as there were hours. But in no imagined scene had this uneasy constraint crept between them. Taverik was staring at her as if she were a stranger, and she could think of nothing to say.

He started to smile, then held his swollen mouth. "I was right," he said around his hand. "You do look good in a dress."

A flash split the air. "The jars!" Marita exclaimed. She seized the guard's feet and tried to drag him into the cell. "Hurry!"

"What jars?" he asked, lifting the limp man under the armpits and coming after her. "And who's she?"

"That's just Soza's first wife," Marita said, dropping the guard's feet and pulling his knife from his belt. "The jars are Soza's *mahiga* jars. He's got a circle of them in a room at the base of the tower. That's where the fire is coming from. We've got to smash them or Balanji won't make it."

He accepted that without question, efficiently tying the guard to the bed and joining her at the door. They met no one on the next landing down. On the next landing, which again had windows facing the courtyard, three men with crossbows leaned out. Over their shoulders Marita could see men lining the palace roof, directing a rain of arrows down into the bailey. Heart pounding, she crept past. Taverik came behind her.

She slipped safely around the curve of the stairs. "Who goes?" cried a strange voice. Blood draining from her face, she looked up. Taverik calmly lifted his hand, but kept moving. He started down toward her grimacing. Marita's scalp prickled but no further sounds came from above. She continued on, cursing her cumbersome skirts. As they approached the ground level, Taverik touched her elbow. She looked up.

"Careful. There are several of Soza's men there, and a lot of servants hiding. You are my prisoner. I'll escort you to whatever door you point out."

She nodded her understanding. He pulled out a ring of keys and assumed a fierce expression. "Just get us to the right door," he said. "Ready?"

"Ready." Marita bowed her head submissively and allowed Taverik to propel her around the final curve into full view of all. She felt sick and exposed.

Silence. Surprised, she gave a quick look from under her lashes. The room was crowded with palace servants, crouching together, cringing as each explosion of light filled the dim room. On the far side of the room ten soldiers hauled food, water and weapons from an opened trap door. Marita began to weave her way through the crowd, toward the door which led to the *mahiga* jars. The servants shifted to let them through. "Marita Vos," she heard. On either side, servants stood. The whispering grew to a murmur. "Marita Vos!"

"Stand back," Taverik said gruffly. He elbowed a man away and pushed Marita on.

Across the room a woman shouted, "You leave the zoja alone!" Voices cried agreement, and the murmur grew to a chant. "Marita Vos! Marita Vos!" The soldiers stopped hauling bags. "Quiet there!" one yelled. Marita reached the door and felt heat radiating from it. Taverik tried the knob, swore and snatched away his hand. "Marita, shut them up!" he said. "They'll bring Soza on us!"

The servants hemmed them close. Marita turned to them. "My friends," she began.

"Marita Vos!"

Marita raised her voice. "My friends! Listen!"

Taverik let go of her arm as he fumbled with the keys. Instantly, the man he'd elbowed ran forward, brandishing a knife. "To me, Marita Vos!"

"Stop it!" Marita screamed. She flung herself against Taverik, protecting him with her body. "He's a friend!" she shouted over her shoulder. "Listen, he's a friend!"

The servant drew back, bewildered. "He's Soza's man."

"He's not," Marita said low and urgently. "He's just dressed like that."

"What's going on here?" demanded one of the soldiers. He stood, hands on hips, on the pile of sacks, the better to see.

A guard skidded around the last curve of the stairs. "Stop those two!"

"Vos!" shouted a servant. "For Zojikam and Vos!"

The crowd seethed toward the soldiers, grabbing the weapons hauled from the storage room below. Metal rang against metal. Marita found she still gripped Taverik in a great bear hug. She released him.

"They love you," he said in a soft voice. An odd expression flickered across his face. Then he bent to the door and once more tried the keys. Marita pulled out her knife to guard his back. The servants, she saw, had actually managed to kill the soldiers who had been on the floor, and were now pursuing the others up the stairs. The servant who had tried to rescue Marita shouted above the din. "You all, stay here!" he said, flinging his arms wide. "The rest of you, to the palace! Marita Vos! Zojikam! Balanji!" With a roar, men and women took up the cry and swept away.

"Got it," Taverik said. He took the tattered black cloak from around his shoulders and wrapped his hands in it, then pushed open the door. A wave of heat washed over Marita. Flames licked the walls, shining off Taverik's tangled yellow hair and sweat-streamed face. "Zojikam, what *is* this?" he muttered.

Marita crowded past him, feeling resistance in her spirit as she did so. Shielding her eyes with her hand, and feeling the hair on her fingers shrivel, she saw the eight jars standing in the same semi-circle as before. Flames licked across the chair she'd sat in the night Soza had brought her there. From the jars rose a squealing protest that hurt her ears.

"We've got to smash them!" Marita shouted over the noise. She snatched Taverik's cloak from his hands. Holding it before her face, she approached the nearest jar. The heat burned her fingers right through the fabric, the air hurt her lungs. She grit her teeth and raised the jar high and hurled it to the pavement.

Instantly a raging scream tore the room. The force of it beat her to her knees, hands over her ears. A whirlwind whipped the flames into a spiral of fire and a spout of flames burst through the window and was gone.

Taverik took the cloak from her and approached the next jar, walking as if into a high wind. The noise increased in volume until it beat in Marita's head. With trembling, blistered fingers, Marita sliced through her skirt with her knife and staggered to her feet, wrapping the heavy fabric around her hands. They had to break them all.

Chapter 20

Balanji

Again and again Balanji scrambled to his feet only to be thrown down by another explosion. Around him, deep shouts turned to screams. Soza's men, as well as his own, writhed on the ground, burned by the blasts of fire. Soza didn't care who he hit.

Light flashed in Balanji's eyes. A fireball hurtled directly at him. "Zojikam!" he cried in despair. He'd never dreamed it would end like this. So easy for Soza. He dropped his sword and threw up his hands in a futile warding off of the blaze. The fire hit his palms. It split into a rain of sparks which sizzled and danced across the bloody cobbles. In amazement Balanji stared at his hands. They were blackened, and hurt, but otherwise he was unharmed.

The warning shouts of the men defending him brought him to. Another gout of flame had exploded from the roof. "Zojikam!" he shouted again, this time battle cry and prayer combined. Leaping deliberately under the next fireball, he again split it.

"Zojikam!" His men took up the chant. Heartened, they fell on the enemy, who still outnumbered them. A fireball hit the stable. Flames rose roaring, and above them, the terrified trumpeting of the animals within. The flames flared higher and higher, spreading to the roofs of the city.

Balanji left his sword and concentrated on deflecting the fire wherever he could. His men formed a tight guard around him, a core of determined fighters who steadily pushed back Soza's troops toward the palace. And always above them, the black-clad figure on the roof hurled fire. That small corner of Balanji's mind which always remained aloof wondered at himself. It didn't make sense, what he was doing. Not rationally. But then, neither were Soza's fireballs rational. Somehow he'd never thought Zojikam would interfere in such a way, and use *him* of all people to do so.

Was it his imagination, or were the flames weakening? Yes, yes, each burst of fire was smaller, fell shorter. Suddenly from above came a great cry of rage. Soza disappeared from the parapet. "For Zojikam!" Balanji's men shouted, and redoubled their efforts.

With the fireballs gone, someone handed Balanji a sword. He grabbed it and immediately dropped it, pressing together his agonized hands. Blackened and blistered, they hurt with a growing, stinging hurt. What had he done to himself? His men faltered, noticing his pain. Balanji thrust it aside and, surrounded by guards, guided them with his voice.

Slowly they pushed Soza's troops to the palace, but suddenly the black uniformed men surged forward again. Behind them came an army of servants, barring doors and windows, fighting with anything that they could grab. "Marita Vos!" they shouted, "Zojikam! Balanji!"

Squeezed unexpectedly, Soza's men panicked. Many tore off their uniforms and fell on their former comrades, shouting "Death to Bcacma!" A messenger pushed through to Balanji, shouting. "The gate, they're attacking the gate from the city!"

He'd expected it, and turned immediately to the new emergency. "Mamos!" he roared over the unbelievable din. His commander turned a black-streaked face to him. "Take as many men as you can to the wall. *Keep the turncoats away from the gate!*" He couldn't trust them. But so few men left!

It was past noon before Balanji felt he'd gained a semblance of control. All but thirty of Soza's men had died or surrendered. That thirty had massacred their way through the untrained army of servants, forcing entry into the tower. Barricaded there, they shot from the windows at anyone who approached. Balanji was pretty sure Soza was among them.

He drew back his men and counted them. A little more than fifty on their feet, including those defending the gates and those guarding the surrendered soldiers. In the palace, the servants apparently searched from room to room, a roar going up whenever they found a hiding enemy. They still shouted "Marita Vos, Zojikam, Balanji!" It grated suddenly that he was mentioned last—without him all this wouldn't have happened. He spun on his heel and strode through the rows of wounded men to the gate.

Mamos turned to meet him. "We've done it," the commander said wonderingly. "I can't believe it. But we couldn't have done it alone. Look, the citizens of the town have thrown up barriers. It's they who have kept Soza's men off the gate for us."

"Shouting 'Marita Vos, Zojikam?' " Balanji said dryly.

"And 'Balanji,' " said Mamos. "But the city burns."

But it did. Across the carnage of the plaza, flames

leaped from building to building. Balanji watched, shaking his head in sorrow. And being a just man, he had to admit that he couldn't have gotten this far without Zojikam, or without the citizens rallying to Marita Vos. He'd like to know what she'd been doing to make them so loyal.

Wind stirred the flames higher. Above the gate tower a flag flapped. Balanji glanced up and scowled. "Get Soza's flag down, Mamos. Put up ours."

He watched his flag rise into the smoke, wrap itself around the pole, then leap free like a bird. Brave scarlet snapped in the dark billows. The fortress was his! Moved suddenly past the point of self-consciousness, Balanji threw wide his arms. "Ah, Zojikam!" he shouted. "Preserve my poor beloved city!"

A rain drop fell. Another. From the serene blue sky, rain gushed like a bucket upended. Hissing and smoking, the fires died. Men stood in wonder, streaming faces turned upward.

Suddenly a nerve-shattering, inhuman scream went up from the tower. Again the scream—directly overhead. Balanji set his face against it, resisting the urge to fling himself flat. Mamos reeled against the wall, covering his ears. The keening wail faded gradually, reluctantly. When it was gone a great oppression lifted from Balanji's soul. The very air seemed easier to breath, and his thoughts came clearer. The Black Eagle was gone. Inside Balanji a great exaltation grew and struggled to find expression. He knelt where he stood on the parapet, in the midst of the downpour and the exaltation overflowed as the Thanksgiving Praise of the temple service. He shouted the words aloud, part of his life since childhood, yet never one with him until now. Not until he finished and looked up, did he realize that all his men had likewise knelt in the pouring rain and had chanted the passage aloud with him. He stood up, embarrassed. He was getting as emotional as Akusa. Then, with a queer shock, he remembered his grandfather, kneeling to give thanks before all his subjects, while a little boy looked on uncomfortably.

His rule would never again be the same.

Kintupaquat

Even as Soza's forces pushed his men back from that first breach of the wall, Kintupaquat aimed a new attack at the second weak spot, all the way across the city from the first. The defenders were slower to respond than Kintupaquat had anticipated. His men, breaching the wall by noon, soon discovered why. The citizens of Illiga, pressed into service to haul rocks and keep fires burning under tar pots, instead revolted. They built barricades in the streets and threw rocks at Soza's men as they passed. Soza's men killed as many as they could reach, but others took their places, hampering the movement of the army as much as they could.

With the breach, Kintupaquat steadied his men, curbing their impulse to rush into the city. He concentrated instead on building up their numbers inside the wall so that the advance, when it came, would be less vulnerable. But the build-up of men went agonizingly slow. The enemy had rallied and the fighting grew fierce around the breach. Kintupaquat lost his brave Pemintinuchi, who had led the rush.

They were losing ground. To keep that precious breach open he'd soon have no choice but to send in his reserves. He chewed his lip, glancing nervously toward the walls of the fortress where Soza's flag yet flew. Had Balanji failed? No matter. He turned to his aid. "Please request Commander Enas to send the reserves to the breach."

A roar of joy broke out around him. Kintupaquat whirled and looked where his men were pointing. There, above the fortress, Soza's flag had disappeared. As he watched, the scarlet flag of Illiga snapped open above the billowing smoke of the burning city. Kintupaquat shouted with his men. They would not fail now! "Forward!" he cried. "We'll meet Balanji at the gates of the fortress!"

Thunder cracked. Rain fell in a great gush from the blue sky. Kintupaquat gathered his men and hurled them on the city.

Soza

Soza threw back his head and laughed as Balanji fell once more. He enjoyed toying with the zoji, throwing fireballs just to the left or the right and seeing him jump. Now the time came to finish him, then to answer the call of the Black Eagle who wanted to absorb him and attack the army without the city wall. He drew back his hand—tomorrow it would be blistered beyond use, he knew—and hurled fire square at the zoji.

Balanji threw up his hands in a last futile gesture. Then, incredibly, the flames split and ran down each side of him and sizzled harmlessly across the cobbles.

"How—?" Soza started.

He threw another and the zoji once more deflected it. In a rage of frustration, Soza aimed at the stable roof and set it ablaze. Below, Balanji's men had begun to call Zojikam's name. The power of the Black Eagle began to weaken.

In fury, he hurled the largest fireball he could towards the knot of men around Balanji. It flew sluggishly, with nowhere near the strength it should have had. Balanji purposely leaped beneath it to deflect it. Soza threw again and again, and Balanji deflected them all. Some power was protecting him, and he in turn used it to protect his men.

Each fireball grew weaker. "Something's happening to the jars," he snarled as Abado rejoined him.

"Master, they have breached the wall again. They have men in."

Soza shouted in frustration and looked once more into the courtyard. His men were backing to the palace, pursued and cut down by Balanji's small band. A swarm of his men scrambled out onto the roof. Commander Ucherik ran to Soza and bowed low. "Zoji," he panted. "The servants have revolted and are trying to hold the palace."

"Servants!" Soza snarled. "You've let yourselves be beaten by *servants*?"

"Master," said Abado, hanging over the edge, "some

of our troops are pulling off their uniforms and fighting with Balanji."

Bad, bad, bad. "Rally as many men as you can," Soza ordered Commander Ucherik. "We'll fight our way to the tower—we can hold it indefinitely."

Ucherik nodded and ran off. Soza thought aloud as he followed him. "Once in the tower, I'll better control the jars. They'll help me win yet. And if not, I'll withdraw to Ormea and begin again."

Abado kept pace. "How, Master?"

"Does not the badger build a secret escape route?" Soza enjoyed the dawning admiration in Abado's face. "You, faithful one, may come with me."

The men Ucherik gathered formed a desperate cluster around Soza. Fighting for their lives, they easily mowed down any servants in their path and brought Soza safely to the tower. Rebellious servants controlled the tower as well. His men slaughtered them and barred the door.

Soza let Ucherik take over the tower's defense. He strode across the bloody floor to the room where the jars were kept.

The door was unlocked. Scowling, he entered and stopped dead. The Vos woman and one of his men straightened quickly and stared at him. No, not one of his men, it was Zandro, whom he'd ordered executed. Around their feet lay heaps of broken porcelain and only one remaining jar. They'd smashed them all.

Marita

It had been slow work, destroying the jars. Approaching each one seemed like heading into a gale wind. The jars weighed heavier than was natural, as if they willed themselves back to earth. And the heat, even through the layers of thick cloth, blistered Marita's palms and fingertips. She and Taverik had been forced to work together, moving in a dreamlike slowed motion, lifting together, hurling. The *mahigas* screamed and wailed and the room had darkened, but they'd pushed on until only one jar remained.

Then Soza entered. Marita stiffened, her fingers still touching Taverik's around the jar. Taverik looked over his shoulder then straightened, pulling her behind him.

Abado slid in, stared, then kicked shut the door. Soza started for them, flexing his fingers, then seemed to change his mind. Eyes blazing, he raised the claw talisman from his chest and began to chant.

The remaining jar broke into flames. Soza pointed from it to the floor. The flames obediently raced across the room, slowly rising into a wall of roaring fire. Marita gasped for breath—the heat hurt her lungs. Taverik backed away, pulling her to him to shield her from the heat. Just as the yellow curtain closed she saw Soza unlocking the small door that led to the cliffs.

With a jolt, she understood. "Taverik!" she yelled over the roar and crackle. "Taverik, he's escaping! He's got a rope over the cliff!"

His fingers tightened on her arms. Then he pushed her aside and started toward the wall of fire. "Taverik, no!" she cried and dragged him back.

"Fire," he shouted. "Flood, darkness and fire!" He broke her grip and leaped directly into the flames.

Crooking her arm over her face, she tried to follow, but the heat thrust her back. She kicked at the jar. It rocked but remained upright. Her underdress caught fire. Coughing, she beat it out. In desperation she seized the jar, ignoring the agony in her hands. She strained to lift it, then hurled it to the floor. The fire curtain dropped. Shards still spun crazily underfoot as she leaped for the door.

She burst out into the open, just as rain gushed. The force of it nearly buckled her knees. It fell from the blue sky, cold and soothing to her blistered face. She shielded her eyes and peered through the pelting wet.

On the very edge of the cliff, Taverik grappled with Soza. The servant circled, trying to get at Taverik's back. Shouts echoed from the windows of the tower above. An arrow struck the rock at Marita's feet and rebounded into the gulf beyond.

Gradually Soza maneuvered Taverik around until he was fully exposed to Abado's knife. An arrow hit the rocks at their feet with enough force to remain upright, quivering. Abado crept closer.

"Look out!" Marita shouted. Her warning went nowhere in the hissing roar of the rain.

Taverik tried to pull free but Soza held him. Abado's arm drew back.

Marita threw Idbca's knife. It struck Abado between the shoulders. With a cry of pain and frustration he fell. At the same moment, Taverik pushed. Soza stumbled backwards, heels over the cliff edge. He flailed his arms, catching at Taverik for balance. In awful silence, both disappeared over the edge.

The silence shattered. A wailing, keening cry shook Marita to the core. The Black Eagle! She cowered, trying to disappear inside herself as the *mahiga*'s enraged scream rose directly overhead. Then, amazingly, it faded and dispersed in the rain. *If the abode of a* mahiga *is broken, it will disperse.* Was Soza then dead?

Marita flung herself flat beside the unmoving Abado and peered over the cliff. Ten feet below, a ledge jutted from the cliff face, holding a rope ladder and several iron rings. It had caught the two men and they lay, tangled together as if embraced. Neither moved.

The rope! It lay coiled just beyond Abado's upturned hand. Marita scrambled over him and seized it, only dimly aware of movement above her. Something, a sledgehammer, perhaps, struck her in the shoulder and sent her sprawling. She had only enough thought to thrust out her hands in a desperate attempt to stop her skid towards the edge.

Balanji

As Balanji came down from the gates, a delegation of servants knelt before him, presenting their weapons. "Welcome back, My Zoji," said their spokesman, whom Balanji recognized as his stablemaster. "We missed you sore." He spoke broken Massadaran and wore his stable clothes, but his grim, fierce eyes reminded Balanji of pictures of Pakajan warriors of old.

"Thank you," he said thickly. He reached for the sword but couldn't take it because of his blistered, shaking hands. Motioning to Mamos to take it for him, he switched to Illigan Pakajan. "Without your brave loyalty, this day might have ended quite differently."

"We had always been true," said the stableman proudly—Pakajan to the core—"but especially when the Tet-zoja Marita Vos told us the truth about Soza and the Black Eagle. She told us to organize ourselves, in case you returned. Not bad for *mere* Pakajans."

Balanji noted the ironic stress on the word, mere. "Most worthy indeed," he said, and raised his voice for all to hear. "My loyal friends, without the help of Illiga's Pakajan subjects, I might not be here today. The time has come for Illiga to become one race. A new race, created of the best of Pakajan and the best of Massadaran."

A roaring cheer drowned out even the rain. Balanji felt a sudden qualm. No turning back now—come what may. He noted that many of his Massadaran soldiers, who worked side by side with Pakajans, also cheered. But some darkened and muttered to each other.

Balanji lost no more time but dispatched servants to search the palace from top to bottom. Others he set to tending the wounded, guarding prisoners, and cleaning up the stomach-turning butchery. He strengthened the guard on the gate. Kintupaquat, he knew, had breached the outside wall and routed the enemy, but it would be some time before old Ironbiter would finish cleaning out the city.

Now for the tower. Nikilo Vitujak picked his way toward him around the tangled bodies and bloody pools on the pavement. Seeing Vitujak by daylight for the first time in almost two weeks, Balanji was startled by how much gray had crept into the russet hair. Perhaps his own—tangled into dripping rattails at the moment—looked the same.

"Where's Soza?" said Vitujak.

"In the tower with about thirty men."

Vitujak frowned. "What's he planning?"

"We shall see, immediately," said Balanji. He motioned to his bodyguard and cautiously approached the tower. "Hail them, Commander Mamos."

Mamos stepped forward. "Hello the tower!" he bellowed.

A long silence. Mamos inhaled once more, but before he could repeat himself, a face appeared at a narrow slit window just above the roof line of the palace. "What do you want?" the man yelled in Vosa Pakajan.

"We speak only to Soza."

"He's not here. What do you want?"

"You can last in that tower only a short time," Mamos shouted. "We will slaughter you in the end. Surrender and deliver Soza and all other traitors into our hands."

The face disappeared. In the long wait that ensued, Balanji pressed his throbbing palms together. The pain was growing.

"Hello!" came the voice from the tower at last. It sounded desperate. "We can't find Soza. He's not anywhere."

"Who are you?" shouted Mamos.

"Commander Ucherik."

"Swear by your Black Eagle this isn't a trick."

"I will not swear by that *ikiji*," said the man proudly. "I will swear by Zojikam, we cannot find Soza, this is no trick."

"For one loyal to Zojikam," said Mamos, "you choose strange leadership."

"We were deceived."

"Stick to the subject, Mamos," said Balanji curtly. He looked at Vitujak. "Is he telling the truth?"

"Wait!" called Ucherik. Once more the pale face disappeared, then reappeared. His voice took on a harder edge. "We have the Tet-zoja Marita Vos."

"Oh great," muttered Vitujak.

"We will deliver her to you safe if you'll spare our lives."

"Mamos," warned Balanji softly. "Nothing without Soza."

"Deliver Soza, all other traitors *and* Marita Vos to us, and we will spare your lives."

"How do we know you won't kill us?"

"You have our word, and no other choice."

The window darkened for many minutes, then, "We've found Soza, and the others," called Ucherik. "We're coming out. Remember your promise."

"Leave your weapons behind," Mamos shouted. "Come out one by one. The first ones out, bring the traitors and Vos."

"Good, Mamos," Balanji said. "Prepare your men to receive them. Ah, best guard them from the servants. Watch out for arrows still."

The first man to appear at the tower door looked hesitantly out upon the armed men surrounding the door, then stepped forth, hands raised. Commander Ucherik, thought Balanji, noting his uniform. Behind the commander came two men bearing a body between them, a body dressed in splendid black. Vitujak drew in his breath. "That's Soza," he said. "Did they murder him?"

"Not by the look of his neck," said Balanji. "It's broken." Mamos pointed to the cobbled pavement and the two men laid the inert form there, and allowed themselves to be marched away. Next came a burly man carrying a limp and bloody Marita Vos in his arms. Mamos gestured to one of his men, who took her and carried her directly to the palace. The next man easily carried over his shoulder the little wizened pawnbroker who had attacked Balanji in Novato. The body was dumped unceremoniously beside Soza's. Beside it soon lay Donato Zandro and Viti Malenga. A line up of traitors indeed, Balanji thought. He squinted at the next body, carried by two large Pakajans. One of Soza's men by the black uniform. Who?

Not until the inert form was laid beside Malenga did he recognize him. Taverik Zandro. For a horrified moment he wondered if Zandro had indeed been a traitor. Then reason asserted itself, just as Vitujak started forward. Balanji grabbed Vitujak's sleeve and hung on, though it cruelly hurt his hands. "Wait. Don't give them any more hostages."

Not until all the men surrendered and had been marched away did Balanji release Vitujak. He himself strode forward, staring down at Soza, the Agash Itzil Farasoza, scarcely daring to believe his enemy lay dead at his feet. He looked up as Mamos rejoined him. "This victory indeed belongs to Zojikam, Commander," he said. "We were but tools. Cut off his head and impale it at the gate."

As Mamos gave the order, Balanji crossed to where Vitujak knelt beside his nephew. "He lives?"

"Zojikam! Yes," said Vitujak, his soul shining in his eyes. "Concussion, and I suspect a broken collar bone. And his hands are burned."

"We'll have a doctor soon," said Balanji. He pressed his own shaking hands together and the world rippled.

"You need a doctor, yourself," said Vitujak, springing up to grasp him tight under the elbow.

Balanji pushed him away. "Find one. I can't stop yet. Mamos!"

"Zoji?"

"Take those two," he pointed to Malenga and the pawnbroker. "Hang them from the walls of the fortress."

Mamos pointed to the pawnbroker. "Zoji, this one still lives."

"Hang him."

"Yes, Zoji." Mamos nudged the elder Zandro's body. "What about him?"

"Bury him."

"Bury him!" Mamos looked shocked. "But Zoji, they say this is the traitor."

Balanji gave Mamos a level stare to remind him of his place. "His debt," he said, "is paid."

Chapter 21

Marita

Fever mounted from the jagged wound. Marita grew confused. Her shoulder hurt and the worried faces of Sahra and Bibi hovered over her—but hadn't the attack on the caravan occurred months ago? Had everything in between been a fever dream?

Taverik wasn't there. In the dream, he'd been with her, a watchful guardian against the blackness. But though she called and called, he never came. And the blackness itself had rolled back and bothered her no more. She should have been glad, she dimly knew, but she wasn't. The world tasted flat and she didn't want to wake.

But wake she did, the next morning, fever barely lingering. She'd been struck by a spent arrow, but the wound was glancing rather than deep. Though it hurt well enough. Thick bandages immobilized her hands.

Sahra smiled down at her and Bibi beamed from the foot of the bed. "You're better," Sahra said. "I'm so relieved."

"Tell me what happened," demanded Marita. "Start at the beginning."

"Well, when Taverik came back without you, I wouldn't believe it at first." The mattress sank as her sister sat beside her. Sahra talked on and on, Marita listening hungrily, until Bibi cleared her throat. Sahra laughed and hurriedly finished. "They're already singing about Balanji's victory. And I've heard three different songs about that rainstorm. And songs about *you*, Marita. Whatever were you doing?"

Marita fingered her bandage, wondering where to start. Instead she said, "Where's Taverik?"

Sahra looked confused and exchanged a quick glance with Bibi. "You need to eat," she said quickly. "We'll talk more later."

"Is he dead?" Marita squeaked.

Sahra hesitated. "No. I'll ring for food." And with that Marita was forced to be content.

The third morning she woke early, feeling much better. For the first time it came home to her: she had stood up to Soza, to her nightmare—and lived. She'd won! After years of fear-filled running and hiding, at last she was free. And without Taverik it wouldn't have happened. Why wouldn't they let her see him, or even tell her about him? *Was* he dead?

She'd find out for herself. Sliding shakily from her bed, she began to dress, wincing as she strained her shoulder. The activity woke the pain in her bandaged hands. Two attendants found her leaning against the carved bedpost, panting as she tied her shoes. They put up such a dither she became cross. "Out!" she demanded, pushing away their hands. And when they demurred, she raised her voice. "Get out!"

They backed away, faces reflecting both fear and disapproval. The old sensation of being trapped swept over Marita. "Go on, you heard me!" she snapped.

They gave up and left with dignity, curtseying as they passed, to someone at the door. "Bullying you, are they?" said the priest. "Will you banish me, too?"

Their eyes met in the special understanding they shared since the banquet when both had defied Soza. In the priest's eyes now shone a peaceful clarity instead of the tortured self-hatred of before. Released from his cell, he'd quickly made himself useful among the wounded, and Marita could remember his face in her fevered dreams. The blessed water he brought was the only thing that soothed the burns on her hands.

She sank into a straight chair and tried to unwrap her left hand. "Give me a straight answer," she said. "Is Taverik Zandro alive or dead, and why won't they tell me?"

The priest put down the bottle and helped her. "Since you and I seem to have practice at defying zojis, I will tell you that is was Zoji Balanji's strict orders not to say a word to you about Taverik Zandro until he has had a chance to talk to you himself."

She went cold. "He's dead then."

"No, not dead. In bed these days with a concussion, broken collarbone and hands burned like yours."

The blessed water trickled coolly across her throbbing palms. Marita closed her eyes with the relief. The priest examined her hands. "I believe we can leave the bandage off now," he said. "The blisters are gone. I have, however, done a little research along with Kali Vitujak (an excellent man), and we both suspect that your hands will feel pain off and on for the rest of your life."

"Why?" Marita asked, startled.

"Such is the nature of *mahiga* fire. It seems the blessed water is the only thing that will ease the pain. But," the priest added earnestly, "you may bear the burden as a reminder of your courage."

She laughed wryly. "Say rather, as a reminder from Zojikam of who is in charge. Tell me now what has happened."

"Balanji and Marshal Kintupaquat have cleaned up Illiga, scoured the countryside and gotten many of Soza's men fleeing to Ormea. Kintupaquat has taken the army to Ormea, but we have not yet heard the outcome."

He leaned forward and put a medallion in her lap. Marita knew it even before she picked it up—an identical medallion lay in the bottom of her father's strong box. The falcon of the Vos family flashed under her fingers. She looked at the priest inquiringly.

"The delegation from Vosa has arrived," he said. "They have been talking with your younger sister, and they have asked for you. They gave me this to give to you."

"I won't see them," Marita said. "They scorned my father for marrying my mother, a Pakajan and a merchant. Well, I am half Pakajan and a merchant to boot. Will they take me now?"

"You'll find that times have changed. For good or for bad, who knows? But changed. Irrevocably."

"I don't want to be embroiled in the sneaky machinations of politics," she said, nettled at his disagreeing with her. "All I want to do is live my life simply and quietly."

"The world is not simple nor quiet," he said. "I also am confused and repelled by political maneuvering. But I love Zojikam deeply. And just as you once urged me to face the enemy bravely, now I'm urging you. The people love Marita Vos. To them, she stands for more than you can know. They chant her name as often as Balanji's and Zojikam's. *She* was the one that inspired Illiga to fight against Soza, and without that, Balanji might not have carried the day. Even now, a crowd stands outside the fortress, calling for her."

She bent her head under the weight of his words. She wanted to shut him up but knew she couldn't. Not after her loud-voiced scorn of his own cowardice.

"Ormea is without a leader," the priest went on gently. "Vosa has but you and your sister left of the old order which has been turned on its ear. You represent the blend of old and new."

Marita turned the medallion over and read the motto under the coat of arms: I keep my own. She stilled. Just what did that mean to the people of Vosa?

What did it mean to her?

"But—Balanji?" she asked.

"Balanji will no doubt now rule both Ormea and Vosa, uniting the Giss Valley. And Zojikam knows, considering the current emergency, we have need of united leadership. But meanwhile it is Marita Vos who gives the people courage."

"What current emergency?" she said. "Soza's dead."

"Bcacmat ships attacked Novato. Last we heard, the city was beginning to fall. It may be in Bcacmat hands even now."

Marita's stomach tightened. If she had stayed in Novato—but Zojikam had seen to it she hadn't. He'd gotten her out of Illiga just in time, then pried her out of the seeming safety of Novato just in time. Even though it always seemed to mean facing her worst fears. And now? "It's easy to look back," she said thoughtfully, "and know that Zojikam worked everything out. Hard to apply the knowledge to the future."

The priest sighed agreement. "Vita," he said, giving her a sympathetic look, "you are tired now. Won't you return to your bed?"

"No, now I will see Taverik," she said, rising.

He laughed ruefully. "In that case, you must see Zoji Balanji first."

"My cousin," Balanji said, rising to meet her. "I am glad to see you so well. But perhaps," he added, searching her face, "it is too soon. Please take this chair."

"I am not tired," she said, though she was. She took the chair gratefully however, and studied him as he dismissed the servants with a bandaged hand. The last she'd seen him had been in the tunnel, the night she'd been captured by Soza. He'd looked grim and determined then, his face darkened by an unshaved shadow, dressed in worn and mended black. His eyes, however, had been sparkling alive. They still were. But now, he was bathed and barbered, and he wore a surcoat of red edged with silver.

His hands lay bandaged on the arms of his chair, and Marita remembered that he also had handled *mahiga* fire. Would he also feel pain for the rest of his life—pain which only Zojikam's blessed water would ease? Hard to think of a zoji's independence curbed in such a way. What would it mean for him?

He'd been studying her as well. "You make a handsome woman, cousin. Last time we talked, you were a fierce young man. In Novato, I had no idea of who it was, kneeling before me to swear fealty."

Now why had he brought that up first thing? Wary, Marita sidestepped. "Why have you denied me news of Taverik? Why won't you let me see him?"

"You are blunt," he said. "I also will be blunt. You,

Marita Vos, and your sister, are a problem. I do not know what to do with you." He examined her broodingly. "You are zojas by birth, yet your father was disinherited. You are now much beloved by two cities, one of which is leaderless. Yet you have not been brought up to rule, and wouldn't, I suspect, enjoy it."

This last might be true, but she wasn't willing to admit it. She remained silent, watching him.

"I owe you much," he said, almost to himself, "in restoring my city to me. Do I owe you a city in return? I think not. For, Marita Vos, I will tell you frankly, it is time the Peninsula was united. It *must* be, to face the threat of Bcacma's attack. You have heard?"

He paused so long she had to answer. "Yes, I have heard. And you are the man to unite the Peninsula?"

His answer surprised her: "If Zojikam allows it. You know better than most that this war has more at stake than mere physical land and rule." He lifted his bandaged hands and looked at them, then allowed them to drop.

"You have not yet told me why you've denied me news of Taverik Zandro or let me see him. You owe him much more."

"I will begin my answer by asking you this: why do you refuse to see the committee from Vosa?"

Marita shifted with impatience. "I do not wish to talk with the men who disinherited my father," she said curtly.

"They did not disinherit him," Balanji said. "Those who did are now dead. They are merely citizens of Vosa, leaderless with war close, looking for direction. You are their last link with the old, their bridge to the future."

There it was again, a reminder of obligations she did not want. If she'd been a mule she'd have put down her head and bucked. As it was, she sat still and expressionless as Balanji leaned forward. "Marita Vos, I want to do right by you. I want to do right by Zojikam. And, I want to do right by the Peninsula. Vosa wants you or your sister to rule them, for you are one of their own.

However, they want my protection, and are willing to swear fealty to me, providing you give sanction."

"*I* give sanction!" she said. She gaped at Balanji, absorbing the ramifications.

"You yourself, have sworn fealty to me," Balanji said mildly. "But considering the circumstances, I will not hold you to that unless you request it."

She stumbled from her chair to the window, staring over the roofs of the town. She didn't want to rule, yet presented with opportunity to do so, what should she do? Zojikam help her. She'd said so often that all she wanted was a quiet safe life. Did she mean that? If she passed up the opportunity would she regret it the rest of her life? She found herself fingering the medallion with its hawk and motto, turning it over and over in her pocket.

She turned from the window. "How does all this answer my question?"

"I cannot be everywhere. Vosa needs a governor, who would report directly to me. The committee has asked for you. We have already discussed possible husbands for you, men I trust and who have been raised to govern."

"You have discussed this with the committee without my knowledge!"

"They came, after all, for a wedding, cousin. Would you like to hear some of the men we have suggested? Perhaps whoever you choose can take your name, though I would prefer you to take his and allow the Vos name to rest."

In high anger, Marita paced to the window and back. Manipulated at every turn, was this what awaited her? Fah, the whole business was disgusting.

Balanji watched her sympathetically, and this she hated too. "Perhaps," he said, "this was sprung on you too soon. Would you like time to think it over? I can give you that time. You don't have to decide on a husband today, though I do wish to consolidate our grip on Vosa before facing whatever Bcacma provides for us in Novato and—"

"I am engaged," she interrupted.

"Soza is dead."

"I don't mean Soza," she said. "I am engaged to Taverik Zandro. He asked me to marry him, and I accepted."

"He, ah, withdraws his request."

"What!"

Even zojis could look sheepish. "Once I knew you were a woman," he said, "I began to suspect what might be between you and young Zandro. When he was awake enough for visitors, I sat beside his bed to chat. He confessed he'd asked you to marry him. He agreed quite readily to call off the engagement."

"So that is why you separated us," she cried. "How dare you!"

"My dear cousin," Balanji said, "I want to give you both the best start I can. You made this engagement before your identity was discovered, when you had no other future. Now you have wide horizons. You don't want those horizons curtailed, do you, by a regretted engagement you are too proud to back out of? Zandro has relinquished any hold on you, and I have separated you so you may remain free of embarrassment. Cousin, do you realize you may look anywhere in the Peninsula and in much of Massadara for a husband? Do not, I beg, for the sake of sentiment, throw this away."

"You owe your throne to Taverik Zandro. Is this how you reward him?"

Balanji bowed his head. "Without Illiga's citizens, and specifically that young man, I would not be here today. I'd probably be dead, in fact. I'm much impressed with him, and will reward him, and see to it he will go far. I envision a world where he may indeed go far. I wish to abolish the *Sadra* Laws. Pakajans will have access to all that was once limited to Massadarans. I intend to open the university to them. I will form a city council composed of the worthy kalis of the city. We need to become a new people, not Massadaran and Pakajan, but something united beyond."

"That's wonderful!" Marita cried impulsively. "May Zojikam bless it!"

"Bless it?" Balanji snorted. "I suspect he led me to

it with a ring in my nose. But it will not come without conflict. Massadarans will fight it. I am leading my city into great turmoil with only a vision and a hope it will succeed."

"And you see Taverik there, but not married to me?"

"My dear, you may look anywhere for a husband. Taverik Zandro has no training, no experience. He is of not impeccable background."

"You didn't scorn that background when he risked his life for you. And my background, I remind you, is not exactly impeccable." Even as Marita spoke certain matters became clear to her. The muddy remainders would take care of themselves. "Zoji Balanji," she said, "you must let me see Taverik Zandro. If to me he will still relinquish his engagement, then I will allow you to choose me a husband from the horsemarket. Otherwise I will marry Taverik Zandro."

Balanji started to thump his bandaged fist then thought better of it. "Soza didn't know what he was getting into with you, woman!" he cried. He glared at her, then suddenly laughed. "All right then, I will tell you something I must demand you keep private for a while. I am divulging it only because I don't want you thinking you had anything to do with the decision.

"Since Soza devastated my viti, whole estates are going to ruin. My court is practically empty. I suspect the same will be true of Ormea and Vosa. I need to fill these places. Among the new viti will be many deserving Pakajans—including Kintupaquat, Vitujak and ah, Zandro."

Marita gaped then recovered. "Will Massadara let—?"

Balanji shrugged. "Massadara has paid less and less attention to us lately because of Bcacmat pressures all along its border. But indeed they might not allow it. Further, these Pakajans will face lifetimes of hot prejudice from Massadarans here. They are more to be pitied, perhaps, than congratulated. One more reason for you to look elsewhere for a husband."

"No," Marita said, more and more sure. "My lot is cast with the Pakajans for better or for worse."

"I won't concede that yet. By the way, I had intended to meddle—make Vitujak's grant depend upon his adopting Zandro as his legal son. However I have seen an attraction between Vitujak and your sister, and it is unfair to rob their issue of the inheritance. Do I shock you?"

"No," Marita said. "And if you forbid a match between the younger Vos and Vitujak, how can you forbid it between the older Vos and Vitujak's nephew?"

"My cousin, have you considered the ramifications?"

She smiled wryly. "My sister becomes my aunt?"

Balanji laughed. "There are more complicated genealogies than that, believe me. No, the ramification is this. I will have no viti that has not sworn fealty to me."

Marita looked inside herself. If she passed up the opportunity to govern Vosa would she one day regret it? Perhaps. And if she proudly insisted on her "right" no doubt she would regret that too.

"I will marry Taverik Zandro," she said.

He sighed and stood up, offering his hand to help her to her feet. "I warn you," he said. "You will not find it easy to gain your will. Zandro is very conscious of the difference in your backgrounds. I did not have to persuade him to relinquish the engagement—he did it willingly. But you are exhausted now, you are up too soon. Won't you return to bed and rest?"

She *was* exhausted. But if she delayed, something very important to her might slip through her fingers and be gone forever.

Balanji read her expression. "You'll find Zandro through that door to your left," he said.

Chapter 22

Marita

The door led her to the long balcony along the sunny south of the palace. She passed quietly through the rhythmic shadows of the pillars and didn't see Taverik until she was almost upon him.

He stood, one arm in a sling, the other propped against a pillar, gazing off across the river valley. The clear sun spilled over his taut, wide-cheekboned face and Marita suddenly knew what he'd look like when he was old. Her heart tightened. Had the laughter in his eyes been extinguished forever?

He became conscious of her presence, gave her a glance, then suddenly looked again. His face lit up. "Did I tell you you look handsome in a dress?"

"You did," she said, coming to stand beside him.

"Yes, I vaguely remember. Got a good bang on the head," he explained. "Knocked some sense into it, though."

"What do you mean?"

"I mean, it was foolishness for me to ask you to marry me. I knew that the moment I found out who you are. I'm setting you free, Marita Vos, to become all you could be."

"What if I don't want to be set free?"

A little V appeared between his eyes. "Best for you."

"How do you know? Without you, I might have died, or been absorbed into Illiga's slums. Then no one, including me, would have known who I was anyway. Listen, Taverik, I wasn't raised to be a vita. I am a middle-class Pakajan merchant. The only thing I'm proud of is that I managed to support myself and my sister and my servant—as a merchant. And without you I couldn't have."

He shook his head, and her anger sparked. "Listen, damn you!"

"Watch your tongue, Zoja," he said in mock disapproval.

"I'm in a cage!" she exploded, then lowered her voice. "It is unladylike to press love on a man, but remember, I lived three years as a man. I'm going to fight for what I want. You made me admit at last I loved you and couldn't live happily without you. Are you going to abandon me now?"

"But you have so much more." His eyes suddenly widened. "Mari, you're turning green. You better sit, look here's a bench."

He put his good arm around her, and Marita, who hadn't been feeling bad at all, leaned into it willingly and allowed him to escort her to the bench. From the way he sat, she suspected it was welcome to him, too, and he forgot to remove his arm afterwards. "Balanji is against our marrying," he said. "And are you proposing to relinquish Vosa?"

"I never had Vosa, and never will. I would be given a husband picked out by a committee, and he would rule Vosa. As for Balanji, I did not escape Soza to be hounded by another zoji."

"I have nothing to give you. What would people say?"

"That by your own hands and integrity you became a great man."

"Ha," he said flatly and turned away. "Think realistically. Balanji will give me a monetary reward, and send me off. He's even asked me to leave the palace—tonight I go to Uncle Nik's to finish recuperating."

Her arms tightened. "That's just another way of separating us. Listen, Taverik, do you love me? Tell the truth, not what you ought to say."

He made a sound, half groan, half exasperation, then pulled her close and kissed her hard. She responded warmly and it was some time before Taverik spoke again, his voice a rumble above her head. "I seem to have spent my entire life on the wrong side of authority," he said. "Must have been practice for this. But my love, I don't want to come to you empty-handed. Will you allow me time to make something of myself, to be able to offer you something to live on?"

Marita clamped her lips tight on her exultant answer. Balanji was right to demand silence—Taverik must never think he won his title because of her. "All right," she said calmly. "I will fend off all suitors until you come for me. But, oh, make sure you come!"

His answer made it slightly hard for her to breathe.

LIST OF CHARACTERS AND GLOSSARY

Key: P = Pakajan, M = Massadaran, B = Bcacmat, U = Unknown, II = Characters First Appearing in Part II

Abado—a pawnbroker, among other, less honest, occupations (U)
Achicha—a smuggling crony of Skaj (P,II)
Agash Itzil Farasoza—a Bcacmat general under the old Tlath, but who disappeared when the new Tlath ascended the throne of Bcacma (B)
Akusa Ormea—Zoja of Ormea (M)
Alka—one of Skaj's two daughters (P,II)

Balanji—Zoji of Illiga (M)
Barsatta—one of Balanji's bodyguards (M,II)
Bibi—Marko's servant (P)
Boy—Skaj's younger son (P,II)

Chado Zandro—Taverik's brother (P)
Chisokachi, Gunnar—a young Textile Guildsman (P)

Dervi—a viti at the court in Illiga (M)
Donato Zandro—Taverik Zandro's father (P)
Dula Familo—unmarried daughter of Familo (M)

Echin—a young Textile Guildsman (P)
Efila—a physician (M)
Ela—Zoja of Illiga, Balanji's wife (M)

Familo—a clinging, poor relation of Malenga (M)
Familo, Dula—Unmarried daughter of Familo (M)
Farasoza, Agash Itzil—see Agash Itzil Farasoza
Ferco Ormea—Akusa's son, heir to Ormea (M)
Frez—Taverik's ornery mule, named after Frez Ittato
Frez Ittato—see Ittato

Gentle Philosopher—the pen name of an author who writes poetry and philosophic essays, and who engages in anonymous literary debate with the Humble Kali (U)
Gunnar Chisokachi—a young Textile Guildsman (P)

Humble Kali—the pen name chosen by Sahra Kasta for her poetry and essays (U)

Idbca—wife of the Agash Itzil Farasoza (B,II)
Ikatabalcha—the priest of Ervyn (P,II)
Ironbiter—Nickname for Marshal Kintupaquat, a literal rendition of his name from the Pakajan language (P)
Ittato, Frez—president of the Textile Guild (P)

Kaja—Skaj's wife (P,II)
Karaz—a foreign student at the University at Illiga (U)
Kastazi, Marko—see Marko
Kastazi, Oma—see Oma
Kintupaquat, Yuot—Marshal of Illiga (P)
Kishstash—a member of the Copper Guild (P)

Little Skaj—Skaj's oldest son (P,II)

Malenga—a proud, discontented viti at court in Illiga (M)
Mamos—Commander in the Illigan Army (M,II)
Mano—short for Manokichit
Manokichit—Nikilo Vitujak's man of all work (P)
Marita Kastazi—a daughter of a prosperous Vosazi merchant (U)

Marko Kastazi—a young, struggling merchant, befriended by Taverik (U)

Nalama—a viti at the court in Illiga
Namina, Ali—the name Marko Kastazi assumes in Novato (II)
Namina, Sahra—the name Oma Kastazi assumes in Novato (II)
Nikilo Vitujak—Taverik's uncle, secretary to Zoji Balanji (P)

Oblatta—Zoji of Novato (M,II)
Oma Kastazi—Marko's younger sister (U)
Ot—Marita's father's stableman (P)
Ouasi—one of the Widow Pardi's friends (P)

Pardi—Nikilo Vitujak's housekeeper, a widow (P)
Pemintinuchi—a captain in the Illigan army (P,II)

Rinatto—one of Balanji's bodyguards (M,II)

Sahra Kasta—a daughter of a prosperous Vosa merchant (U)
Sanisman, Amaro—Textile Guild member (M)
Skaj—a smuggler who helps Taverik (P,II)
Soza—Former marshal of Vosa who took over Vosa in a bloody coup, and who is bent on expanding his territory still farther (U)

Taverik Zandro—a young merchant of Illiga (P)
Tazur—Pakajan for hawk, the name Taverik travels under
Tlath, The—the ruler of Bcacma (B)
Tlele—a servant of the Agash Itzil Farasoza (B)
Tsaksil—wesh-agash (second-in-command) in the Bcacmat army (B,II)

Uali—the son of the Zandro stableman (P)
Ucherik—a Pakajan mercenary, originally from Vosa (P,II)
Ulmo—an older, conservative Textile Guildsman (P)

Vitujak—see Nikilo Vitujak
Vos—The name of the ruling dynasty of Vosa (M)

Whitey—Marko's sturdy old mule

Zandro, Chado—see Chado
Zandro, Donato—see Donato
Zandro, Taverik—see Taverik
Zilvrik—a servant at the palace in Illiga (P,II)
Zojikam—Creator God

GEOGRAPHICAL TERMS

Ao River—joins the Giss River at Illiga. Navigable only to the Illiga Bridge
Bcacma—(PKAK-mah) a country east of the Sarian Sea, warlike and aggressive
Dark Lady—one of two high mountains east of Illiga, beloved by the people
Ervyn—the village on the east slopes of the Giss Valley, one day's journey from Illiga
Giss Valley—the broad, fertile rift valley of the Giss River
Giss River—important river which travels from the mines in the north, down almost the length of the Peninsula. Important trade/travel route.
Great Ocean—the ocean to the west of the Pakajan Peninsula
Illiga—(ILL-lee-gah) a city in the Giss Valley of the Pakajan Peninsula. Situated at the junction of the Giss and Ao rivers, and on the northern trade route, it is a growing, bustling, merchant city.

Massadara—(mah-SAH-dah-rah) the powerful and imperialistic country to the south of the Pakajan Peninsula

Novato—(no-VAH-toh) coastal city to the east of Illiga

Pakajan Peninsula—(pah-KAH-jahn) the narrow, extremely mountainous jut of land cutting off the Sarian Sea from the Great Ocean. Once inhabited by the clans of the Pakajan peoples, it has since been colonized by Massadaran outposts. The Pakajans have either been subjugated, driven into the mountains, or north to mountainous, inhospitable lands.

Pale Lady—one of two very high mountains above Illiga, beloved by the people

Perijo—(per-EE-joh) coastal city to the west of Illiga

River Road—the important road crossing Illiga from river bridge to river bridge, and passing through the Great Square

Sarian Sea—the inland sea cut off from the Great Ocean by the Pakajan Peninsula

Vosa—coastal city southwest of Illiga, at the mouth of the Giss River

Yassa—small city in the far north of the Pakajan Peninsula

FOREIGN TERMS

Key: M = Massadaran, B = Bcacmat, all other terms are from the Pakajan language

Agash—the highest rank in the Bcacmat army (B)

Ihiga—(ee-HEE-gah) spiritual beings, the servants of Zojikam

Ikiji—(ee-KEE-jee) lit. "one settles for less." A derogatory Pakajan merchants' term for foolish buyers, or for those who allow themselves to be cheated. Also, anything second best. Also used of those who turn from the Creator, Zojikam, to worship things Zojikam created.

Kali/kala—Mister, Mrs., ma'am, sir, etc.
Kam—high, great, most important. A suffix affixed to Pakajan nouns.

Hama—the dress worn in hot Massadara: short tunics over leggings or knit hose. It is becoming a fad among the viti in Illiga, though unsuited for the cold climate of the Giss Valley. (M)

Lita—a small Illigan coin. Ten make one pelli. (M)

Mahiga—(ma-HEE-gah) spiritual beings who hate Zojikam

Pakajans—a race of people who dwelt in the Peninsula before the Massadaran trading colonies took over
Pelli—a Illigan coin. Middle-range money. (M)

Rizi—lit. "interloper." A Pakajan term for the Massadaran colonists.

Sadra Laws—the laws designed to keep the Pakajans and the lower classes in their place (M)

Tazur—hawk
Tet—little, younger, less important, again a Pakajan prefix
Tet-zoji, tet-zoja—children of a zoji
Tlath, The—the ruler of Bcacma (B)

Vidlas—a big Illigan coin (M)
Vidyen—round stone buildings with conical roofs of either rush or slate favored by the Pakajans. Many vidyens are large, composed of several connecting rounds built over the years. Each round has a center chimney

and a center hearth which the Massadarans find very quaint, but barbaric.

Viti/vita—male/female nobility. Viti refers to them collectively.

Wesh-agash—the next rank from Agash (B)

Zoji/Zoja—male/female royalty

Zojikam—the Creator God, from the Pakajan roots, *zoji*, lord; and *kam*, highest thus literally, "Highest Lord." Worshipped throughout the world, but in late years, knowledge of Zojikam is fading, and idolatry has crept in.

SOME NOTES ON THE LANGUAGES IN HAWK'S FLIGHT

During the period represented in *Hawk's Flight*, pure Pakajan is spoken mostly by country people and stubborn nationalists, and among the Pakajan tribes who fled north. Everywhere else, Pakajan has been modified by Massadaran, with varying regional accents. These accents are usually identified by the city state which controls the area where the accent developed. For example, Taverik Zandro speaks Illigan Pakajan.

Pakajan priests teach pure Pakajan, of course, and there is a growing Pakajan nationalistic movement which insists on it. Nikilo Vitujak writes poetry in both Massadaran and Pakajan.

Throughout the Pakajan Peninsula, pure Massadaran has been modified by contact with Pakajan. Young Massadarans in these colonial outposts often learn both languages, and salt their Massadaran with convenient Pakajan words and grammatical patterns. Needless to say, their accents are ridiculed by true Massadarans. Young viti sent to Massadara to gain polish find themselves ridiculed until the accent is knocked out of them. As soon as they return, the accent creeps right back. Old-school Massadarans despair at curbing the growing influence of Pakajan, which they view as barbaric.

Coming from a separate language family, the Bcacmat language uses quite a different word order than either Pakajan or Massadaran. Instead of Subject-Verb-Object, the basic order is Subject-Object-Verb. Adjectives and adverbs come behind the word they describe. Bcacmat also uses double negatives and double question words.

Bcacmat has several consonant clusters not found in Massadaran or Pakajan:

Bc, is formed at the front and the back of the mouth simultaneously. It is the sound a hen makes—Bk, Bk, Bk, Bkdawkit!

Ts is a sibilant formed by pronouncing S with the tongue starting right behind the upper teeth.

Tl is pronounced by saying T and L at the same time.

FRED SABERHAGEN

Fred Saberhagen needs very little introduction these days. His most famous creations—the awesome Berserkers—are known to SF readers around the world. He's reached the bestseller lists several times, most recently with his "Book of Swords" series, and his novels span the territory from hard science fiction to high fantasy. Quite understandably, Saberhagen's been labeled one of the best writers in the business.

These fine volumes by Saberhagen are available from Baen Books:

PYRAMIDS
A fascinating new twist on the time-travel novel, introducing a great new series hero: Pilgrim, the Flying Dutchman of Time, whose only hope for returning home lies in subtly altering the history of our own timeline to more closely reflect his own. Learn why the curse of the Pharaoh Khufu (builder of the Great Pyramid) had a special reality, in *Pyramids*. "Saberhagen's light, imaginative and enjoyable adventures speed along twisting paths to a climax that is even more surprising than the rest of the book."

—*Publishers Weekly*

AFTER THE FACT
This is the second novel featuring the great new series hero, Pilgrim—the Lost Traveller adrift in time and dimensionality. His current project: to rescue Abraham Lincoln from assassination, AFTER THE FACT!

THE FRANKENSTEIN PAPERS

At last—the truth about a sinister Dr. Frankenstein and his monster with a heart of gold, based on a history written by the monster himself! Find out what happened when the mad Doctor brought his creation to life, and why the monster has no scars.

THE EMPIRE OF THE EAST

A masterful blend of high technology and high sorcery; a world where magic rules—and science struggles to live again! "Ranks favorably with Tolkien. Exceptional in sheer unbridled zest and imaginative sweep!—*School Library Journal* "*Empire of the East* is one of the best science fiction fantasy epics—Saberhagen can be justly proud. Highly recommended."

—*Science Fiction Chronicle*

THE BLACK THRONE with Roger Zelazny

Two masters of SF collaborate on a masterpiece of fantasy: As children they met and built sand castles on a beach out of space and time: Edgar Perry, little Annie, and Edgar Allan Poe. . . . Fifteen years later Edgar Perry has grown to manhood—and as the result of a trip through a maelstrom, he's leading a much more active life. Perry will learn to thrive in the dark, romantic world he's landed in, where lead can be transmuted to gold, ravens can speak, orangutans can commit murder, and beautiful women are easy to come by. But his alter ego, Edgar Allan, is stranded in a strange and unfriendly world where he can only write about the wonderful and mysterious reality he has lost forever. . . .

THE GOLDEN PEOPLE

Genetically perfect, super-human children are created by a dedicated scientist for the betterment of Mankind. As the children mature, however, they begin to wonder if Man *should* survive. . . .

LOVE CONQUERS ALL

In a future where childbirth is outlawed and promiscuity required, one woman dares fight the system for the right to bear children.

OCTAGON

Players scattered across the continent are engaged in a game called "Starweb." Each player has certain attributes, and can ally with or attack any of the others. But one player seems to have confused the reality of the world: a player with the attributes of machinelike precision and mechanical ruthlessness. His name is Octagon, and he's out for blood.

You can order all of Fred Saberhagen's books with this order form. Check your choices and send the combined cover price/s to: Baen Books, Dept. BA, P.O. Box 1403, Riverdale, N.Y. 10471.

PYRAMIDS, 320 pp., 65609-0, $3.50 ______
AFTER THE FACT, 320 pp., 65391-1, $3.95 ______
THE FRANKENSTEIN PAPERS, 288 pp., 65550-7, $3.50 ______
THE EMPIRE OF THE EAST, 576 pp., 69871-0, $4.95 ______
THE BLACK THRONE, 304 pp., 72013-9, $4.95 ______
THE GOLDEN PEOPLE, 272 pp., 55904-4, $3.50 ______
LOVE CONQUERS ALL, 288 pp., 55953-2, $2.95 ______
OCTAGON, 288 pp., 65353-9, $2.95 ______